No Leaves in Autumn instantly tr
World War II with a heartwarmir
Impeccable research and vivid writing combine in a book brim-
ming with faith and romance. A solid choice for historical romance lovers!

~ Roseanna M. White,
bestselling author of *The Imposters* series

Terri Wangard's action-packed book, *No Leaves in Autumn*, transports us to Iceland in a little-known World War II setting. Wangard paints such a realistic picture of the setting and events that you tend to believe the author was there herself. With suspenseful drama and romance, the book's well-developed characters and intriguing plot are guaranteed to keep you engaged. I highly recommend this book to anyone who enjoys reading historical fiction, especially stories based on true events in World War II.

~ Marilyn Turk,
award-winning author of *The Escape Game*

Not many think about the Land of Fire and Ice in relation to World War II, but the unique island nation of Iceland had a special part to play. Through her immersive novel, *No Leaves in Autumn*, Terri treats readers to a lovely book that sets an enduring love story against the backdrop of Iceland's majestic landscape. As the wife of an Icelandic Viking myself, I was delighted to read about this era in the country I love and lived in. Fans of World War II stories will not want to miss out on this distinctive story.

~ Jenny Erlingsson,
author of *Her Part to Play* and
Milk & Honey in the Land of Fire & Ice

Unsung Stories of World War II - Book Two

TERRI WANGARD

Published by Scrivenings Press LLC
15 Lucky Lane
Morrilton, Arkansas 72110
https://ScriveningsPress.com

Printed in the United States of America

Paperback ISBN 978-1-64917-452-9

eBook ISBN 978-1-64917-453-6

Editor: Amy R. Anguish and Denica McCall

Cover design by Linda Fulkerson - www.bookmarketinggraphics.com

"A father to the fatherless, a defender of widows,
is God in his holy dwelling.
God sets the lonely in families."
Psalm 68:5-6

Chapter One

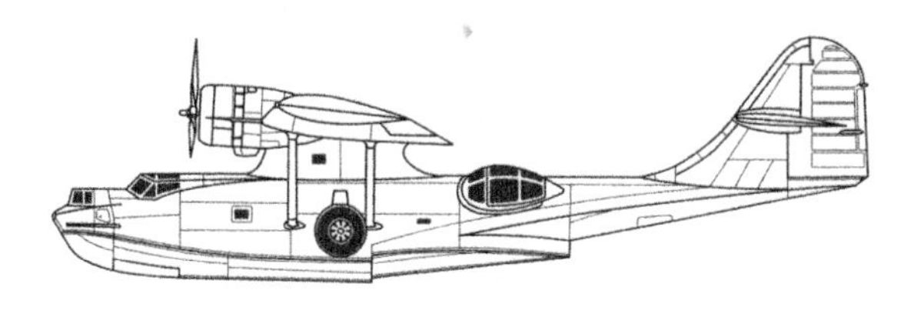

Reykjavik, Iceland
April 1943

Disbelief filled Marie Foubert as she watched her date scurry from the dining room. Again. Before he left the first time, he'd offered a weak excuse about phoning someone. But the other four times? Did he need to continually visit the toilet? He should see a doctor.

She lowered her fork before spilling her food. Fish and potatoes, Icelandic staples, lay unappealing on her plate. Still, it was better fare than if she had stayed at the naval air base and eaten in the mess hall with her Red Cross colleagues. Dinner would have been some version of Spam and dehydrated vegetables. Fresh vegetables and fruit didn't exist in Iceland. They weren't in season, of course, but she craved a juicy apple, or a tender pear, or succulent strawberries.

Don't go there.

The doorway remained empty. Why had George invited her to dinner if he wasn't going to eat with her? Was she such awful company that he had to keep escaping? She should have suspected something when she had to find her own way into town.

She dragged her fork through the remains of the potatoes and scooped up a bite. The food may be boring, but she should be grateful she didn't go hungry. The war in Europe was destroying people's homes and larders, leaving them to subsist on minimal rations. Her shoulders rose and fell with a deep sigh. A beady-eyed gull stared at her in censor from the print on the wall beside her.

The waitress brought an order to the neighboring table and sent a quizzical glance in Marie's direction. After depositing the meal, she turned back and spoke in limited English. "The man eat woman other room."

What?

The waitress waved toward the other side of the dining room, hidden from view by the kitchen on one side and the cloak room on the other. "Table other room."

Understanding dawned. George was eating with another woman on the other side?

That explained a lot.

She balled up the napkin on her lap and slapped it onto the table. On shaky legs, she followed the waitress through the passageway. The change in décor served to form her first impression. Instead of waterfowl, soothing prints of Iceland's spectacular waterfalls covered the walls.

Her eyes landed on George and—was that Lettie James, a member of her Red Cross recreation group? The woman wore the blue-gray Red Cross uniform, which was required at all times. Her red hair gleamed in the soft lighting. It had to be Lettie. Marie struggled to inhale.

The recreation workers had traveled together to Iceland in early March, crammed into the same storm-tossed troopship.

Lettie laughed when they were instructed on wearing life belts. Cross their arms and their legs if they had to jump? Lettie would cross her fingers.

When the ship bucked and rolled during particularly rough weather, they and two others had ended up in a tangle, sliding across the floor. A steward joked that they resembled arm-wrestling octopuses. Lettie received a bloody nose from someone's elbow or knee, and Marie was poked in the eye. She was sure they hadn't wounded each other, but the incident didn't create a bond between them, either.

Now they had something to bond over.

Hands clenched, Marie straightened her shoulders. She approached the table with dignity, her head held high.

"Good evening, Lettie."

"Why, Marie, I didn't know you planned on coming here tonight." Eyes bright, Lettie turned to George. To introduce them?

Marie grabbed the initiative. "George, I was concerned you weren't feeling well with all your mysterious disappearances. And here you are, having a second meal."

George opened and closed his mouth like a fish in an aquarium. The color leeched out of his face.

"Second meal? Disappearing?" Lettie's cheeks blossomed into a bright red that clashed with her hair. She slapped the table and shoved back her chair. "That's why you keep running off? You've been two-timing?"

She snatched her clutch, stood, and linked arms with Marie. "Are you ready to go?"

They strode out of the Borg Hotel's restaurant like they owned the place. Bright smiles hid their consternation. No one would guess Marie's heart pounded like a bass drum, battering her chest. She sucked in the cold air as they stepped outside.

Lettie dropped her arm and whirled to face the hotel.

"Ooh, that really blows my top. How dare he treat us like this? What was he thinking?"

"I don't think he was thinking. When his mouth stopped doing the fish act, he didn't have a word to say." Marie pulled on her coat and buttoned it up to her chin. "Do you think he would have left both of us to pay the bills?"

"Ha. I'll bet he planned exactly that. I didn't bring any money. Did you? Did you have to meet him here? How are we going to get back to base?" She shivered and hurried into her coat. "It's so cold. By late April, I'm used to temperatures in the sixties, not the forties."

Now Marie remembered why she hadn't spent much time with Lettie. The gal chattered nonstop.

"Sunsets after nine-thirty are what I'm not used to. In two more months, the sun will barely set at all." Marie glanced around. "An officer from the base gave me a ride. If we start walking, someone's bound to offer us a lift. At least it's not raining at the moment."

The rain was another Icelandic feature Marie found difficult to adjust to. Rain fell and stopped and fell and stopped again. The sky often wore a sullen gray guise. She'd quickly learned to appreciate periods of sunshine.

After a brief hesitation, Lettie nodded and fell into step beside her. "I hope we'll be transferred elsewhere before winter. I know we're supposed to be here for a year, and I don't mind twenty-four hours of sunlight, but I don't fancy having twenty-four hours of darkness. That will be so depressing."

The long daylight hours offered an advantage. Outside of Reykjavik, the roads of red-lava gravel were rough for driving. Marie did not care to walk here in the dark. Thoughts of tumbling and suffering a sprained ankle, a skinned knee, or worse, a broken tooth, caused her to shudder.

A Jeep pulled up alongside them. "Good evening, ladies."

A corporal doffed his cap. "May I offer you a ride to Camp Kwitcherbelliakin?"

"You most certainly may." Lettie clambered into the Jeep before it came to a complete stop.

Marie squeezed into the back seat. "Actually, our quarters are by the hospital."

"Of course. I'll give you door service." The corporal drove, letting the Jeep bounce over the rocky road. "Did you ladies have a nice evening?"

"Oh, my." Lettie prattled away, enlightening the poor man to every aspect of their double date. "And we ate horsemeat stew. Can you imagine?"

"Horsemeat?" Marie swallowed hard. She'd heard large herds of ponies called the island home, as well as sheep, but they slaughtered the horses to eat?

Her mind drifted back to the year she was eight. She'd received a battered copy of *Black Beauty* for Christmas. The book ignited a love for horses. How she'd longed for the chance to visit a farm just once and see a real, live horse.

But apparently in Iceland, they ate horses.

The corporal's words pulled her out of her memories. "Have you had any whale meat yet? That's common here-abouts. Fairly cheap, and of course, now easy to get."

"Why is that?" The wind picked up, and Marie snatched off her garrison cap before it blew away. "Isn't it dangerous for whalers to hunt while submarines are torpedoing anything that floats?"

The driver chuckled. "I don't know about whalers. It's the Allies that are killing the sea life. All those depth charges dropped to sink U-boats, you know. The shock waves travel and wallop the whales. Or sometimes, the flyboys think they see a sub beneath the surface and fire away but ... heh, heh, heh ... it's a whale. Some of them wash ashore. The seabirds are gorging on them."

"I thought whales were mostly blubber." Lettie looked a little pale. Her horsemeat must not be settling well.

"Oh, sure, but there must be some muscle." Their chauffeur shrugged. "Horsemeat, whale meat. Think of it as an adventure. You're in Iceland! Live like the natives."

"Yes. Aren't we lucky?" The fish Marie had dined on wasn't whale. It was like any of the fish pulled from one of the lakes of Quebec, where she had grown up. "A convoy should arrive soon from the States. I look forward to the brief respite from our monotonous diet."

"Emphasis on brief." Lettie was off again, jabbering about what they'd had for breakfast and what family breakfasts back home in Texas featured.

Marie tuned out the food talk and gazed around the barren landscape. Not a tree in sight. In Reykjavik, a few trees struggled to grow. Outside the city, however, nary a one. She sighed. She'd see no leaves budding in the coming weeks. Iceland was covered in moss instead. She wasn't sure if it was because the island was created from volcanic rock or if centuries ago, settlers had cut down all the trees. Maybe the gale-force winds she heard whipping across Iceland kept trees from growing. How could the people live without them? She would miss the colorful leaves in fall.

Her drifting thoughts skidded to a stop when Lettie's words broke through.

"I haven't had a decent night's sleep since we arrived nearly two months ago. I can't believe how noisy our barracks is at night. Women aren't supposed to snore like some of our esteemed colleagues do." She twisted in her seat. "Doesn't it bother you, Marie?"

"No, but I grew up in a noisy environment. Silence would likely awaken me."

"Not me. I had my own room until I went to college, and then I had one roommate. Now I have to share a tiny space with a dozen women."

Did Lettie realize how rude she sounded? Was she including Marie among the snorers? No one had ever complained about her nocturnal respirations.

The corporal must have noted Lettie's *faux pas*. He glanced back. "Are you from a big family?"

"No." Marie laced her fingers together. "I grew up in an orphanage."

Lettie spun back around. "An orphanage?"

She sounded outraged, like Marie should have told her before. Did she consider orphans to be riffraff? Plenty of people did.

The driver stared at Marie, his eyes wide. With pity? The smile he aimed at her resembled a grimace. "Why were you in an orphanage?"

"My parents and little sister were killed in a car wreck. The other driver was drunk and didn't suffer a scratch. I was not quite four years old."

Lettie gasped. "How awful. What about aunts and uncles? Couldn't anyone take you in?"

"No one wanted me." Marie exhaled and fought to keep the bitterness out of her voice. She parroted Sister Marguerite's well-meaning words. "Times were hard in the years after the last war." Resentment flared. "No one needed another mouth to feed."

A vague memory rose. A sad-eyed woman hugged Marie, but set her down in the orphanage office and walked out, never to be seen again. Who was she?

She'd once heard Sister Marguerite tell another sister about the woman who asked how much money Marie's parents left. "She'd gladly take the inheritance, but not the poor child. Good riddance of her."

"How many girls slept in your room?" Bless the corporal for his attempts to divert her.

"We had twelve beds, and they were usually filled. Occasionally, someone was placed with a family."

No one ever expressed interest in Marie. And fortunately for her, no one asked about her best friends, Francoise and Ozanne. They'd pretended they were sisters.

The Jeep arrived at the sprawling US naval air base, passing the sign proclaiming Camp Kwitcherbelliakin. When Marie had first seen it, she dismissed the name as an Icelandic word. Only later did she learn the humorous moniker was English, sort of, for "quit your bellyaching."

Before the driver could head for the Quonset huts that served as the American Red Cross quarters, Lettie directed him elsewhere. "Please let us out at the headquarters. I need to drop something off, and I think we should file a report about George, don't you, Marie?"

"Good idea. Especially if he tried to sneak out of the restaurant without paying for one or both meals."

The driver chuckled. "I'd like to be a fly on the wall to see how he fared."

Marie stepped carefully out of the Jeep. "We never asked your name."

He tipped his cap. "Wilmer Case, at your service."

"Thank you for your gallantry." She raised her brows as she smiled and shook his hand. He inclined his head and winked.

Inside the office, Lettie hurried off to deliver her paperwork while Marie wrote a quick explanation of their evening. As she slid her account through the adjutant's mail slot, an arm snaked around her and spun her about. A man smelling of cigarette smoke, beer, and sweat pulled her close. His mouth attached to her neck, and adrenaline shot through her. Was he biting her? As she tried to punch at his head, she imagined fangs.

The man let out muffled words in puffs of hot air. "Ah, sweetheart, let's find somewhere private."

She thrust her elbow into his chest and shoved hard, yanking the arm from around her at the same time. He stumbled back, and she saw pilot's wings glinting on his uniform.

"What's the matter, baby doll?" His smirk broadcasted his assurance that she must find him attractive.

More like revolting.

He advanced and slipped his arms around her again. He must have as many arms as a centipede. The more she fought, the tighter he gripped. Where was Lettie? If she screamed, would anyone hear?

"Let go of me." She forced her hand upward, and her fist connected with his jaw. "Help!"

"What's the matter with you?" The man glared, rubbing his jaw.

She ran for the door. Cool air bathed her face. She raised trembling hands to her lips as her breath came in gasps.

A Jeep pulled up. The pilot hadn't followed her outside, but maybe whoever was in the Jeep would help if she needed it.

A man strode toward her. He wore pilot's wings too. He smiled, showing straight white teeth. "Good evening, miss."

"Stay away from me. I don't like Casanovas."

His eyebrows shot skyward. He raised both hands as if in surrender, or maybe to ward her off. "Pardon me, ma'am." His voice turned stiff and formal. "Don't have a good evening."

Before he disappeared inside, he skirted around Lettie, who stood stock-still at the door.

Lettie's face was mottled with ... confusion? Disgust? "Why did you do that?"

Marie blew out her breath. Leaning forward, she braced her hands on her knees. "Did you see the pilot inside? He-he tried to ravish me."

Lettie's face cleared. "Tony Dever. Yeah, he thinks he's every girl's dream."

"Nightmare is more like it."

"Hmm. He gave you a hickey." She smoothed Marie's hair, too short to hide her neck. "But why were you so rude to Stefan Dabrowski? He's the sweetest navy pilot here. He really *is* every girl's dream. I'd love for him to notice me." Lettie paused to take a breath. "He flies the PBYs, you know. Did you know the *P* and the *B* stand for patrol bomber, but the *Y* doesn't stand for anything? That is so strange."

Marie stood still as Lettie continued to prattle. His smile had been friendly, not slimy. Her shoulders sagged. What else would go wrong this evening?

Chapter Two

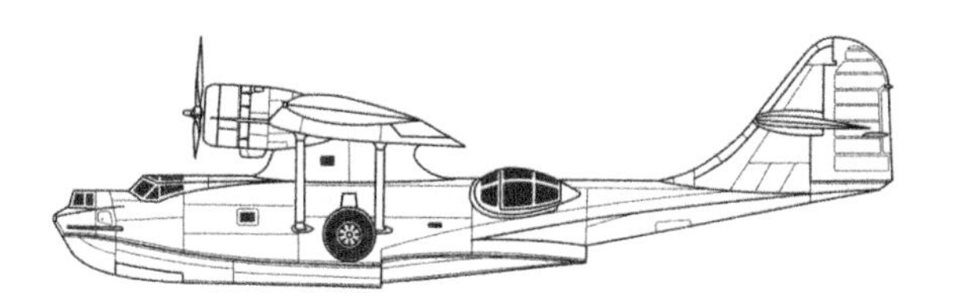

"U-boat reported on the north side of the convoy, toward the front."

Radioman Bruce Jenz's words electrified Stefan Dabrowski. Their squadron had yet to sink a submarine. Their commanding officer, disgusted with their pathetic performance, had closed the officer's club. The club's closure didn't bother Stefan, but their failure did. Ships, men, and supplies succumbed at an alarming rate to the unseen enemy.

He was no different from the rest of the men in hoping he would be the plane captain to break their string of bad luck. He nosed his PBY amphibious airplane into a northeasterly direction and raced to the head of the convoy.

"Jenz, do you have the coordinates?"

As he spoke, Stefan watched a merchantman plow through the North Atlantic chop. The ship appeared to have an airplane lashed to its deck. As he watched, the vessel jerked up in the waves. A fireball exploded out of it.

He stared in disbelief.

Torpedoed.

They'd arrived too late. Again.

Fire engulfed the back two-thirds of the ship. No way would it reach England. As they flew past the stricken ship, he spotted men on the deck. Men on fire. Some jumped overboard into the icy water to extinguish the flames.

Stefan's heart clenched as he imagined their pain.

"From too hot to too cold," Roy Pennington commented from his ringside seat in the bow. "They won't last long if one of the destroyers doesn't pick them up real quick-like."

"If they can even tread water with the pain of their burns," Mel Lawrenz responded from the blister window in the back of the plane, where he manned the waist gun. "Although I suppose cold water numbs the pain."

"There." Beside Stefan in the cockpit, his copilot Andrew Grant thrust a finger at a slight disturbance on the ocean's surface. "A periscope. It hasn't gone deep."

Stefan angled their flight into position. He released four depth charges attached to their wings in the spot where the sub should be.

"One of the depth charges is hung up," Lawrenz yelled through the headset.

Botheration! The hanger may have been the one to hit home. Stefan circled around. Heaving waves prevented them from detecting the sub's presence.

"Jenz, any word from the destroyer?"

"They think that one's going deep, but there's another possibility on the other side of the convoy. Stand by."

They flew over the stricken ship. Other ships in the line detoured around them. A corvette—one of the convoy escorts—stopped to pick up survivors.

Stefan sighed. "I sure wouldn't care to be a merchant seaman in wartime. They have no way to defend themselves."

"And yet lots of men dare to risk it. Just look at all the ships here." Grant waved at the armada. "There are thirty-four, right? Only one's been torpedoed. Do you think there's more than one U-boat down there?"

"Maybe it just found the convoy," Allan Ramsey chimed in from his engineer's cubbyhole in the pylon attached to the overhead wings. "It's probably radioed the location and one of those wolf packs is heading this way."

Stefan and his men maintained their patrol over the convoy for five more hours as it plodded eastward. The lead destroyer detected no more submarine activity. Odd. What happened with the one that torpedoed the merchantman? Might their depth charges have caused some damage?

After another circle around the ships, Stefan squeezed his eyes shut. He needed a break. He tapped Grant's shoulder for him to take over, eased out of the cockpit, arched his back, and stretched out his arms. He paused by the navigation-chart table. "McQuaid, I'm heading for the galley. Want anything to eat?"

David McQuaid set aside his pencil and ruler, leaned back, and rubbed his belly. "Why, yes, now that you mention it. I'll have duck l'Orange, grilled asparagus, and a glass of chardonnay."

"Ha, ha, dreamer. How about a bowl of tomato soup with a slightly stale slice of bread?"

"Ugh. How pedestrian. Bring me back a chocolate bar."

Lawrenz and their tail gunner, Lucius Poulos, were drinking coffee, and Poulos poured Stefan a cup without interrupting his conversation. "I'm telling you, Mel, that girl didn't even look at us. It's like we weren't even there." He shouted to be heard over the roar of the engines. "Most Icelandic girls are rude."

"Can't blame them for not being friendly. Iceland was occupied against their will. Remember what that British sailor said? They sailed into the harbor and fired a shot over the town. I wonder where that shell landed." Lawrenz cradled the steaming cup and blew across it before testing the coffee. "Did she speak English? Maybe she didn't understand you and was intimidated."

Their comments brought to mind the Red Cross girl Stefan had greeted last week. Icelandic girls weren't the only ones to be rude. *Stay away from me.* Wow. Just for saying good evening. And she was here with an organization to raise morale among the men?

He raised the heat on the hot plate and stirred the pot of soup.

The girl's red-haired friend had run after him and pleaded for mercy for her teammate. Said she'd just been assaulted by another pilot who had grabbed her and latched onto her neck.

Okay, he could see how that would upset her. That also explained the Casanova remark. It wasn't like she'd been raped, though. Why was she so hysterical?

Stefan braced himself as the plane banked. Turning off the hot plate, he poured a bowlful of soup and grabbed a spoon.

Maybe he was being too harsh. What had the redhead called her? Mary? What if it had been his sister who was attacked? Dorota surely wouldn't have panicked. She was feisty. Had to be with three brothers.

But if the assailant had overpowered Mary, if she couldn't fight back, yes, that would have shot up her blood pressure. Her adrenaline would have soared.

Maybe that explained her actions. She was still wound up when he crossed her path.

Grant her grace. That's what his mother would say. She'd had a dreadful fright and wasn't thinking clearly. Blessed are the merciful. Let it go.

He blew out his breath and tested the soup. The metal spoon burned his tongue.

What really bothered him was how she equated him with the assailant. Tony Dever was the only other pilot Stefan had seen that night. She insulted him with the comparison. To think she expected him to force himself on her simply because he smiled. He heaved a sigh. That Dever was the guilty culprit didn't surprise him. Stefan had never met a more arrogant bully who delighted in belittling any and everyone.

Stefan grimaced. He understood his problem now. She'd hurt his feelings.

Get over it, Dabrowski. Be a man. Show some compassion.

He, probably more than all the others in his squadron, understood mankind's cruelty. The Nazis and Soviets had teamed up to destroy his ancestral homeland. His relatives knew unbelievable suffering. Some had vanished, no doubt tortured and executed. What was a little thing like a hysterically offered insult?

He gulped down his soup and headed to the lavatory in the tail of the plane. Time to quit moping and return to work.

The weather deteriorated in an instant. The plane bounced all over the sky as the wind approached hurricane strength. Stefan's arms ached as he wrestled with the control column, fighting to keep the aircraft from flipping over.

"I won't be a bit surprised to arrive back in Reykjavik and discover Iceland has blown away." Grant added his muscles to the effort of remaining airborne. "I suppose they'll tell us this wasn't in the weather forecast."

Stefan smiled. "By the time we get back, we'll have sunny

skies with barely a hint of a breeze. They'll say, 'Oh, did you have a spot of weather?'"

Growing up in Wisconsin, he had often heard, "If you don't like the weather, wait five minutes." The saying never made sense to him as he lay shivering in bed, listening to a blizzard howl all night long. Iceland, however, had a perfect claim to the motto. He gritted his teeth as another gust hurled them fifty feet down.

Jenz broke into his tumbling thoughts. "Just heard from base. The weather's grounding a lot of the trans-Atlantic traffic. They're running out of parking space. We'll have to land in the bay and, if the beach is too crowded to go ashore, we'll have to remain onboard."

"Stay onboard? You mean all night?" The waist gunner groaned. "Will a caterer come around with some supper?"

"Man up, Lawrenz." Stefan worked to keep amusement out of his voice. "We've got soup and bread's that getting staler by the minute."

"Oh, yummy." As the baby in his family with five sisters, Lawrenz had been granted every wish, so military life proved to be a challenge for him. Still, he maintained a happy attitude most of the time, much to Stefan's gratification.

They landed in the bay without incident, and Pennington set an anchor from the bow with Lawrenz's assistance. They headed to the back of the plane to check on the deployment of the rear anchors.

Stefan and Grant completed the post-flight checklist when Jenz called them. "They want us to beach after all."

Stefan sagged in his seat. "Well, at least we don't have to warm up the engines. Reel the anchors back in, fellas."

"I'm back here," Pennington responded.

"What he means is, he's in the lav," Poulos said.

Grant was already flipping through the switches, so Stefan hauled himself out of his seat and dropped down into the bow compartment. The plane rocked in moderate swells as he raised the hatch on top of the turret. Cool air swirled around him as he leaned out and grabbed the lizard line. The anchor refused to budge. Sighing, he hoisted himself out of the turret and balanced on the tiny walk rail on the side of the fuselage. He leaned forward in an effort to see what held it and unhooked the line. The plane rose on a wave and dipped, dousing Stefan. Just as suddenly, another wave smacked the plane. The anchor line pulled taut in his hand and yanked him off his feet to tumble into the icy water.

The air whooshed out of his lungs, and the water stabbed him like knives. His soaked flying gear weighed him down as the waves pushed him away from the airplane.

Served him right. Working with the anchors was a two-man operation. And why hadn't he hooked up to the safety belt?

Did his crew even know he was in trouble? Did Grant, the only one forward, realize he was no longer inside?

Stefan tried to swim, but his arms seemed to weigh a hundred pounds each. The plane lumbered toward the beach. Lawrenz wasn't in the blister window. Where were they? Stefan would drown right there in the bay, and they wouldn't be the wiser.

A nurse layered another blanket on him, but it failed to stop the shivers as knives of agony stabbed Stefan's body. The nurse prodded him to open his mouth for a thermometer. "Do you remember what happened?"

"Swimming."

She smiled. "You were in the water for half an hour before a local fisherman pulled you out." She checked the thermometer. "One hour out of the water, and your temp is up to ninety-five degrees."

Thirty-four minutes, and without a life vest. How had he survived?

The sequence of events remained hazy. The overwhelming stench of fish still filled his nostrils, and a vague memory of Icelandic chatter teased his mind.

A groan to his left snagged his attention. A sailor lay with severe burns, from a torpedoing most likely. Now there was some serious suffering.

And here he lay, shivering like a leaf. The doctor said something about keeping him for observation. Pneumonia posed a threat. His lungs didn't sound clear, and he couldn't take deep breaths without coughing.

A louder groan emanated from the wrapped bundle of misery next to him. Stefan huffed in frustration and coughed. His own "injuries" hardly merited him occupying a bed.

From beyond the doorway came a voice he recognized. Lieutenant Commander Arnett, the squadron's commanding officer, spoke at full volume as though he stood on the deck of a heaving ship in a storm.

"Why is Dabrowski lazing about here? Are you afraid he'll catch a cold?"

Stefan flinched. They might have matching thoughts, but did Arnett have to be so crass and loud about it?

Whoever the CO conferred with countered in a moderate tone, which was indistinguishable to Stefan in the ward.

"Aw, well, he's not one of our best pilots. Boring as last night's bathwater, he is."

Heat surged through Stefan, suddenly curing his chills. He

might have jumped out of bed if a wave of lightheadedness hadn't messed with his equilibrium.

Boring as old, dirty bathwater? The CO didn't even know him. What justified his claim?

A face flashed across his mind. A sneering, arrogant face. Dever didn't only accost women. He was probably telling the CO stories to undermine Stefan.

Chapter Three

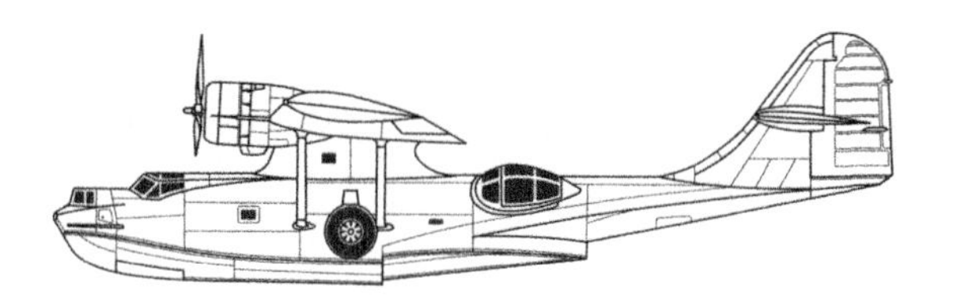

Stefan clenched his fists beneath the stiff hospital sheet. He shouldn't be surprised. Dever specialized in half-truths and untruths. He excelled at twisting facts to make his targets appear ridiculous.

Stefan fidgeted in the bed. Why had Dever targeted him? Sure, he never joined the guys for a drink. He had to guard his alone time, for privacy was hard to come by in the military.

After twelve or more hours flying with his crew, he cherished the chance to lose himself in a good book or write to family and friends. Sitting in the officers' club, rehashing the flying and the weather and the dreary food, and stinking like an overflowing ashtray because of all the cigarette smokers held no appeal for him.

He frowned at the arched ceiling. His first week in Iceland, someone had offered him a cigarette. He refused it, explaining he didn't care for the smell of tobacco due to visiting his chain-smoking grandfather's house while growing up. After that, Dever delighted in blowing smoke in his face. He may as well have a bull's-eye painted on his back.

Stefan longed to walk beyond the base and breathe the fresh, bracing air. Granted, the air often stank of sulfur, a consequence of living on a volcanic island. But that contributed to Iceland's fascination. This was a geologist's jewel box. The lava fields, the barren mountains, the mind-boggling absence of trees. He itched for the chance to explore the geysers, waterfalls, and hot springs existing here in abundance.

"Hey, Frenchie. You came."

A patient's exuberant greeting pulled him from his musing. Surprise rocked Stefan when he realized the man was speaking to her—Dever's victim, Mary. Why did they call her Frenchie?

She grinned at a trio of patients. "I knew you boys wouldn't go to sleep without a bedtime story."

Her smile dazzled his tired eyes. She looked the same yet different, with brown hair somewhere between straight and curly. Maybe an inch above average height. And did she have freckles? Gone was the hysteria that had tinged her voice. She acted at ease with the bedridden sailors. Of course, men confined to bed were unable to attack her.

"How can we go to sleep when the sun is finally shining?"

"We've been in utter darkness without you."

"Only your sweet smile gets us through these wearisome days."

Oh, brother. These three could be the Curly, Moe, and Larry of the lovelorn. Stefan chuckled through his foggy thoughts.

Frenchie ignored their foolishness as she perched on Curly's bed and clasped her hands primly in her lap.

"Once upon a time, Goldilocks wandered, lost in a forest, when she discovered a ramshackle cottage. Inside, she found Len working on his stamp collection. The moist, heavy bandages on his hands attracted the stamps like glue, and he became verily frustrated as they all stuck to him."

Moe held up his bandaged hands. "Boy howdy, you better believe it, sweetheart."

"In the kitchen, Jack wanted to bake cookies, but the casts on his arms made him clumsy indeed, and more flour coated the counter, the floor, and himself than could be found in the bowl."

"Say you'll help me make those cookies." Larry sported casts on both arms and a leg. Stefan didn't want to think about how he'd gained those injuries.

"Randy attempted to cross the living room but tangled his crutches with a throw rug and fell with a mighty thud. In his frustration, Len snarled, 'Having a rest?'"

Curly, his leg up in traction, hooted. "Len, she nailed you. Never a lick of sympathy."

Before their squabbles got out of hand, she rose and patted Curly's arm. "Nighty-night, boys."

* * *

Marie rose from Len's bed with a laugh. They probably wouldn't appreciate knowing they reminded her of boys she'd grown up with in the orphanage.

A man lay in bed four, his gaze fixed on her. She swallowed a gasp and blinked once, twice. It was him—the man who'd said good evening and then rescinded his greeting when she snarled at him. The man Lettie called the sweetest man in Iceland, whom she'd love to have notice her. Too bad Lettie wasn't here now. Marie had his full, undivided attention and, judging by the stormy-blue eyes, he was not happy to see her.

Shuffling forward, she raised her chin and straightened her shoulders. She'd made an honest mistake. If he wasn't man enough to overlook it, that was his problem.

Pausing beside his bed, she fought the urge to flee from his steady gaze. Her fingers hurt. No wonder, with the way she clenched them. Smoothing her hands down her skirt, she cleared her throat. "I, um." Her voice cracked. Confound it! She tried again. "I owe you an apology."

He quirked his right eyebrow. "Is that so?"

His voice hadn't sounded scratchy before. On closer inspection, she noticed the spiky condition of his short hair that, if longer, would likely curl.

Amusement flared in those mesmerizing blue eyes. Sapphire blue. How had she missed that the other day?

"Why are you sorry?"

She pulled over a chair. No need to entertain the whole hut. "I was rude. Last week." Breathe in, breathe out. "A Lothario had just given me a hard time. But you were being friendly. I realize that now. One of my colleagues told me you're one of the gems." Exhale.

He stared at her for the longest time. He must be wondering why she'd joined the Red Cross if she couldn't handle an overdose of testosterone.

"A gem. Would you put that in writing? My fourth-grade teacher claimed I was part of an unholy trio."

That's all he heard? As one of her college professors would say, *well, alrighty then.*

"A little devil, were you?"

"We were little angels."

"Of the fallen variety?"

He grinned, then laughed. And then he coughed. And coughed. His face turned red, and still he coughed.

Marie scrambled to her feet. What should she do?

A nurse rushed to his side, pulled him upright from his slightly inclined position, and smacked his back. A basin appeared on his lap. "Cough it up. Come on, now. Get under it and cough it out."

After another mighty thump that had to hurt, a dribble of water trickled from his mouth. A doctor pushed Marie away and added some whacks of his own. Stefan convulsed as seawater gushed out. He panted while the doctor pressed a stethoscope to his chest, then his back, and ordered him to breathe deeply.

"Very good. Your lungs are almost clear." He scribbled on Stefan's chart and left.

Marie should leave as well. He'd probably prefer privacy rather than an audience to the indignities of hospital affairs. She certainly would. But her feet remained stuck to the floor.

When the nurse left, he eyed her. "Did Dever give you that bruise?"

She stifled a gasp. Lettie chattered too much. "Hmm. What happened to you?"

He smirked but allowed her to change the subject. "I went for an ill-advised swim."

"Ah. That explains the spiky hairdo."

He patted his head all over and sighed. "I lost my comb."

The man in the next bed groaned, and Stefan winced. "The staff hasn't been by to check on him, and he keeps moaning. Can't they do something for him?"

"I'll ask." He probably wanted her to leave. "And I'll find you a comb. By the way, I'm Marie Foubert."

"Marie?" His eyes clouded as he rubbed his chin. "Marie it is. I'm Stefan."

Odd reaction. She mentally shrugged. Stef-an. Not Steven. Alrighty. She nodded. "Nice to meet you, Stefan."

* * *

Marie departed hastily, her cheeks burning. After telling a nurse about the groaning burn victim, she slipped back into the room to leave a comb on the stand by Stefan's bed. Before exiting, she glanced back and found the man's blue gaze on her. She pressed her hands together and laid her head on them, indicating sleep. He grinned but closed his eyes again. He must think her a real ninny. But why should she care?

She marched across the base to the Red Cross barracks. Inside, the Red Cross women were all present. Lettie jabbered away to Helen, who nodded now and then as she read a letter. Marie wiped a grin off her face. Poor Helen. She and Lettie were assigned to an army camp several miles from their base. Daily traversing muddy, bumpy roads often resulted in endless delays, during which Lettie likely subjected Helen to her ceaseless monologues.

Marie joined Betty at their side-by-side cots. Their semicylindrical Quonset hut came equipped only with beds, a shelf stuck to the curved dome of the hut above each bed, and a potbellied stove. She stored her purse in the upended packing crate she'd commandeered for use as a bedside bookcase. A soldier had added two shelves and applied a blowtorch to the bare wood, giving it an antique look.

Betty set aside her letter writing. The petite blonde hailed from southern California with a large, happy family and a love for the beach. Despite being opposites in many ways, they'd become good friends. "How are the patients doing?"

"No new gruesome injuries today, but word came that several burn victims are arriving from a torpedoed merchant ship." Marie plopped down on her bed and glanced around. No one seemed to pay them attention. "I met Lettie's 'sweetest man in Iceland.'"

Betty leaned forward. "Is he sweet?"

"Hmpf. He asked if Dever gave me a bruise. It was a bite mark, like a vampire. What must Lettie have said to him?" She covered her face with her hands at the memory of

Dever's touch. "Stefan does have the bluest eyes I've ever seen."

"What are you two whispering about?" Lettie sauntered over. "Have you heard we're having our Monday-morning meeting tomorrow instead? The field director's back from wherever he went. We need some new ideas for programs for the men."

Across the hut, Anne watched them through narrowed eyes. The woman was too outspoken for Marie's liking, claiming personal credit for all the Red Cross women had accomplished, no matter how tenuous the likelihood. The field director ate it up like a cat in cream and admonished the rest of them to carry their weight and not make Anne do all the work.

Betty touched Marie's hand. "Tell Lettie your suggestion and see what she thinks."

"We should see if any musical Icelanders can provide concerts. It might be a way to promote friendly relations between them and us. Of course, piano concerts aren't possible, not with our wheezing, rinky-tink upright."

"Oh, yes." Lettie clasped her hands and nodded. "Maybe a choral group?"

Marie tilted her head. "If they know English-language songs. Icelandic lyrics wouldn't be understood."

"Do share that. It's a great idea."

The following day, all twelve women gathered in a room at base headquarters. The director, Mr. Perry, and his assistant, Mr. Walton, sat at the head of a long table. Both men appeared to be of appropriate age to serve in the military. Lettie often speculated about their excuses for not being in active service. Red Cross work was important, surely, but neither man seemed indispensable. Lettie's guess that Mr. Perry fainted at the sight of blood amused Marie.

Mr. Perry droned on about the past week's accomplishments, often praising Anne, even when they all knew she hadn't been at a particular camp. Some of the women fidgeted while others stifled yawns. Even Mr. Walton seemed bored, staring out the window.

"Now then, does anyone have any new thoughts on raising our military men's morale?" He looked straight at Anne.

Marie had her page of notes ready and started to hold up her finger when Anne jumped in. "Oh, I've got a great idea. We can involve the natives and ask them to give concerts for the men."

Marie's jaw dropped.

Lettie scoffed. "You got that great idea by listening to Marie last night. She came up with it."

Mr. Perry pointed at Lettie. "Don't be rude. Give Anne the opportunity to explain her idea."

Several of the women gasped. Even Mr. Walton frowned as he shifted in his chair.

Anne preened. "They probably wouldn't be able to bring a tuned piano or sing in their own language, but possibly a string quartet."

Marie's blood boiled. "No, no string ensembles. They're too ..." She laid her hand on the table near Betty. "What did you call it?"

"Longhaired. Too refined for our boys to fully appreciate. Most of them, anyway."

"Right." She directed her words to Mr. Walton. "My idea is for brass ensembles, maybe with drums."

Helen laughed. When all eyes turned her way, she said, "Loud music that will keep them awake."

Before Mr. Perry could regain the floor, Marie continued. "A lot of the men like guitars and wish they had brought their own with them. I don't know if there are any Icelandic guitar groups, but if there are, they'd find a receptive audience here."

"Good idea." Mr. Walton nodded as he jotted notes. "Even one or two guitarists might be willing to have a jam session with small groups of the men. Anything else?"

She took a deep breath. This one could open her to Mr. Perry's scorn. "I attended an Easter service at a church in Reykjavik. While I didn't understand the words, being in the church was ..."

"Soothing." Betty supplied the right word.

"Yes. Some of the men who were churchgoers at home may enjoy the formal atmosphere found in a church. It would be a huge imposition, but it would be nice if a church could offer something. Maybe just the building, and our own chaplains and a small choir ..."

"Ha." Anne sat back with crossed arms. "There isn't a choir."

"There could be." Betty refused to yield. "Memorial Day is coming up. That would be a nice occasion to have a special service."

"It would indeed." Mr. Walton glanced at Mr. Perry with a raised brow.

The director scowled as he looked around the table. "Are you quite finished?"

When no one spoke, he smiled at Anne. "Write up your idea, would you, dear? Now then, any other matters of business?"

Marie pursed her lips. He acted like she'd hijacked the meeting. She stiffened her spine. "We continue to have problems keeping our mimeographed song sheets, because the men like to take them." She paused. No need to point out that Anne's idea of chalking lyrics on a blackboard would only work for one song and not be visible to those beyond the front of the room. "I heard the army has an overhead projector. I doubt they'd let us use it, but we could ask."

"You're right. The army won't share it." Mr. Perry dismissed her idea, but Mr. Walton scribbled on his notepad. "Anything else worth our while?"

Beside her, Betty scoffed quietly. Mr. Perry couldn't have been clearer that Marie was wasting their time.

Marie refused to back down. "Can we obtain kites?"

Mr. Walton lifted his head. "Kites?"

She nodded. "Several of the boys were talking about flying kites. They feel Iceland is a good place to do so because there are no trees for them to get stuck in."

Lettie snickered, prompting everyone to laugh. Everyone except Anne and Mr. Perry. Mr. Walton declared he'd send the suggestion to headquarters.

As they rose to leave, Anne approached Marie with her hand out. "I'll take your notes for the minutes."

"The minutes? Mr. Walton writes the minutes." Lettie made quote marks with her fingers. "All Mr. Perry expects from you are the details of Marie's idea for concerts."

Marie shoved her notes into her pocket. She'd never do well at committee work. Someone always had to cause contention and dampen the mood. So much antagonism made her head ache. She needed air.

Slipping away from the others, she set off on a brisk walk. Rounding a supply shed, she collided with a solid chest. The impact knocked the wind out of her. Hands caught her arms, and her gaze rose to tangle with the bluest eyes she'd ever seen.

Chapter Four

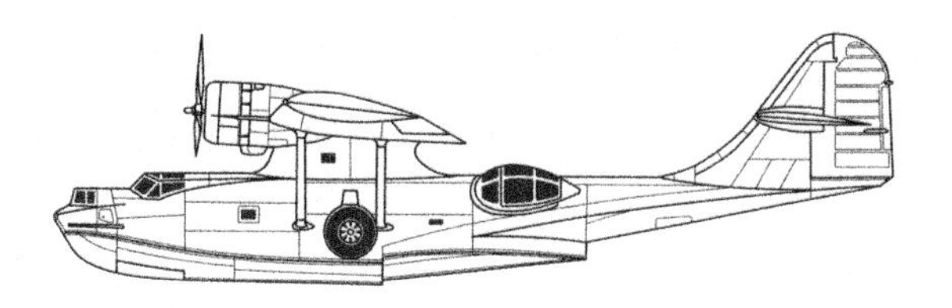

"Good evening, Marie?"

His greeting came out as a question, but not because he expected her to reject his pleasantry this time. Their hospital visit had shown him her amiability. Still, the way she barreled around the corner ...

"Dever bothering you again?"

"Dever?" She blinked. Sighed. "No. No." She sighed again and splayed her fingers across her breastbone. "I wonder who's worse."

Did he want to know?

"Someone else bothering you?"

Her shoulders sagged. "None of the military men." Tilting her head to the side, she studied him and nodded. Apparently, she'd decided to trust him. "We just had a Red Cross meeting. One of the ladies fancies herself our leader and thinks she has the only good ideas for our programs. Of course the director believes her and tells the rest of us to be nice when we try to claim ownership of the ideas."

"Ah. The joys of working with people."

Marie tried to laugh but ended up sputtering. "If it was only Anne, I'd understand. But the way Mr. Perry panders to her ..." She waved her fist in Stefan's face. "I'd like to give him a knuckle sandwich."

Stefan laughed and stepped away. "Is he smitten with Anne?"

Her eyes bulged. "Smitten? You mean, is he in love with her? I hope not." Her hands fluttered up and back down. "He's married. With children."

He snapped his fingers. "You didn't grow up in America, did you?"

She stepped back. "No. I'm from Quebec."

"Aha." He clasped his hands together and scrutinized the sky. "Hmm. *Parlez-vous français*?"

Laughter bubbled from her. "*Oui. Mieux que toi.*"

"If you say so." He wouldn't admit he didn't know what she said besides "yes."

"You are out of the hospital, so no danger of pneumonia?" She mercifully returned to English.

"Pshaw. I didn't need to stay there overnight." He took a deep breath and experienced no need to cough. "I'm in the pink. Now I'm out for my constitutional."

When her face clouded, he hid a smile. "You know, periodic review of America's fundamental principles of governance. Don't Canadians do that?"

She crossed her arms, eyes narrowed.

He relented. Maybe they weren't well enough acquainted to tease like that.

"I'm out for a walk. Walking is beneficial to our overall well-being. Did you know North Americans walk less than any other civilized nation?"

"Is that so? North Americans? You are including Canadians in your lazy habits?"

"I don't want you to feel left out."

She snickered. "How very thoughtful of you. How do you know about Americans' lack of exercise?"

She'd left out the *North*. He smiled to himself. "I read an article in the newspaper back home."

"And this is a special interest of yours?"

"I like to be informed." He shrugged and changed the subject. "Where are you headed? Your barracks? You need a walk first. One of the benefits of walking, besides strengthening muscles, is the diminishing of stomach upset. Surely you don't want to stew in your juices over your bossy coworker." He prodded her forward. "Come along. Swing those arms. Deep breaths to drive out the stale air."

She laughed again but matched him stride for stride. And coughed.

"Uh-oh. I know of an open hospital bed that comes with entertainment from three stooges."

Marie waved away the air in front of her. "It's the smell of sulfur that irritates my lungs. I think it's the wind from the north bringing us that stench."

"Is it now? Except today, the wind is from the south. The Gulf Stream, which keeps Iceland from becoming the iceberg its name suggests."

She eyed him for a long moment. "You know this because you're a pilot, and pilots need to understand wind patterns?"

"Especially in Iceland where the wind can blow you upside down and inside out."

She grinned, then a giggle escaped, followed by a gale of laughter. Gasping for breath, she explained, "On the ship coming here, when we were informed we were destined for

Iceland, one of the soldiers claimed he knew all about this country. After all, he'd attended a full year of college. Iceland is an island made up of one huge volcano with flowing lava." She brought her hands up in a cone shape. "Snow and ice cover it year-round."

"Wait a minute. What about the flowing lava? Doesn't that melt the ice?"

She shushed him. "Denmark owns Iceland and uses it as a penal colony, like Australia. Oh, and people ride on wild reindeer."

"Right. Do they live in igloos?" Stefan shook his head. "Doesn't say much for American education. I remember social studies in junior high. World history in high school. I don't remember anything about Iceland, though. Leif Erikson, maybe, or was it Eric the Red? We should have spent more time on geography than Latin."

His friend John wouldn't agree. John had excelled in Latin. He still spouted Latin phrases that no one understood. Were there any appropriate phrases for a fighter pilot in the Pacific? An ache formed deep in Stefan's gut. He missed his pals John and Daniel. As a cargo pilot in the south Atlantic, Daniel shouldn't be in danger, but John ... Aerial combat was deadly. Of the three of them, John was least likely to make it home.

Stefan paused at the corner of a Quonset hut, peering around it as he held up a hand to stop Marie. "Coast is clear. No hard-charging Red Cross ladies."

"Very funny." Marie pointed to the administration hut. "I'm hoping mail arrived with the convoy that came in today."

Mail. He took her arm and veered toward the potential windfall of news from home. "What are we waiting for?"

* * *

Arriving in the officers' mess, Stefan fanned out six letters on the table. He read the return addresses and savored the moment before picking up the fat letter from his mother. He paused before opening it.

Marie had found one letter waiting for her. One. Sadness flickered in her gaze, but she offered a brave smile as she told him he had a busy evening to look forward to. Who did she anticipate hearing from? Her mother? A boyfriend?

Matka sent eight pages of cramped writing. He skimmed through the letter, planning on spending more time with it later. Laying it aside, he opened his sister's missive. In the interest of keeping him informed, she made an amusing gossip.

Matka's letter disappeared from his periphery.

"What have we here? Could Stevie D actually have a girlfriend?"

Dever. No mistaking that sneering voice. Stefan refused to react.

"What is this?" Dever shook the letter in his face. "This isn't English."

"You don't say." Stefan snatched his mother's letter from Dever's grasp. "I wondered about that."

"Is that Polack?" Dever pressed into Stefan's personal space. "Sharing military secrets?"

Stefan couldn't stop a snort.

"Use your brain, if you have one." Andrew Grant spoke up from across the table. "Poland is an ally with more at stake in this war than the US."

"If they want to live in America, they should use English. What do they have to hide?"

"Our privacy?" Stefan shook the letter before tucking it into his pocket. "This keeps people from sticking their noses in our business where they don't belong."

A moment of blessed silence lingered as if Dever couldn't decide whether he'd been insulted. Finally, he emitted his I'm-so-clever laugh.

David McQuaid cut him off. "Huh. My kid brother must have had a chicken do his writing." The navigator shoved a letter in front of Stefan. "I can't make heads or tails of that scratching."

Stefan examined the page. "This might be 'furnace.' And this looks like a five. Is this a dollar sign? Five dollars? Maybe someone threw money in the furnace."

"Well, if that's what he did and he's asking me to replace it, he's barking up the wrong tree." David took back the letter and studied it before stabbing it with his finger. "Ah, Lester. The kid next door." He slid a glance at Dever. "Reminds me of someone here."

Dever gave no indication he realized he was being referred to. "Must be a Polack. Everybody knows they're lacking in the smarts department." He head-slapped Stefan. "Isn't that so, Stevie boy?"

Andrew scoffed. "I know no such thing. Copernicus was Polish. He realized the earth revolves around the sun instead of vice versa. I'd say he had plenty of smarts in mathematics and science."

"He probably would have been a great navigator."

Stefan laughed at David's musing. Trust his crewmates to deflect Dever's taunts.

"Hollywood knows they're worthless. Watch any movie and you'll see the Polacks are cowards at heart." Dever never quit. "That's why Stevie here will never be a great pilot. He's a cowardly Polack. Especially with a name like Dumbroski."

Stefan shuffled one of his letters to the bottom of his pile and scooped up his mail. "Time to see if the cleaning service tidied up our hut."

"Yeah, this place has the atmosphere of junior high." David shoved his chair back into Dever.

He and Andrew followed Stefan out the door. So did Dever. He would have followed them into their Quonset hut, but after allowing his crewmates to precede him inside, Stefan shut the door in Dever's face. He grinned. God forgive him, but that glimpse of shock on Dever's face before the door clicked shut was satisfying. Thank goodness he bunked elsewhere.

Officers from other crews who shared their hut were absent. Good. The loss of privacy ranked right up there with things to dislike about the military, like overbearing commanding officers and cold showers.

David threw himself onto his cot, which creaked a loud protest. "I don't get it. Why are Dever and so many others hostile to Poles?"

Stefan shrugged. "There aren't that many Poles in the US, and they're from Eastern Europe. They came late, after Western Europeans had settled and built up the States. Most Eastern Europeans are not welcomed with open arms."

"But why is Poland so disparaged?" Andrew settled on his cot with more decorum and spread out his mail like a handful of playing cards. "We don't hear Hungarians or Czechoslovakians being maligned like the Poles."

Stefan tightened his lips. This wasn't his favorite topic, but these were his friends. They stuck up for him and were genuinely curious.

"The Soviet Union is going to help us win the war, not Poland. You think Roosevelt's going to acknowledge Soviet atrocities against Poland? Washington sees Poland as a useless ally who isn't worth creating trouble with Moscow."

The reality rankled him. The Western European nations overrun by the Nazis had quickly capitulated. Not Poland. The Poles fought back harder and longer than any other country.

Even after Poland finally fell, many of its pilots escaped to Britain to form one of the RAF's best Spitfire squadrons.

Stefan pulled out the bottom letter from his pile from Greg Wolton, previously known as Grzegorz Wolanski. His second cousin, Greg now served as a Spitfire pilot and one of Stefan's best sources of information concerning the happenings in Poland.

"That doesn't explain why we hear so many Polack jokes. Or why Dever is such a pain in the neck about the Polish." David twirled a letter on his fingertip. It flew off and dropped to the floor.

"A lot of Hollywood bigwigs are Communists. They won't malign Russia with the truth, so they portray Poles negatively. Washington's okay with that. Russia's a big ally, so it has to be presented positively. Anyone who reveals what Russia is really like is silenced."

David snapped his fingers. "That Bogie film we saw the other day. The merchant marine ship made it to Murmansk and one actor says, 'The Russians are our friends.' Was that written by a Commie?"

"You better believe it. And any character with a Polish-sounding name is portrayed as an emotionally unstable loser. No one said life is fair." Stefan shucked off his shoes and sat cross-legged. "Say, did I tell you Humphrey Bogart traveled through Brazil where my buddy is based, and Daniel got his autograph? He also got the First Lady's signature when she pinned a medal on him for sinking a U-boat."

"He got a medal for that?" Andrew flipped the letter he'd been reading onto his cot. "What are we doing freezing our tootsies in Iceland when we could be lollygagging in the tropics and still hunting U-boats?"

David stabbed the air. "I've got it. I know how you can prove you're superior to Dever. Bag the first U-boat."

Stefan slapped his knee. "Why didn't I think of that?" With effort, he kept a straight face and nodded. "Tomorrow, boys. Tomorrow, we'll bag us a U-boat."

More men trickled into the hut as he finished reading his mail. Not interested in their boisterous talk, he headed outside and wandered down to the shore where they beached the planes. An upended barrel perched near the edge of the launch apron, and someone sat upon it.

Marie.

He watched as she fiddled with something, gazed around the area, and fiddled some more. She was the picture of aloneness.

He inched closer until he could see what she held. A ball of pale-blue yarn?

"Did you enjoy your letters?"

She hadn't turned around. How had she known he'd joined her?

"I did. My mother's roses are blooming, my sister's erstwhile boyfriend went AWOL to convince her not to break up with him and ended up being arrested by MPs, my cousin in England had to bail out after his Spitfire's engine seized and British farmers nearly stabbed him with their pitchforks because they thought he was a Kraut, and my subscription to *Popular Mechanics* will expire if I don't renew now. I didn't know I had a subscription."

She let her hands drop to her lap as she stared at him. "Is your cousin all right?"

"Yeah." He inched closer to the water, stopping before the lapping waves could wet his shoes. "He'd like to quit the RAF and join us. Since Americans have so many accents, he thinks he'd blend in better. Maybe. There are still bigots like Dever."

He gazed at the sea. "On the other side of the world, my buddy John ended up on a hospital ship where one of the nurses turned out to be Gloria, our friend Daniel's cousin. He embarrassed her in front of the medical staff by waking up and saying, 'Glory hallelujah.' She and Daniel's sister Theresa followed us everywhere, the personification of nuisances."

"You enjoy your memories."

To the west, the sun hung low, ready to plunge into the ocean. Twilight was the loneliest time of day, when he missed his family the most. Did Marie miss anyone? He turned back to find her busy with her yarn.

"What are you doing?"

Her brows arced upward, but she lifted her project. "Crocheting a mitten. A friend sent me a new pattern. They'll be appreciated in autumn. I should have them finished by then." She glanced down. "Are you considering a constitutional swim?"

Stefan looked around and jumped back, shaking his damp shoe. "One dip in that water was quite enough for me, thank you." He plopped down on a rock that appeared fairly clean. "My mom always made us mittens, but she used two things."

A slow grin spread across Marie's face. "Knitting needles? We weren't allowed to learn to knit at the orphanage because the needles could be used as weapons."

Orphanage?

"Ah. They didn't want to referee any swordplay. But what about now? Do you know how to knit?"

"Never learned, although the benevolent widows wanted to teach us. But anything that can be knitted can also be crocheted. And carrying around a crochet hook is easier than needles."

He wrinkled his nose. "Were the benevolent widows a bunch of do-gooders?"

Humor filled Marie's laugh. "You could say that. They offered to teach us poor, motherless girls womanly skills. It made them feel useful. I always liked one lady in particular. She told me stories of when she grew up. I imagined she was my grandmother." She pursed her lips, and her shoulders rose and fell with a sigh. "She died when I was sixteen. I miss her."

After a moment, she straightened. "Anyway, my friend who wrote keeps asking where I am, and don't I trust her to keep a secret? Writing is so hard. We can't say anything that would offer a clue to our whereabouts. We can't even mention that reliable old icebreaker, the weather. All I can write is, 'I am fine, how are you?' No wonder she's upset with me."

Stefan watched the waves lap placidly at the shore. "I hear you. I want to write about the scenery here, which is so different from Wisconsin. But not a whisper is allowed. You know why, right? If the Germans board a ship before sinking it, they look for mail. Or they may find a mailbag floating on the ocean after a sinking. They gather all the mail and take it to Germany for analysis, searching for clues that indicate troop location and strength. You can bet they wish they'd grabbed Iceland before the British did. Had they known how sparse our manpower was last year, they probably would have attacked."

"Do mailbags really float? And with the convoys now, do they risk boarding ships?" She offered a dainty shrug. "If my letter to Ozanne was opened, the censor didn't object to my request for a mitten pattern." She dropped her yarn and folded her hands. "Do you have any musical ability?"

He gaped. "What does that have to do with mittens and censors?"

"Not a thing. We need acts for the shows we stage for the men. What's your talent?"

"Sitting in the audience and applauding." He filled his lungs with the brisk air and laughed. "Actually, a friend and I did take part in a talent show during basic training. It was more of a comedy act, though."

"Comedy is good. What did you do?"

"My friend recited 'Paul Revere's Ride.' You know, during the Revolution, when ..."

"I know Longfellow's poem. What did you do?"

"I played the drums to accompany him. Only I mixed in Morse-code messages. Like when he said, 'If the British march,' I beat out 'with pants on fire.' The guys who knew Morse laughed, and those who didn't couldn't figure out what was so funny."

"Did your friend know what you were doing?"

"Nope. He thought I was giving him a military beat."

"You were a naughty boy."

"I was an angel."

"Yes, yes, of the fallen variety." She grinned and rubbed her hands. "Where can I find a drum? And you—find a friend to recite with."

He sighed. He and his big mouth. Oh well. It had been pretty funny. "Yes, ma'am." He rose and stretched. "Right now, though, it's time to turn in. We fly early, and we have to bag a U-boat tomorrow."

"You have to?"

"Yep. To prove Poles are superior to Dever."

Marie opened her mouth, then closed it. She exhaled. "Be careful, Stefan."

He touched the brim of his hat. On his way back to the hut, he paused.

An orphanage! That's where she grew up? How old had she been when she lost her parents? Would it be rude to ask?

He recalled a friend of Matka's who was recently widowed. She complained that everyone avoided mentioning her husband, afraid they would upset her. But she wanted to talk about him.

Maybe Marie wanted to talk about her parents.

Stefan pictured his family. Ojciec and Matka, his brothers, Jedrek and Bronislaw, his sister Dorota. His stomach hollowed as he imagined losing them.

Next time he saw Marie, he'd ask about her parents. First, though, he had to find a U-boat to sink.

Chapter Five

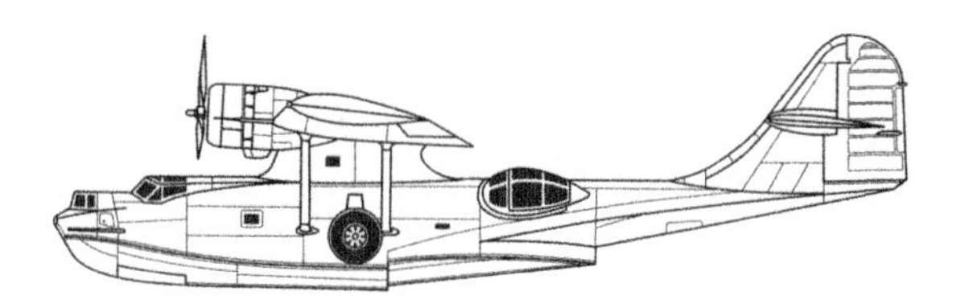

Marie waited until the doctor left the ward before approaching the sailor propped against the wall and staring at his bandaged hands lying limp on his lap. She'd never seen a more woebegone expression.

She summoned a bright smile. "I understand you're ready to exercise your hands."

A spark of emotion crossed the young man's face, and it wasn't a happy one.

"I don't know what you're talking about." He raised his hands. "These are useless."

Marie swallowed a laugh. "That's more like it. Now you remind me of my neighbor's kitten back in DC. All spit and snarl."

His eyes widened before a hint of menace flickered. "You think you know ..." He turned his head to the side while keeping his gaze locked on her. "I'm not spitting."

His voice had softened as though acknowledging that he had snarled.

She clasped her palm to her breastbone and looked up. "Thank you, Lord."

The patients in the surrounding beds hooted.

"She's got your number, Burkhart." The guy in the next bed practically drooled as he eyed Marie.

She kept her attention on Burkhart. "I've been asked to help you get your hands back into shape."

He snorted and raised them again. "They're burned. Stiff. Scarred. I was a pianist. I'll never be able to play again."

"Never is nebulous." Marie unfolded a mat and laid it across his lap. Retrieving a canister from the basket at her feet, she unscrewed the lid and dumped the contents onto the mat.

"Pick-Up Sticks!" The patient on Burkhart's other side struggled to sit up. "I haven't played that in ages."

Burkhart's shoulders slumped. "Are you kidding me?"

Marie wiggled her fingers in his face. "This requires dexterity. Pick up the sticks without disturbing any of the others." She waited a moment while he glowered. "What's the matter, sailor boy? Are you afraid?"

More hooting rose from the other beds. Burkhart scowled. He picked up a blue stick that had landed away from the others and poked her with it. "Satisfied?"

She snatched it away. "Blue sticks are worth five points. Next?"

He released a long-suffering sigh and flexed his stiff fingers. Oh-so-slowly, he extracted a red stick. Clenching a loose fist in triumph, he stared in wonder as he stretched out his fingers. He leaned over the pile in determination. "How many points are red sticks worth?"

"Ten. Green are worth two points each and yellow are only one point. The black one is worth twenty-five points." Marie clasped her hands together to avoid reaching for the blue stick that begged to be next.

"Too bad the black stick is on the bottom of the pile," the eager patient in the next bed said.

Another stick shifted as Burkhart attempted to lift a green one. Before he could snarl, Marie grabbed the blue stick.

"Five points for me." She waved it in his face, prompting a rueful grin. For her next move, she allowed the stick to bump another. This game wasn't for her benefit. "Pity."

As Burkhart considered his next move, she pointed her blue stick at his neighbor. "Lessman, right? How about taking him on?"

She winced as he launched himself off his bed. Her task was to help these men recover from their injuries, not gain new ones. Lessman landed in the bedside chair and took her blue stick. As the game continued, she picked up her basket and searched the ward for someone else who needed distraction.

One man lay staring at the ceiling.

She stopped beside him. "I have a few books. Are you interested in reading?"

The Red Cross' small selection of books was in constant demand. Even nonreaders took their turns.

The man rolled his head back and forth.

"How about some stationery? Would you like to write to someone?"

That garnered a response as his sullen gaze zeroed in on her. "Write to who?"

His dark-brown eyes wavered. A letter lay on the stand. A Dear John? She sat on the edge of his bed and picked it up. *Dear Charles.* Her gaze strayed to his patient chart. *Michael.* Uh-oh.

He nodded at her realization. "I'm so special, am I? She doesn't even remember my name."

Marie fingered the paper. "How long have you known ..." She checked the signature. "Olive?"

"We met at a train depot while my unit traveled to our next training camp. The ladies served sandwiches and stuff. Olive gave me an apple. We got to talking and she gave me her address, asked if I'd like to write to her." His voice trailed off.

"This letter is mimeographed. See how the ink with the name is a little different? Olive must be writing to several men. She mixed up the letters and envelopes." The girl's heart might be in the right place, but her technique needed work.

Michael reverted to studying the rounded ceiling. "I'm a sucker for a pretty face."

"I wonder what Charles thought when he received a 'Dear Michael' letter." Marie scanned the letter. "You can write her back and let her know you're on to her. Address it 'Dear Jane.'"

He frowned. "Jane?"

"Isn't that the woman's equivalent of a Dear John? Or keep writing as a casual acquaintance. This is an amusing letter. Did you read the whole thing? This part here about her mother backing the car into the trash cans and a bunch of cats howling and waking up the neighborhood? Can't you picture the cats leaping out of the cans?"

He took back the letter. "Huh. Yeah, that is pretty funny. Casual acquaintances, eh?" He shrugged. "It is nice to get mail. And it's not like I would ever see her again. She's in Ohio and I live in Idaho."

Accepting sheets of stationery, he began scribbling. Marie smiled as she backed away. He would be all right.

The Pick-Up Sticks game had gained another player. Burkhart crowed at retrieving the black stick. Maybe he wouldn't become a concert pianist, but for today, his mood was lifted. And she had something to do with that. She raised a mental fist. This was what made her job so fulfilling.

She found Betty in the next ward. "What are you doing here? Am I finally getting some help in the hospital?"

"Dream on, Marie." She attempted a stern look. "You haven't been actively recruiting talent for our shows."

"Betty, these are wounded patients. Even if they have talent and are ambulatory, they can't go out to wherever the shows are held."

Her friend wilted. "True. But we can keep them in mind for when they're healthy."

Marie crossed her arms. "Not really. When they are ready to leave the hospital, they'll go back to the merchant marine or the navy. Few of them are based here."

"Aren't you a ray of sunshine?" Betty pouted and cleared her throat. "Actually, I'm here for another reason. I seem to be coming down with the Reykjavik Rasp."

"Oh no."

Most of the Red Cross women had suffered through a debilitating cold that left them with a hacking cough, dubbed by the soldiers as the Reykjavik Rasp. So far, Marie had been exempt. Lettie insisted it was because she'd grown up in the cold north. Marie believed the sulfur-laden air was unhealthful. Now, with her best friend under the weather, she'd find out if it was contagious.

"Oh!" Betty clapped her hands. "I found something you need." She pulled Marie to the kitchen and, with a proud grin, placed two pots on the counter upside down.

The Rasp must have affected her brain. Marie looked from the pots to her friend and back. "I'm guessing you don't expect me to make dinner."

"Marie!" Betty squealed, then coughed. "You need drums for your friend." She patted one pot, then the other. "Here you go. Kettle drums."

When Marie imagined Stefan banging on the pots, the image tickled her funny bone. She giggled. "I can't wait to see his face. All he needs is a beat, though, to transmit Morse code.

I wonder if he ever played with his mother's pots." She clutched her sides with a full-blown belly laugh. "She'd be so proud to see how far he's come."

Betty laughed too and doubled over with a cough. "I have to get outta here." With a wave, she left.

Marie checked her watch. She was scheduled to conduct a quiz show among the ambulatory patients. Helen had supplied her with pages of questions, and she'd procured three chocolate bars as prizes. Were the boys really interested in parlor games? Maybe no one would show up.

She pushed through the door of a small foyer and skidded to an abrupt halt. The benches along the walls and the numerous chairs scattered about were filled with red-robed patients. She took a deep breath. "Hello, boys. Are you feeling smart today?"

When they saw her, they peppered her with questions about why didn't she visit more often, did she have a boyfriend, where was she from. They must be really bored.

She allowed them five minutes of banter before posing the first question. "Time to test your knowledge, and I have three sweet prizes. Number one, what constellation has a belt of stars?"

"Orion," yelled a freckle-faced redhead.

"What kind of tree can be called melancholy?"

"Willow." The redhead wasn't giving anyone else a chance.

"In 1775, the shot heard round the world was fired where?"

"Lexington."

"No, Rodger Dodger, it was Concord." A pale boy slumped against the wall grinned at Marie. "I'm from Massachusetts."

"And you're right." Next was her favorite question. "What is a dead-end street meaning 'bottom of the sack' in French?"

A tall, lanky man who could use a longer robe responded, "Cul-de-sac."

"I was going to say that." Rodger was getting grouchy.

Half an hour later, Marie passed out the prizes. The first winner ripped off the wrapper and gobbled up the whole chocolate bar. The second man carefully peeled his open and, closing his eyes, inhaled the delicious fragrance. He broke off a tiny piece, placed it on his tongue, and savored it. Then he broke off a piece for the man beside him.

Rodger won the third chocolate bar, but the sweet treat didn't meet with his approval. "Come on, miss. Give me a kiss."

She stepped back. What was the appeal in kissing a stranger? "Sorry, big boy. I've been exposed to the Reykjavik Rasp."

He scowled but to her relief didn't press his suit.

Marie left the hospital drained. Remaining upbeat around the men's emotionally challenging injuries took the starch out of her. Not for the first time, she considered asking to be reassigned. Of course, then she'd have to attend more dances. The fellows tended to get possessive when they finally had a partner, and Marie had heard enough complaints from the other women about being treated like rag dolls.

Did Stefan like to dance? Would he want to kiss her?

He'd said he *had* to get a U-boat today. What did that mean? Her stomach churned, and she crossed her arms tight across her abdomen.

Oh, Stefan, don't do anything foolish.

Chapter Six

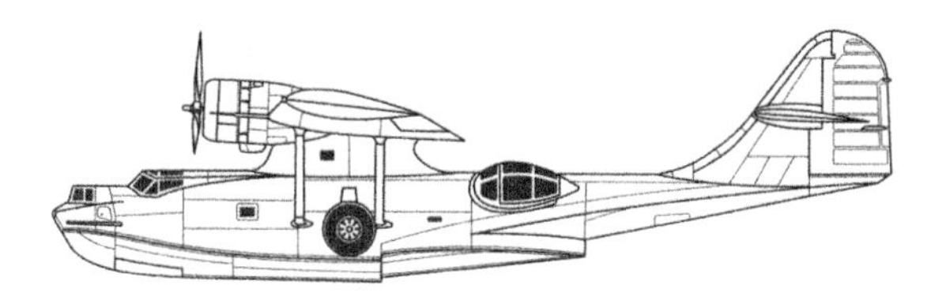

"How do you know we're going to sink a U-boat today?" Lawrenz's voice warbled through the interphone. "Are we getting secret messages or something?"

Stefan glanced at Andrew beside him in the cockpit. They shouldn't have told the crew their plans.

"We don't know we'll sink a sub for certain today, but we're sure going to try. The squadron's performance has been abysmal, and that's got to change. We have to take greater risks."

"Why now?" Curiosity filtered through Jenz's voice.

"Because we're going to prove the superiority of the fighting Poles over clowns like Dever." McQuaid injected his voice with a note of hauteur.

"What nationality is Dever?" Pennington joined the conversation from his spot in the bow.

"I believe he's Irish," Andrew said.

"No way!" A thump sounded. McQuaid must have tried to

jump up from his navigation table. "I refuse to share my ancestral honors with that fool."

"So being first to sink a sub is supposed to prove who's smarter?" Jenz didn't seem to share McQuaid's philosophy.

"Either smarts or stupidity, if we get shot down." Andrew searched the horizon with binoculars.

"May I point out something?" Poulos hesitated. "I have no Polish ancestry."

"Duly noted." Reaching up to adjust his throttles, Stefan wished McQuaid hadn't shared his philosophy. They needed everyone on their toes, not worrying about their ethnicity.

He'd spent a long, restless night reviewing their usual attack procedure. They usually approached U-boats perpendicularly. Most of the depth charges fell too far beyond the sub to do any damage. However, if he attacked along its length, he could maximize the potential for destruction. With no margin for error, he had to be precise in his positioning. By the time he circled back, the sub would have dived.

It was all theoretical, but he believed he could accomplish this maneuver. And while he was at it, he intended to nail the U-boat.

McQuaid's voice sounded in his headset. "Convoy should be ten miles ahead."

Stefan took a deep breath, held it, and released it slowly. "Okay, everyone, keep your eyes peeled. Restricted visibility and moderate sea swells will make spotting subs mighty difficult."

Long minutes passed with only the drone of the Pratt & Whitney engines filling his ears. He swept his gaze back and forth, hoping he'd notice anything that didn't belong to the ocean and not become hypnotized by the repetitive waves.

Wait! What was that?

"Andrew, check to my left. Eleven o'clock."

Before Andrew could focus his binoculars, Pennington hooted from the bow.

"Whoo-wee! A U-boat on the surface. Boy, is he brazen!"

Stefan slipped the plane to the left to line up with the sub. He guessed it to be four miles ahead. "See any activity around their machine guns?"

Andrew steadied his binoculars with his elbows on the control yoke. "No sign of movement on the deck." He adjusted his focus. "There is someone in the conning tower. Lookouts, probably, but I don't think they've spotted us."

Stefan flexed his fingers. Despite the chill, sweat trickled down his back. Doubt tried to shake his resolve, but he gritted his teeth. He could do this.

He pushed his PBY down into a 180 miles-per-hour dive. The sub continued on its course. Why weren't they shooting at them or making an emergency dive? He saw the men in the conning tower now.

Lots of men.

At 125 feet, he released four depth charges in salvo. The simultaneous discharge of nearly two thousand pounds made the plane bounce like they'd flown over a bump. Pulling up, he raced over the U-boat from stern to bow, getting a fleeting impression of shocked, upturned faces.

Stefan banked into a sharp turn and nearly banged his head on the side window as he tried to view the results. He clenched his fist. The depth charges straddled the sub just short of the conning tower, as he'd hoped. For a moment, nothing happened. Then, huge geysers exploded out of the sea on either side, momentarily hiding the U-boat. As the water settled, the German vessel rolled to the side. It began to submerge, stern first.

He'd done it. He'd actually sunk a U-boat.

Lawrenz spoke up from the blister window "There's men in the water."

With a start, Stefan realized no one had cheered or said anything during the enemy's destruction. Were they awed by the spectacle? Imagining the scene inside the submarine? In total disbelief?

Disbelief, he understood. He had destroyed an elusive, menacing submarine. A tingly feeling grew in his chest.

Oil spread across the sea. Odds and ends meant to support the deadly missions of the cramped submersible floated in the gunk. The boat seemed to go down in one piece, but the depth charges must have blasted some big holes in the vessel to allow the stuff to escape.

Men in the water, Lawrenz said. Focus, Dabrowski!

He circled low. "Poulos, Lawrenz, drop a life raft to them."

Andrew jerked his gaze to him. "You planning to pick them up?"

"No. The swells are running too high to risk a landing. Jenz, radio our position to the convoy. They can have the honor."

They watched as seven men hauled themselves and each other into a raft that became more cramped with each addition.

"Tight squeeze, although being huddled together may warm them," Ramsey said from his engineering post.

Stefan doubted that.. The memory of his own dip in the bay sent shivers convulsing through his body.

"Are those the guys who were in the conning tower?" Jenz asked.

"Yeah, the tidal wave from the explosions washed them overboard," Poulos said. He'd probably watched from the blister window with Lawrenz, which was the best seat in the airplane to observe the Germans' catastrophe.

Stefan studied the sailors. Most folded their arms tightly across their bodies or around their drawn-up knees. One man was allowed extra space as he lay stretched out—maybe unconscious or injured, thrown against the sub when he was tossed off.

The Germans watched him. Were they inwardly cursing their misfortune or Stefan's good luck? Well skill, actually, if he may be so bold. Perhaps they wondered what would happen next. Prisoner-of-war camps in the United States had to be a whole lot better than those in Germany.

He glanced at his watch. "Almost time to return to base. Jenz, did you receive an acknowledgement?"

"Yeah, but they didn't give any indication of when they'd pick these guys up."

He waggled his wings at the Germans and turned northwest. "Lawrenz? Did you have your camera plugged in?"

"You betcha." Excitement infused the gunner's voice. "I sure hope they turn out. I snapped one right when the water towered over the boat."

"What do you suppose all those Krauts were doing out there? Gabbing?" Ramsey said, always the analytical one. "They should have been looking out, but they didn't see us, and we didn't fly out of the sun."

"Count our blessings. I don't care to return the plane to base riddled with holes."

"Not to mention us." McQuaid had been strangely quiet until now, leaving Stefan to wonder if he'd dozed off. "I have an aversion to anyone putting holes in me."

Stefan monitored his instruments as the gunners chattered.

"Hey, Jenz, what did base say when they heard we sank a sub?" Lawrenz's question caught his attention.

"Roger."

"Huh? I asked a question."

"And I answered. They said, 'Roger.'"

"That's it?" The gunners' voices rose as they expressed their indignation.

Stefan shifted in his seat and glanced at Andrew. Why the lack of enthusiasm from base?

The comment he'd heard in the hospital replayed in his mind. *He's not one of our best pilots. Boring as last night's bathwater, he is.*

Stefan tugged at his collar, his neck suddenly warm. The brass didn't believe they'd sunk the U-boat. If Lawrenz's photos didn't turn out, would they accuse him of being a liar?

"Finish your roll of film, Lawrenz. We may need proof."

Silence reigned. Finally, Pennington said, "If Dever claimed to sink a sub, they'd throw him a party without any verification."

Andrew drummed his fingers on the control column. "No one said life is fair, fellas."

* * *

Arriving at Reykjavik, they landed and taxied to the dispersal hut. Waiting there were Captain Hopley and Lieutenant Commander Arnett.

Stefan blew out his breath. This could get ugly. "David, bring your chart, please."

"You got it."

They filed off the plane. Before their superior officers could say anything, Stefan touched Lawrenz's shoulder. "Run the film over to the photo lab and request immediate development."

The captain's eyes widened. "You think you got a sub?"

"Yes, sir. We watched it sink, dropped a life raft to the survivors, and radioed the location. They haven't been picked up?"

"Not that we've heard." The captain considered him for the longest time, and Stefan forced himself to not fidget under his perusal. Finally, Hopley said, "I'm surprised, Lieutenant. I wouldn't have picked you to be the first to bag a sub."

He may have meant to be complimentary, but Stefan viewed the comment as an insult. He cut a glance at the CO. "I may be as boring as bathwater, sir, but I do know how to fly."

The captain rocked back on his heels. "Boring as bathwater. That's interesting. Why do you say that?"

"I've heard it mentioned."

"By whom?"

Stefan looked at the CO again, who was staring into the distance, his shoulders twitching.

"I see." Captain Hopley nodded once. "Report to the ops room for a debriefing."

The whole crew saluted.

Tension knotted Stefan's muscles. Too bad he didn't have time to drop in at the hospital. He could use a smile from Marie. Exhaustion dogged him, but he had no time for rest, either. He needed to detail their flight for the brass.

Lawrenz's photos received priority. By suppertime, they had their proof. In one photo, the bow protruded from the explosions of water on either side of the sub. Another showed the conning tower exposed, but the sailors had disappeared. A crucial photo portrayed the U-boat lying on its side, stern submerged.

Captain Hopley grew more animated with each photo. "This is more like it. We've had too many muffed attacks for weeks. Let's hope we're turning a corner now and this isn't a fluke. Keep up the good work, Dabrowski."

His joviality wasn't shared by Arnett. The CO's dark scowl might be cause for concern.

Stefan kept his head down, examining a shot of the

survivors in the life raft. Where were they now? The convoy may not have released a corvette to find them. Dropping a raft hadn't done them a favor, for it would only keep them marginally warmer than in the ocean. He sighed. He had simply prolonged their icy ordeal.

Dinner at the mess hall grew boisterous as more crews returned and heard the news. Everyone wanted to examine the enlarged photos. Stefan was about to take a drink when David gave a rapid shake of his head. Stefan lowered the glass and, *whop!* Dever—it had to be Dever—slapped him on the back, no doubt hoping to break Stefan's teeth on the glass.

"Well, well, well. Stevie D is trying to win a medal."

Stefan didn't acknowledge the man but said to David, "I can't let my cargo-pilot pal outpace me by sinking a sub off the Brazilian coast and being awarded a DFC by the First Lady."

The navigator chortled. "Don't expect her to come here for another ceremony."

"Oh, I don't know, David." Andrew scooped up a spoonful of dehydrated potatoes. "She travels so much that she may pass through Reykjavik."

Stefan pushed his Spam slices and mushy canned peas around his plate. Matka's constant admonition rang through his mind. *No dessert if you don't clean your plate.* The vanilla pudding tempted him to gulp down another bite. He shook his head at the men's banter. "We did what's expected of us. Sinking U-boats isn't expected of cargo pilots."

"Can you prove you sank a U-boat?" Dever never gave up.

Another airman held up the photo of the sub beginning its death dive. "Come on, Dever. Does this look healthy?"

The bully's face darkened. "Don't let it go to your head, Stevie boy."

Stefan's eyes drifted shut as he visualized the press release. *"Pilot as Boring as Bathwater Sinks Squadron's First Sub."*

Ojciec would counsel that opposition meant he was doing well. Matka would react more like a mother bear. He chuckled, picturing Dever with a black eye the size of her fist.

Chapter Seven

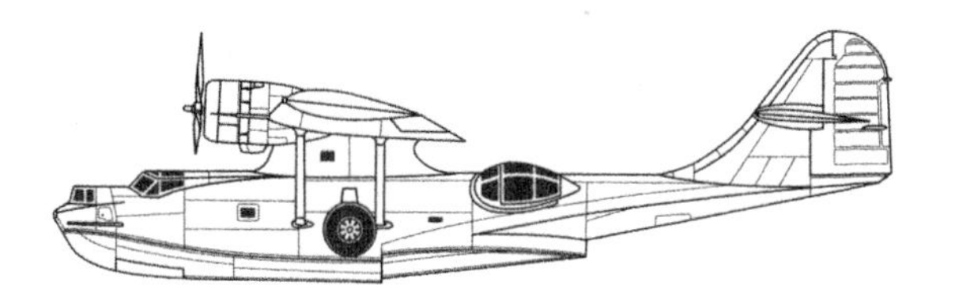

Marie watched Burkhart pick up sticks like he was gathering acorns under an oak tree. His doctor wore an ear-to-ear grin as he observed his patient's dexterity.

A portly, older man in civilian attire nudged her. "I hear you got him started with the Pick-up Sticks."

She had noticed the gentleman right away. He carried a fancy camera and had been photographing many of the patients and asking where they were from. "Are you a reporter?"

He stuck out his right hand. "Chase Rollins, *New York Times*. I'm doing a profile on our troops in Iceland."

"*The New York Times.* I've heard of that." She regarded him with greater interest. "Are the patients' local papers able to pick up your article and run it in their hometowns?"

"That's the idea. Where are you from?"

The question was a standard conversation starter with the military men.

"Quebec City."

"You're a long way from home."

She tried not to let her surprise show. "Actually, I'm closer to home than most of these boys are."

Rollins cringed. "Ugh. You're right. My knowledge of Canadian geography isn't very good. How'd you end up in the American Red Cross?"

She'd lost count of how many times she'd had to explain her background. Remembering the Red Cross edict to always present a happy face, she offered a big smile. "I went to school in Maine, then worked at a hospital in Washington as a dietitian, which led to recreational hospital work with the Red Cross."

"That's where you learned to use Pick-up Sticks?" At some point, he'd pulled a notebook and a stubby pencil from his pocket.

"My primary task is to keep up morale. When the men are seriously wounded, they're often depressed. Rather than merely trying to take their minds off their injuries, I like to present them with something that might help, like the sticks. We have a limited supply of books and games, so I rarely see results like this. But yes, I believe I can take a little credit for his recovery by bringing him the game."

"What does your family think of you being here?"

Marie shifted and scanned the ward, hoping to find someone who could benefit from her presence. "I have no family. I grew up in an orphanage."

"Oh, that's too bad." He didn't sound sympathetic. "I'd be glad to give you my wife's family. Heh, heh, heh."

Wasn't he clever. Before her brittle smile cracked, she excused herself to help a patient whose playing cards had spilled on the floor. She'd once considered dreaming up an imaginary family to shield her from all the thoughtless comments thrown her way, but she'd risk being caught in her own lies if she didn't keep the details straight.

After supper, she wandered outside with the intent to walk along the shoreline. She stopped short when she spotted a tall man leaning against a Jeep. Stefan!

She skipped across the parking area. "You're back. In the mess, I heard about a U-boat sinking. You really did it."

He pulled back in mock affront. "You doubted my skill? Marie, you wound me." He straightened and crooked his arm. Only after she tucked her hand around his elbow did he say, "It was a strange experience."

When he remained silent, she asked, "How so?"

They paused at a runway, and he hugged her hand against him to stop her. "Look both ways before you cross the runway."

She laughed. "Stefan, we're at its end. No plane will be coming from our left."

"It's when you let down your guard and get careless that *whop*, something hits you out of the ballpark."

He used the oddest metaphors.

They arrived at a stretch of shoreline away from the PBYs' landing beach. He stared out at the distant horizon. The water lapped at their feet, too tranquil to be called waves. Marie filled her lungs with the sea air. Beside her, Stefan stood silent, hands shoved in his pockets.

She squeezed his arm. "Will you tell me about it?"

"I've seen torpedoed ships explode." His words came out in a sigh. "I've seen men on fire, dropping into the icy water to douse the flames. I've seen men still on the ships, or parts of them, as they sank, their mouths open in screams. The Germans did that to them."

He shifted his gaze to the west. "Today it was their turn to experience the horror. I dropped depth charges that must have opened up some big holes to make the submarine sink so fast.

The men inside had no chance to escape. Lots of men die out there, either from water rushing in to drown them or by being set ablaze. Either way is a painful death."

She watched a pair of seabirds perform an aerial ballet. An airplane swooshed in to land, and the birds scattered.

"I heard there were survivors."

He grunted. "Seven men on the conning tower didn't go down with the ship. We dropped them a life raft, and I saw them pull themselves aboard. But no one came to pick them up. By now, they've died of hypothermia."

His tone held a hint of anger.

She touched his arm. "Patients in the hospital have talked about a British seaman who machine-gunned U-boat survivors in the water, saying he put them out of their misery. They've known U-boats to surface, and the Germans machine-gunned survivors of the ships they torpedoed. The British take a hard attitude now about rescuing the enemy."

"Understandable." His shoulders slumped. "I've seen some prisoners who were glad to be out of the war. One of them ... In other circumstances, he and I might have been friends. Maybe one of the men who died today was like that." He glanced around. "Of course, if Dever heard me say that, he'd be howling about the traitor in his midst."

He hunted for a smooth stone and pitched it over the water. It skipped twice before sinking. He turned back toward the camp. "I rarely see any of the other Red Cross ladies out in the evenings."

"That's because they're responsible for programs. There's one going on now. We could join them. They're playing charades."

"Charades?" He recoiled like she'd said a dirty word. "That's the most ridiculous game." He pantomimed something.

She clapped. "You'd be great at it. I have no idea what that represents."

"Good, because I don't either." He caught her hand and continued walking toward the landing beach.

He held her hand like it was the most natural thing in the world. She performed a giddy twirl in her mind.

Maintaining a sedate pace, she latched onto a mundane matter. "Well then, are you flying tomorrow?"

"Nope. My plane's down for routine maintenance."

"Good. I'm doing a small program at the hospital. Low key, in deference to the wounded. I'll be reciting a poem. I've penciled you in to do one too."

"A poem?" This time his reaction was more like he'd bitten into raw steak.

"What's the matter?" She poked his ribs. "Are you afraid?"

"Hmpf."

"Afraid you won't seem like a big, strong man because you know a little poetry? And it is little. Only four lines. I wrote it out on this card. Memorize it. Practice it. Put feeling into it."

Stefan snorted.

This should be fun. She rubbed her hands together.

Maybe.

* * *

Marie tapped her foot, though not in time to the music. Helen sat on the dais, singing "Don't Sit Under the Apple Tree" with her own guitar accompaniment. The men leaned forward, gazing at her with love in their eyes.

Marie was next. She'd thought it would be cute, reciting a poem about trees in a treeless land. Now it seemed like a stupid idea. Most of these men were sailors who weren't based in Iceland. Did they know about the absence of trees?

"What's the matter?" Stefan sat beside her.

"What was I thinking?" she whispered back. "They'll think this is silly."

"Want to do mine? It's only four lines."

"And you'll do this one?" She held up the paper. She'd memorized it but didn't trust herself to remember the words in front of a crowd, small as the crowd may be.

"No, thank you. I'll lead the applause."

"Snips and snails."

"Huh?"

She bounced one shoulder. "The sisters never let us swear at the orphanage."

Helen curtsied and stepped down, wreathed in smiles. "You're next."

Taking a deep breath, Marie climbed onto the dais and peered at all the faces watching her in anticipation. *Don't look at them. Look at the far wall, or the floor, or... Get a hold of yourself.*

"'Trees,' by Joyce Kilmer.

'I think that I shall never see
a poem lovely as a tree ....
A tree that looks at God all day,
and lifts her leafy arms to pray;
A tree that may in summer wear
a nest of robins in her hair;
Upon whose bosom snow has lain,
who intimately lives with rain.
Poems are made by fools like me,
but only God can make a tree.'
Unfortunately, he overlooked Iceland."

Her added line at the end garnered some laughs.

"And now, Lieutenant Stefan Dabrowski."

They changed places. Instead of facing the men, he faced the nurses and Red Cross women.

"'Ladies, to this advice give heed—
In controlling men:
If at first you don't succeed,
Why, cry, cry again.'"

The room exploded in laughter. Stefan offered a playful bow to the men and saluted the ladies. He nudged Marie as he slid onto his chair. "Thanks. I always wanted to be a comedian."

"Funny. At least you have the talent. I wouldn't have the nerve to be so animated. The way you raised your hands for the last line? That was effective. It didn't occur to me to use hand motions."

"Next time."

Like there would be a next time. Public speaking wasn't Marie's forte. Avoiding the spotlight was more like it. She sighed.

"Hey, don't beat yourself up about it." Stefan patted her hand kneading her thigh. "You have other talents. Concentrate on those, and you'll be happy."

What talents? She crocheted well. She loved to grow flowers, but here ... She'd enjoyed watching things grow in school science classes. Maybe the hospital patients would enjoy caring for seedlings. All she needed were little pots, soil, and seeds. Maybe Mr. Walton would help her find them.

Stefan watched her with his right brow quirked. How did he manage to do that without moving his left brow?

"Thank you. I'll do that. Do you like to plant seeds and watch them grow?"

Now he lifted both brows. "Can't say I've had much practice."

She didn't require much convincing after the show to join him in a walk along the shore. With sunset around ten thirty and sunrise at four thirty in early May, the nights were no longer completely dark. That was fine with Marie. Walking in sunlight was much preferable to stumbling around in the gloom.

"Soon, the amount of daylight will become shorter."

"Yep. Couple more weeks." Stefan looked to the west. "I won't mind the days and nights balancing out, although when we fly for thirteen hours, it's nice that God leaves the light on."

Marie tucked her hands into her coat pockets. All that sun didn't lift the temperature out of the fifties. "God leaves the light on? Cute."

"Actually, I think my grandmother meant the moon when she said that."

"Too bad he doesn't leave the light on during the winter months. When we arrived in March, the sun rose two hours later than in America. Waking up in the dark is hard for me. I'm dreading the continual darkness."

"Think of what we'll gain. Have you seen the Northern Lights? Magnificent."

Marie studied him. "You always look for the bright side, don't you?"

"I suppose I do. I remember my father telling my brother, who complained a lot, that life is more enjoyable, or at least bearable, when we're happy. He'd ask him if he enjoyed being grumpy. So what if his friend knocked his bicycle into the mud? A momentary inconvenience. At least he still had a bike. Anytime one of us was out of sorts, he'd make us count our blessings. Minimum of ten."

"Did you often have to count your blessings?"

Stefan laughed. "I remember one time. I must have been twelve years old. Ojciec read my list and said, 'These are all on the negative side.' I'd written stuff like, *I'm glad I don't have to play the tuba like Ralph Eggers in the school band.* Or, *I'm glad Matka doesn't like lamb chops, either.*"

"Oy-jests? Is that 'father'? It's so different from Matka."

"Yes, Ojciec is Polish for 'father.' When we were little, we called him Tata. That'd be like calling him daddy. We're too old for that now, although I think he wishes we still used Tata. Sometimes we call him Pops."

Stefan tugged her hand out of her pocket and enveloped it with his. She liked it, but she needed to think about something other than the tingles dancing up and down her spine.

"When you fly for twelve or more hours, doesn't that get boring?"

"Yep. Couple of times, I nodded off. Once, both Andrew and I drifted off at the same time. I jerked awake almost immediately, my heart pounding. I like to think my guardian angel head-slapped me."

"The same scenery of endless ocean must become dull. Can you tune into any radio shows?"

Stefan shook his head. "Probably be too distracting. Since then, I've made sure Andrew and I both get up, walk around, sack out at least twice. Not at the same time."

Marie stroked her chin. "You can't enjoy private conversations, right? You have to use the intercom, and everyone hears you. So what do you think about, besides whether you see a periscope or not?"

"Family, friends like Daniel and John." He nudged her. "My unholy-trio buddies. Books I've been reading. Bible verses. I try to meditate on them like the pastor back home says. Not sure how that works exactly, because my mind always wanders.

I try to pray for family and friends. Never had so many conversations with God before."

He stopped to select a smooth, flat stone. With a flick of his wrist, he sent it skipping across the water's surface. Five skips. Marie clapped. When he offered her a stone, she tried to imitate his technique, but the stone disappeared with one plop.

"Not my talent." She brushed off her hands. "Maybe I should pray about my lack of talents, but I doubt God would answer. People always say, 'what does God tell you?' He's never told me anything."

Stefan nodded. "I've never heard him speak audibly to me. But I do believe He brings things to my mind. Like with Dever. I was praying ..." He grimaced. "Okay, I was ranting, and I immediately thought of a verse in Colossians. 'Set your mind on things above, not on things on the earth.' I need to quit obsessing about jerks and concentrate on God instead, who loves me."

Marie gazed at the horizon. When was the last time a Bible verse had come to mind at an opportune time? Maybe when she decided to join the Red Cross? She'd read something about God being with a patriarch and watching over him wherever he went. Did that apply to her too? Had the verse influenced her?

To remember Bible verses meant she had to already know them. When was the last time she'd read the Bible?

Uncomfortable with her thoughts, she turned to Stefan. "Tell me about your family."

Chapter Eight

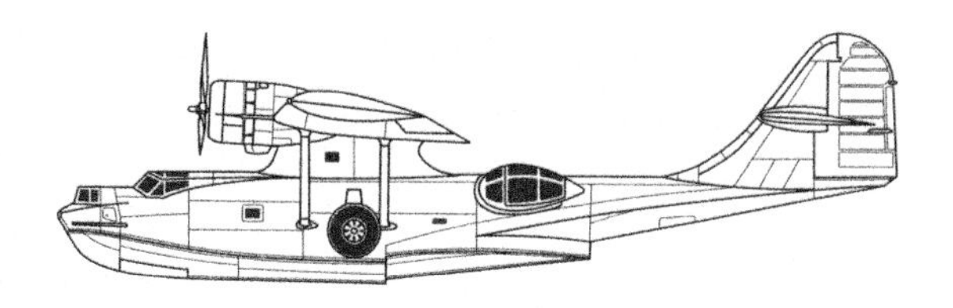

Stefan ran his hands along the fuselage and looked up at the engines. The covers had been removed and stowed, as well as the pitot head covers. The nose wheel lined up with the keel. He checked its pressure. Forty-three pounds. Good. They were ready to fly.

He hoisted himself aboard through the blister window in the waist compartment. The crewmen were already inside, readying their compartments for action.

Lawrenz greeted him with a furrowed brow. "No bombs have been hooked up to the wings. How are we gonna bag another sub without an arsenal?"

"We're not hunting for U-boats today. Our assignment is a little different." Stefan whistled toward the front of the aircraft. "Everyone come on back to the blisters so I can show you what we're doing today."

"Is it safe to fly without depth charges?" Poulos asked. "What if a Kraut plane is flying this way?"

Not that long ago, a single German airplane out of Norway had flown over Iceland and dropped a few bombs. With his long flight distance, he had to carry more fuel and less ordnance, making his attack more of a nuisance and a scare tactic than an effort to cause major damage.

"In the unlikely chance that we'll see a German plane, we won't drop depth charges on him, so it doesn't matter. Like the German flying to Iceland, we're carrying the maximum load of fuel. Our destination is Little Germania, an island off the northeast coast of Greenland, where there's reported to be a German weather station. Our task is to determine if the report is true and photograph the station. If we find it, a Coast Guard cutter will be sent to commandeer it."

"So we're going sightseeing over Greenland." David McQuaid spread out his navigation map. "Here's Little Germania, almost halfway between the Arctic Circle and the North Pole."

"Greenland ain't green and Iceland ain't ice." Pennington leaned against the bulkhead. "They got their names mixed up."

Stefan ignored him. "We'll fly over the Denmark Strait, keeping the coast in sight, but once we approach the Greenland Sea, we'll overfly these islands up to Little Germania. Any questions?"

"It's gonna be a looong day." Lawrenz yawned, already bored.

"Yes, it will be, especially with the summer solstice in a few days. Take turns hitting the sack. Use eye masks if you need to. I want everyone alert when we're in the vicinity of that weather station. Just in case they start shooting at us."

The men straightened at Stefan's words, like they hoped they'd see a little action. But having an engine shot out or a man wounded that far from home would be disastrous.

As Stefan made his way forward, checking each compartment, Jenz looked up from his radio. "Are we being sent away from the U-boats because Dever wants to bag the next one?"

Stefan shrugged. "It's a job that needs to be done, but I wouldn't be surprised if that's the reason we were tabbed."

If true, the CO was petty. Punishing them for sinking a sub? Maybe Captain Hopley had words with him about the bathwater comment, and this was Arnett's retaliation.

He and Marie had this in common. The Red Cross director, like the CO, had his personal favorite and didn't mind disparaging all the others.

From the cockpit, he called back to Jenz to start the auxiliary power unit. Stefan made sure the propellers were at full rpms, the throttle was one-fifth open, and the ignition switches were both on. He called to Ramsey, "Start the starboard engine."

Flying the PBY was a team effort. The flight engineer responded promptly. "Starting the starboard."

In short order, they headed north. Stefan flew over the western side of Iceland, gazing at volcanic mountains and vast, empty spaces. He wanted to see more of the country than Reykjavik. Maybe the Red Cross could organize tours. He'd ask Marie.

Marie.

His heart ached for her. Orphaned at three. Left in an orphanage with a battle-ax for a director. No contact with extended family. Thank God for this Sister Marguerite who gave her hugs.

Had he been orphaned, he had a passel of aunts and uncles, none of whom would have hesitated to take him in. The house may have been bursting at the seams with children, but they would say, "what's one more?"

He missed his family, but he would see them again in a year or two. All Marie had were a couple of sketchy memories. Her dad tossing her in the air. Her mother reading to her. At least she'd made two close friends in the orphanage.

Iceland disappeared behind them, and the flying grew monotonous. Time for a break. Stefan left the plane in Andrew's capable hands and headed back. The galley was empty. Beyond, Lawrenz snoozed in the blister window. After a few calisthenics to get his blood pumping, he poured a glass of lemonade. His mouth puckered at the bitter taste. What did he expect from the powdered stuff?

He found a can of peaches and sighed. What he wouldn't give for a fresh, crisp, juicy red apple. Stretching out in a bunk with his snack, he closed his eyes and relived sitting in the tree fort with his best friends, Daniel and John. He imagined the crunch as he bit into the luscious apple, the juice dribbling down his chin.

His eyes popped open, and he swiped a hand across his face. Nope, he wasn't drooling. Would have been embarrassing, even if he was alone.

His hunger quenched, Stefan crossed his arms beneath his head and continued torturing himself with memories of home. Like that spark of citrus scent when ripping open an orange skin. He breathed in. The plane definitely did not smell like an orange. More like a gym locker room full of aviation fuel.

He grinned as he recalled eating bananas in the tree fort. They'd peel them halfway down then toss them in the air with a twist to see who could get the peels to spread out like flower petals without breaking off the banana like they'd seen a man do at the park. Daniel came close, once. Mostly, they wasted good fruit.

They'd done such stupid things as kids. Did Marie have any fun memories like those?

The sun hung high overhead when they approached Little Germania island. In June, the nation of Greenland was indeed green. They sighted occasional buildings, but it had to be a lonely life down there.

Time to rouse the crew. "Everyone awake and on your toes. Have your guns ready if we take fire. McQuaid, is the camera ready?"

"It is, and I'm in the starboard blister. Lawrenz has his own camera in the port blister window. Let's hope there's something for us to record."

"Why do the Krauts need to know about the weather way up here?" Poulos asked.

"We're not that far from the route to Murmansk. And Norway." Andrew handed his binoculars to Stefan. "Nothing on this side."

"I see something." Excitement filled Pennington's voice. "There's a boat down there. And a building."

Stefan trained the binoculars on the boat. "A trawler. With an antiaircraft gun. Lots of stuff on the ground. Could be scientific equipment. Someone came out of the building."

Keeping a safe distance from the possible reach of the gun, Stefan circled lower. More men emerged from the building. One of them uncovered ... "Another gun on land, to the right of the building."

"I'm getting lots of photos, but we're too far away for good detail." McQuaid hesitated. "Are those antennas on that ridge? Radio equipment?"

Four men so far. At least two guns. Probably more of each. Stefan weighed his options. "Jenz, are you sending this?"

Ramsey answered. "Yes, he is. As we speak."

"Okay, here's the plan." Stefan paused to take a breath. They were entering combat. "I'll approach from behind the building. Have the cameras rolling, and the rest of you, be prepared with suppressing fire. Everyone ready?"

A chorus of agreement filled his ears, and he exchanged glances with Andrew. This was it. The PBY was a notoriously slow bird, but he throttled to gain as much speed as possible.

Two Germans rounded the corner of the building, and one raised a rifle to his shoulder.

"Whoo-ee! Here we go." From the bow, Pennington's gun stuttered. The Germans scattered.

The plane swept over the weather station. Stefan saw flashes from the German guns and heard the clatter of his crew's guns. "Report! Any damage?"

"Nah. They're lousy shots." From the front of the plane, Pennington was least likely to see any damage.

"I see a bullet hole or two in the portside horizontal stabilizer," Poulos said.

Stefan moved the yoke slightly, and the plane responded as desired. Apparently, no harm done. Fortunately, the stabilizer was metal-skinned, unlike the fabric-covered elevators.

"Camera crew? How'd you do?"

"We shot some lovely scenes. Even got one of a Hun yelling at us." McQuaid laughed. "Just as well we couldn't hear what he said."

"Poulos trashed the German gun, and Pennington shot one of the Krauts. I didn't have time to notice anything else." Lawrenz sounded more subdued than usual. "I just hope the cameras worked as advertised."

"Hey!" Grant glared out the window. "No negative vibes. We did good."

"And we're going home." Stefan tried to stretch. Their mission was only half over. "What are our coordinates, McQuaid?"

* * *

While Stefan enjoyed his return-trip rest time, he tried to read. He'd found *Wind, Sand and Stars* in a collection of paperbacks printed for servicemen. A French aviator's account of crashing in the Sahara Desert and nearly dying of thirst before a Bedouin saved him and his companion, it had grabbed his interest. His friend Daniel in Brazil had to land his cargo plane in the Sahara when sand clogged the engines. Daniel's adventure sounded much more exciting than this.

Stefan snapped the book shut and stretched his arms out and overhead. He missed his friends. Often, he daydreamed about them being together instead of scattered around the world flying very different aircraft. What was the likelihood they'd all return home? A line from a Civil War song came to mind. "*When this cruel war is over, pray that we meet again.*"

Did Marie look forward to returning home? She'd gone from a Quebec orphanage to a New England college to Washington. Who looked forward to seeing her again? She hadn't seen her friends in Quebec in seven or eight years. At least they still wrote to her. She'd probably like Milwaukee, even if it did get colder than an ice cube.

A full hour elapsed before he pried himself from the bunk. He paused at the navigation desk, and David pointed out their location on his map. They were approaching the Denmark Strait. Almost back to Reykjavik. He stopped by the engineer's compartment, and Ramsey assured him that, with a tailwind, they had plenty of fuel.

The northwestern most tip of Iceland came into view as Pennington asked, "Does anyone see what I think I see?"

Stefan searched the water with binoculars. "I see a floating mine."

"Yeah, I saw that too. Two of 'em, actually. But look to the one o'clock position from there. It appears to be a periscope, because there's a dark shape below it."

"I do believe you're right, Pennington." Grant turned the PBY slightly east. "And here we sit with no depth charges."

Stefan throttled back. "Jenz, see if anyone is patrolling this area."

"There's a plane nearby that will be here momentarily."

Something about Jenz's voice gave Stefan a bad feeling. "Who is it?"

Silence.

He tried again. "Don't tell me it's Dever?"

"It's Dever." Jenz's reply came out in a sigh.

"Well, that's a fine how do you do," McQuaid groused. "He'll be bragging about how we couldn't manage one little sub without his help."

Stefan silently agreed as he watched a glistening speck in the sky grow into a PBY. "He's too far west."

"And the U-boat's going deep," Pennington said.

Stefan circled around the U-boat's last known position. "Jenz, tell them it's diving."

As he spoke, he spotted a depth charge drop from Dever's wing. Not even close. Water erupted harmlessly. If the U-boat captain was smart, he'd hightail it out of there.

"What the ..." Lawrenz watched from the blister window. "Look at that. What's happening?"

Eruptions occurred all over the sea. As Stefan and his crew watched, the water spouts happened farther and farther away.

It wasn't funny, not really, but Stefan couldn't stop laughing. "That idiot blew up a mine. The shock waves travel out and detonate other mines. Dever's clearing the strait for the Germans. I hope they send him a thank-you card."

"Do the Krauts in the U-boat know what's going on?" Poulos asked.

"Oh, they hear it. Probably even feel it." Andrew grinned. "They must be wondering what new weapon we've unleashed."

"The Dever mine buster." McQuaid wheezed from

laughing so hard. "I have the most direct route back to base. We need to return first and spread the news before Dever has a chance to sweep this under the rug."

Stefan pressed his microphone switch. "Jenz, radio in our return. Add that the mine field has been decimated by a depth charge."

Andrew turned to him. "Don't you want to say that PBY-1 dropped the depth charge?"

Stefan shrugged. "Base knows Dever answered our call for someone with weapons. They'll know. And we don't have to point the finger at him."

"Who laid those mines? The Brits?" Lawrenz asked. "They won't be happy about this."

Stefan grinned. The CO's golden boy had tarnished his halo, and it didn't bother Stefan one bit.

Chapter Nine

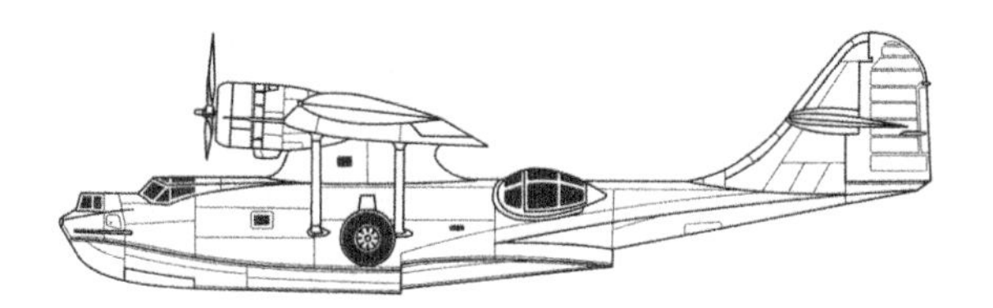

When Marie slipped into the officers' mess, the subdued atmosphere surprised her. Usually the men were boisterous, bragging about their exploits, or holding debates on flying tactics. Never had she known them to be this silent.

She spotted Stefan's navigator, David McQuaid, grinning down at his plate. Next to him, the copilot held his coffee cup in front of his face, his shoulders shaking in silent laughter. Stefan sat with his back to her, but he turned his face toward the wall and brought his napkin to his mouth. Wiping away a smile?

Outside, a gale-force wind howled around the Quonset hut, and the curved structure shuddered. Airmen's gazes rose from their breakfasts to the corrugated walls. Maybe they wondered, like her, if the hut would suddenly fly away, leaving them exposed.

David noticed her and spoke to Stefan while spinning a chair from another table to theirs. Marie scurried over to join them.

Stefan's welcoming smile warmed her heart. The early-morning blueness of his eyes captured the sky. She shook the silly thought from her mind.

"Why is it so quiet in here?" She whispered to avoid drawing everyone's attention.

"Did you hear about yesterday's debacle?" The copilot—oh yes, Andrew was his name—nodded to indicate the other side of the room. "Dever aided the Germans, and now he's stewing in his juices."

Marie looked to Stefan for an explanation.

His sapphire eyes twinkled. "He blew up a mine field, clearing a substantial portion of the Denmark Strait for U-boats to traverse unimpeded."

She blinked. "That's bad. Why were the three of you laughing?"

David snickered. "We've been imagining different scenarios of the meeting between Dever and the brass. Our CO thinks the world of Dever, but even he can't be happy about the loss of a dozen mines."

Marie raised her brows. "Another unholy trio."

Andrew frowned. "Huh?"

Stefan flicked his fingers at the copilot. "What's up?" he said to Marie.

"We're having the show today. Did you ask someone to read the poem?"

He pointed at David. "He'll do it."

The navigator straightened. "What will I do? Did you say 'read a poem'?"

Marie sighed. "Why do men act like poetry is going to kill them? You know, don't you, that many of the best-loved poems were written by men?" She pulled a sheet from her folder. "'Paul Revere's Ride.' You don't have to memorize it. Just familiarize yourself with it and practice with Stefan. The show's at three o'clock."

David's gaze swung to Stefan. "What are you going to do?"

"Provide you with a kettle drum accompaniment."

Andrew leaned back, crossing his arms. "This ought to be rich."

A crash sounded from across the room. Marie jumped, expecting the wind had damaged the hut, but then saw that Dever had leapt to his feet and upended his chair. He jabbed a finger in another man's face.

"You think Stevie D's boys have a magic touch? Well, let me tell you something. That dumb Polack does not have any magic. My men never saw a sub yesterday, and neither did he. He lied. He wanted to cause trouble."

The room erupted in laughter.

"Don't make excuses for your blunder, Dever," an officer wheezed through his guffaws. "We saw the photo they took of the periscope riding above the long, dark shape of the U-boat just below the surface. You should have followed their coordinates."

David dropped his fist on the table. "Hear that? He has men. We have boys. I think Ramsey might object to that."

"Yeah, did you hear?" Andrew spoke to the man beside him. "Our engineer turns thirty-five next week."

Stefan drummed his fingers on the table. "So what should we do? Gift him with a cane?"

"Say, not a bad idea." David rubbed his hands together.

Marie smiled. "How about one of those Icelandic walking sticks? Nice souvenir."

The man next to Andrew asked, "Does he have a family back home?"

"He was married with no kids," Stefan answered. "His wife died, though. Day after the funeral, he enlisted."

The man grimaced. "That's rough."

"Yeah. He worked in auto repair. Figured he'd do some sort of engine maintenance." Stefan shuffled the mail he'd picked up earlier into a neat stack. "He discovered he loved flying and was assigned to our crew."

Dever suddenly reached over Stefan's shoulder and snatched the letter from the top of his pile. "More Polack letters, Dumbo? Still passing secrets and aiding the enemy?"

"Look who's talking," someone yelled as laughter filled the room again. Dever frowned at the letter.

"Who's the dummy?" David said, grabbing the letter. "Can't you read?" He pretended to peruse the words. "Aw, talk about rough." He tapped the letter. "Stefan's sister's friend gave birth in the morning and received a telegram in the afternoon. She's a widow."

As Dever stalked off, Marie leaned toward David. "You know Polish?"

David grinned. "Nah. Stefan read this to us while we ate."

"So there really is a widow with a new baby? That's so sad." She stood and placed her hands on Stefan's shoulder. "Practice. Three o'clock."

* * *

Waltzing through the door of the Red Cross ladies' hut, Marie stumbled to a halt and stared. Everything stored in her bedside crate had been tossed onto her cot. Books lay willy-nilly with no concern for their pages. Her crochet yarn spilled out of its box, and stationery and letters from friends rested on the floor.

Betty gasped as she entered the room behind her. "What happened?"

Seated on her bed across the aisle, Anne didn't look up.

"You're lucky we don't have inspections like the military. You'd fail for sure."

Sara, Anne's only friend among the Red Cross ladies, widened her eyes at Anne's words. Her gaze skittered over the newcomers, but she didn't look them in the eye. She knew something.

Marie noted the way Sara fidgeted and picked at her fingernails. "The mouse that sneaked into the hut the other night didn't do this."

"Certainly not." Lettie crowded in behind her. "A rat did this."

With Betty's help, Marie put her belongings back into place. Smoothing a wrinkled page, she closed the book. "Only one thing seems to have been stolen."

Anne snapped her head up before quickly looking away.

Marie checked her wristwatch. "We have a little time before the show. Want to come with me to the RC director's office? We can have some fun."

Anne jerked and positioned herself away from them. Definitely guilty.

Betty, Lettie, and Helen followed her out the door.

"What are we going to do?" Helen asked. "Are you going to file a report about the vandalism?"

"No. Mr. Walton informed me that we've received half a dozen kites. They need to be tested. Now that the wind has settled down to a gentle breeze, we're going to fly kites."

Lettie squealed. "Oh, we'll have such fun. Maybe some cute guys will give us a hand."

As they dashed to the office, Betty asked, "What was stolen?"

"A pink bookmark. My list of ideas for activities."

Helen whistled. "Anne has to know she can't get away with that."

Mr. Walton joined them and helped assemble the kites. "No, no. Pull the loop up to the notch at the end of the stick. It should snap into place. Don't yank on it. You don't want to tear the fabric. These are delicate."

Marie tugged on the binding sewn into the hem around the edge of the kite. She eased it up to the vertical bar. It dropped into place so readily she nearly lost her grip. "That's not so hard."

"Of course not." He handed her a ball of string. "Tie this to the crossbar."

Soon, five kites soared through the air. And sure enough, men converged on the field to "help."

Marie recalled the one time in the orphanage when they had a kite. Someone donated a beat-up old thing that should have been junked but was deemed good enough for orphans.

They'd been so excited. After watching other children run through fields with their colorful kites in high pursuit, they now had a chance to do likewise. They struggled to get their battered kite airborne, and it soon crashed into the street. It was damaged beyond repair. More than a few children shed a tear.

That evening, Marie heard the sisters talking about it. Sisters Marguerite and Yvonne wanted to replace the kite since kites cost only a few cents. Sister Martha scorned their desire. What was one kite among so many children? It wouldn't last much longer than this one, anyway.

No other kite appeared at the orphanage.

Helen sidled close to Marie. "We need to begin preparing for the show."

Marie thought she recognized a man from Stefan's crew. She handed him her kite string just as a PBY roared overhead, coming in to land. The turbulence in its wake blew the kites out of the sky.

In the sudden silence, Mr. Walton grimaced. "We need a

field farther away from the runways." He picked up a kite that had taken a nosedive. The crossbar had snapped. "And we need to order more kites."

Marie smiled ruefully. She wasn't at the orphanage anymore. Here, morale came first. She tried to count the men who had gathered and relaxed her smile. Her kite idea was a big success.

"Next, we have Ensign David McQuaid reciting a dramatic poem, accompanied by Lieutenant Stefan Dabrowski on the kettle drums."

The announcer's words garnered a laugh when the curtain was pulled back to reveal Stefan with two kitchen kettles.

David stood at a podium and held a lightly clenched fist to his chest. "'Listen, my children, and you shall hear of the midnight ride of Paul Revere.'"

Stefan thumped a rhythm on the kettles. Marie knew he would use the smaller, higher-pitched kettle for dits and the larger one for dahs. His cadence changed when David said, "'Hardly a man is now alive who remembers that famous day and year.'" Snickers rose from the audience.

Marie wished she knew Morse code. Many of the men apparently did. Some laughed so hard, tears rolled down their cheeks. At David's last line, Stefan rapped out: dit dah dit, pause, dit dah, pause, four dits. Marie recognized the pattern when he repeated it twice. The men stood to their feet and cheered. David remained erect, hand at his chest, nose in the air. He must have known what Stefan was doing.

One of the nurses came alongside Marie. "One of the sailors had to tell me your boyfriend's messages. He's really good."

Her boyfriend? Marie grinned. She wouldn't argue with that.

After supper, she joined Stefan for his evening constitutional. They walked their usual route along the shoreline. "What was your first Morse message?"

Stefan tilted his head back. "Let's see. Listen, my children, you'll hear of the ride of Paul Revere." He snapped his fingers. "Oh, goody."

A laugh sputtered out of Marie. "That's what you tapped? No wonder they laughed so hard."

A smile stretched across his face. "It was fun. I'm getting rusty at Morse, though. I had a little cheat sheet with my messages written out in code. Remembering Morse is not like riding a bicycle. You can forget."

He paused, and an uncertain expression clouded his eyes. He wove their fingers together. "I suppose you didn't have a bicycle while growing up, did you?"

"No." Marie sighed. "I've been thinking about the orphanage a lot today." She told him about flying the kites. "And before that, Anne dumped out all my belongings on my cot. She was looking for my list of ideas."

"She told you that?"

"Oh, no. But the list is the only thing missing. It was my bookmark in *Anne of Green Gables*."

Stefan stopped walking. "Anne. Green Gables. Aha!" He swung their joined hands. "The orphan who longed for a bosom friend."

Marie gaped. "You read it?"

"Nope. My sister did. Dorota thought it was so silly to want a bosom friend. She thought it sounded scandalous, even if it mean a kindred spirit." He studied Marie. "Did you bring that book along, or find it here?"

"It's mine. I left a few clothes behind with a friend but

brought my books—a grand total of four. Silly, maybe, but Anne ... the one in the story ... is a kindred spirit in a way, both of us being orphans. She was sent to live with families—not to be a family member, but more as a servant. That happened, sometimes, at the orphanage. Boys especially were sent to farms to be farmhands. I'm glad I wasn't sent away to be a maid or babysitter."

Stefan nodded. He swaddled her hand between both of his. "Never doubt your worth, Marie. Your value is far above rubies. Don't forget that."

Heat spiraled through her. If she wasn't careful, she'd start grasping for an impossible dream—a rosy future. Dare she think it? She loved this man.

Chapter Ten

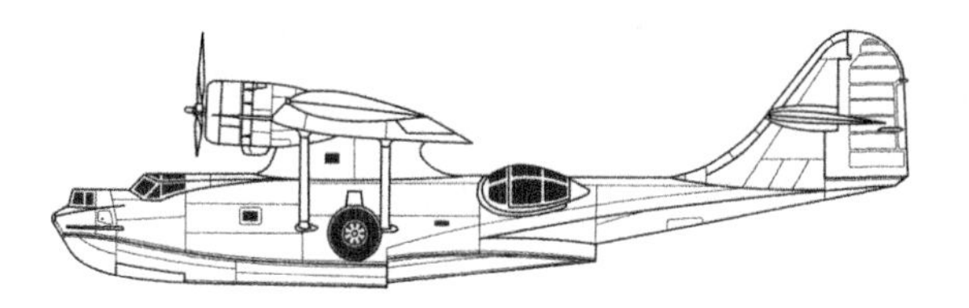

The photographer's mistake was Stefan's windfall. The man had accidently made copies of photos from the Red Cross show. And what did he do with them? He threw them away. Two photos of Marie laughing at a performance. Beautiful photos.

Stefan just happened to enter the photo lab with Lawrenz to expedite a repair of one of their N4 aerial cameras in the waist compartment. While Lawrenz explained the problem, Stefan wandered over to a bulletin board of pictures and noticed the waste basket, where he saw duplicates of nine photos, including the two of Marie and even one of him playing the kettle drums. They found their way into his pocket.

Now Marie's smiling face sparkled at him from the instrument panel—a touch of beauty in the plane's functional environment. John and Daniel would howl with laughter if they knew he waxed poetic.

The convoy he was shepherding through the treacherous North Atlantic stretched from horizon to horizon. There had to be one hundred ships down there. Clustered in the center were a couple of former ocean liners. Troopships. Very precious cargo.

Stefan flew over the escort aircraft carrier, a tiny brother to the huge combat carriers in the Pacific that John flew from. The extra protection declared the Allies' determination to bring this convoy safely to England. Even with the PBYs' long-range ability, a gap still existed where the ships had no air cover. With the carrier, the convoy possessed its own gap protection.

Off on the fringes, three low-riding cargo ships plodded along at a farther distance from the rest. Two destroyers nipped at their keels, ever vigilant. Stefan knew what that meant. Ammunition ships. No one wanted to be close by if those babies blew up.

Jenz called from the radio compartment. "Possible radar contact starboard side. Stand by for coordinates."

Opposite side from the ammo ships. The Germans weren't stupid. They'd love a big fireworks show. Stefan angled to the right.

Another PBY burst through the cloud cover at three thousand feet. Immediately, the warships escorting the convoy opened fire.

Grant gawked at the fireworks. "What the ...?"

Stefan keyed his mic. "Ramsey, fire the day's colors with the Very pistol. Poulos, transmit the recognition signals on the Aldis lamp. That's got to be Bradley."

Smoke streamed from one of the PBY's engines. Those ship gunners were good.

"Jenz, contact them. Ask if they can get back to Iceland. Ask the carrier if they'll launch a plane to replace our esteemed colleagues."

Stefan continued to the site of the contact, his thoughts scrambling. The ships had stopped firing, but Bradley was in trouble. Why hadn't Bradley followed normal procedures?

Why hadn't he identified himself and made his presence known by flying in a wide circuit? Those guys down there were jumpy enough without having a friendly aircraft suddenly pop out overhead.

"Four direct hits wounded six of the crew. One engine and the rudder control are gone. Two guys have chest wounds, but they're gonna try to make it back to Reykjavik." Jenz paused. "They misjudged the wind and were closer to the convoy than they thought they were." A hint of incredulity laced his voice.

"They bagged a sub last week," Grant mused. "Maybe that led to sloppiness."

Careless mistake, but it could happen to the best of them. They'd be lucky to reach Iceland before any of the wounded died. A doctor or two was surely among the ships down there, but returning to base made sense.

Stefan noted the ocean chop. Landing a damaged plane on those swells would likely result in disaster. And if they did succeed and a ship rescued them, they'd end up going all the way to England with the convoy.

Something teased his eyes. Something that didn't resemble waves. He angled closer. A life raft?

"Pennington, grab your binoculars and check out what's bobbing around at our ten o'clock position."

"On it." Ten seconds passed. "Whoa! A couple dead men in a raft. They're not moving. And that's not one of our yellow life rafts."

Stefan circled around the raft. Both men's arms were folded tightly against their bodies. This far north, they'd surely froze before starving. "Jenz, notify a destroyer."

He recalled telling Marie about U-boats searching for Allied mail. They would do likewise. At the very least, the corpses might carry identification, and the Red Cross could notify two families that they wouldn't be seeing their loved ones again.

One of the ships headed in their direction, and he turned back to the convoy. "Jenz, what happened with that radar contact?"

"Lost it. If it had been a U-boat, they could have gotten in some mischief while the ships were firing on Bradley's plane."

"There's some mischief." The excitement in Lawrenz's voice sent a shiver down Stefan's spine. Mischief wasn't good. "There's a plane skulking around in the clouds, forward on the port side. It's gotta be a Kraut."

Stefan blew out his breath. On Tuesday afternoons, the Germans made reconnaissance flights over Iceland from a base in Norway like clockwork. The planes flew high over the harbor, no doubt checking out the ships gathering to convoy together and photographing everything. Before returning to Norway, they dropped a few bombs and sometimes machine-gunned a convenient target, usually an Icelandic fishing trawler or a lighthouse. Peaceful targets of a neutral nation. He hadn't heard of them attacking any military installations.

"Jenz, let the convoy know we're going into the clouds and will try to sneak up on the enemy. Ask them not to shoot at us. And to track it for us."

The cloud cover wasn't solid. A few small cumuli. More mid-level altocumulus with wispy altostratus. Stefan spotted the German plane just as it ducked into a cumulus. Fine. He throttled up and raced for the altocumulus above the enemy.

Through a break in the clouds, he registered the outline of the convoy. Ammo ships. Great. The possible sub missed them, but the German fliers realized what juicy targets they had. If they unloaded their bombs on one of those, *kaboom!* At the least, they'd inform the Kriegsmarine of the convoy's location.

Resolve stiffened his spine. Not on his watch. He maneuvered among the altocumulus, hopscotching from one powder puff to the next. A glint of metal in the sun grabbed his attention. "Is that a Junkers 88?"

"Yep. Matches the recognition silhouette." Ramsey was their crew identification expert. "Machine guns in the nose and a couple in the fuselage or tail."

Jenz relayed the convoy escort's tracking coordinates. "We're about five thousand feet above them. They should be popping out of that cloud any moment."

Stefan maneuvered behind the cloud. If the Germans were unaware of their presence, he could get a jump on them. "Be ready at the guns. Make the first pass count. I really don't want to get into a dogfight."

From his window, he saw Pennington open the bow turret. A chill swept through the cockpit. Lawrenz and McQuaid would have the blister windows rolled back. Opening up was a necessity for shooting, but with no heating system, the plane grew cold fast. Stefan shivered despite his layers of flying clothes. He'd love to try one of those electrically heated flying suits he'd heard the bomber crews in England had. Closing the watertight bulkhead doors might make the temperature a little cozier, but they were left open during flight for unrestricted movement. Instead, he wiggled his fingers in his gloves and his toes in his boots.

Poulos would also be ready with the tunnel gun in the rear. Four gun sites. They could do this.

"We're just about even with them." Jenz paused. "Maybe fifty feet above them."

The German bomber popped out of the clouds.

The PBY rattled with the burst of machine guns.

The German bomber danced around the sky. Smoke streamed back from one of its engines. A crewman fired his gun, a little too tardy and a little too wide. The pilot tried to turn away but lost altitude.

Stefan pulled away from the Junkers, away from the convoy. "Jenz, tell the ships to have at it."

A dozen ships opened fire. Chunks blew off the enemy aircraft, and half of a wing disintegrated. When the plane spiraled down, a man bailed.

"Seriously?" Lawrenz said. "Isn't he too low for his parachute to open? And if it does, does he think the convoy will stop to pick him up?"

"One of the Brits' corvettes will snag him. The intelligence guys would love to interrogate him," McQuaid said. "Did you know the British name their little warships after flowers?" He affected a British accent. "'Why, yes, during the war, I served on the RMS *Tulip*. Thanks for asking.'"

The plane hit the water, losing more parts. Stefan saw what might be another man tossed out of the wreckage. There was no way to know whether he was alive or dead. He glanced around the sky. "Fellas, make sure you scan around and above us. I don't want to be jumped in turn by any of their friends."

"Another PBY is approaching," Jenz said. "P-1. It's Dever."

Stefan pursed his lips. His crew was designated P-8. Crazy eight, as Dever like to taunt. He, of course, claimed number one. Even in the air, Stefan couldn't get away from him.

"The convoy's picking up intermittent contacts on the starboard side." Jenz interrupted Stefan's glum thoughts. "The carrier's planes are landing to refuel, so P-1 says it will take care of the new intruder."

"Of course Dever will," McQuaid said. "I'll bet he's drooling."

Stefan silently agreed as he continued patrolling the port flank. He stayed far away from the ammo ships, watching the sea for dark shadows that might indicate a submerged submarine. Nothing. Then he noticed the *Tulip*, er, corvette approach the middle ammo ship. The seamen unrolled a Jacob's ladder down the side of the vessel, and the German aviator climbed aboard. Hmm, putting a prisoner on the most dangerous ship in the convoy? That couldn't be reassuring to the German.

"Dever's dropping depth charges," Lawrenz whined.

Stefan glimpsed plumes of water shoot upward.

"They're claiming they bagged a U-boat," Jenz reported. Two minutes passed before he tried to clarify the situation, but his laughter made him hard to understand. "One of the ships congratulated him on dispatching a whale."

McQuaid chuckled. "The seamen should all feel much safer. Wow. First he sets off a mine field, then he kills a whale. What is he doing to aid the Allied war effort?"

Stefan smiled grimly. "He'll be hard to live with. Angry that he blew it. Angry that we share credit in downing that Junkers."

"No joke." Andrew nodded. "And we witnessed both his gaffes. Best to keep our distance."

Except that Dever would likely seek them out and accuse them of showing off. Stefan sighed.

"Status check," Ramsey called in from his engineering compartment. "We've been out for six and a half hours. Time to head back to base."

The PBY had a fifteen-hour endurance, but most missions stayed within twelve hours to allow a safety margin. Stefan rotated his shoulders. He was ready to return to Reykjavik. To Marie. "Jenz, bid the convoy farewell."

"They say, sorry to see us go, but thanks for our expertise."

"That's got to rile Dever," McQuaid snickered. "Too bad."

Stefan tried to stretch in the cramped cockpit. Another hour and he'd take a break. Marie's happy visage caught his eye, and he smiled back. Her birthday was in October, he'd discovered. How had the orphanage celebrated birthdays? Did they note the day at all?

How could he make her day special? October was a few months away, but if he needed something sent from home, he should put in a request now.

He pushed away his mic. No need to let the whole crew listen in. "Andrew, you're married, right?"

His copilot's look told him he was an idiot.

"Yeah, yeah, I know you are. What I mean is, what is a gift your wife would really appreciate?"

Andrew's gaze wandered to Marie's photo. "Don't make it practical."

"Huh?"

"My brother-in-law gave my sister a new vacuum cleaner. He viewed it as something to make her life easier. She viewed it as a rebuke for not keeping his house clean enough. What he should have done was take her shopping for a new dress." He pointed at the photo. "But you can't do that with her."

So something frivolous that she liked. Stefan's sister liked music boxes. Marie probably didn't have one and might enjoy that, but being deployed meant she couldn't accumulate a lot of stuff. Especially fragile things like music boxes.

He'd noticed several shops in Reykjavik sold packets of scenic views in Iceland. He'd purchased a few with scenes of the hot springs, waterfalls, and geysers. Would she be interested in a souvenir like that?

Pennington broke into his musing with a shout. "Periscope at one o'clock long."

Stefan grabbed his binoculars and searched the sea. There it was, lowering. He sideslipped to line up with it and descended. "Jenz, inform the convoy it's being shadowed, but we'll try to make life difficult for the unwanted company."

He dropped two depth charges ahead of the diving U-boat.

The outline of the sub was still visible when two explosions detonated on either side of the stern, but when the water settled, the submarine had disappeared. He circled. No oil slick rose to the surface.

"There, on our port. No, starboard. Toward the sun."

Despite the serious nature of their business, Stefan grinned at Lawrenz's directional confusion as they circled. He shifted over to where the periscope stuck out of the water. Since it wasn't diving, they must have hurt it. "Jenz, is a destroyer coming back?"

Poulos answered. "Yeah, there's a tin can charging our way."

"Dever announced his intent to join our hunt, but he was ordered to stay with the convoy," Jenz added.

Poor Dever. Stefan chuckled silently.

As he continued to circle, the periscope lowered out of sight, but the sub's outline remained visible.

"The tin can's lobbying garbage cans," Lawrenz announced.

Stefan watched one of the depth charges hit the water near the U-boat's bow, and the boat heaved from the explosion.

"It's surfacing." Lawrenz's voice rose in pitch.

The destroyer idled nearby, all guns trained on the emerging submarine. Hatches on the U-boat opened, and enemy sailors scrambled out. None of them ran for their anti-aircraft gun.

They were surrendering. Stefan sagged in his seat. They'd probably scuttle the sub, but at least their torpedoes wouldn't kill anyone. He asked McQuaid for a heading and swung the plane around.

"A good day's work, men. Time to head home."

And time to finesse an idea out of Marie as to what she might appreciate as a gift.

Chapter Eleven

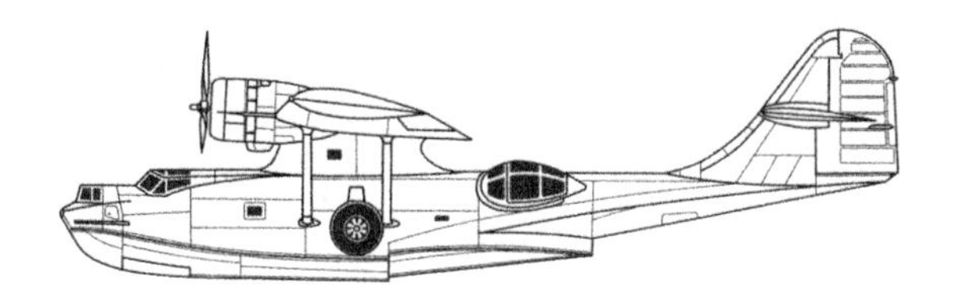

Mutinous. That was the perfect word to describe the man in bed three glaring at the curved ceiling above him. Marie paused at the foot of his bed and rubbed her hand across the metal bed frame. He didn't acknowledge her presence.

This ward held men based in Iceland, so she knew he wasn't a torpedoed mariner. His hand resting on top of his navy blanket had been wrapped like burn wounds would be. She tipped up the placard attached to the bed frame. Sergeant. Army.

"What are you in for, soldier?"

That grabbed his attention and earned her a scowl. His arm twitched. "Kitchen accident," he growled.

"Ha!" The man two beds down pushed up on his elbow. "He was whipping up a batch of poison for us."

Grumbling agreement rose around Marie. She turned to a patient wearing an amused and sympathetic expression. "Poison?"

The man shrugged. "Chow is lousy, but I haven't heard of anyone dropping dead from it."

The victim of their scorn clenched his healthy fist. "We can only serve what we're supplied with."

"Which is slop," said the outspoken complainer.

She let the comment pass. "What's a typical meal like?"

The polite man reached for a book. "I have an old menu here that I use for a bookmark."

Marie accepted it and read, "'Breakfast: juice, coffee, S.O.S., toast, dry cereal. Lunch: Spam, bread, beans, gelatin. Supper: fish, potatoes, corn, bread, carrot salad, rice pudding.'" She raised a brow at the mess sergeant. "Rather vague and not too exciting."

"That's what we have to work with."

She pulled a pen from her pocket and sat at the foot of his bed. "All right, let's work with it. You can list breakfast as 'chilled grapefruit juice, creamed chipped beef on toast ...'"

Several men hooted. She knew they wanted her to say the cuss word they used to describe what she considered one of their better meal options. She refused to give them satisfaction.

"Why toast? How about biscuits? They'd be a big improvement." She crossed off "toast" and wrote "biscuits." "And then a *choice* of dry cereal with milk and sugar, and coffee."

She couldn't read the mess sergeant's expression. A little dazed, a little doubtful. Like, what was the use? It was all the same slop.

"On to lunch. 'Baked luncheon meat a la Ruby sauce.' Or would 'saucy baked luncheon meat' sound better?"

"What's Ruby sauce?" the outspoken man asked.

"Red sauce. Tomato sauce." Marie shrugged. "'Ruby' sounds more highfalutin, doesn't it? Or would you prefer 'scarlet'?" She tapped the mess sergeant's knee. "Baking Spam with sauce isn't a problem, is it? And these beans. Are they green beans? Pork and beans? Be specific. And then, let's see, nothing much we can do with bread, except say 'white bread and butter.' And *fruit* gelatin dessert. Okay, boys, who's hungry now?"

Cheers rose, along with, "What's for supper?"

"Hmm. Baked fillet of halibut, Hawaiian style. Or you could call it 'Aloha baked fillet of haddock.' Bake it in pineapple sauce. Whipped potatoes. Is the corn whole kernel or creamed? Again, be specific. The bread. Is it always white? How about Icelandic rye bread? I'm not normally a fan of rye, but the local bread is dense and quite sweet. Let's see. Do you put raisins in the rice pudding? Call it 'rice pudding with raisins.'"

The mess sergeant took her list and gazed at it with reverent awe. "Do you think this will really help?"

"Why not? Mix things up and use your imagination. Like the canned Chicken a la King. Add corn and call it ..."

"'Corny Chicken a la King,'" shouted a patient.

"Or 'Chicken a la King, Iowa style,'" another said.

Marie nodded. "There you go. And mutton. How about 'herbed leg of lamb'? Ask your mess officer for ideas."

"Hey, we need some fancy names for the Fourth of July." One of the men grinned. "How about 'Independence cake with red, white, and blue frosting'?"

As the men threw out ideas and the mess sergeant scribbled them down, she stood to leave the ward. Mr. Perry and another man with a Red Cross insignia watched from the door. Oh dear. She could imagine what Mr. Perry might be telling his colleague.

Mr. Perry's narrowed eyes, crossed arms, and fidgety foot screamed his annoyance with her. Why? She was doing her job, raising morale. The patients had been irritable, but now they laughed and joked, and the mess sergeant was no longer in danger of being the target of a slugfest.

She drew abreast, and the stranger smiled. "Well done, miss." He paused and glanced at Mr. Perry. When the man remained silent, he stuck out his hand. "I'm Harold Britt. I remember when you received your orders to report for training. Everyone thought you were making a mistake to leave the hospital and give up being a dietitian, but here you are, still planning menus."

Marie stared as a memory clicked into place. "You were the man standing in the shadows, wearing a red tie."

Mr. Britt tilted his head back and laughed. "I thought that red tie was patriotic, but it only caused more problems. So you're still in a hospital. Do you work with the kitchen staff?"

She nodded. "I've been asked to attend the weekly meetings with the staff. Some of the seriously wounded have no appetite, and it's a challenge to find something that will tempt them to try even one bite."

"I can imagine. Well, good job, Miss ..."

Mr. Perry straightened. "Miss Foo-bert."

Marie couldn't stop a double take. He knew better. She returned her attention to Mr. Britt. "It's Foe-bare, Marie Foubert."

"*Enchanté*, Miss Foubert. We'll see you this evening at the Red Cross meeting."

"This evening?"

"Yes, this evening, six o'clock," Mr. Perry fairly growled. "Be there, Foubert." He still stressed the first syllable.

Marie pressed her lips together but managed to offer a nod to Mr. Britt before escaping to the nurses' station.

* * *

One of the last women to arrive at the meeting, Marie slid onto the chair between Betty and Helen. Lettie, as usual, provided a running commentary about how her day had gone. Beyond her, Anne folded her hands over a paper. Marie sucked in her breath when she realized it was a piece of pink paper.

Mr. Perry led Mr. Britt and Mr. Walton into the room. "Looks like everyone's here. Good. Good. How'd everything go this past week?"

He didn't introduce Mr. Britt. Helen speculated that the visitor came in order to learn the ropes from an experienced director. Marie hoped he wasn't expected to learn from Mr. Perry. Maybe he'd be evaluating Mr. Perry's job performance. Her brief encounter with him convinced her that Mr. Britt would do a better job.

Mr. Walton scrawled notes on their activities. Marie had seen his handwriting and knew only he would be able to interpret it. He finished by dotting an *i* and probably missing before looking up. "What's on the schedule for the rest of the month?"

"I have some ideas." Anne lifted her chin as she picked up the pink paper and unfolded it. She froze, staring at it.

Lettie leaned over her shoulder. "Anne, I didn't realize you knew French. Pink paper! Marie, weren't your stolen notes written on pink paper?"

Anne's face flushed a deeper pink than the page Lettie snatched out of her hand. Lettie handed the notes to Marie.

"What is the meaning of this?" Mr. Perry glared at Lettie, then at Marie.

Marie smoothed out the paper. "Several days ago, my belongings were ransacked. This was the only thing missing. I wrote my notes in French as a safety measure."

Clear as day, she was accusing Anne of being the ransacking thief. Mr. Perry probably didn't take umbrage, because Anne refused to look up or defend herself.

Mr. Walton braved the awkward silence. "I'm glad you've recovered your list. You always have the best ideas. What do you have for us today?"

Taking a deep breath, Marie referred to her notes. "One of the soldiers who arrived in '42 told me each company in the army has a company recreation kit containing all sorts of sports equipment." She enumerated the sports on her fingers. "Badminton, baseball, football, horseshoes, basketball, croquet, volleyball. The soldier was telling me this because whoever packed the crates didn't include enough for many of the games. For instance, his company received two rackets each for tennis and badminton, along with one ball each." She glanced up. "The lone birdie quickly wore out. Anyway, I haven't been able to learn if the navy also supplies sports equipment. They may have only one baseball and one bat, but we could encourage the formation of teams."

Mr. Walton tapped his pencil on the table. "I've heard of these recreation kits. I'll scout around, see what bats and balls might be on the island. The Red Cross supplied kites. We may be able to acquire the equipment. Basketball shouldn't be as difficult to equip."

"Boring," Lettie said.

"Croquet is fun." Betty grinned. "I'd play with them."

"I'll see what I can scrounge. Promoting league play is a good idea." Mr. Walton glanced at Mr. Perry, who remained stone-faced, and Mr. Britt, who nodded. "Marie, what else?"

"The same man told me what it was like before most of the British pulled out." She picked up her paper. "They had the NAAFI, which stands for Navy, Army, Air Force Institutes. He said it's similar to our Red Cross but in his opinion, far better."

Lettie slapped the table. "Ooh, them's fightin' words."

"What made the Brits better?" asked Mr. Britt.

"They had live shows with performers who came out of retirement to do their bit for the war effort. Acts included jugglers, tap dancers, singers, and comedy teams. All the Red Cross offers, according to him, are games like checkers and table tennis, and card tables, plus the occasional movie."

Helen twisted a lock of hair around her finger. "Could we entice older performers to brave the Atlantic to entertain the troops?"

"Why not? If the Brits can do it, so can the Americans." "No" wasn't in Lettie's vocabulary. "What about when they're *en route* to England and stop over here? They could do a show then."

"We wouldn't be able to plan in advance, because we never know who's passing through." Betty turned to Mr. Walton. "Would the Red Cross be able to learn who's traveling and schedule something?"

"I'll include that question in my report." He avoided saying yes or no.

"Anything else this soldier had to say about the NAAFI versus the Red Cross?" Mr. Britt leaned back in his chair, seemingly relaxed.

"Well, yes." Marie hesitated, knowing they wouldn't like this. "He said older women served as hostesses for the NAAFI, and they were a lot more fun than we are. They joked and danced with the boys, but we only talk to them."

Groans and protests arose.

"What they really want is dances. And girls." Betty's voice rose above the rest. "Obviously not us. Most of them are just out of high school. We must seem like big sisters to them."

Lettie sputtered. "The British ladies sound old enough to be their mothers."

"What they'd like are dances with the Icelandic girls,"

Marie said. "But the Icelanders pretend we're not here and don't speak much English, besides."

"So we have a conundrum." Mr. Walton paused and looked at Mr. Perry, who appeared oblivious. Shrugging, he continued. "With summer nearly here and the days growing longer with extra sunshine, getting the men outside for sports is a great idea. I'll look into equipment, and we'll take it from there."

The meeting broke up, and Marie headed for the shoreline, craving alone time and privacy. No doubt Lettie wanted to speculate on whether Anne would be sent home in disgrace. Maybe even Mr. Perry. Who was Mr. Britt, anyway? The beginning of silver wingtips at his temples hinted he was at least forty. He must be from Washington if he'd seen her at the hospital there.

Pushing all thoughts of the Red Cross from her mind, she dashed across the end of a runway and scurried down to the beach. The water gurgled quietly in a half-hearted tide. Overhead, a bird squawked. Behind her, an airplane roared in to land, but she'd learned to tune them out.

Off to her left, a man loitered at the shore. He stooped down, fingering something in the waves. She was about to head right when he straightened and she recognized his physique. Broad shoulders, lean hips. Firm biceps too, if his jacket hadn't been hiding them. Her heartbeat sped up. Forget about alone time. He was the one person she wanted to see. She skipped to the shoreline.

"Good evening, Stefan." Her heart stuttered at his slow smile as the day's trials faded away. "Finding seashells?"

"Something better." He held out his hand. A wet, worn tenkronur note featuring a blue-toned view of a waterfall lay on his palm. "Someone must have been laundering his money."

Marie poked the bill with a gentle finger. "Good thing it's

not one króna. Those notes seem to be made of tissue paper. I don't think it would survive a dunking."

Stefan pulled out a handkerchief and blotted his find. "You know, some couples designate a song as *their* song. I think this beach qualifies as our place." He tucked the money in his jacket pocket and grinned. "We do rendezvous here frequently."

"It's my favorite spot." Marie sighed. "Of course, I haven't seen anything beyond Reykjavik."

Stefan had been scanning the horizon, but now he stared at her. "You haven't been anywhere else in Iceland? Scandalous! We're in a foreign country with a very foreign way of life. You need to see what Iceland has to offer."

She shrugged. "Some of the girls are assigned to various distant posts. They complain about long, difficult drives on roads that are mostly ruts and are either dusty and bumpy or muddy and slow. Oh, and the same boring scenery of endless lava fields."

"Psh. What I've seen from the air has been fascinating." He shoved his hands in his back pockets and offered a sheepish smile. "Of course I would say that, being a geologist. But today, we flew past a sharp-peaked mountain on the eastern coast—lava rock, naturally—with a black sand beach. I would have loved to land there and do a bit of exploring."

"I wish I could go sightseeing."

She'd heard Iceland had numerous waterfalls and fjords. Barren lava fields, yes, but also dozens of volcanoes that still erupted from time to time. The largest volcano stood not far from Reykjavik. She'd gladly forgo watching that one spew lava into the air.

"Know what? There's an area not far from here. It has waterfalls, geysers, a rift valley, hot springs, all in close proximity. I don't fly day after tomorrow. Try to get the day off.

Consider it as scouting possibilities to recommend to the troops. We'll take in the sights."

Take in the sights. With Stefan. She'd ask Mr. Walton, maybe with Mr. Britt nearby. Surely they'd agree that a day off would be beneficial.

Practicality crashed in. "How would we get there?"

"A Jeep and driver might be possible, but hiring a local makes sense." Stefan eased the damp kronur banknote from his pocket and fluttered it in front of her. "This is a portent of good things to come."

"Maybe we should look for more discarded laundry."

"Keep your eyes peeled." He took her hand, sending chills up and down her spine. She could get used to this. They strolled the length of the harbor in quiet companionship, then sat on a large boulder.

"I expected mail today, but I guess the ship didn't arrive." Stefan rubbed her palm with his thumb. "Do you hear from your friends at the orphanage often?"

"My best friends were Ozanne and Francoise. They both married, but Francoise's husband died in the war. She's working in a factory now. So did Ozanne, but she couldn't tolerate the noise. Now she clerks at a fraction of the wage, a fact her husband doesn't let her forget. They don't write often. When they do, it's to say they're still alive and that I'm so lucky to be away from Quebec."

Francoise's husband had been a fellow orphan. Honoré was wonderful. If he showed interest in her instead of Francoise, Marie may not have gone to college. Instead of being here with Stefan, she'd be the widow working in a gritty, noisy plant.

She didn't know Ozanne's husband. Her dear friend had married quickly, probably anxious to have someone to call her own. *Marry in haste, repent at leisure* seemed to sum up Ozanne's life. Marie's heart ached for her.

"What about college friends?"

Stefan's question pulled her out of the past. "Oh, um, a couple classmates and I exchange birthday cards. Or Christmas cards. Someone from the hospital in Washington always lets me know what I've missed by gallivanting off on my big adventure. Lucretia keeps asking where I am. In her last letter, she speculated that I'm in New Guinea battling mosquitoes, lizards, and other creepy crawlers, and am too proud to admit I made a colossal mistake."

"Like my friend John in the South Pacific, battling fighters, boredom, and bullets."

Stefan expected to see John again if he survived, back home in Wisconsin. And his other friend, Daniel. But Marie didn't know if or where she'd see any of her friends again. A familiar loneliness wrapped around her.

Friends were wonderful, but nothing like family. She'd left the orphanage for college, then moved on to Washington and finally the Red Cross. Friends didn't leave her. She left them. Of course, she'd aged out of the orphanage and couldn't go back. School friends graduated and moved on. Her life didn't consist of the same neighborhood with white picket fences where everyone always came home to visit.

"I wish I had a family to go home to. When my parents died, none of the relatives claimed me. An aunt may have wanted me, but no one was willing to take me in. I always wondered why. What's wrong with me? Am I so unlovable? Most of the children adopted from the orphanage were chosen for work, not as family members. Like Anne of Green Gables."

Stefan didn't say anything. Instead, he wrapped his arm around her and pulled her close, stroking her arm up and down. She leaned her head on his shoulder, and a sense of belonging stole over her. An alien feeling, but wondrous.

He pointed out a bird high overhead. "I believe that's a

puffin. I didn't think they were in this part of Iceland." He allowed a moment of silence before saying, "You mentioned once that you brought all four of your books along but left some things behind. Was that because of luggage restrictions?"

"Yes. We received a list of all the things we needed to bring. Mostly wardrobe concerns. So many blouses, so many skirts, and, um, undergarments. Everything had to fit in a duffel bag and a footlocker."

"What do you wish you could have brought along?"

"Hmm." Marie squinted at the sky. "Craft supplies, maybe. Although, maybe not. I like pressing flowers and leaves and making greeting cards with them." She shivered as a memory surfaced. "Once, I made a birthday card for Mother Superior using petals that had fallen from her rose bushes. She was furious and scolded me for picking her roses. Sister Marguerite defended me, saying the petals had fallen off during a recent storm. Mother still looked grim, which actually was her usual expression, and never apologized. After she died, the birthday card was found framed in her room."

"And she never thought to encourage you in your artistic ability?"

Marie shook her head, blinking back a tear and sniffing. "Anyway, around here we have no flowers and no leaves. I really miss that. I'm from Quebec and New England, where the fall leaves are spectacular. Here, we'll have no leaves in autumn. Or in spring, when everything back home turns green and fresh."

Stefan chuckled. "Reminds me of a conversation I had with a man from the Southwest. Iceland's green moss amazes him. In Arizona, they don't have grass in their yards. Or trees. But they do have a huge saguaro cactus."

"The desert gets cold at night, right? Maybe Iceland doesn't seem as foreign to him as it does to us." She squeezed his hand. "What do you wish you could have brought along?"

"My telescope, and I did bring it."

"Really?" She hadn't expected that. "You'll have to wait a few months before you can use it in this land of the midnight sun."

"True. I've made use of it to check out the bird life." Stefan waved in the direction the puffin had flown. "Once, I took it up in the plane for a closer look at Icelandic features. That didn't work out so well, with Lawrenz and his greedy grubbers."

Marie twirled a lock of hair around her finger. "Will you be able to see Saturn with its rings when it gets dark?

"Absolutely. Interested in taking a peek at the planet?"

She clasped her hands together. "Yes."

"It's a date."

Suddenly, she couldn't wait for the darker days.

Chapter Twelve

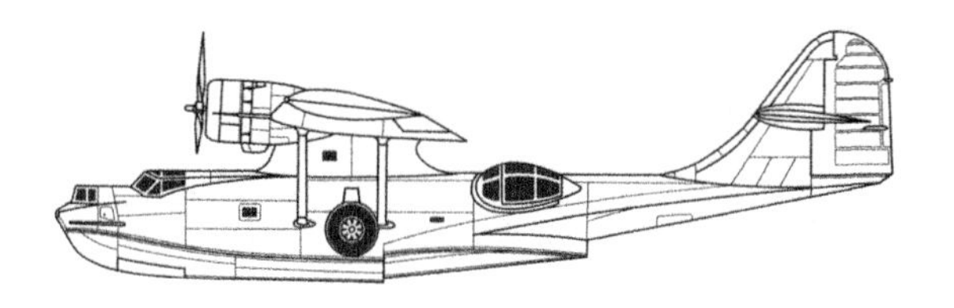

Bang!

Stefan jerked in his seat. A bang in an airplane was never good.

"We've got falling oil pressure and a rising temperature in the port engine." Stress colored Ramsey's voice. "Something must have come loose. We need to shut down the engine."

They were three hours from Reykjavik. The plane could fly on one engine, but Stefan didn't like that option. He eyed the placid surface of the ocean. "Can you fix it? Should I land?"

"Yes. Maybe. I don't know."

The engineer's flustered response put Stefan on edge. "Would it help if we landed and you take a look?"

"Yeah, go ahead and land. I won't know what's wrong until I open the access panel."

"Couldn't ask for better wind conditions," Andrew said.

"Yeah. Jenz, send our position in code. Everyone, prepare for landing. Floats down." Stefan eased the big plane down, flaring out his rate of descent so their motion was parallel to the surface.

"Floats lowered." Ramsey's usual calm returned.

Stefan glanced out his window. The wingtip floats had extended down into position to provide stability on the water. They reminded him of little boats.

Andrew called out their speed and altitude as Stefan guided the seaplane lower, into the docile wind. The belly kissed the ocean, and the contact provided braking. Spray flew out on the sides but not onto the windshield. Stefan imagined Lawrenz and Poulos enjoyed quite a show from the blister windows.

Their speed diminished until finally, the plane—now a boat—stopped, rocking lightly. The floats kept them from rolling over. Silence reigned when the engines fell quiet.

While he and Andrew went through the post-landing checklist, Stefan called out, "Ramsey, grab whoever you need to help you. The rest of you can climb out, but don't fall if you're not wearing a life vest."

"Oh. We can go for a swim if we wear vests?" Trust Lawrenz to be a smart aleck.

"It's your choice, but not one I recommend."

With the PBY secure, Stefan opened the overhead hatch and hoisted himself out. From atop the fuselage, he noted Pennington now stood in the open bow turret. Ramsey, McQuaid, and Poulos had exited from the navigator's hatch and the open blister. Ramsey had already removed a panel off the engine housing. Jenz poked his head out the navigator's hatch, still wearing his headset.

Stefan and Andrew raised their binoculars and scanned the area in a full circle. Total solitude. Like they were the only people left on Earth. Nothing here but water and sky in shades of blue, gray, and white.

Was this what his parents experienced when they crossed the Atlantic, dreaming of a new life in America?

When Stefan took a deep breath, the briny scent of the sea filled his nostrils. The smell was distinct—not fishy like in Reykjavik. He wracked his brain to recall the minute details from his college classes that explained this particular sea smell —the stale, sulfuric scent of organisms, produced by bacteria as they digested dead plankton. Sounded awful, despite the pleasing aroma. He imagined explaining it to Marie. Would she decline to loiter at the shore with him if he waxed eloquent about the contents of the water at their feet?

Lawrenz stuck his head out of the blister and sniffed the air. "We should have brought along some fishing gear. Coulda caught us some fresh fish for dinner."

"Like a whale?" Poulos asked as he disappeared back into the plane.

Lawrenz scanned the water, only moving his eyes. "There might be whales around here, right? Like the one Dever killed? Would a whale attack us, like in *Moby Dick*?"

"Let's not worry about that." Stefan twisted to face Ramsey. "Do you see a problem?"

"Loose pipe. Oil's all over the place except where it's supposed to be."

"The plane was in for an overhaul yesterday." Pennington wiped his window with a not-so-clean rag. "Didn't they put it back together right?"

"Maybe. I don't know. The threads look worn. Maybe should have been replaced." Ramsey sorted through the crate Poulos had brought out and selected a part. "I'll replace it now and see if that works."

Stefan continued searching the horizon, confident that Ramsey knew what he was doing. During yesterday's downtime, he and Marie had taken their sightseeing trip. He recalled her laughing when they got too close to Gullfoss waterfall and were enveloped by the spray. Not that it mattered. A rain shower had already soaked them through. Three rainbows shimmered for their enjoyment. They hiked around the circle of thunderous falls, gazing down into the gorge of turbulent white water with hints of turquoise below. It was his favorite stop on their tour.

A disturbance on the calm ocean surface caught his attention. Lawrenz's whale? *No.* His heart thundered. Heaven help them.

"U-boat surfacing!"

His crew froze. Beside him, Andrew murmured, "I doubt they're going to offer to lend us a hand."

Stefan spun to face Ramsey. "How soon can we get underway?"

The engineer's hands shook as he poured oil into the engine. "Fifteen minutes? Maybe less."

"Jenz, is anyone nearby? Gunners, limber up your guns. We'll return fire. Poulos, have the life raft ready to push out. They may want to sink the airplane. Or they may try to take over. We cannot let them take the plane."

"Think they want to fly it over the convoy and attack it?" Andrew asked. "We could heave-ho the depth charges."

"Not yet. Their weight may help sink the plane."

In front of them, Pennington had his 0.30 caliber machine gun ready. It was pitifully inadequate against a submarine's 20-millimeter and 37-millimeter antiaircraft cannon. And the bow gunner's exposed position made him an easy target. Pennington glanced back toward the cockpit. "If we board the life raft, they're likely to machine-gun us."

Stefan grimaced. Yes, they likely would. The Germans knew the men in the PBYs were responsible for locating and bombing many of their U-boats. They must thirst for revenge.

The submarine had fully surfaced approximately two miles away. As it steadily drew closer, men appeared on deck, clustering around their gun. Facing the sub's superior firepower, the PBY didn't have much chance. The blisters boasted 0.50 caliber machine guns, still woefully underpowered against the enemy. Nevertheless, Pennington and Lawrenz waited resolutely at their positions.

With furious movements, Ramsey screwed the engine panel back into place. One screw dropped, rattled down the side of the aircraft, and plopped into the sea.

"Forget it. It'll hold." From his hatch, McQuaid reached over and slapped Ramsey's leg. "Get in and start up the engines."

Stefan breathed deeply. They hadn't been down long. Hopefully, the engines hadn't cooled off completely and would start quickly. To Andrew, he said, "Drop down and start the checklist."

Satisfied that the engine was back in working order—albeit missing one screw—and the navigator's hatch was closed, Stefan dropped into the cockpit and secured his hatch. His gut tightened when he saw how much closer the U-boat was now. Would they aim for the engines? The wings, still full of fuel? Or the fuselage, hoping to decimate the soft bodies inside?

About to take his seat, a shove caused him to stumble. His left thigh stung like a hive of bees had attacked him, and blood stained his pants.

A bullet had pierced the fuselage. And him.

He fell into his seat while Andrew and Ramsey continued through the start-up checklist. Stefan increased the throttles to one thousand rpm, ignoring Andrew's raised brows.

The PBY's engines were mounted close to each other, making directional control easier when one engine failed. Unfortunately, their closeness reduced the effect of differential power, making steering on the water more difficult.

The throbbing in his leg distracted him. Focus. Steer. Water takeoff.

"Lower the port main landing gear to pivot our turn. We have to put distance between us." Stefan gasped for air. "Turn into the wind. Which way?"

Grant gave him a hard look, then gasped. "Stefan, you've been shot."

"I know." He glanced down. So much blood. Had the artery been clipped? "There's so little wind, we'll need a longer takeoff run. Then we should circle back and drop depth charges."

"Right. We've got this." Grant shook his head. "McQuaid, Pennington, get up here and haul Stefan back to the bunks. Jenz, grab the first aid kit. Is anyone else in the vicinity?"

"Dever's the closest, but he's not coming. Plane number six is a half hour away. A destroyer's ten miles out."

Stefan watched the blood pool around the fingers he had pressed to his leg. Reykjavik was three hours away. If he was bleeding out, he'd be dead by the time they returned. "We'll drop our depth charges after taking off with little wind."

"Relax, Dabrowski," Grant ordered. "I know how to do a sticky water takeoff."

Stefan stayed quiet as Pennington grabbed him beneath his arms and hauled him from his seat. McQuaid gripped his uninjured leg and delicately raised the wounded one. The pair would never qualify as ambulance workers. They wrestled him back to the living quarters, jarring him against two watertight passageways. He groaned when they dumped him onto a bunk.

"Sorry, old boy." McQuaid said, mimicking a poor English accent. "You're not exactly a featherweight, and I'm not exactly in shape for weight lifting."

The plane accelerated. Slick, glassy water wasn't easy to take off on, hence the label "sticky water." Their best course was to cross their own wake to get airborne. Did Grant know that? The plane wobbled. Yes, of course Grant knew what to do.

Jenz waited with the first aid kit. "Raise him up so we can remove his pants."

Stefan understood how a rag doll felt as McQuaid yanked down his trousers.

Jenz dropped the bandage he held and rummaged in the box. "His femoral artery must have been nicked. We have to get a tourniquet on quick."

McQuaid grabbed Stefan's right foot. "You mean he could bleed to death?"

Jenz didn't reply. He wrapped a belt around Stefan's thigh and pulled it tight.

Stefan winced. "If it's too tight and no blood reaches my toes, I'll lose my leg."

"I'll loosen it now and then, but right now, we have to save as much blood as we can." Jenz's face wore an ashen hue. His first time serving as medic and he faced a life-and-death situation.

McQuaid didn't look much better. Stefan wiggled his foot. "You don't have to hold on to me. I'm not going anywhere."

"You better not." McQuaid's eyes glittered with panicky determination.

"What are you going to do? Hold me back from Heaven's gate?" A cartoon image made Stefan grin even as he shivered. He was so cold.

Jenz covered him with a scratchy blue wool blanket. At home, Matka would have tucked him in with one of her fluffy quilts.

Matka. Home. Good chance he wouldn't see them again this side of Heaven. No more walks along the lakeshore, no more games of checkers in front of the fireplace. And Marie. Might they have carved out a life together?

Sleep crowded his thoughts. If this was how he was going to die, it wasn't so bad. One bullet hole instead of being torn apart. No burning to death in a fiery crash. No lengthy, debilitating illness.

He would simply drift off to sleep and wake up in Heaven. He would see Jesus. Would He say, "Well done, good and faithful servant?"

A verse from Revelation threaded through his mind. *"God shall wipe away all tears from their eyes, and there shall be no more death, neither sorrow, nor crying, neither shall there be any more pain: for the former things are passed away."*

His parents would grieve, but he'd be full of joy. He'd see the street of gold, gates of pearls, and foundations garnished with colorful jewels. Heaven had no sea. That was a troubling thought, for he loved the sea. He mentally shrugged. There'd be so many other wonders that he wouldn't miss it.

He shifted his shoulders and rolled his head. No pillow. Jenz had swept it away, saying Stefan had to lower his head for better blood flow and keep the wound elevated. Lovely. Nothing about this constituted a heroic death in battle. He'd been shot while running from the enemy. Cowardly? Or was discretion the better part of valor?

A sharp odor pricked his nose, and his eyes snapped open. Lawrenz waved something in front of his face. Smelling salts?

"Stay with us, Lieutenant."

"Not going anywhere." Had he nodded off? "Did we bomb the sub?"

"They got away to fight another day."

Lawrenz didn't answer his question. Did that mean they hadn't dropped the depth charges? At least his crew got away to fight another day too.

"This bird's never flown so fast. Lieutenant Grant got it up to two hundred miles an hour. Isn't that swell?" Awe filled the kid's voice. "The PBY's supposed to have a maximum speed of one ninety-five. We'll get you back to base and into the hospital in no time."

Stefan groaned. "Needles and knives."

Lawrenz shrugged. "Can't be worse than a bullet, right?"

Pennington poked his head into the compartment, grinned, and retreated back to the front.

Stefan realized he didn't hear anyone else speaking. He touched his head and didn't feel his usual headset. When he tried to pull it off, Lawrenz stopped his hand.

"These are Buck's and my special headphones that we wear to talk privately back here without shouting. Aren't they swell? Ramsey calls them our 'Flash Gordon and Buck Rogers gear.' I'm Flash and Lucius is Buck. All the guys at base call him Buck. He likes that better than Lucius."

Stefan stared at his gunner. How had he not known any of this? His crew got along well, but there obviously remained some distance between officers and enlisted men.

"I always liked those comic strips better than *Tarzan of the Apes*."

"Oh, yeah. Science fiction is the way to go." Lawrenz nodded earnestly. "They're a lot better than those new ones, *Superman* and *Batman*. They're just crime fighters. No space adventures at all."

Stefan explored the headset with his hand. "Where'd you get these?"

"Buck made 'em. He's real clever."

"Maybe he should have been a mechanic."

"Nah. He doesn't like to get his fingers greasy."

Stefan laughed and winced. The slightest movement sent

stabbing pain through his leg. "Right. Actually, radioman would be likelier."

Lawrenz scrunched his face. "He's not exactly an ace at Morse code."

Jenz returned and fiddled with the tourniquet. He was probably loosening it, but Stefan felt no difference. The way the radioman stared at it sent queasiness through his gut.

Pulling away a thoroughly red length of gauze, Jenz grimaced and gave Stefan a shrug. "I need to keep the tourniquet tight. The blood isn't gushing now, but you're still leaking."

Gushing? Stefan hated this helplessness, this dependence on amateur medics. He didn't realize he had the blanket clenched in his fist until Jenz asked, "Would you like a shot of morphine?"

"No. And no more smelling salts. I'm not a swooning Southern belle."

A grin cracked Jenz's face. "For sure. My sister would need the salts."

Stefan recalled that Bruce Jenz hailed from Virginia. "Broken fingernails throw her into a tizzy?"

Jenz chuckled. "Something like that."

"How's the plane?"

"We found a few bullet holes, but no vital damage." Jenz finished applying a new dressing. "We're about an hour out of Reykjavik. An ambulance will be standing by to take you to the hospital."

A silver lining suddenly glowed in Stefan's mind. Marie worked at the hospital. He wouldn't mind being laid up for a while.

Chapter Thirteen

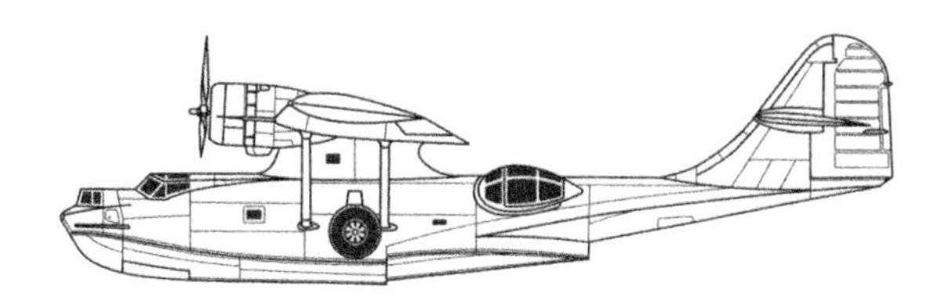

"Helen, what is the name of that bookstore where you found a good English language section?" Marie stood at the foot of her friend's cot after supper, paper and pencil ready.

"Something like Edmundson. No, Eymundsson. It's on Austurstræti." Helen watched her scribble the name. "Why?"

"Lots of men ask me where to find things or where to go. One sailor wanted to know where to have his watch repaired, although I think his watch is beyond help. Anyway, I'm making a list of places they might be interested in." Marie placed the scrap of paper on the far left corner of her bed, starting a pile of *B* words. "Besides shopping needs, I'm including places like museums, a gymnasium, and a swimming pool. Did you know there's an indoor swimming pool open for Allied troops only on Thursdays from six to seven thirty? It's a big pool, the water's warm, and it's never crowded."

Betty looked up from her letter writing. "How do you know about that?"

"Stefan mentioned it yesterday. He goes there often. He

likes water sports of all kinds. Swimming, sailing, rowing." She snickered. "Seaplanes."

"You're awfully chummy with him." Lettie wiggled her eyebrows.

"Hmm." Marie's romantic life wasn't open for discussion with the talkative Lettie. She pinpointed the bookstore on her Reykjavik city map. "I'll be sure to point out the bookstore tomorrow on my city sightseeing tour."

"Sightseeing tour?" Lettie hopped up and walked over to read Marie's notes.

"What tour is this?" Betty laid her letter aside.

Helen's eyes widened. "I didn't know we gave tours. Am I missing out on something?"

"One of the doctors asked me to take some of the ambulatory patients out to see a few points of interest in the city. Breathe fresh air, get a little exercise, have a glimpse of normal life outside the hospital. I plan to show them where they can buy souvenirs or gifts. I know of an art exhibit that might be interesting, but they may not have the stamina. This will be a short walking tour, under an hour including the ride into town."

"Oh, that sounds fun." Helen fiddled with her bracelet. "Maybe we could offer sightseeing tours for the healthy men. I'll bet some of them want to see the town. I'd be glad to lead a tour. May I use your notes?"

Marie grinned. "I'm alphabetizing everything, and then I'll make copies of the list."

"Don't forget to run this by Mr. Walton," Betty said.

Off in her corner, Anne observed their conversation. Most of the girls had shunned her since the revelation that she'd stolen Marie's notes. Even her friend Sara preferred to spend more time with the others. Marie almost felt sorry for Anne. Almost.

Lettie brightened. "You could organize tour groups to see those nature sites you visited yesterday."

Nature sites. Marie chuckled at Lettie's moniker for Iceland's natural phenomena but shook her head. "I'm sure there'd be lots of interest, but it's more complicated than a city tour. It would be an all-day excursion and require transportation for a group."

Betty grinned. "Another thing for Mr. Walton to arrange."

Two of their group had left for the Red Cross Center directly after the evening meal. One of them rushed back into the hut. "Marie, where are you? Ah, Marie. Your pilot is Steven, right? Or Stefan?"

A spidery feeling crept across the back of Marie's neck as she stepped forward. "Why?"

"I heard he's in the hospital, badly wounded."

Marie gasped. Her notes fluttered to the bed. "Did his plane crash?"

"No. They were in a firefight with a U-boat."

Marie pressed a hand to her chest and struggled to inhale. Then she grabbed her coat and sprinted from the hut.

Bursting into the ward where she'd been told she'd find Stefan, she saw him lying still in the fourth bed down the aisle, below a window. An IV bottle hung above him, containing amber fluid. Plasma, not medicine. Dizziness crashed through her, and she groped for a chair.

His eyes were closed, but his head moved on the flat pillow, like he was having a bad dream or was in pain. Marie lifted his hand resting on top of his blanket and clasped it between hers. His eyes flickered open.

"Stefan, I'm so sorry."

"Did you shoot me?" His voice was barely audible. His eyelids slid down.

"No!" Marie pressed his hand. "Remember the U-boat?"

Again his eyes opened, but they didn't seem to focus. He tried to lick his lips. She brought a glass of water to his mouth and lifted his head so he could take a sip.

"I dun like ana sted ic." His mangled speech rode on a sigh as he closed his eyes again.

In spite of the situation, Marie smiled. "I don't know anyone who likes anesthetics."

"Makes my stomach sick, my head stuff with cotton, and my shoulder ache."

She rubbed his arm. "How does your leg feel?"

"Hurts." He swallowed hard. "Can't even say we sank sub. Turned tail and ran."

Tears pressed against Marie's eyes. "That's all right. I saw your copilot as he left the hospital, and he told me you landed on the water. A landed seaplane is hardly an equal opponent to a submarine. That's like David versus Goliath, but without the slingshot."

His lips twitched, but his eyes remained closed. He twisted his hand around until he held hers. She moved her thumb back and forth across his hand the way she imagined her mother used to do to her. Finally, his hand relaxed as sleep claimed him.

She let her tears overflow. *Thank you, God. He's alive. Thank you.* She repeated the prayer several times in her mind. There was nothing else to say.

* * *

Three days later, Marie guided Stefan's wheelchair outside to a sheltered spot between two Quonset wards. He heaved a great sigh. "Fresh air."

"It smells like sulfur."

He inhaled and coughed. "Which do you prefer—sulfur or antiseptic?"

She tapped his shoulder. "How about the scent of roses? Or bread baking? Or chocolate cake?"

"Or the seashore? Or pine trees after the rain? Or plumeria?"

Marie laughed. "Or *what*?"

"Plumeria. It's a fragrant flower in Hawaii. My friend John wrote about them. They make leis with them, and a Hawaiian girl looped one around his neck when he was there. The scent was so strong it gave him a headache." Stefan sighed. "He's been wounded a lot worse than me. Keeps flying, though."

"So will you. Your leg will heal, and your body will replenish the missing blood." She gulped. "That sounds awful. You nearly died from loss of blood."

He grabbed her hand and interlaced his fingers with hers. "I thought I would. But my life didn't flash before my eyes. Instead, I thought of the future. Of Heaven. Of my parents' grief." He paused. "Of you, what we might have had."

He locked his eyes with hers, and Marie could scarcely breathe. A life with Stefan. She bit her lip. He hadn't said he loved her. He wasn't proposing. But he might, just might, in the future.

No. No one wanted her. Not since her parents died. Stefan was in a euphoric state due to surviving a near-death experience. Reality would soon bring him down to earth. Wouldn't it?

He played with her hand, running a finger down one of hers and up the next, down the other side and up the next finger. Hardly a romantic gesture, but she shivered anyway.

"Andrew and David stopped by this morning." Stefan leaned his head back and closed his eyes.

When he said no more, Marie prompted him. "And?"

"Our plane underwent maintenance while we were sightseeing. The engines were exposed to salty seas and lava grit, so they required cleaning. During reassembly, the mechanic tightening a bolt went to the aid of another guy. When he returned to his work, he forgot he hadn't finished off that bolt. A pipe came loose, allowing oil to spew. Such a little thing, with such potentially lethal consequences." He spoke in a monotone.

Marie pressed her abdomen as a chill swept through her. If the German sailors had killed the crew, no one would have ever known what went wrong.

Stefan's shoulders rose as he inhaled. "I watched the sunrise this morning. Somewhere else, the sun was setting. The sun rises and hastens back to where it rose."

He must be referring to a Bible verse. Something about nothing new under the sun.

He sighed. "I've been trying to visualize what my family is doing. Right now, Matka might be making bread. I have no idea what my little sister is up to." He brightened. "Have I told you my brother Bron is in the navy? He's on a rescue and salvage ship. Still on the East Coast, but they'll be aiding stricken vessels. Mostly torpedoed ships, I presume. Doubt they'll be able to help any stricken PBYs."

When he shivered, Marie stood and turned his chair around. "I think it's time for your afternoon nap."

"Psh. Do I get a teddy bear?"

She patted his arm. He sure made a cranky patient.

After an orderly helped transfer him to his bed, Marie glanced around the ward. One man, obviously in agony, kept repeating, "'Yes, sir, yes sir, three bags full.'" If he was trying to distract himself, he wasn't succeeding. She grimaced as Stefan clapped his hands over his ears.

Two men played Chinese checkers, their board balanced precariously on one man's legs. When the board tipped, he exclaimed, "I lost my marbles."

Stefan slapped his hands down on his bed.

Marie shot a pleading look to the nurse in her station at the end of the ward. The nurse entered the ward, suggested the two men ought to rest, and soothed the hurting sailor. Stefan's fists remained clenched.

Marie laid her hand on the side of his face. He opened his eyes slightly before he grabbed her hand and kissed her palm. He closed his eyes again, and his hand dropped to his side.

Marie stood as still as a statue. Such a dear man. When their lengths of service in Iceland ended, they'd go separate ways. He'd be nothing but a special memory. A tear slipped down her cheek.

It was a sad truth, but Marie Foubert was alone in the world.

Chapter Fourteen

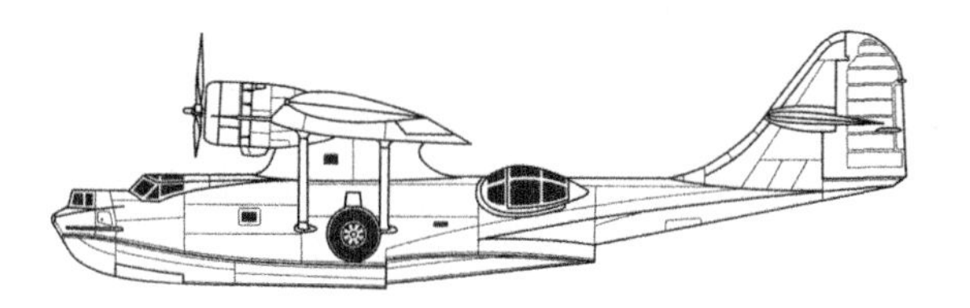

Stefan clumped up and down the aisle between cots in the hospital ward. Adjusting to crutches wasn't as easy as he'd expected. If he had been hospitalized in Milwaukee, he would have been released and at home under Matka's care. He grinned, thinking about her suffocating care. Right now, though, he'd really enjoy her cooking. His mouth watered at the thought of her pierogi, especially when she stuffed the dumplings with cheese or beef.

She'd make sure his bedding was clean and open the window for fresh air. She'd even put a bouquet of flowers in his room to gladden his heart. Homesickness clawed at his throat.

The hospital ward was dingy, stuffy, and smelly. With temperatures rarely topping sixty degrees Fahrenheit even in summer, windows stayed closed. Pity, since some of these guys were pungent. He plopped down on his cot and casually sniffed his shirt. Maybe not fresh as a daisy, but not ripe enough to bowl Marie over.

He eyed the nearest window. Surely opening it a crack and freshening the air in here would do them all good.

A balding chaplain paused at the door and scanned the room. "Good morning, gentlemen."

His benign smile sparked a flash of irritation in Stefan. Every time he saw this man, he thought of the saying "too close to Heaven to be of any earthly good." Except the chaplain didn't talk about Heaven, or even God. He acted more like a cheerleader, assuring everyone that they'd soon win this war and have the Germans on the run.

An enlisted man slipped in behind the chaplain with a guitar in his hand. Stefan straightened. A classmate in college who owned a guitar had shown Stefan how to play. Maybe he could find one in Reykjavik along with a simple songbook. It would fill some of the long hours when he wasn't flying or spending time with Marie.

"Any requests?"

Stefan blinked. Had the chaplain already given his homily? He raised a finger. "'I Need Thee Every Hour.'"

The chaplain froze momentarily and glanced at the guitarist, who strummed a few chords as he neared Stefan. When he opened his mouth, Stefan did the same.

"'I need Thee ev'ry hour, most gracious Lord; No tender voice like Thine can peace afford. I need Thee, O I need Thee. Ev'ry hour I need Thee! O bless me now, my Savior, I come to thee.'"

They moved on to "Near to the Heart of God" and "O Love That Will Not Let Me Go." The chaplain didn't sing at all but rather smiled and nodded. Several of the patients joined in, especially on the refrains.

When the chaplain suggested "America the Beautiful," Stefan wasn't the only one to blink. Nothing wrong with patriotic songs, but today was Sunday, the one day of the week they should concentrate on glorifying God alone.

He leaned back, content to listen to the others and catch his breath. Maybe because he'd come close to knocking on Heaven's door, he found the hymns more meaningful. What had Ojciec told him before he'd left for basic training? "Keep your eyes on Jesus. Don't let anything distract you."

Stefan thought Ojciec referred to all the temptations that might entice him away from his faith. Perhaps so, but he may also have meant that Stefan needed to be ready to die in the war.

He shifted around, uncomfortable on the very hard cot. His shoulders ached, which could be from using crutches. Except his knee hurt too. His stomach roiled and, come to think of it, he had a headache. He swiped a hand down his face. Why was he sweaty? And why did he need to catch his breath?

The sing-along ended and the ward quieted. A nurse meandered down the aisle, checking each patient. When she paused at his bed, her eyes widened. Hurrying forward, she felt his forehead, whipped back his blanket to check his leg, pushed up his sleeves, and muttered, "Nooo."

She rushed back to the nurses' station and placed a call. Then she returned with a basin of water and sponged his face as he shivered.

A doctor took over, poking and prodding and asking him how he felt. *Lousy, thank you.* Stefan would prefer to curl up and sleep, but he really did feel rotten.

"What is this?" The doctor's irritated voice penetrated Stefan's malaise. He uttered a curse. Not good. "This man was to receive a tetanus toxoid booster. According to this, he received a tetanus antitoxin."

Activity increased around him. He wished they would leave him alone.

"What happened?" Marie's anguish pierced his fog.

The nurse pointed to his arm. "Injection reaction."

Hmpf. Go ahead and admit it. *Wrong* injection reaction. A

medic jarred his cot as he hung an IV bottle overhead. Lovely. More medicine to react to. *Everyone, just go away. Leave me alone. Except Marie.*

They finally left, and he struggled to open his eyes. Marie settled onto the chair beside his bed and took his hand, tears glistening in her eyes. "You were doing so well."

"That's when the devil throws in his pitchfork. He wants to dance on my grave."

She flattened her lips as if trying not to smile and stroked his hand.

"Matka used to stroke my hand like that." He gripped her thumb when she tried to pull away. "Don't stop. It makes me feel like everything's going to be all right."

The nurse returned and handed Marie a tube. "Spread this salve on his rash and any swelling. It should ease his discomfort."

The salve's coolness made him shiver, but Marie's light touch caused his nerves to do jumping jacks. He could get used to this.

Finishing her task, she set the tube aside. "How are you feeling?"

"In the pink. And tired. I can't sleep, though. It would be very rude to sleep while you're here."

She may have laughed, but he couldn't be sure. She did pat his head like he was a little boy. "Then I'll visit with other patients and let you snooze."

Wait. What? He didn't mean to imply she should leave. Stefan opened his mouth to protest, but a yawn escaped. Must be the stuff in the IV.

In the end, sleep won.

* * *

A week later, Stefan sat at the shore on an uncomfortable chair with an empty gallon can to serve as a footstool, elevating his wounded leg. He was bored stiff. Bored into a stupor. Bored to tears. His crew was flying on patrol with a replacement pilot and Marie was on Red Cross duty at the hospital. He was tired of reading. Tired of writing letters. He'd sleep if he weren't so tired of that too.

The sun shone nearly all day. They'd passed the summer solstice a month ago. While the sun did disappear below the horizon for a whopping five hours, the sky didn't grow dark. He was used to the sun rising in the east and setting in the west. Here, it dipped below the horizon and almost immediately popped back up alongside where it had set. Instead of traveling across the sky in a straight line, it made a giant circle around the heavens.

The men weren't used to the midnight sun. They'd played volleyball late into the evening one day, only to discover it was three thirty in the morning. Now they had a time keeper to tell them when to go to bed. And they needed to use dark blinds on the windows—not to block any light from shining out, but to keep the sun from shining in.

Stefan massaged his leg. He'd like to play volleyball too. Or baseball. Or take a hike. Instead, he twirled a cane.

Quit whining, Dabrowski. He still had his leg, and it was healing just fine, so said the doctor.

"Look who's lazing around." A tall, blond man dressed in a Royal Air Force uniform loomed over him, the omnipresent sun behind him. "Are you contemplating life's unanswerable questions?"

The man spoke in Polish.

"Greg?"

Stefan pulled his leg off the can and pushed to his feet. "Greg?" Soon, he was captured in a bone-crushing hug that expelled the air from his lungs. Finally, he pushed back. "Oh, man, it's good to finally see you in person," he said to his cousin. "But what are you doing in Iceland?"

Greg grimaced. "I had my own recovering to do. Crash landed two months ago after my Spitfire was all shot up. Should have bailed out, but I didn't realize how torn up it was. I went rolling across the field in a ball of scrap metal. No injury was life threatening, but I had many lesser ones, and the medics wrapped me up like a mummy."

Stefan looked him up and down. "And now? Everything's working as normal?"

Greg spread out his arms. "Lots of scars, but a medic said ladies like scars. I am not sure I believe this." He shrugged. "I will feel aches and pains for all of my life. A small price for freedom." A shadow crossed his eyes. "The bigger price is never seeing Poland again. Never seeing my father again in this life."

Stefan's heart sank. "You're sure he's dead?"

"Yes." Greg watched a bird soar out to sea. "We don't know where or when he was killed, but yes, he is surely dead. The professionals were an early target when the Russians rushed in. And they will not leave when the fighting stops. The Allies will pacify them. Just like they gave away Czechoslovakia to pacify Hitler."

"What will you do?"

Greg shoved his hands into his pockets. "The RAF wants me to instruct. I do not wish to. I prefer to support the Polish squadrons. And after the war, I want to go to America."

"Good idea." Stefan nodded once. "What about your mother?"

"She is still in Sweden. It is safer than England. I write to her that she and my sister must come to America with me." He shoved his hands into his pockets. "She is lost. She wants her old life back. I hope my sister talks sense to her, but Adela has a Swedish boyfriend now."

They began walking, silent at first as a plane roared overhead, coming in to land. Stefan tried to imagine life in the United States if they were invaded by a neighbor. What if the Canadians invaded? With a smaller population, they couldn't expect a conquest. More realistically, if each state was independent, the Canadians might try to grab Michigan or New York. Would Wisconsin go to Michigan's aid? Or sit back, glad to be spared?

His whole imagined scenario was ludicrous. For more than one hundred years, the two countries had been peaceful. If the United States was like Europe, each state would be ready to fight with its neighbors. Most Americans didn't realize their good fortune of life, liberty, and the pursuit of happiness, along with a friendly neighbor to their north. A friendliness that allowed him to dream of a future with Marie.

Stefan turned to his cousin. "You know we'll help you and your mother. And Adela. We can sponsor you. Matka fondly remembers growing up with your mom. They were cousins but acted more like sisters."

Greg nodded. "My matka was so disappointed when your parents emigrated. Now she wishes she'd been braver. Ojciec dreamed of going to America, but Matka was fearful. She doesn't speak much English. So they stayed. And now Ojciec is dead."

As suppertime drew near, they headed for the mess hut. "How long can you stay?"

"I must find a plane heading to England tomorrow." Greg laughed. "When I was told to take the weekend off, I do not think they intended that I would leave the country. Why not? My uniform allowed me to board a plane for a free trip to see some other part of the world and meet my cousin." He spread out his hands. "If I cannot hop a plane tomorrow, I will have trouble."

They entered the mess hut, still speaking Polish. The first person they encountered was Dever. Of course. Stefan pointed to his crewmates. "Those are the men I want you to meet."

"Well, well, well." Dever wore his sneering smile as he followed them across the room. "Planning a little sabotage? Undermining authority?"

Greg studied him with a blank stare. "This is what you say crawled out from under a rock?"

A grin raised Stefan's lips. "Indeed it is."

Dever's sneer transformed into a scowl. "What are you saying?"

Stefan switched to English. "Nothing that would please you." With a hand at Greg's back, he directed him to a table. "David McQuaid, Andrew Grant, meet my cousin, Greg Wolton of RAF Spitfire fame."

Other officers gathered around to hear Greg's observations on combat during the Battle for Britain and flying over enemy territory. Questions flew through the air as fast as Spitfires, leaving Greg little opportunity to eat. Dever loitered at the back with narrowed eyes.

Stefan ate with a smile on his face, soaking up his cousin's experiences. Times like these reminded him how much he missed his pals, Daniel and John. He envisioned similar conversations with his friends when they returned home after the war. *If* they all returned. He fingered his pocket, feeling the outline of the letter he'd received yesterday. John had been wounded in the Pacific. Again. He'd be lucky to survive.

At least Greg probably wouldn't find himself in combat anymore.

By the time they escaped Greg's audience in the mess, Stefan was eager to introduce him to Marie. "She's French-

Canadian but has lived in the US for several years. I'm hoping to introduce her to Milwaukee."

They found her at their usual meeting place at the shore, and Greg raised her hand to his lips. "*Enchanté.*"

Stefan inhaled slowly. Maybe it was just as well for Greg to return to England in the morning.

Chapter Fifteen

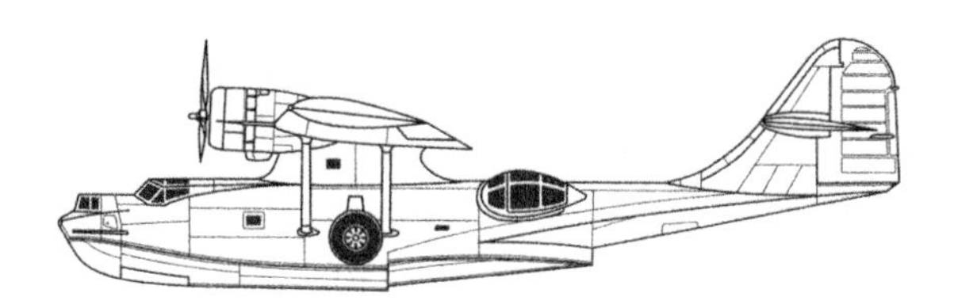

Marie dribbled water into the grapefruit juice can she'd salvaged from the mess hut. Her friend Francoise had sent her a tiny packet of marigold seeds, and Marie was determined to coax a few buds of cheery color to bloom.

When she moved on to the fruit cocktail can, she gasped. One of the seeds had germinated. She spun around in a circle. Would Stefan share her excitement?

The spinach can didn't have any sprouts. She touched the soil. It didn't need water. She set aside her watering can—a yam can with a hole punched near the lip.

"What do you expect to do with all those?"

Marie jumped and turned to see Sara, whom she hadn't heard enter the room. "Enjoy some flowers, I hope."

The Quonset hut didn't qualify as a greenhouse. She doubted the temperature ever rose above seventy degrees, so the big potbellied stove had no time off even during the cool summer months. Little sunlight entered through the small dormer windows due to the slope of the hut. Marie was fortunate to have a window between her cot and Helen's. The top of her packing-crate bedside table hosted her five cans of seeds, but they might do better in the warmer hospital.

Sara poked at the seedling. "You'll be lucky if that spindly thing can support a flower."

Marie pulled the can away. "It's doing just fine. Marigolds sprout quickly but can take about eight weeks to bloom."

She set up her drying rack fashioned from the skeletal remains of a crate by a patient. A sweater draped over the rack protected her plantings from drafts and hopefully warmed the air within. She'd taken a few botany courses in college but stuck to dietetics because it seemed like a better career option. Now she wished she knew more about growing plants.

"What are you doing here? Aren't you supposed to be in ..." Marie circled her hand in the air.

"Hvalfjord today, yeah," Sara finished for her. "I guess the roads are bad or the weather's bad." Sara shrugged. "Something's up. We were told to stay put."

Anne entered the hut and sneered when she caught Marie's eye, but then stuck her nose in the air and headed for her own bed. Marie sighed. Time to go to the hospital.

* * *

A U-boat had torpedoed a destroyer. The *Dobbins* succeeded in reaching safety in Iceland, and several sailors now resided in the hospital. Their eyes were clear and they chatted among themselves, so they probably weren't traumatized.

"Hey, look, a canary has come to visit," one of the man called.

Marie stopped herself from rolling her eyes. Being called a canary was so much better than being called a crow. She'd been shocked the first time she heard a sailor refer to one of the nurses as an old crow. The nurse wasn't ugly, merely firm in carrying out her duties. Still, this sailor bolstered Marie's esteem by considering her beautiful. On second thought, he may have been at sea for so long, he'd think she was pretty even if she wasn't.

She paused at the bed of a particularly morose man and laid her hand on his. "How are you feeling, sailor?"

He didn't respond at first. Could it be shock? His other arm was burned, and the side of his face sported lacerations. What other injuries couldn't she see?

Finally, he muttered, "Kasten coiled up his ropes."

Marie looked to the man in the next bed.

He twisted his mouth to one side. "His buddy died."

Oh, dear. She patted the man's hand, hoping her touch provided some comfort.

After a quick survey of the ward, she stepped over to the other man. "I'll take a guess that you all were belowdecks at the wrong time."

"Big time, wrong time." The man sighed. "One minute, everything's hunky-dory. The next, there's this almighty crash and water's pouring in. I wasn't even in the compartment the fish barged into."

She really needed to get a better handle on navy slang. The airmen didn't talk like this.

"Oh, miss? Will you hold my hand?" A red-haired sailor tried to look innocent, but Marie caught the gleam in his eyes.

"I don't think my boyfriend would appreciate that." Stefan shouldn't mind if she claimed his protection in this way.

The redhead scowled. "Yeah? Where is he? In the *army*?" He said the last word with a twist like it was a curse.

"As a matter of fact, he's in the navy." She raised her chin. "He's a navy pilot."

The man's scowl deepened. "That means he's an officer."

"He's on a bird boat?" another man asked. "Which one?"

"He's here in Iceland as a PBY pilot."

The scowler scoffed. "Flying coffins. They're low and slow, and easy pickings."

"And yet here *you* are, in the hospital." Marie shivered. Stefan had lain in a hospital bed not so long ago.

The man's pals hooted. He narrowed his eyes, but then his lips twitched. "Ha, ha. It's the only way I can get some time off."

While the men traded insults, Marie moved down the aisle. A man with both hands bandaged wrestled with a letter. "Do you need some help, sailor?"

Relief washed across his face. "I sure do. I can't get everything stuffed into the envelope without wrinkling it."

When she took the letter from him, several coins fell to his bed. She picked up a króna and aurar in one, five, ten, and fifty values.

Marie jingled them in her hand. "You can't send this out of the country."

"Why not? They're great souvenirs. I already have English, Norwegian, Russian, and French coins." He reached for them.

She closed her fingers around the coins, which combined silver and bronze metals and were stamped with the Icelandic crest. "You can't send them home. It's against the law. So many military men sent coins home that Iceland started running out of available currency."

"So why don't they make more?"

Marie couldn't help but laugh. "That would cause inflation. Remember, this is a small country, and not a wealthy one. Their money is made in Denmark, and they can't get more while the war continues. Leave their coins here. If you don't, the censors will remove them."

The man pouted.

She reluctantly returned his money. He'd likely hang onto the coins until he left Iceland. Then he'd send them home.

"Hey, miss."

She turned to the patient behind her.

"I have some coins to put back into circulation." He held up a handful of change. "Will you find an art store and buy me some watercolors?"

Marie didn't have an art store on her list of Reykjavik establishments. Scrounging for toiletries, candy, cigarettes, or even a case of fruit juice was easy enough, but going into town required more planning.

Maybe Stefan would be game for the mile or so hike from the hospital. They'd have to take it slow, so it might fill their whole day. But they could always thumb a ride back. She smiled and held out her hand. "I'll see what I can do."

The next man wore a morose expression. Uh oh.

"Bad news from home?" she asked him.

"My wife's selling our house. Moving in with her parents. She says it will be cheaper. Well, sure, but what happens when I go home? I bet her parents are behind this. They didn't want her to marry me." He dropped the letter.

Marie pointed at the paper. "May I?" At his nod, she picked it up and perused the tiny handwriting. "She writes that she can't make ends meet."

"I don't know why not. Clara gets almost all my pay."

Something wasn't right here. "If her parents are urging the move, they may be telling her she's not capable of managing on her own." Marie tapped her chin. "Do you think Clara wants to return to her parents?"

"She was glad to leave 'em. Her mother especially." He lowered his voice. "She's a witch."

"The Red Cross chapter in your area can check in with her.

Maybe help her create a budget, if it's finances that concern her."

"They'd do that?" The man brightened. "Boy, that'd be swell."

After collecting the necessary information, Marie left the ward. In the main hospital building, a petty officer called to her. "You've received a package in the mail."

"Delivered here?" She accepted the box. The return address proclaimed C. Rollins in New York. Mystified, she borrowed scissors and opened the parcel. Several issues of *Life* magazine slid out. They were all the same current issue, and a letter accompanied them.

Marie gasped. "They're from Chase Rollins, the photographer who was here a few months ago. The hospital is featured in here."

Handing a copy to the petty officer, Marie flipped through the pages of another. There it was. There she was—standing at the bedside of Burkhart, the pianist with injured hands who was playing Pick-up Sticks. The camera captured his look of triumphant wonder as he held up a stick. Beside him, Lessman's face wore its usual eagerness to have a go at the sticks.

They were all named.

Marie Foubert, who grew up as an orphan in Quebec and is now with the American Red Cross, got George Burkhart started with Pick-up Sticks to exercise his fingers. Burkhart had been a pianist with the Pittsburgh Symphony before the war.

How about that? She didn't know Burkhart's given name was George. Was he back in Pittsburgh now? Was he playing the piano again?

Did Rollins have to mention she was an orphan?

Turning the pages, she found herself in the background of another photograph. She must have been writing a letter for a patient. Too bad the photographer hadn't been here while

Stefan was a patient. Other photos featured scenes of the vast base, including the beach where she and Stefan often met. What a wonderful souvenir. Walking into another ward, she shared copies with the staff members who were pictured.

"Oh, thank you, love," a nurse said. "Be a dear and deliver this mail to the burn patients." She walked away without waiting for Marie's assent.

For the men in the burn ward to receive mail meant they were long-term patients. Many were torpedo victims with serious burns. Despite the agonizing recovery process, they joked and razed each other with a cheerfulness Marie found hard to understand.

Though the smell of burned skin appalled her, she couldn't show it on her face. The nurses often asked her to encourage the men to drink lots of water, and she'd been asked to assist a nurse with changing a patient's dressing. Marie hadn't been able to eat for the rest of the day. The nurse later apologized, saying she thought Marie had received medical training as a Red Cross member.

She walked to the center of the ward. The men lay still, their gazes following her. Selecting a letter from her basket, she asked, "Anyone here named Ralph Piering?"

The men perked up, and one of them lifted his arm six inches. "I'm Ralph."

"Bill Peterson?"

"That's me."

"Oh, here's another one for you. How about Mason Furth?"

She kept returning to Bill with more letters. Finally, she stood by his bed and shuffled through the stack. He'd received over thirty. "You're popular."

Other patients hooted. "How many girlfriends do you have, Peterson? Can I borrow your address book? What do the dames see in you?"

Marie helped some of the men open their mail while keeping an eye on Bill. He'd open a letter, scan it, set it aside, and reach for another. With a sigh, he finally pushed them away.

Marie wandered over. "Is something wrong?"

"They're from my mom."

She widened her eyes. Why the disappointment? She'd love to receive mail from her mom. "Does she write every day?"

"Rarely." Bill flicked a finger at the closest letter. "These are all the same."

Marie picked up a letter. "These are V-Mails." To save space in shipping, letters were photographed and rolls of film shipped overseas, where the letters were then printed. It seemed the copying machine had gone crazy and printed multiple copies of Mrs. Peterson's letter. "Well"—Marie dropped the letter back onto his pile—"now you have no excuse not to know you have a new nephew and that he's your namesake."

Bill quirked the unburned side of his mouth in an effort to smile. He took one letter and shoved the rest toward her. "Dump them, will you?"

"Miss, can you read this?" Another seaman waved a letter. "The copy is so light, I can't make it out."

She spent the rest of the day with the burn patients, reading and writing letters for them and reading aloud from *Mr. Winkle Goes to War.*

Returning to her barracks at the end of the day, she headed straight for her seedlings to see if another one had sprouted. Heat flushed through her and she balled her hands into fists when she saw that the fruit cocktail can nearly overflowed with water.

That despicable Anne had drowned her marigold.

Chapter Sixteen

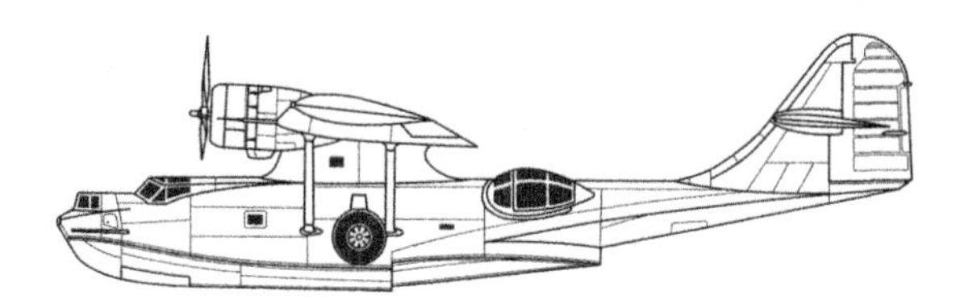

"Why would she do that? Everyone knows she did. She claims I must not have been paying attention when I watered the seeds. Ha! Even Sara, her only real friend here, doesn't want to be with her anymore. It's like Anne is trying to punish me because all her efforts to take advantage of me have led to her humiliation."

Stefan grabbed Marie's arm as she marched down the road to Reykjavik. She'd worked up a full head of steam, which propelled her along much too fast. "Slow down, kitten. My leg is almost healed, and I want it to stay that way."

Marie nearly tripped herself when she stopped abruptly. "Oh, I'm so sorry. Are you all right? Do you need to sit down?" Her hands fluttered as she whipped her gaze around. "There's no place to sit around here."

Another B-17 flew overhead. A squadron must be transitioning. Or it could be a replacement aircraft for those lost in battle. Combat pilots scorned his friend Daniel who flew cargo planes out of Brazil, because he didn't fight. The air crews stayed out of PBY territory here, so Stefan didn't know how they felt about his war role. Probably figured flying patrol over convoys was a soft duty.

He glanced back at Marie and found her watching him with raised brows.

"Kitten?"

He bit back a laugh. "Spit and snarl, right?"

A sheepish grin grew on her lips, and she poked his arm. "I shouldn't have told you about my neighbor's cat. I guess Anne is my cross to bear, and I'm not doing a very good job of bearing her."

They began walking again. A PBY circled above before disappearing to the east. He tucked her hand around his elbow. "Let's keep going. A sedate walk though, please."

Her shoulders sagged. "I'm sorry. She makes me so mad."

"I understand." He paused, turned toward the sea, and found a distraction. "Look at all the ships in the harbor and beyond. Reykjavik has limited docking and a lack of depth at those docks. While I was in the hospital, I heard that sometimes those ships wait seven weeks to be unloaded. Some are even ordered to return home while still fully laden. Can you imagine?"

As he hoped, Marie calmed. She took a deep breath and studied the scene. "The cranes for unloading seem to be idle."

"It's low tide. Ships with deep drafts have to move back into the harbor when the tide goes out."

"Further slowing things down." Her eyes followed a Flying Fortress as it roared in for a landing. "Are the supplies for us, or are they meant to continue on to Europe?"

"Hard to say. We're still eating, so we know our food comes through." Stefan rocked back and forth, testing his leg. Not even a twinge. "My brother Jed works in logistics, figuring out how much to ship where and when. They're frustrated with the bottleneck here, but that should change soon. There's a deep harbor in Hvalfjord, and the army engineers are almost finished with unloading facilities and building a good road leading back to Reykjavik."

"Hvalfjord. That's where Sara and Anne are assigned."

Great. Just when he'd gotten Marie's mind off her nemesis, he had to remind her.

"What do you know of Anne's background?"

Marie brushed wisps of hair off her face as she squinted into the distance. "She doesn't chat with the rest of us. She hovers nearby and listens to our conversations but never enters in. At first, we invited her to join us and attempted to draw her in with questions. She would only turn away or lift her nose." She pursed her lips. "I think she's from the Boston area."

"Hmm. I wonder if she and Dever suffer from insecurity. They only feel good by making someone else look or feel bad, which may also give them a feeling of superiority."

That had been the case with a boy in elementary school. His father always berated him, taking a switch to him for real or imagined offenses. Stefan's parents counseled him to befriend the boy, but he didn't want to be friends. Instead, he unloaded his taunts and punches onto Stefan. Sometimes maintaining distance from bullies was best.

Dark clouds scuttled across the sky, and the wind picked up. They were in for a shower. The rumble of a vehicle made him stop, turn, and stick out his thumb. The army truck stopped, and Stefan helped Marie climb into the cab.

She paused halfway in and stared at the corporal. "I know you."

The driver touched his cap. "Wilmer Case, at your service."

"That's what you said before." She scooted over so Stefan could climb in. "The corporal gave Lettie and me a ride," she said, turning to Stefan, "the day I ran into you."

The infamous day of Dever's attack. Today was a day for revisiting bad memories.

A cloud spattered rain on the windshield. "Your timing is impeccable, Corporal," Stefan said. "Do you know of any art supply stores in Reykjavik?"

"Art? Hmm. Maybe by that photography studio. Lots of guys have their picture taken there even though they can't send them home because they wear their parkas. It's just off Laugavegur, the main street in town."

The sun shone again as they veered away from their ocean view, and houses appeared on both sides of the street. The houses huddled closer together the farther they drove, and then shops appeared among them, until only shops lined both sides of the street. People thronged the downtown area, visiting stores and chatting on the sidewalks. Many glanced at the truck and quickly looked away.

"They still refuse to acknowledge us after all this time," Corporal Case said. "It's eerie, like we're invisible." He paused at an intersection. "You can see the photo shop there on the left."

Stefan and Marie thanked him for the ride, climbed out of the truck, and started down the street. Marie kept stopping to look in windows. She pulled out a notebook. "I haven't been here before. I need to add these stores to my list."

Stefan halted at the photo studio, aware of Marie's quizzical look. He wanted a photo with her. Pulling out his pocket-sized English-Icelandic dictionary, he reached for the door. "Let's see if they can fit us in."

Her eyes glowed as she nodded.

A woman of about thirty stood at the counter. She didn't smile or utter a word. No doubt Stefan mangled the pronunciations of "schedule" and "appointments," but not a flicker of amusement or disgust crossed her face. She'd make a great poker player.

The woman turned and walked away.

"Either she's calling a bouncer or asking the photographer if he wants our business." Being ignored on the street was one thing, but this cold indifference in a place of business was even harder for Stefan to swallow.

"Her dress is pretty." The tremor in Marie's hushed voice made him want to shake these people and tell them it wouldn't hurt to be polite. It wasn't like they expected an invitation to tea.

The woman reappeared and waved them back. The photographer may have been her father, considering the same straight blond hair and green eyes. He eyed them before uttering a clipped phrase that Stefan assumed meant "Stand there."

Marie slipped off her coat and produced a comb, which she hastily drew through her short, wavy dark hair.

"You look beautiful," he told her, and her cheeks turned rosy.

For the first pose, she stood partially in front of him as they both faced the camera. Turning a bit, they gazed into the distance. As they repositioned, Marie glanced back and they smiled into each other's eyes. *Click.* That would be his favorite.

The old man had mellowed by the time he finished taking half a dozen shots. He cracked a tiny smile as he held up four fingers, telling them in how many days the proofs would be ready. His daughter scowled. Stefan nodded farewell and ushered Marie out the door.

Narrow roads, old European-style buildings, and foreign language surrounded them. A few cars traveled the streets, as well as bicycles. "Have you noticed how many buildings have arched windows? And how many roofs are sloped?" He tapped on a wall. "Corrugated iron. That's interesting. And that's why they're painted. The paint keeps the iron from rusting."

Marie nodded toward a five-story building with arched doorways boasting a sign that read APOTEK. "I'm wondering what all the signs say."

"I'm guessing it's a drug store." Stefan thumbed through his dictionary. "Yep. Pharmacy." He pointed to another shop. "That's probably the art store."

Once inside, he attempted to tell a clerk they wanted water paints. The young man waved toward the right side of the store. Stefan gritted his teeth. "Thanks a lot, pal."

After wandering up and down a few aisles, Marie pounced on a narrow metal case holding eight watercolors. Back home, schoolchildren used these. Handing Stefan the container, she pulled out the man's coins and sorted through them. "I can buy three sets. This is probably the best I can do for him."

"He'll be grateful. If he's not, let me know and I'll adjust his attitude."

Laughing softly, Marie patted his arm before heading to the counter. She waited until he set down the paints before she dumped out the coins. Wide-eyed, the clerk slapped down a few rolling coins before they ended up on the floor. Under her steady gaze, his hands twitched as he counted them and handed her a receipt. "Thank you so much for your kind assistance," she said, her voice dripping with sweetness.

The guy stiffened. Yep, he understood English.

Back on the sidewalk, Stefan watched Marie inhale the brisk air. "Maybe I wasn't very nice. I know we're uninvited occupiers in Iceland. Still ..."

Stefan set his hand on her shoulder and squeezed. "Do unto others as you would have them do unto you. You were a lot nicer than that guy's actions deserved."

A small girl running down the sidewalk tripped and fell in front of them. Immediately, Marie crouched and helped the tot regain her feet. She brushed off her little coat. "That was quite a tumble."

Around them—even across the street—people froze and watched Marie, the foreigner, speak to one of their children. Stefan stood tall, shoulders back and ready to challenge anyone who dared object.

The child's eyes widened at the strange words, but since smiles were universal, the little girl grinned in return. Marie patted her arm and straightened. She didn't even give the child's mother a glance as she walked away.

Taking her daughter's hand, the mother dipped her head toward Stefan. He nodded back and caught up to Marie. "I think her mother appreciated your help."

Marie sighed. "I didn't want to risk seeing her glare." She gripped Stefan's hand. "Did you see that? The little girl *smiled* at me." She walked a few paces. "It wasn't the first time an Icelander has been kind to me. At the restaurant before Lettie and I met Corporal Case, the waitress informed me that—oh, I forget his name—our date was two-timing us. Right now, I'm savoring that little girl's smile."

As they left the town, Stefan snapped his fingers. "I have a great idea. Do you have a swimsuit?"

"Y-yes. Do you want to come back and go to the swimming pool?"

"Sure, but that's not what I'm thinking of now. We'll go to the hot springs this afternoon."

Marie made a show of checking her wristwatch. "Back by the waterfall and geyser?"

"No." He grasped her hand and picked up their pace. "There's a hot spring southwest of Reykjavik. You'll enjoy it. And my leg will appreciate it."

* * *

After hitching a ride back to base, Marie rushed to her barracks to prepare. Betty and Helen stared at her as she rummaged through her foot locker. "I need to find my swimsuit. Stefan and I are going to a hot spring."

Helen jumped up. "A hot springs?"

"Can we go too?" Betty already had her own suit pulled out.

Lettie arrived as they were shoving towels into duffel bags and insisted on going too. The driver gaped when four women descended on him.

"Good thing we've got a truck and not a Jeep," Stefan drawled as he handed the ladies into the back. He wasn't alone, either. A somber, dark-haired man wearing pilot's wings hung back. Stefan placed his hand on the man's shoulder. "Ladies, this is Frank Cusson from my squadron. Frank, this is Lettie, Helen, Betty, and Marie." He pointed to each of the ladies.

In a quiet aside that Marie heard, he added, "Marie's mine."

Her face heated. "Hi, Frank." The words came out breathless.

The men climbed in, and Stefan grabbed the seat beside her, leaving Frank to sit next to Lettie. As the truck jerked into motion, Lettie started her interrogation. "Where are you from, Frank?"

"Iowa."

"Did you train with Stefan?"

"Yes, ma'am."

"Where did you train?"

"Norfolk."

Betty leaned close to Marie. "The strong, silent type. Just as well. Lettie talks enough for everyone."

Marie grinned. She might have felt sorry for the poor man, but Stefan didn't seem concerned. Neither did Frank. He leaned his head back against the canvas siding, his gaze shifting to the scenery out back.

Lettie huffed and turned her attention to the rest of them. Marie tensed when her eyes gleamed in Stefan's direction. "Did you have to bring her along?" he whispered to Marie.

"What are you two lovebirds whispering about?" It may have been Marie's imagination, but Lettie seemed to raise her voice in order to garner everyone's notice.

Instead of answering, Stefan asked, "How did you all manage to get away at the last minute?"

That was all Lettie needed. "Oh, Helen and I are working a program this evening, and everything's ready, so we figured why not enjoy a bit of relaxation? I've never been to a hot springs, and who knows if we'll have another chance?"

Under the cover of her duffel bag, Marie poked Stefan's leg. He shifted his hand to interlace their fingers, and his slow smile unleashed a flock of jitterbugging butterflies in her abdomen. Lettie's yammering dimmed to a background buzz.

They arrived at the hot springs, which occupied an old lava field. Marie gazed around in wonder. Bubbles burbled to the surface, and steam rose from the milky blue water. Several men bobbed in the mineral bath, and Marie noticed a few military vehicles waiting in the parking lot. At the lagoon's edge, Stefan claimed a bench and dropped his gear.

"The servicemen know about this place." Marie's fingers hesitated at her coat buttons.

"Must be bath day," Stefan joked while shrugging off his jacket. "The water's hot, around one hundred degrees. Do you want to take it slow, or dive in?"

One hundred degrees? "How about dipping in my toes?"

"Take it slow. All right." He stripped off his clothes, revealing a brick-red swimsuit.

As the women disrobed, catcalls and whistles erupted from the bathers. "Well, lookee here. The Red Cross is by our side."

One man splashed toward them. Would he grab them? Toss them in? Marie bumped against Stefan, and Betty and Helen hid behind Frank. Lettie grinned. "How's the water, boys?"

Holding her hand, Stefan led Marie into the water. "Yep. Hot!"

Marie gasped as her feet tingled. She scooped up some water in her cupped hand and let it dribble down her arm. The cool air cancelled out the fiery sensation. "The air is too chilly for a swimsuit, but the water is so hot."

Stefan kept tugging her forward, inch by excruciating inch. Funny how she shivered on top while her legs sweltered. "What are we standing on?"

He reached down and lifted a handful of white mud. "Silica mud, the result of recondensation. It's beneficial for the skin, if you'd like to smear it on your face. Just like you'd do at a spa."

She eyed the gooey stuff and stuck her finger in it. One sniff, and she wrinkled her nose. "Why am I not surprised to smell sulfur?

Stefan chuckled and smeared a bit on his right cheekbone. "I'll experiment. In five or ten minutes, I'll check to see if this cheek feels softer than the other."

If he did, so would she. No one could accuse her of being a spoilsport. Holding her breath, she scooped up her own handful. But she'd forgotten about the hot water. Her arm, shoulder, and body quailed from the heat. Bouncing upright, she battled dizziness and lost her balance. Stefan caught her arm, and she latched onto his shoulder. His bare shoulder. What was she doing? She let go and stumbled against his chest.

When his arms came around her, the heat in her face rivaled the water.

He released her slowly, and she stared straight ahead. At his chest. She attempted to twist away but slipped on the muddy bottom. He grabbed her again and furrowed his brow. "Marie? Do you want to get out of the water?"

She tried to wave away the suggestion. "Moderation in all things. I just have to get used to this." She raised her hand. "Oh, I've lost my mud."

Stefan tilted his head back and laughed. "Easily remedied, sweetheart."

Sweetheart? New tingles zipped through her that had nothing to do with the hot springs.

He handed her a serving of mud. Using her index fingers, she scooped it up and smeared it on her cheeks. Clasping her hands, she offered a triumphant grin. "Why doesn't dipping down in the water bother you?"

He raised his arms, fists clenched and biceps bulging. "Big, strong men aren't affected by a little discomfort."

It was her turn to laugh. "Next time you get a sliver in your finger, I'll remind you of that."

"You do that." He seized her hand. "Time to wade out farther. Little increments at a time. It's not supposed to be deep —less than five feet—so we needn't worry about going under."

The steam rising from the springs created a foggy, ethereal atmosphere. Wisps surrounded their bodies, hiding the others from view. They could be alone on an enchanted island. As Marie adjusted to the heat, the water crept higher and soon lapped over her shoulders.

Beyond the fog, Lettie screeched, and the sound of splashing filled the air. Laughter rang out from both Lettie and a man. Marie squinted but couldn't see through the fog. "Lettie must have tumbled, and a gallant young man rescued her. Does the water benefit the face like the mud? And hair?" She reached for her own locks before jerking her wet hand away. "All these minerals might be hard to wash out."

"Can't help you there." Stefan traced his fingers along her jawline. His eyes darkened as he moved closer.

He intended to kiss her. And she realized she wanted him to.

She'd been kissed in college by Bill Schwartz. His lips were wet and slobbery. She never dated him again.

Stefan didn't lick his chops, and he didn't have nasty breath.

His lips brushed hers like butterfly wings. She experienced a spinning sensation, like she was about to lose her balance. She clutched his arms, and his lips pressed closer. A jolt passed through her, a momentary chill that had nothing to do with the air.

Someone splashed nearby and they drew apart, staring into each other's eyes.

Stefan ran his fingers through a lock of her hair. "I could get used to this."

The jitterbug started up in her stomach again. "Me too."

When they headed for the beach, Stefan paused and looked around. "A day to remember. Tomorrow, I return to flight."

Marie hugged herself as a sudden chill gripped her. But this time, the chill was fear.

Chapter Seventeen

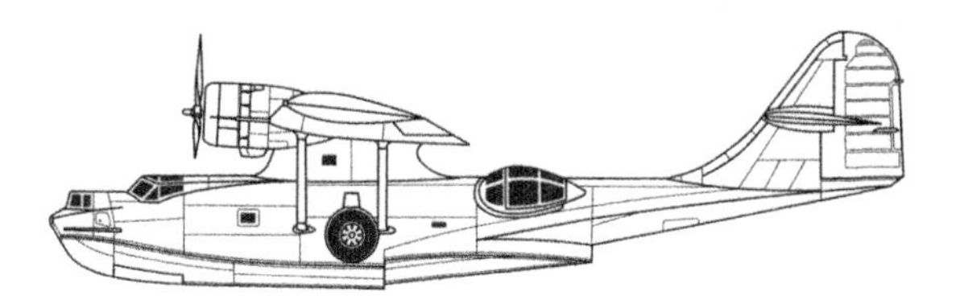

Stefan stifled a yawn as he focused on his instruments. Two weeks off had softened him. No matter how hard and uncomfortable his cot was compared to his bed at home, it called to him now.

"I'm glad you're back." Grant's words warmed him until he added, "The guy who flew with us had sloppy techniques. Taxiing should be done without brakes as much as possible. That's one of the first things we learned in flight school, but this stooge must have been sick that day. Ramsey kept saying the brakes were overheating, but did Stooge get it through his thick skull to back off? Oh, no."

Ramsey chimed in. "Instead of applying a little power for long periods, he repeatedly applied surges of power. Of course, that emptied the accelerator pump, and it never had sufficient time to refill."

"Sounds like you had some hair-raising flights before you even left the ground." Stefan pointed to a clump of white stuff stuck to the edge of the instrument panel. "What's this?"

Grant clicked his tongue. "Chewing gum. Stooge chomped

on it constantly. He'd, uh, set it aside when he had coffee. Even the ground crew complained about all the wads they had to scrape off."

"He always ordered me to bring him a cup of java." Lawrenz's voice was filled with indignation. "He treated me like a mess steward."

"All his sudden braking damaged the nosewheel gear. That really annoyed the mechanics." Grant raised both hands, clenched in fighting form. "And he didn't check to make sure the wheel pointed straightforward before entering the plane. If it's turned slightly, you should begin taxiing in that direction until it starts to pivot. Basic plane handling we learned in the first flight school class, but did he follow procedure? Ha!"

Stefan listened to his crewmen's reports with a growing sense of outrage. This airplane did not belong to him. He knew that. Still, it was his baby. He acted as plane commander, and he didn't appreciate anyone mistreating his airplane. He made a mental note to ask the head mechanic whether a full overhaul was warranted.

They were trundling toward the foot of the runway when Ramsey spoke again. "We should take another turn around the perimeter. The cowl flaps are fully open, but I'm seeing a high cylinder temp."

"Once around the block," Stefan acknowledged. "Jenz?"

"Inform control we're going sightseeing. Roger."

Stefan chuckled as he turned away from the runway. When another PBY's wing swept into view, shock ran through him. The plane following them in the taxiing pattern had accelerated onto the runway before they were safely clear. "Who's the clown behind us?"

"Cardelli," McQuaid answered. "He must think you've been out so long you've got cold feet now. His one-upmanship has begun to rival Dever's."

Shaking his head, Stefan questioned Ramsey on their temperature status. His response encouraged Stefan. By the time they returned to the starting point, their bird's health should be fine.

Letting Grant guide their plane, he watched Cardelli speed down the runway. Their weather briefing had included variable winds. Cardelli lifted off into a strong headwind. His landing gear began retracting when a severe crosswind struck the plane. It wobbled, and the port wing dipped and scraped the ground. The airplane flipped and slammed to the ground. The explosion sent out a shockwave that buffeted Stefan's plane.

"Whoa!" Pennington's exclamation from the bow reached Stefan without the benefit of the headphones.

"What was that?" yelled Lawrenz.

Stefan stared at the wreckage in disbelief. The men aboard that aircraft hadn't had a chance to escape. They'd been ripped into eternity in a heartbeat.

He took a deep breath. During training, a fellow student had reworked the familiar childhood bedtime prayer and it rang through his mind. *Now I sit me in the cockpit, I pray the Lord my skill will fit. If I should die before I land, I pray the Lord to take my hand.*

If a high cylinder temperature hadn't delayed them, they could have been the crew tossed by the crosswind. Stefan didn't pray for skill and protection every time he flew. But now, without bowing his head or closing his eyes, he offered up a word of prayer.

As they raced down the runway and lifted off, the billowing smoke served better than a wind sock. The flaming wreckage taunted him. *That could have been you.* Only one benefit of the sudden crash came to mind. The men must have died instantly, so they hadn't suffered.

He needed to clear his mind of morbid thoughts, and he

should encourage his crew to talk about it. "Did any of you know anyone on Cardelli's crew?"

"Yeah, the enlisted men bunked in the hut next to ours," Poulos said. "Smithers liked to juggle. One time, he juggled lava rocks while barefoot, and he dropped one on his foot. He had to get stitches."

"Nicholson played baseball," Pennington chimed in. "If it weren't for the war, he'd probably be playing professional ball. He'd been scouted by the pros." Envy laced his tone.

"He had us playing ball into all hours of the night when the sun didn't set. Once someone said, 'Hey, we have to get up in two hours,' so we turned in." Lawrenz paused. "But I think Nicholson would have stayed out there all night if anyone kept playing with him."

"Their radioman wished he could join another crew," Jenz said. "He didn't like the way Cardelli was always cussing them out. They were doing their jobs. It wasn't their fault they never bagged a sub."

Stefan didn't realize Cardelli was so tyrannical. The military frowned on fraternization between officers and enlisted men. Stefan understood that if they were all chummy, the enlisted men might not be quick about following orders, especially in critical moments. But that didn't mean officers should act like drill sergeants.

Did his crew grouch about him behind his back? He didn't order them around unnecessarily. Did he? Did he nag them to do their tasks, the way Matka had always asked him if he'd done his homework?

"Would any of you prefer to be on another crew?"

Grant raised his eyebrows, as if wondering if Stefan really wanted an answer to that question.

"We're already on the best crew."

"Poulos is right. We're well-oiled." Trust the engineer to use a mechanical metaphor.

"Well, I'd like to be on an all-girl crew," Pennington said, inciting laughter from everyone.

Stefan donned his sunglasses. He noticed something on the ocean's surface, making tracks and puffing out smoke. "McQuaid, how far are we from the convoy?"

"Forty-five minutes."

The ship made a change in course and started zigzagging. The way it blended in with the water made Stefan think of ... the Gray Ghost. "Jenz, we're overtaking the *Queen Mary*. Let her know we're friendly."

"Where is it?" Lawrenz sounded ready to jump out of the plane. "I don't see it."

"One o'clock position."

A light blinked from the cruise ship-turned-troop carrier.

"They acknowledge us." Pennington sounded as excited as Lawrenz.

"Jenz, blinker them to let them know they're approaching a convoy." Stefan dropped down to five hundred feet and began a wide circle around the ship, mindful that it carried antiaircraft guns.

Grant adjusted the fuel mixture to full rich for their low altitude. "They ought to know about convoys, shouldn't they?"

"I would think so, but they're coming up on the tail of the convoy. Doesn't seem likely they'd want to plow through dozens of slow-moving ships. They'll need to either zig or zag to skirt around it." Stefan hoped he wasn't issuing an unnecessary reminder.

A blast of icy air swept into the cockpit when Pennington opened the bow hatch. He stood in the turret and waved to the *Queen*.

"Crazy fool." Grant secured his collar. "He'll get frostbite on his nose."

"Don't fall out." Poulos must be admonishing Lawrenz, who probably opened a blister window in the back.

Onboard the ship, hundreds of servicemen watched them, many waving back. They were packed in like sardines.

"They want to know the convoy's latitude. Sub activity was reported to them south of here." Jenz and McQuaid worked out the convoy's present location, and Jenz relayed the position to the ship. "They plan on passing to the north."

As Jenz spoke, the *Queen Mary* adjusted course and Stefan flew ahead of it. The *Queen* sailed alone, too fast for a U-boat to catch her. He shook his head. Sure, and the *Titanic* was supposed to be unsinkable. His friend Daniel's cousin, Gloria Bloch, who served on a hospital ship, had grown up next door to a couple who had been aboard the *Lusitania* when it was torpedoed in the last war. It was supposed to have been too fast to be torpedoed.

The British Admiralty remained unconcerned, and the *Queen Mary* traveled alone. She wasn't his responsibility. He asked McQuaid for a direct route to intercept the convoy.

* * *

Intermittent clouds created shadows on the ocean's surface that resembled submarines. Stefan chased one shadow after another called out by his gunners. After the latest false alarm, he sighed. Those seamen down there must think he was drunk considering the way he flew so erratically.

"The cruiser's going to catapult its scout plane," Jenz announced. "It's the big ship at our nine o'clock position."

"Why are they launching it?" Stefan wouldn't be surprised if the navy escort questioned his flying patterns too.

"They're picking something up on their huff-duff. It's inconsistent. Either it's moving around a lot, or there's more than one U-boat."

Grant grinned. "Or it's nothing."

Stefan chuckled, his attention riveted on the cruiser. When the ship flung the small seaplane into the air, he whistled under his breath. That took courage. How often did a plane fail to become airborne and flop into the ocean like a spent cannonball?

"There's a dark spot to our right," Pennington said. "It doesn't seem to move like the other shadows. Lawrenz, do you see it?"

"Yeah, there it is." Lawrenz's voice rose to a shout. "It's got a periscope. That's a sub."

Grant yanked off his headset while McQuaid complained. "For the love of money, Lawrenz, practice radio etiquette and have mercy on our ears."

Stefan immediately turned to starboard, searching for the enemy. There! They knew they'd been spotted and were diving. He lined up his approach. He only had one shot at this. Diving at an angle of sixty degrees, he released four depth charges on the swirling water indicating the sub's location.

Gaining altitude, he circled around. A geyser of foaming white water burst out of the sea, followed by another. The third spit out dirty water.

"We got it! We got it!" Surely the men on the ships could hear Lawrenz scream.

"Please, Lawrenz, no screaming on the radio."

"Sorry, Skipper." Lawrenz's voice was now so quiet Stefan nearly missed it. "We got it."

"The escort sends his congratulations. Their sonar heard the explosion," Jenz said. "Huff-duff still hears something, but it's distant. This U-boat was likely calling for its pals to join in a wolf pack attack after dark. They're altering course for a more northern route."

"One of them may already be on station, so keep your eyes peeled." Stefan needed a break. Motioning for Grant to take over, he pried himself out of his seat and headed back.

McQuaid waved him over and pointed to his map. "We saw *Queen Mary* here. It opted to go north of the convoy. The convoy is here." He tapped a spot. "Now they're angling north. The *Queen* should be about here. They could still make contact."

Stefan rubbed his chin. He couldn't broadcast her position to the convoy in case the Germans picked up the signal. They would bend over backward to sink such a prize. Still, it wouldn't do for the convoy to spot her smoke and send a destroyer racing after her.

He plugged in his headset. "Grant, we need to circle the lead escort ship, and Jenz, blinker them that the *Queen Mary* is north of us. Just so they know there's friendly company in the vicinity."

Jenz scampered past him with his spotlight to work from the blister window. Stefan aimed for a bunk and collapsed onto it. His leg may have been cleared for flight, but manhandling a PBY required strength that he apparently hadn't fully regained. His muscles began to cramp. He rolled his leg, flexed his foot, and tried to relax.

Another trip to the hot springs sounded marvelous. For tonight, though, he looked forward to his beach rendezvous with Marie.

He was nodding off when a bang reverberated through the plane's fuselage. His eyes snapped open. Last time he heard a bang like that ...

"We need to head back. We're running out of gas."

At Ramsey's words, Stefan jackknifed and vaulted off the bunk. There went his evening with Marie.

Chapter Eighteen

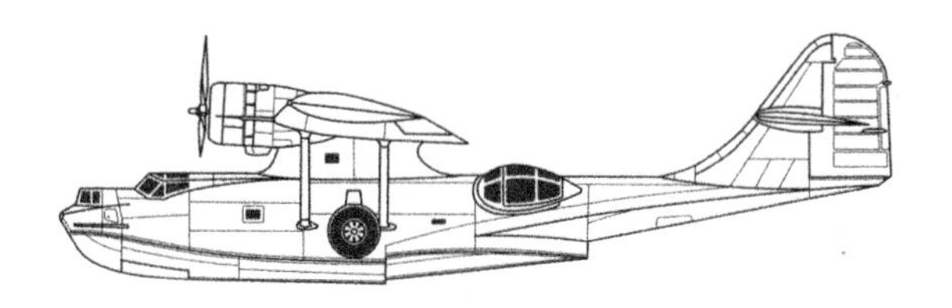

"We're planning something different for Thursday." Mr. Walton beamed at the Red Cross ladies. "For most of you, it will be a new location. For all of you, it will be a new experience."

Marie glanced at Betty on her left, then at Helen on her right as her thoughts swirled. A new location meant outside Reykjavik. They must be going to one of the other bases that at least two of the other women were familiar with.

"Get on with it, Walton," Mr. Perry snapped.

Since he'd been demoted to Walton's assistant position and Mr. Walton promoted to the directorship, Mr. Perry had been meaner than a bear disturbed during hibernation. Marie bit her lip to keep from laughing at the memory of him snarling, "What are you doing here?" when she arrived at the hospital one morning last week. It was her assigned post. What did he think she was doing there? Like Anne, he must blame her for his troubles.

"Most people based in Iceland never see anything outside the city. We'll be going to Hvalfjord base ..."

Anne scoffed. "Big deal."

"... to assist Sara and Anne with moving supplies into our new Red Cross center. Until now, we've had a tiny hut with rough furnishings that once served as a mess hut for an old British camp. Now we have a recreation center. Sailors have already done the heavy lifting. We'll unload a truckful of supplies that will make the men's off-duty time in Hvalfjord more enjoyable."

"Sara and I should do the unloading so we know where everything is." Anne sulked, her arms folded across her chest.

Mr. Walton continued as though he hadn't heard her. "After everything's inside, we'll head for Snæfellsnes Peninsula, which is considered Iceland in miniature. There are mountains, a glacier, a lava cave, and a beach. If you've read Jules Verne's *Journey to the Center of the Earth*, you've read about Snæfellsjökull glacier." He read the Icelandic name from his notes and shrugged. "Something like that."

"How long will we be there?" Lettie asked.

"Not long enough, I'm afraid. Two full days won't do it justice. We are going there to evaluate the possibility of organizing tours for the men. The logistics haven't been worked out, and it's getting late in the year, but Marie's little tour with her pilot has stirred interest among the men in Reykjavik for sightseeing."

Helen raised a finger. "Why are we going instead of some men?"

Mr. Walton smiled. "Because you ladies deserve a break."

"This will be fun," Lettie said before he finished answering.

Betty frowned. "That's a bit of a distance, isn't it? How much time will we have there?"

"We'll stay overnight in pup tents."

Marie sucked in her breath. Pup tents? What about a latrine? Water for washing? She had no experience with camping. She straightened. It was only one night. This would be an adventure. She'd have stories with which to regale Stefan. He must have flown over the area. He'd tell her to go for it.

Her day at the hospital dragged by. Too many patients grumbled about their discomfort, their lack of contact with family and friends, and life in general. Where was their usual good cheer?

Marie fought to keep a smile on her face and not scold them for complaining. The night had been stormy. Maybe they all suffered from sleep deprivation. She finished writing a letter as a seaman dictated. It was hardly a cheery epistle. *I'm alive. I want to go home.* She'd bring her Pick-up Sticks for him to exercise his fingers tomorrow and begin writing his own letters.

A nurse appeared beside her. "Did you hear about the crash?"

"What crash?"

The nurse whispered so the patients wouldn't hear. "One of the PBYs crashed on takeoff early this morning. I heard a wind gust flipped it over. Since it was full of fuel, it caused quite a fire. Of course, none of the crew survived."

Marie's blood turned to ice. She grabbed the nurse's hand. "Whose plane was it?"

"I haven't heard." The nurse shrugged. "All I know is that smoke billowed into the sky for hours."

Marie spun around and strode to the front desk, trying not to run. Arriving breathless, she interrupted two nurses. "Can you find out who the pilot was who crashed?"

The older nurse exhaled a long-suffering sigh. "Really, dear, we're not on the flight line."

"You can phone them. I need to know who the pilot was."

Nancy, the younger nurse, was always friendly to Marie. The petite blonde had taken high school French and liked to practice with her. She picked up the phone. "I'll see if I can reach someone."

Marie clutched the counter, hardly daring to breathe.

Finally, Nancy raised her gaze to Marie. "Cardelli? So it wasn't Stefan Da ..."

Cardelli. Not Stefan. Marie sagged against the counter, and the older nurse came around the desk. Taking her arm, she led Marie to a chair.

"Stefan was just cleared to return to flight. When I heard a wind gust flipped the plane, I thought maybe his leg wasn't strong enough yet to maintain control." Tears slipped from her eyes.

Nancy joined them. "I was told Stefan was supposed to be next to take off, but he pulled off the runway to make adjustments. Cardelli whipped around him. The controller watching was surprised they didn't clip wings." She touched Marie's shoulder. "If Stefan's plane had been ready to fly, it could have been him."

The older nurse continued to hover. "Why don't you take the day off, dear? You don't need to be here."

Did she think Marie's presence was unnecessary? Yes, there was a big difference between laughing with the men and caring for their wounds, but didn't their emotional health affect their physical well-being?

The frown Nancy directed to her colleague bolstered Marie's resolve. "No, the men seem so glum today. I should find the phonograph records. A little music might help them."

She found some Vera Lynn, Andrews Sisters, and Doris Day records. She grabbed a couple by Tommy Dorsey and the Song Spinners as well, which included her own favorite songs.

Her fingers shook as she set the first record on the turntable. Tilting her head back and closing her eyes, she breathed slowly. *Relax.* Stefan hadn't died. He was just fine.

* * *

Stefan hustled up to the engineer's station located high in the pylon, which supported the wings above the body of the aircraft. "What was that clank?"

Ramsey waved at his instrument panel. "Best guess? One of the engine-driven pumps failed. The fuel pressure dropped below minimums on the right engine. We're not out of fuel—we can't be. But I can't transfer fuel from the left side. It'll end up in limbo like the rest of the right tank's supply." He twisted to face Stefan. "This isn't something I can fix on the water."

A burst of relief flushed through Stefan. The last time they'd done a water landing hadn't turned out so well for him.

Ramsey indicated a page of scribbling. "Our usable fuel isn't going to get us to Reykjavik. Near as I can figure, we can reach Búdhareyri on Iceland's east coast. They've got a good landing spot on a lake there."

Stefan nodded. "All right. McQuaid, plot a course to Búdhareyri."

Dropping into the living-quarters compartment, he ducked through the bulkhead doors and returned to the cockpit. He waited while Grant adjusted course to McQuaid's new coordinates, wishing he had Poulos's Buck Rodgers headset. This second mechanical failure concerned him, but he didn't want the enlisted men listening in on his conversation.

As they settled into their new route, he leaned toward Grant and yelled, "Do you think someone is messing with our plane?"

Grant shot him a startled look. "You mean sabotage?"

Clearly, the idea hadn't occurred to Grant. This gave Stefan pause. Was he paranoid? Too jumpy after taking a bullet?

"Last time I flew, we had a loose pipe because a bolt wasn't tightened. Nothing alarming. But twice in a row?" He reached up to adjust a throttle. "I return to flight, and we hear another bang. How likely that it's a coincidence?"

Grant squinted out the windshield, his mouth pinched tight. "No one else has had trouble like this. Do you think it's personal? Someone's out for you? Dever, maybe?"

"It's hard to imagine, but if his aim is to discredit me without killing us all, I wouldn't put it past him."

"Maybe, but he'd need help." Grant flexed his fingers on the control yoke. "I don't see him as capable of damaging an engine in a way that's not immediately noticeable."

True. Who would go along with Dever's mischief, assuming he was behind their problems? From what Stefan had observed, his copilot wasn't thrilled with his assignment to Dever's crew. He wouldn't help him.

A ground crewman was far more likely to assist Dever in a malicious scheme. He could envision Dever chumming up to a mechanic. "Show me how this works." While the mechanic wasn't looking, he could give a little twist here or a loosening there. Still, the scenario was a long shot. The man might hate being upstaged by a Pole, but he wouldn't risk endangering the whole crew. Would he?

They barely made it to Búdhareyri. They'd been poking along just above stalling speed to conserve gas in their one working engine. Stefan commenced a long glide to the lake's surface. He knew the airplane tended to porpoise when landing at slow speed, but he had no choice. A brisk wind created rough water, but the plane settled down as though glad to rest. When their forward motion slowed, he revved the engine to turn toward the dock. The engine coughed and died.

Welcome to Búdhareyri.

Chapter Nineteen

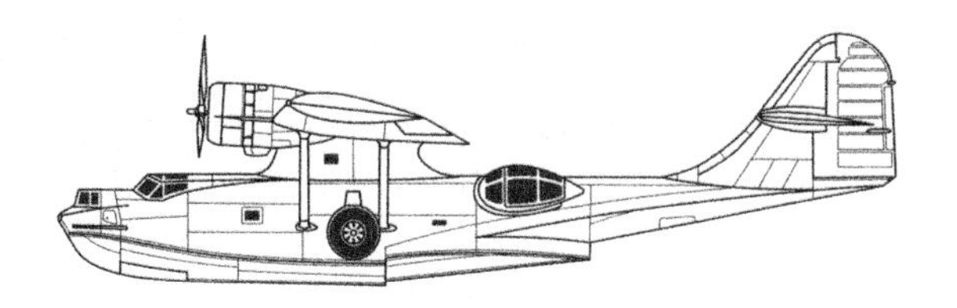

Stefan's plane hadn't returned. Apparently one of the engines didn't have enough gas. What was it last time? Not enough oil? Two mishaps so close together sounded odd to Marie.

She wandered down to the beach, knowing Stefan wouldn't be there. Still, it was their place. Here, she felt his presence. Locating the barrel she often sat on, she wondered about it. Why had no one claimed it? With furnishings so scarce, someone must want to use it. Unless they enjoyed sitting here too.

She filled her lungs with the crisp, sea-scented air. Some sort of gull wheeled overhead, releasing an occasional squawk. The seaplane base was quiet. Across a spit of land, planes ferrying to Europe landed at the Keflavík airfield called Meeks Field, built by American soldiers shortly after US troops arrived in Iceland. She'd learned that today from a ground crewman in an air group. His plane had run off the runway, tossing him around like a beanbag. He insisted he didn't need to remain in the hospital and had to stay with his group. But he lost his appeal and was left behind.

Stefan's crewmen were loyal to each other. That spoke well of him. A good leader set the tone, right? They performed their missions well, and they worked and got along like a well-oiled machine.

The waves splashed onto the beach and reached for Marie's feet. Failing to dampen her shoes, they retreated back into the sea. She scraped out a little trench and watched a wave pounce on it, filling it to overflowing. The next wave washed the trench away. Wave after wave after endless wave, washing away disturbances, steady in their hypnotic rhythm. No wonder Stefan enjoyed living near a big lake.

The crunch of lava gravel warned her that she no longer had the beach to herself. Footsteps stopped beside her.

"Good evening. You look lonely. I can remedy that."

The voice raised the hair on the nape of her neck. She clenched her skirt. Holding her breath, she glanced up into the face of ... Dever, and his charming smile proclaiming he expected her to fall at his feet.

She leaped up and stepped back. With a flick of her hand to indicate the beach, she fought to keep her voice steady. "It's all yours."

"Hey, no need to run off. We can share this lovely evening."

He thought he could charm her out of her shoes and everything else. She pulled her coat more tightly about her as she scurried up the beach. "No, thank you."

"What's the rush, doll?" He caught her arm. "The night is ours. Dabrowski can't keep you company. That dumb Polack doesn't know how to keep his plane in the air."

Dumb Polack? He sounded like the Nazis with their racial superiority. And what did he know about Stefan's plane? He couldn't have heard any more than she had.

She yanked herself away from him, but before she took two steps, he latched onto her again. "Come on, babe. I'll show you a real man."

Her blood, frozen at his approach, now boiled. "Being accosted by you once was one time too many."

He loosened his grip, and she jerked away. Then he grabbed her again. They were playing tug-of-war, with her arm as the prize.

"What are you talking about? All the other canaries agree that I'm gravy." He pulled her closer.

Panic set in. He was about to violate her. She tried to put her elbow between them. Wrong move. Now he had both her arms.

He chuckled. "So you like it rough, eh? Fine with me."

She wrenched sideways and saw movement among the parked seaplanes. Mechanics? "Help! Help me!"

He grabbed her jaw. "What's the matter with you?"

Two men ran toward them. Surely they would help her. If she could just hold him off a little longer. She stomped on Dever's foot.

"You vixen."

He slapped her, whipping her face to one side. Lights flashed before her eyes.

"Hey!" The shout sounded like it came from a tunnel.

Dever shoved her away. "You're such a loser. You and the Polack belong together."

He stomped off as the two mechanics skidded to a stop in front of her. The tall one pulled off his cap. "Ma'am? You all right, ma'am?"

"No." Marie touched her cheek. Her fingers felt wonderfully cool against her stinging skin. She focused on the man before her, and his wavering image solidified. Freckles covered his face beneath a shock of unruly red hair. He took a slow step forward as though he was scared of her, or afraid he'd scare her. What did he expect?

"He would have attacked me if you hadn't come." The left side of her mouth didn't cooperate, slurring her words.

The mechanics exchanged glances. Did they think she'd come out here to meet Dever?

She stood tall, trying not to sway. "He thinks he's charming, but he's not."

More side glances. What were they thinking?

The short one cleared his throat. "Well, he's gone now, ma'am."

Marie tried to nod, but the movement pained her neck. "Thank you for running him off."

They hemmed and hawed, bobbed their heads, and headed back to their work.

Marie turned in a full circle. The beach had lost its appeal, but she didn't want to return to the hut. Didn't want to see Lettie or Anne, if they were in. Maybe she should go to the hospital. One of the nurses had complained about Dever.

When she pushed through the door, Nancy looked up from the nurses' desk with a ready smile that quickly fell into a frown. "Marie! What happened?"

She rushed around the desk and reached for Marie's arm. "Do you need to sit down?"

The nurse's reaction told Marie she must look a lot worse than a slap warranted. She touched her hair. Her cap had slid down. As she lowered her hand, she spotted a touch of blood. A fingernail had ripped to the quick, and only now did she feel the pain.

"He-he kept yanking on my arm. Then he grabbed my face when I called for help." She shifted her jaw and touched it. Her cheek still burned. "He slapped me so hard."

She sagged in the chair. Now that she was safe, all she

wanted to do was curl up in a ball and hide from the world. A tear squeezed under her eyelid, and she brushed it away.

A memory wafted through her mind. A new girl had arrived at the orphanage. She hadn't wanted to get out of bed, and one of the sisters berated her. *"Life is hard. Everyone has problems. Face up to it. No one has time to mollycoddle you."*

The girl was eight years old. She'd needed a hug, not a lecture.

Other nurses gathered around. One asked, "Who slapped you? Dever? I'll bet it was Dever. He had a go at me last week. He doesn't understand the meaning of 'no.'"

A petite blonde nodded. "As my mother would say, he thinks he's the cat's pajamas."

Marie licked her lips. "He thinks he's gravy and I'm a canary."

Nancy patted her hand. "You are beautiful. And he is kind of good looking, until he gets that creepy look in his eyes."

"Well, there's the advantage of being a plain Jane." Another nurse planted her hands on her hips and heaved a sigh. "He'll never bother me."

The nurse nearest her touched her arm but didn't dispute her claim.

A male voice seized their attention. "Have you notified the military police?"

Standing at the edge of their group, a stocky doctor studied Marie.

"No. I didn't report him. They'll say it was my fault. They'll send me home, and I don't have a home to go to." She shuddered at the doctor's stern visage. "He's a pilot, after all, and I'm only with the Red Cross and not doing his morale any good."

Several nurses spoke over each other.

"She's right."

"They won't believe us."

"Stupid little women without serious thoughts in their heads require big, strong men to tell them how to behave, and it's our duty to please them." Everyone paused to stare at the statuesque nurse with fire in her eyes. She must have a story to tell.

Marie pressed her fingers to her forehead, where a headache throbbed.

"Get some ice on her face." The doctor made eye contact with each of them. "Reconsider talking to the MPs. If this man is escalating his unwanted attentions, something worse may happen."

No sooner did he leave them than a policeman entered the hospital. "I understand a report needs to be filed."

Marie nearly stopped breathing. She couldn't file a report. Dever was sure to retaliate against her and against Stefan. She'd have to leave. Would the Red Cross reassign her? Dismiss her? Could she get her job back in Washington?

The first nurse to comment folded her hands and raised her chin. "Yes. Several of us have been subjected to the unwanted attention of one of the PBY pilots. He thinks we're here to satisfy his, er, baser needs."

Four nurses told stories of being grabbed by Dever. The military policeman frowned mightily when the tall nurse described how Dever had cupped her bottom and pressed her against him so she was left without a doubt of what he wanted.

By the time Marie trudged to her hut, the ice had left her cheek cold and numb. Her brain didn't fare much better. Crossing her arms, Marie hunched her shoulders against the chilling image. Her insides quivered at the thought of Dever dragging her out of sight and ... *Stop! Just stop! He didn't do it. I'm safe.*

Overhead, the sky deepened in color. Soon, normal

sunrises and sunsets would return as summer waned. They would see stars and the Northern Lights. At least that was something to look forward to.

Think about what is true and honest, pure and lovely. Things of good report. That's what Sister Marguerite always reminded them to do in the orphanage. Don't think about Dever. Think about Stefan.

And her flowers. She needed to water her flowers. Anne had drowned one can of marigolds, but Marie planted more seeds. All five cans now flourished. Two buds had opened yesterday, thrilling them all. Well, all except for Anne.

A quick survey of the hut revealed everyone accounted for. Marie shrugged off her coat and headed straight for her garden. She grinned at four new blossoms. Turning to ask Betty if she'd noticed, Marie stopped at her friend's wide-eyed look. She covered her cheek and gave a minute shake of her head.

Betty joined her at the flower cans. "What happened?"

Marie whispered back, "Dever." She pointed to one of the cans. "This one will have three new blooms tomorrow."

She didn't notice Lettie come up behind them. The gregarious girl's voice rang out loud enough to raise the dead. "Marie, what happened to you?"

Chapter Twenty

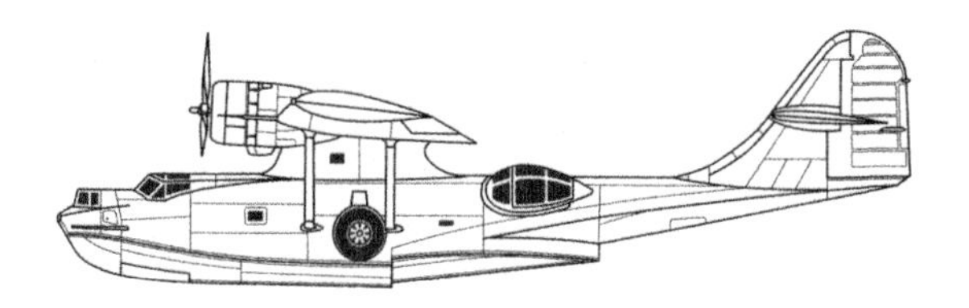

The aircraft roared into the air, good as new, and Stefan's grin broadened. Mechanics unknown to him had performed their magic on his ailing engine, and now it sang like an opera star.

His grin faded. Did he really not trust the ground crew in Reykjavik? Surely no one was guilty of sabotage, not even Dever.

They usually flew over water. Now they flew over Iceland. A stirring of excitement rose within him. Here was his chance to see more of the country. They'd fly over Vatnajökull glacier, which lay on top of a volcano. White ice and black sand. He knew the black sand beaches resulted from glaciers grinding against the basalt rock. He could already see the glistening mountain of ice. And there, just to his left, a hydrothermal eruption shot jets of water high into the air. Must be sixty feet high.

Jenz's voice crackled in his ears. "A U-boat's been reported sniffing around to the north, probably heading for the Denmark

Strait between Greenland and Iceland." He offered the last known coordinates. "We're supposed to find it."

Stefan sighed. So much for his aerial sightseeing. Banking to the right, he settled into the route McQuaid gave him. He grabbed his map of Iceland to find anything of note, and his pulse quickened. If he angled their course slightly, they'd pass over Dettifoss and see the largest waterfall in Iceland.

"Talley ho." Pennington's voice came through the headphones. "There's a lifeboat."

Five or six men waved at them. Here off the northern coast of Iceland, there weren't likely to be any naval vessels. Only fishing boats. Stefan studied the waves. He'd have to land and pick up the survivors if they had any hope of staying alive.

"There's the sub at ten o'clock. It's getting ready to submerge."

Pennington's announcement shot a burst of adrenaline through Stefan. No wonder those men on the lifeboat waved so energetically. He turned toward the U-boat. Men raced to the hatches, but one man didn't make it in time. The hatch closed, and the submarine sank beneath the surface. The man spun around, no doubt hoping the conning tower was still above the waves, but he was swept into the sea.

"Did you see that?" Stefan asked as he lined up to drop depth charges on the still visible shadow of the enemy boat.

"At least he's wearing a life jacket," Grant said before calling out their altitude.

The depth charges blew the stern of the sub out of the water, but it quickly disappeared again. Oil stained the water's surface. Those men weren't returning to Germany.

Stefan located the sole survivor. He must have been far enough away from the depth charge explosions that they hadn't crippled him. Depth charges could turn a man's innards into mush. "Floats down."

"We're landing? The waves are pretty choppy." Despite his concern, Ramsey lowered the floats.

"We've landed in worse," Grant said.

"It's okay," Lawrenz added. "They gave me a bunch of pencils at that base last night."

Stefan chuckled to himself. Pencils fit nicely into the holes of popped rivets.

The PBY banged down on the crest of a wave and bounced back into the air. Stefan cut back on power, and Grant pulled on the control column with all his strength. They plopped down with a softer bang and soon wallowed in waves. Stefan angled toward the German. "Lawrenz, Poulos, be ready to throw a line to the swimmer and reel him in. I don't want to stop."

"First chance I get to fish and what do I catch? A Kraut." Lawrenz sounded like he was pouting.

"He's alongside now. Oof." Poulos was breathless. "He's in, and he's sopping wet."

"What did you expect?" McQuaid clicked his tongue. "Grab a blanket off a bunk."

"Lawrenz, coil the rope and prepare for another toss." Steering was hard enough on placid water. With the chop, Stefan had his work cut out for him.

The men in the life raft continued waving. He could tell they were yelling too, the way their mouths kept opening. And even considering the risk Stefan was undergoing for them, they didn't look happy. No gratitude.

"Lawrenz, how's our guest doing?"

"His teeth are clicking like cassinettes."

"You mean castanets, boyo?" McQuaid must be nervous about their situation, because he didn't usually didn't lose patience with Lawrenz's pranks and foibles. "Give him some coffee."

"Make it quick." Stefan's own nerves stretched thin. "The raft is coming up." Finally.

A moment later, Poulos whistled. "You should see him guzzle it down. He acts as if he never drank coffee before."

"Probably hasn't for years." Jenz said. "Aren't they making coffee out of acorns because they can't import the real stuff?"

"Yum."

Poulos's weak rejoinder lightened Stefan's mood. "Be ready with the rope."

It took three tosses before the survivors latched onto the monkey's fist, enabling Lawrenz and Poulos to pull them to the seaplane. Stefan felt the tail bob as they clambered onboard.

"Hey! Sit down!" Lawrenz's shout could be heard without headphones.

Stefan yanked off his seat belt and dashed through the bulkheads to the gun compartment. Five angry men dressed in rough seamen's garb stood with clenched fists. "What's going on here?"

"They're Russkies and want to tear apart our Kraut." Lawrenz's chest heaved.

One of them—a big, burly man—thrust out his chin and said something defiant in Russian.

Stefan jerked his thumb at the open blister. "Get out."

The big man gaped before swelling in anger. One of his fellows held up his hands. "We friends. Allies. Not him."

"Polska." Stefan thumped his chest. "Polska. No friend of Russkies."

The Russians shifted around. Some sat. The burly guy subsided but didn't unclench his fists.

Stefan borrowed Lawrenz's headset. "Jenz, come escort our German to the bow. Pennington can sit on him. And bring me a pistol. Poulos, you and Lawrenz remove these guns, put them in the tunnel, and close the bulkhead. If these clowns give you trouble, toss them out."

"Me?" Lawrenz squeaked. The burly guy had to be at least twice his weight.

When Jenz arrived, Stefan took his gun and handed it to Lawrenz with a grin. "Ask him nicely to step outside." After Jenz and the German moved forward, Stefan surveyed their Russian guests. With the prisoner gone, the burly man finally sat down. Stefan turned to Lawrenz. "I don't want to close this bulkhead while we're in flight. If anyone tries to go forward, shoot him."

The conciliatory Russian shook his head. "No need. We are here."

Stefan nodded and returned to the cockpit. The German looked up through the entrance to the bow as Stefan settled into his seat. Fear and exhaustion warred for supremacy on the boy's face. He was just a kid, all alone in a hostile world.

Grant had kept the seaplane moving to avoid swamping. Stefan brought it up to speed and thundered through the waves. They had to get atop the crest of the waves to lift off. The plane plunged through four waves as water splashed onto the cockpit windows. He hoped the bow windows didn't leak. Finally, they hit the top of the fifth and staggered into the air.

Once they were headed to Reykjavik, Grant asked, "How are things back there?"

"There's a big, mean guy who looks like a bar brawler. I think he'd relish eating Lawrenz for breakfast."

Lawrenz's voice broke in. "That's not a comfort, Skipper."

Some of Stefan's tension drained away. "Jenz, call in that we require a police guard for one wet German and five Russians on the unruly side."

Their flight progressed quietly. In the bow, Pennington

talked to the German, who apparently knew English. Pennington caught Stefan's eye and crawled up to the cockpit.

"Dietrich says the Russian ship wasn't going fast, and they heard strange sounds from it," Pennington reported. "Like someone was giving a speech and everyone was cheering. One of the Germans understood Russian and said they were extolling the virtues of Communism. The U-boat was on the surface, and they didn't even see it."

Stefan indicated the prisoner, Dietrich. "What was his job?"

"Cook's assistant."

Lawrenz piped up. "Maybe he can make us some sandwiches."

"The way our galley rivals Mother Hubbard's cupboard?" Stefan laughed. "That's wishful thinking."

Reykjavik loomed into view when Ramsey called Lawrenz. "Lean out the window and check our port wheel. The indicator light isn't happy."

A moment later, he received his answer.

"Hey, we caught a fish, but it just fell out of the wheel well."

Stefan burst out laughing. That was the perfect note on which to end their flight.

* * *

"Have you heard?" Nancy skidded to a halt in front of Marie. "Of course you haven't. It's causing quite a stir."

Marie stared at the normally unflappable nurse. "Goodness, what happened? Did the war end?"

"Don't we wish." Nancy heaved a dramatic sigh. "Alas, no. But, ta-da, Lieutenant Stefan Dabrowski is coming in. And they've requested a police escort. They're bringing in a

German sailor and five Russian seamen who want to kill him."

"Kill who? The German, or Stefan?" Marie asked the question to stall for time. She wanted to race off to the airfield. Stefan was returning! But she didn't want to act like a lovesick teenager.

Nancy planted her fists on her hips. "Duh. The German, of course. It'd be fun to watch them deplane, but we're on duty." She pouted. "Oh well. We will get to see the German, maybe. They'll bring him here to check him out. He may have suffered hypothermia before they fished him out of the sea."

Nancy needed to stay on duty, but as a Red Cross worker, Marie could slip away. "Is an ambulance going to fetch him? Maybe I'll ride along. Then I can describe the big, bad Russians to you."

Nancy clasped her hands together. "And maybe a sweet greeting with a handsome pilot?"

"Oh, no. I won't be describing any such greeting." Marie tucked her basket of supplies under the counter at the nurses' station and hurried to the entrance.

With a squeal from the hydraulics, the PBY eased to a halt. As Stefan and Grant worked through the post-landing checklist, Grant nodded to the windshield. "What's with the mob scene?"

"Can't be a celebrity passing through. They always land at Meeks Field." Stefan surveyed the crowd. A group of MPs awaited their passengers, along with a photographer. Stefan's gaze stopped on the ambulance pulling alongside the crowd.

Word must have gotten around about their guests. Maybe they wanted to see the German? Not many prisoners came through here. The Russians who hailed from that mysterious country with the demanding, paranoid leader whom Roosevelt kowtowed to? Did the people want to see a fight between them? Not that it would be much of a fight. The Russians would tear the kid apart before he could put up his dukes.

The seamen deplaned first. Stefan grinned as some of the spectators stepped back at the Russian roughneck's menacing appearance. The man stopped and faced the plane, his fists on his hips. Waiting for a chance to beat up the German? Nothing doing. Stefan prevented Pennington and the German from exiting the bow.

McQuaid stepped down from the blister window and spoke with ... the base commander? Why was the general so interested?

Stefan turned to Grant. "Something's up. There's too much interest here for a simple sea rescue." His thoughts scattered when he spotted Marie by the ambulance.

"Maybe we should take the German through the blister on the other side. If he disappears, that might defuse whatever the situation is." Grant leaned across Stefan to see out his window. "The Russkies look so boastful, don't they? They lost their ship and had to be picked up by Americans. What do they have to be proud about?"

Pennington pushed the pilots' legs aside and squeezed out of the bow into the cockpit. "Did I hear you say Dietrich will leave from the other exit? He's still shivering. He should go to the hospital."

Stefan slid open his window and waved Marie over. Her welcoming smile warmed his heart. "Hey, beautiful. What's going on with the Russians?"

Marie kept her voice low too. "They seem to be making demands. Before you landed, I heard a Russian ship had attracted attention from Intelligence. They don't think it was an ordinary cargo ship, and this may have been it."

Men drifted closer, and Stefan leaned further out. "Can you get the ambulance to quietly drive around to pick up our German? He needs medical care."

She nodded. As she headed back, he closed his window and stood. "Okay, fellows. We're finished here. Let's make a show of leaving."

Grant crouched through the bulkhead, followed by the others. One advantage to small windows was less likelihood of the German being spotted. In the waist compartment, Pennington helped Poulos with post-flight cleanup. Stefan glanced around. "Where's Lawrenz?"

Poulos snickered. "Checking the wheel well for evidence of the fish."

Stefan let his eyes slide shut and he shook his head. "We'll be hearing fish stories for a week. All right. Here's the ambulance. Everyone off."

While the others hustled Dietrich into the ambulance, Stefan managed to quickly kiss Marie. The vehicle pulled away before anyone realized what had happened. The burly Russian noticed first and started yelling. At a nod from the general, the MPs herded the seamen into the back of truck and hauled them off to the merchant seamen survivors' camp.

The intelligence officer approached Stefan's crew. "Did they tell you anything?"

"They wouldn't even give us their names." McQuaid bounced his fist on his opposite palm. "I told them we needed their names to inform Russia of their survival, that they were responsible for getting the men back to Russia." He scowled. "'*Nyet. Nyet.* We go US.' That's all I learned."

Stefan repeated what Pennington had said, and the Intelligence man frowned. "So there was a crowd on that ship?"

McQuaid smacked his palm with more force. "Maybe they were Communist infiltrators planning to jump ship and cause trouble among factory workers."

"Maybe we should have thanked the Germans for torpedoing them." Grant shrugged. "Instead, we sank 'em."

As the interview wound down, Stefan spotted Commander Arnett—his arms crossed and eyes narrowed—standing with Dever. The smart-alecky pilot was talking nonstop. When Dever noticed Stefan's gaze, he offered a self-satisfied smirk. He was up to something.

Chapter Twenty-One

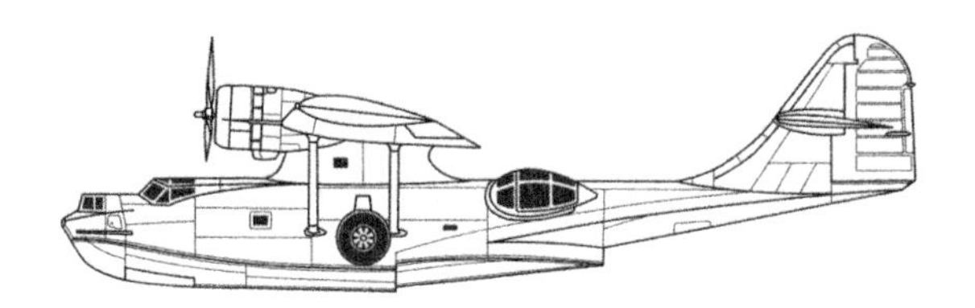

Marie grabbed onto a supporting rib of the truck's canvas roof as the vehicle bounced into a rut on the unpaved, single lane. She didn't consider herself prone to car sickness, but this ride challenged her equilibrium.

From the bench across from her, Sara grinned. "This is the worst part. The army's been dumping crushed lava on the road as well as widening it for two lanes. This is the last section."

"What happens if you meet oncoming traffic?"

"Someone has to pull off on one of those turnouts." Sara pointed out the back, where they'd just passed a widened area complete with lava gravel.

"You mean those aren't scenic viewpoints?" Marie swallowed hard as her stomach rolled.

Sara laughed. "Be glad it hasn't rained much lately. You do *not* want to travel this route when all the holes are filled with muddy water."

When they arrived at Hvalfjord, a truck waited, its bed full of boxes. What could possibly fill so many crates? Red Cross supplies didn't arrive in Iceland often.

Marie wasn't the only one who wanted to peek inside the crates. When Lettie tried to pry open a box, Anne brushed her aside. "We're not opening them now. Just stack them inside."

The recreation center appeared spacious, but the Hvalfjord camp wasn't small. The men would fill it to overflowing on opening day. Helen ran her hand across a ping-pong table. "I wish we had this in Reykjavik. Instead, we have a pool table. The guys always ask me to play with them, but I'm no good at pool."

Marie pushed another box beneath the table. "Would you want to play ping-pong with them? I imagine they'd whiz the ball through the air at fifty miles an hour. I'd never be able to make a return."

"Maybe. Yeah, I can see that happening. But if they wanted to enjoy the game instead of constantly stopping and retrieving the ball, they'd play nice."

Sara joined them. "I grew up playing ping-pong with my older brothers. I can handle any guys who try to impress me with their prowess." She eased a box onto the table and flipped open the top.

"Hey, we're not opening boxes now." Anne stormed over but came to an abrupt stop when she realized her partner was the guilty person.

"Oh hush, Anne." Sara pulled out a carton of Lucky Strike cigarettes. "Phooey. This is the fourth box of cigs. Where are the candy bars?"

"The truck is empty." Mr. Walton clapped his hands at the door. "Let's close up here and be on our way."

The drive to Snæfellsnes took longer than any of them anticipated. Even Mr. Walton seemed discouraged. Back in the

States, a thirty-five mile per hour speed limit was in place during the war to reduce gas and rubber consumption. That speed would have enabled them to make the trip in less than three hours, assuming the roads were in good condition. Iceland's unpaved roads didn't allow such a fast pace.

Another rut nearly bounced Marie off the uncomfortable bench seat. "Maybe the navy will allow small sightseeing groups to use a seaplane for travel."

"They won't take a plane off patrol duty for recreational uses." Lettie was uncharacteristically glum.

"True, but after a plane undergoes an overhaul, it's taken up for a test flight." Marie focused her gaze on the horizon as queasiness welled up. "Why couldn't it drop off a group at this peninsula during its test? The next overhauled plane could pick them up."

"That's a thought, as long as the sightseers don't mind the risk of taking a test flight," Betty said.

Helen shrugged. "Why not? War is full of risk."

Lettie snickered, and the sound soon had them all giggling. All except for Anne. Marie studied her through narrowed eyes. Why was she wound so tight?

* * *

After the rough ride, camping in a pup tent didn't faze Marie. Stretched out on solid ground and not having to sit on the hard wooden bench, she slept undisturbed by the chill. She and Betty rose before dawn, eager to romp around the peninsula before enduring the ride back.

Mr. Walton gathered them for a briefing after their picnic breakfast. "I've been informed of a dozen must-see spots. Obviously, we won't be able to visit them all or stay long at any single one, but we'll view mountains, waterfalls, gorges, craters, and beaches. We'll see why this is regarded as Iceland in miniature. Our route will loop around the peninsula, starting from the south. Let's be off."

They stopped at a black church in a lonely setting, all that remained of a nineteenth century village. Marie turned in a full circle within the empty vista. Why had everyone moved away? She adjusted her camera lens and snapped a few pictures.

Lettie hovered at her shoulder. "Where'd you get the camera?"

"Stefan loaned it to me last night. If we expect to interest the men in sightseeing, we need to show them what to expect." She grinned. "I think he wants to see the sites himself. If we do set up a tour, he'll be the first in line."

"Must be nice to misappropriate military equipment."

Anne. Of course. Marie ignored her and headed back to the truck.

The Lóndrangar rock formations straddled the southern shoreline. The basalt cliffs boasted two towering pillars at the edge of the shoreline. She thought of Stefan, knowing he would love to visit the geological wonders. Marie declined to venture too close to the edge, but Betty inched forward. Marie took a quick picture with an especially tall rock behind her. "Okay, that's far enough. Please, please, please, come away from the ledge."

"Aw, you don't want to rescue me if I start to fall?" Betty laughed but scrambled back. "I think the edge started to crumble."

Marie scrutinized the ledge. "I don't think so. But no, I wouldn't try to rescue you. We'd both end up falling. Let's stay upright on *terra firma*."

They laughed and headed back to the truck, arms linked, while Anne glared at them.

Djúpalón Beach was even better, with its black sand they could walk across right up to the water. Marie had to keep reminding herself not to use up all of her film. At one point, she surrendered the camera to Mr. Walton so he could include her in a picture with Betty and Helen in front of a natural arch.

A few miles north, Skarðsvík Beach featured golden sand and black rocks. Marie scooped up a can of the golden sand to add to her can of black sand.

"What will you do with them?" Helen asked.

"I don't know. Maybe find decorative little jars. Stefan will like to see the sand varieties."

"As if he cares about your silly stuff." Anne was becoming a real pain. She obviously didn't realize exploring Iceland was a geologist's dream.

Saxhóll Crater didn't interest everyone. As they approached a pathway winding up to the summit, a climber slipped and slid down several feet. Helen and Marie persevered and made it to the top, where Marie gazed into the crater. Hard to imagine lava spewing out. The view around them extended for miles, with the sea in the distance. When clouds scudded in their direction, they started their descent.

Rain fell as they journeyed to their last stop on the northern coast. Marie recognized free-standing Kirkjufell Mountain from photos Stefan had purchased in Reykjavik. The steep slope was too dangerous to climb, especially while it was wet. Instead, they stopped by Kirkjufellsfoss, the nearby waterfalls, as the sun broke through.

For the best photo angle, Marie followed a footpath along the river. The others followed, but it was Anne who stayed closest to her. Marie framed her shot, pressed the button, and heard it click. She advanced the film while deciding on her next viewpoint.

"You think you're so clever."

Marie didn't realize Anne was speaking to her right away. How was taking pictures supposed to make her clever?

"You're a fraud. You don't belong here. The way you suck up to Mr. Walton is disgusting."

"Excuse me? You're the one dillydallying with the married Mr. Perry." Marie headed for the rickety bridge. Warped wooden slats showed gaps between them. Testing them with one foot, she grimaced when they wobbled but scurried across. The river was narrow and didn't appear deep, but she didn't care to experience its temperature.

Anne followed close behind. When Marie heard a wail and a splash, she hopped off the bridge on the opposite bank and spun around. Anne was thrashing in the river, the water streaming over her head. She must not be able to swim.

The others weren't close enough to help. Marie carefully set the camera down on a rock. After a slight hesitation, she pulled off her shoes and socks, removed her coat, and took off her wristwatch. When she waded into the river, she gasped. The icy water stole her breath.

With grim determination, she plunged into the water and utilized rapid strokes to reach Anne. When she grabbed Anne's arm, the panicked woman tried to climb on top of her. Marie wrestled her so she was able to get behind Anne. Wrapping her arm around her, she kicked for shore.

Mr. Walton jogged down to the river's edge to pull Anne out. He turned to Marie. "Are you all right?"

"Yes." Marie squeezed water from her hair. "Aside from the bruises that will certainly appear on my shins from her kicking me."

Betty and Helen had retrieved Marie's belongings. Betty held up her coat. "Do you want to put this on now, or wait until you remove your wet clothes?"

If Marie put it on now, she'd be wearing a wet coat for the long ride back. Though her teeth chattered, she shook her head. "Race you back to the truck."

Her friends shielded her from any onlookers while she stripped off her sodden clothes and wrapped herself in a towel. Helen used another towel to dry her hair. Her coat helped, but still she shivered.

"I sh-should wear th-that c-coat." Anne glared at Marie.

Mr. Walton handed her a towel. "Dry yourself off and wrap up in your bedroll."

Anne grabbed the towel but pointed at Marie. "She pushed me in the river. She tried to drown me. Aren't you going to do something about that?"

Marie gaped at her, as did the others.

"You're crazy." Lettie stood with her arms akimbo. "You must have hit your head."

"We saw you, you know," Helen said. "You have it backward. We saw you put out your arm like you were going to push Marie into the river. Only you fell in, and Marie saved you."

Wow. Anne had tried to attack her? Marie wrung the water out of her clothes and rolled them up. She couldn't wait to take a shower, but that was at least six hours away.

Mr. Walton stared at Anne. "How ironic that the Red Cross is here to bolster the men's morale, but you perform a first-rate job of ruining our own."

He used the radio in the truck's cab for several minutes while the girls huddled in the back. Betty loaned Marie her knit cap, but her body still trembled.

"Why'd you do it?" Sara asked. "Why did you go in after her when she's always been nasty to you?"

Why indeed? No one would have blamed Marie if she hadn't jumped in. No one but God.

"Growing up in the orphanage, one of the sisters always told us if we had the opportunity to do good and failed to do so, it was the same as if we had done evil. In this case, if I hadn't pulled her out and she drowned, it would be like I killed her." Marie huddled deeper into her coat. "She's not worth having her death on my conscience."

Betty snickered.

Whoops. Had Marie said that last bit out loud? If looks could kill, Anne would have slain her, sitting on the opposite bench with clenched fists.

Mr. Walton came around to the back. "We'll head for the coast. One of the PBYs is in the vicinity and will pick you two up to take you back to Reykjavik and the hospital quickly. Lettie, you'll go too."

Sugar and spice! Marie didn't think a hospital visit was necessary, but avoiding that long, bumpy ride? She'd take the hospital.

From the shore, they watched the seaplane splash onto the ocean's surface, and Marie experienced her first qualm. She'd never flown before.

A crewman opened a blister window and launched a raft. She swallowed hard. How sturdy was that thing?

The plane's designation painted on the side was P-6. Stefan's plane was P-8. She stifled a sigh. She hadn't really expected him, had she? At least it wasn't Dever.

As Mr. Walton handed Lettie into the raft, he told her, "Make sure they're not misinformed about what happened."

Lettie responded with an ear-to-ear grin. Marie had wondered about her presence here. Obviously, Mr. Walton anticipated Anne telling a tall tale, and Lettie was his safeguard.

Clambering into the waist compartment would have posed a challenge without the slacks she purchased and wore especially for their outing. A crewman took her box with the camera and cans of sand. She needed both hands to grip the ladder.

Inside, she sat with the waist gunner on one side and Lettie and Anne on the other. When the plane headed farther out for its takeoff run, she grabbed the camera. Concentrating on framing shots kept her from overthinking about the way the plane rode the waves as it sought to become airborne. This was what Stefan did all the time.

"Who's your pilot?" Marie asked the gunner.

"Lieutenant Cusson."

"Frank Cusson? The man of few words?"

The crewman stared at her with raised brows. "You know him?"

Marie nodded. "He came with Lieutenant Dabrowski to the hot springs near Reykjavik."

"Ah." The crewman nodded sagely, but his eyes appeared puzzled. Maybe this crew wasn't as close as Stefan's and he couldn't imagine his pilot having a social life.

When he donned his headset, Marie became aware of Anne's sullen stare. How had her life taken such a bizarre turn?

The man beside her stepped into the next compartment, and Lettie rushed to take his place. "What a swell way to travel back! This is my first time flying. Is it yours?" She didn't wait for an answer. "I think the Red Cross should fire Anne, don't you think? At least she should be sent back to the States. Like Mr. Walton said, she's bad for morale."

As she prattled on, Marie tuned her out and watched the scenery. They flew south over Faxaflói Bay. To the left stood Iceland's coastline of mountains and fjords. Stefan probably saw views like this every time he flew. No wonder he loved it.

The plane altered course, and she spotted a line of aircraft approaching from the west. They must be ferrying to England and coming into Meeks Field for fuel. She caught a brief glimpse of the bustling airfield before the PBY turned slightly and lost altitude.

"Are we going to land on the water?" Lettie asked the gunner who returned to sit at the blister window, but her shout pierced Marie's ear.

The man shook his head, and Lettie pouted.

Marie grinned and raised her voice. "Less likelihood of popping rivets on land."

Lettie hopped up. "What?"

"Don't worry. We're landing on the runway." Marie recalled Stefan's comments. "Besides, the crews carry pencils to stuff in the rivet holes to keep water from flowing in."

"Pencils?" No shout this time. Instead, Marie read Lettie's lips. Lettie sank back down on the seat. "Are these planes safe?"

The crewman laughed. "I wouldn't trade the PBY for a B-17."

Lettie screwed up her face. Her thoughts probably paralleled Marie's. The PBY was safer because it wasn't as likely to be shot down.

An ambulance met the plane. Lettie lost no time informing anyone who cared to listen that Anne had fallen into an icy cold river and Marie waded in to save her.

The driver helped Anne into the ambulance. "You're lucky to have such a good friend," he said.

"She's no friend," Anne spat.

"That's right." Lettie's retort came quick. "Anne has no friends."

At the hospital, a nurse stuck a thermometer into Marie's mouth before directing her to a shower. "Oh good. Your temperature is normal. You'll probably be back in your barracks tonight unless the doctor wants to keep you under observation for pneumonia."

Marie longed to dally in the shower, but the doctor waited. He pronounced her fit and said she didn't need to stay.

"Hail the heroine." Stefan stood in the doorway of the exam room. "I brought you flowers." He held out a vegetable can of blooming marigolds.

Now her day was perfect.

Chapter Twenty-Two

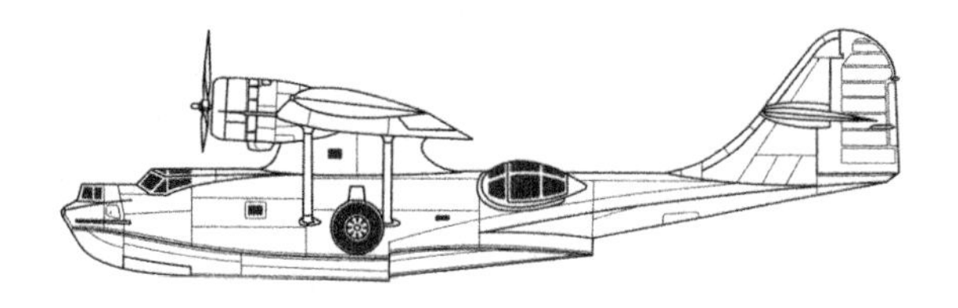

Marie's eyes brightened. Good. She didn't object to Stefan's rash decision to bring some of her precious marigolds out into the chilly air. The occasion seemed to call for flowers, and these were the only ones available, even if they did belong to her.

He dropped a duffel on the exam table. "I come bearing more gifts." He shrugged. "Actually, Lettie sent this."

Marie's mouth formed an O as she pounced on the bag. "Clean, dry clothes. How heavenly." She pulled out something white before shoving it back in, her face reddening. "Oh ..."

Stefan pointed to the door. "I'll just wait out there."

In the hallway, he leaned against the wall and studied the flowers he still held. A half-dozen blooms overflowed from the can. He pressed aside the leaves to examine the dirt. It had to be ground lava. Her determination to grow the marigolds impressed him. She didn't let things like inclement weather, crowded living quarters, or hostile roommates deny her this scrap of beauty. Maybe growing up in the orphanage had taught her to assert herself because no one else would, yet she hadn't become bitter or beaten down.

"Aren't they pretty?" Marie stood beside him, smiling at her flowers. She wore her required Red Cross uniform. She did look good in blue, but he'd like to see her in a pretty dress for a change.

"Ready for a night on the ... base?"

She grinned. "On the base and not the town? Fine with me. Let's leave the marigolds and my things at the front desk."

"Do you want to go to the beach?" Their conversation from two nights ago flitted through his mind. He clenched his fists at the thought of Dever assaulting her. Again. "Or is it tainted with bad memories now?"

"We'll overlay them with good memories. It's still our place." A question lingered in her eyes. Surely she didn't wonder if she was being presumptive.

"Yes. Our place." He clasped her hand as they set off. "Some couples have a song. We have a place." He glanced at her. Time to let her know his thoughts for the future. "Of course, having a place isn't helpful at a reception. You can't dance to a place."

"A recep ... tion?" Her cheeks pinkened. Message received.

"You're up for a walk, right? You don't need to rest?"

Marie's eyes widened. "Rest in the barracks? No, thank you. Only chatty Lettie and angry Anne will be there. The rest won't arrive until tomorrow. I don't want to be in the same room as Anne."

She went silent for a moment. "Did Lettie tell you what happened?" At his nod, she said, "Sara asked me why I rescued Anne. It's possible she could have survived if I hadn't. The river had a bit of a flow that may have taken her to the bank. Or Mr. Walton might have been able to pull her out in time. I did it because I could have been blamed if she died."

Stefan squeezed her hand to acknowledge her words but waited until they reached the beach to respond. Platitudes were well-meant but not helpful. This was not a situation for flippancy.

"I think you're looking at it the wrong way."

Her mouth dropped open. "How else can I look at it?"

Stefan pretended to adjust a pair of eyeglasses on his nose. "God desires all men to come to repentance. We're all sinners—you, me, Anne, Dever. Christ died for all of us. However, if Anne had died today, where would she be in eternity now, do you think? God's home, or the devil's? By saving her, you afforded her another chance at salvation. God used you to help Him accomplish His work. Don't begrudge that."

"Really? God wanted me to help save Anne's soul?" Marie's shoulders slumped. "As you said, we're all sinners. Who am I to look down on Anne? Love your enemy, right?"

"God does seem to enjoy asking the impossible of us. Pray for those who persecute me? I'd much rather punch Dever in the nose."

Marie chuckled before a belly laugh burst forth. "I'd like to watch that." She took three deep breaths. "Sister Marguerite said something like 'difficult people are put in our lives to grind away our own rough spots.'"

"She sounds like a wise woman." Stefan considered the difficult people he'd encountered throughout his life. He must have a lot of rough spots if God needed to keep grinding away on him. What flaws were men like Dever and Commander Arnett supposed to be filing down? Impatience? Resentment toward the unlovable? Pride in his accomplishments?

Marie broke into his depressing thoughts. "You once mentioned your grandmother's wise words. Did she tell you to consider everyone's eternal destination?"

"No. Not directly, anyway. Pops did, but he probably

learned it at Granny's knee." He scuffed his toe in the sand. "As boys, my pals Daniel and John and I built a treehouse. We found lumber from a house that had been burned and razed. Other boys stole our prime pieces. Some of those boards were actually rotten and caused their treehouse to collapse. One of the boys suffered compound fractures." He shrugged. "His injuries have kept him out of the war, but at the time, I thought, serves him right."

"Did your dad tell you to pray for his healing?"

"Yes. He pointed out that our rivals did us a favor by stealing our wood. Our treehouse might have collapsed, and we would have been the ones badly injured. He, uh, *urged* me to make a condolence call on Tommy." A niggle of remorse swept over Stefan. "I shocked Tommy's mother by thanking him for stealing our lumber and saving us from disaster."

Marie gasped. "You didn't! Was she upset with you?"

"His parents hadn't known where Tommy and his friends found the boards. After that, the lot with the razed house was cleaned up and parents in the neighborhood were warned to check whether their children had taken any dangerous debris."

"Wow." A gull captured Marie's attention, until it flew off. "Did that prevent any other harm?"

"Unfortunately, no." Stefan chuckled. "One of Tommy's friends had taken some wiring and stuck it in a socket in his family's garage. The good thing is, the garage wasn't attached to their house. So when it caught fire, it didn't spread to their home. When the fire hit the car's gas tank, it made quite a *whoomph*."

"So the unholy trio struck again?"

"Oh, no." He shook his finger. "We did not take any wiring. The kid stole that on his own. We were innocent lambs."

Marie laughed so hard that tears came to her eyes. "What about now? Are you and Tommy friends?"

Stefan slid his hands into his back pockets. "Tom turned into a nice guy." He angled his gaze toward her when she snickered. "As I said, he's not in uniform, but he works for the railroad, keeping the trains on schedule to carry troops and war material. He's written to me a few times, keeping me informed of happenings with classmates. Who's shipped out, who's died, who's widowed."

Too many classmates were dead, missing, or grievously wounded. Some of the boys he'd grown up with had been so gung ho about rushing off to battle. War was not glorious, though. It was full of senseless loss. The faces of those now gone forever rose in his mind. He closed his eyes to keep from weeping.

Shaking aside the melancholy thoughts, he snapped his fingers. "Say, I forgot. Mail came. I received a care package from Matka but forgot about it when Lettie informed me you were in the hospital. Matka likely sent cookies or brownies. Ready for dessert?"

Surprise flashed across Marie's face. Did anyone send her care packages? Yes, her friend sent flower seeds, but would she send goodies? Her birthday was a month away. He'd quickly mail a note to Matka and ask her to send a package of treats to Marie.

"I haven't eaten supper yet."

Stefan waved away her concern. "Life is uncertain. Eat dessert first."

"You're trying to corrupt a dietitian." Arm in arm, they retraced their route and followed a lane of identical Quonset huts. Marie looked up and down with a slight frown. "Do you ever go into the wrong hut?"

"I haven't, but we've had confused, uninvited guests. Here's where I call home." He pointed to the hut with a six-inch drawing of a cartoon elephant beside the door. "McQuaid drew that. Some people call the PBY 'Dumbo,' because that's the nickname for any air-sea rescue planes." He shrugged. "I like that better than 'pigboat,' which too many people like to call it."

Stefan disengaged his arm from Marie's. "I'll be right back."

He ducked inside and grabbed the box.

"Time for snacks?" Lounging on his cot, Grant must have been drooling over Stefan's package since he'd tossed it on his bed a couple hours ago.

"Great." McQuaid bounced to his feet. "We've been debating how mad you'd get if we opened it for you."

Snips and snails! Why did his friends expect him to always share his goodies? His annoyance faded. Maybe because he always had. Grant received lots of letters, but he'd never received a package. Until now, Stefan hadn't minded sharing with them.

"Marie's waiting outside."

"Okay." McQuaid grabbed his jacket. "We'll share with her."

Stefan shook his head and headed back out, his crewmates trailing in his wake. No cozy tête-à-tête today.

Marie's eyes widened at their appearance. "I thought you guys might be playing baseball."

McQuaid turned toward the direction where considerable yelling arose. "Nah. That's for the enlisted men."

"Today, it's officers against enlisteds." Marie smirked. "The officers demanded a rematch after their poor performance last time." Her grin widened. "I doubt they'll do much better the way they're so outmatched."

"Is that a fact?" Grant offered a shrug. "Must be what our gunners were nattering about. I guess Poulos specializes in home runs."

The foursome meandered toward the playing field and settled on a board balanced on two barrels. Stefan didn't miss the way McQuaid elbowed Grant out of the way so he could sit next to him and his treats.

The scent of cinnamon wafted out as soon as Stefan opened the box. His mouth watered. Snickerdoodles—his favorite. The bundle of cookies was wrapped in a pair of colorful socks, one in red-and-white stripes, the other blue with white stars. Seriously?

McQuaid guffawed. "You'll look snazzy, but you'll be out of uniform."

"They're probably meant for sleeping. My mother's convinced that feet serve as the body's thermostat. If your feet are cold, you won't sleep."

"Does your mother know you're in a cold climate?" Marie nibbled the cookie he offered her and chewed slowly as though savoring it.

"I possibly mentioned the sun not setting in June, so she knows I'm in the north."

Grant clicked his tongue. "Naughty, naughty. Didn't you attend the Army Intelligence lecture about self-censorship and avoiding such so-called harmless topics like weather?"

Stefan bit into a cookie and flicked his hand at Grant's chide. "I also wrote things I'd learned about Alaska from a flight school friend who passed through there. My request for a book on Icelandic geology may have given her a hint." He chewed his cookie. "I also asked for a Brazilian book because my buddy Daniel is based there. I keep them guessing."

Marie finished one cookie in the time it took McQuaid to gobble down three. Stefan moved the box away from him. He offered Marie another, and her eyes brightened.

She pointed to the field. "The first baseman is from Frank Cusson's crew."

Grant and McQuaid both stared at her. Stefan gave them a recap of Marie's day.

"Huh." Grant studied them. He nodded first at Stefan, then at Marie. "You've got Dever on your case, and Anne's after you. You two must be living right. Darkness hates light, and you've earned their enmity."

Nice thought, but it didn't make the antagonism easier to bear.

Grant leaned over to address Marie. "You were lucky to be picked up by Cusson. He's almost as good a pilot as Stefan."

"Hear, hear." McQuaid slapped Stefan's back. "Although I don't know if I've ever heard Cusson put more than two words together."

"Quiet's fine," Stefan said. "I'm used to my quiet friend John. He doesn't say much, but when he does, he's worth listening to. My mother calls him a deep thinker." Stefan looked through the other items in his box. Letters, a paperback, news clippings. What was this from Dorota? Whoops! He shoved the thick envelope under the book. His little sister had succeeded with the birthday gift he'd requested for Marie.

"Say, isn't *Command Performance* on tonight?" McQuaid jumped up, looking at his watch. "I don't want to miss that radio program. We need to get over to the mess hall."

They arrived as a technician fine-tuned the radio. Frank Cusson nodded and scooted over so Stefan and Marie could squeeze in.

Stefan liked having her at his side. Abbott and Costello's "Who's on First" dialogue had never been funnier as he listened to her giggle nonstop. His whole body tingled when Bing Crosby sang "I'll Be Seeing You" and she whispered it should be their song. He felt ten feet tall when she snuggled close and Dever glowered at them from across the room.

The hour ended, and someone shouted that tomorrow's assignments were posted. When Grant returned with theirs,

Stefan unfolded the page and winced. "Three AM wake-up. We need to hit the sack."

First, he needed to walk Marie to her barracks. Grant and McQuaid rose with them, and Stefan cocked a brow.

"We noticed the way Dever's been glaring at you. We'll be your bodyguards," McQuaid said.

"Exactly," Grant added. "I don't want that substitute ever stepping foot in our plane again."

Well, okay. That put everything into perspective.

Chapter Twenty-Three

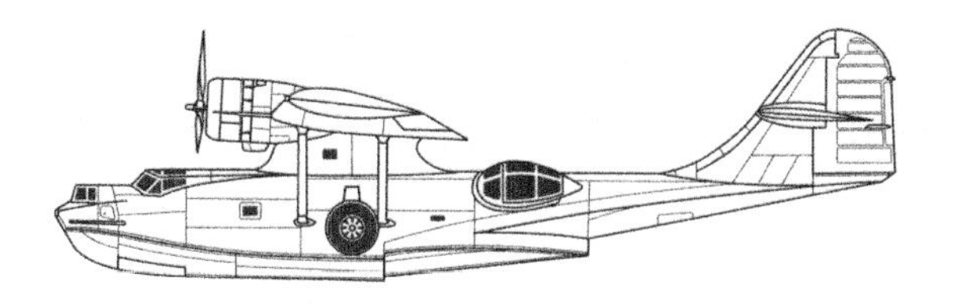

Anne stormed out of the barracks, slamming the door behind her. The windows rattled, or it may have been Marie's imagination. She exhaled.

Helen whispered into the silence, "We will never see her again."

Lettie whooped, startling them all. She danced around in the aisle between their beds. "It's time to party, party, party."

Marie laughed with them but couldn't shake her troubled feeling. Why did Anne dislike her so much? Anne complained that Marie wasn't an American. No, she wasn't a citizen of the United States, but she lived and worked there, and the Red Cross had recruited her.

She let her gaze travel around the hut. Everyone else was friendly. They worked well together as a team. That was the problem—Anne wasn't a team player. Still, to be sent home in disgrace while the war still raged. "How embarrassing."

Betty heard her. "She brought it on herself."

Marie nodded. "Do you think she learned anything? I have this awful premonition of her going to a reporter and complaining how that Canadian, Marie Foubert—an orphan no less—is pretending to run the Red Cross programs somewhere in Europe."

Betty laid a gentle hand on her arm. "No reporter worth his salt would print such rubbish. He'd verify it and learn what a liar she is." She clapped her hands. "And now you get to help me at the recreation center."

Marie stifled a groan. They expected a trio of new girls to join them, but in the meantime, their schedules had been rearranged to cover Anne's duties in Hvalfjord. "I don't want to go to that dance."

"Hmm." Betty twisted her mouth to one side. "Maybe I made the dances sound worse than they are."

"*Worse* than they are!" Marie tried to laugh without any hysteria slipping into her voice. "That means they are bad. I can readily imagine five hundred men packed into a hut, all wanting to dance, but only two or three Red Cross women available. One man grabs you, only to have another cut in before you take three steps. Packed in like sardines and probably smelling about the same."

Helen joined them. "It should be better now that the Icelanders are allowing their girls to come. We're hoping thirty, maybe forty girls will attend."

"And we'll have MPs to keep out gate crashers. Only the men in the outfits organizing the dance will be allowed in." Betty sighed. "I only hope they aren't so eager that they scare the young ladies away."

Those poor girls had no idea what they were getting into. Now, if this were an officers' dance ... But no, Marie couldn't devote all her time to Stefan. She'd have to dance with others and, horrors, what if Dever latched onto her? He'd be there, sweet-talking the girls and expecting them to fall all over him.

She shook away the thought. The Red Cross was here for

the enlisted men, not the officers. She and Stefan only danced alone on the beach.

"The nurses don't attend these dances, do they?" Marie asked.

"They're given officers' ranks, and officers and enlisted men aren't supposed to fraternize." Betty twirled a lock of hair. "Too bad they can't leave their ranks at the door."

Marie thought about that as she walked to the hospital. She faced no restrictions with the wounded men. Good thing too, or she would not have had the chance to get to know Stefan. He would forever think of her as that hysterical woman who told him to stay away from her. *Thank you, God, for second chances.*

Entering the hospital, she waved to Nancy behind the desk and headed for the burn ward. A patient stepped in front of her, wearing the familiar red robe. Marie wondered if the garments had been left behind by the British. The Brits no longer rushed into battle wearing red coats, but maybe they still liked red.

Her fanciful musings slammed to a halt when the patient grasped her arms. "Darling, you're late. I've been worried."

He leaned forward, and she realized he meant to kiss her. His brown eyes were wide and overly bright.

Marie bit back a squeal as she jerked out of his hold. "Mister, what are you doing?"

The man stroked her hair, dislodging her cap. "Sweetheart, what's wrong? You look frightened." His brows lowered. "Has someone been harassing you?"

You are!

She took a deep breath. *Stay calm. This man is delusional.* "Nancy?"

The nurse advanced toward them. "Corporal Morris, what are you doing out of your ward? And where is your arm sling?"

The man gripped Marie's wrist hard enough to leave a

bruise. She kept backing up, but he stayed in step, his eyes devouring her. "We need to have a talk."

His eyes darkened, and fear danced up Marie's spine.

Nancy waved over two patients hovering nearby. "Keep him from hurting Marie while I call for help."

One of the men balanced on crutches, and the other shuffled along too slowly to win a race with a turtle. How could they help her? Marie tried to square her shoulders, an impossible task under the man's wrenching grip. "Are you trying to break my arm? Let go of me, seaman."

"Don't be so highfalutin with me." His voice turned into a hiss. "You've been acting like a shameful whore. You admitted it."

He dragged in a breath and seemed to wilt. "We'll work this out, darling. You're just confused."

"*I'm* confused?" Telling him he was crazy wouldn't help.

A doctor strode into the entry room. "Corporal Morris, let go of the nice lady and we'll see if you're ready for the next phase of your recovery. Come along. You need to return to your ward."

Morris's grip tightened further, and Marie winced. If he didn't release her soon, she'd be an orthopedic patient.

Another patient hustled in. "Harry, old buddy, what are you doing? Come on. The poker game's about to begin."

Uncertainty flickered in her captor's eyes as his gaze wavered between Marie and his "old buddy." The doctor stepped between them and flexed Morris's wrist, breaking his hold on Marie. An orderly took a position on Morris's opposite side, and they propelled him down the hall.

His friend shrugged. "Sorry 'bout that, ma'am. He just got a *Dear John* from his wife."

Marie rubbed her arm. "Do I resemble her?"

"Yeah, brown hair"—he squinted—"blue eyes. Same as Meg."

Nancy probed Marie's wrist, rotating it back and forth. "You'll be black and blue, for sure, with an emphasis on black."

Marie barely heard her. She'd been mistaken for someone else because of her hair and eye color? Was this Meg the same height and weight, and did she have the same light sprinkling of freckles across her nose? "Why did she jilt him?"

"Messing around. I guess she's pregnant. Wants a quickie divorce to marry the other guy."

A headache stirred to life. Marie sympathized with Meg for not wanting to remain married to a charmer like Harry Morris, but having an affair? No wonder Harry suffered delusions. "Wait a minute." She turned to Nancy. "You said something about a sling. Doesn't he have a head injury?"

The nurse spread her hands. "Not that I'm aware of. I think it best if you avoid ward six today."

"I planned on visiting the burn ward."

"Good idea." Nancy started to nod but shook her head. "If he willingly heads into the burn ward, he's a candidate for a straightjacket."

"How was your day?" Stefan looked ready to nod off as he plodded toward the beach with Marie. Even after an exhausting day of flying, he asked about hers. His mother or his father, or both, had done a fine job instilling impeccable manners in him. Marie didn't want to think about all she'd missed with her parents.

"Did you hear the news?"

Stefan took the bait. "What news?"

"We're going home on the first."

Puzzlement knit his brow. "The first what?"

Marie clasped her hands. "The first chance we get. Ha, ha, ha."

They hadn't reached the beach, but Stefan stopped. "Are you all right?"

She spun around in a tight circle. "If I've heard that stupid joke once, I've heard it a thousand times. And today, I heard it three times in one hour. We have to play along like we've never heard it before. Those boys think they're so clever, but they don't have an original thought in their heads."

Stefan settled his hands on her shoulders. "Anne left, right?" At her nod, he said, "I thought you'd be on top of the world." He held up his hand. "And I don't mean because Iceland is near the top of the globe."

"Anne has a replacement." Marie sniffed. "I didn't get even one day off."

"The replacements arrived already?"

"Not from the Red Cross." She pushed up her sleeve, displaying the encircling bruise. "One of the patients went psycho on me. He thinks I'm his unfaithful wife who wants a divorce because my hair is brown"—she twirled a lock around her finger, then pointed to her eyes—"and my eyes are blue. Isn't that just hunky-dory?"

She swiped away a tear. "I did expect that with Anne gone, I wouldn't have so much trouble. The other ladies don't seem to attract problems like I do. Instead, I have a new one. At least I know he'll be shipped home as soon as the doctors clear him to travel."

Stefan interlaced their fingers and started for the beach again, tracing her hand with his thumb in soothing circles. "Maybe that's good."

"Of course it's good that he'll leave, so you must mean it's good I have trouble?" She wanted to pull her hand away.

"Like your Sister Marguerite said, all the troubles the devil throws in our path can sharpen us, filing away our rough spots. God allows them because he wants us to become like his Son."

"There's a Bible verse about that."

Stefan chuckled. "Of course there is. Your faith, tested by fire, proves to be worth more than gold. Paul said that. Or Peter. Maybe John."

"Covering all your bases?" Marie grinned but considered his words. "Betty and Helen don't have the problems I do. I must need a lot of work."

"Don't go there." Stefan looked her in the eye. "Don't compare yourself with others. Ojciec has a lot to say about comparison. Doing so leads to discouragement or pride. More likely, God sees something extra special in you and He's allowing polishing."

Her shoulders slumped. "That thought in itself is discouraging. Like I'm a slow learner."

"No rest for the weary. Yes. That's why the Savior's words are so encouraging. '*Come unto me, all ye that labor and are heavy laden, and I will give you rest.*'" He took her hands in his. "Let's pray about it."

At the Red Cross hut, Stefan kissed Marie, laid his hand against her cheek, winked, and headed for his barracks, humming an unrecognizable tune.

Marie dallied at the door, reluctant to turn her eyes away from him. She had never prayed with a man before. She'd never prayed with anyone. In the orphanage, they'd recited prayers, and sometimes someone would be asked to pray. She hated that, hated praying out loud—trying to sound intelligent to an ethereal being she couldn't see while other kids snickered.

Stefan didn't pray like that. He prayed like God was right there with them. Well, yes, He was. The Holy Ghost was always with them. That sounded so ... ghostly.

Surround us with your peace, Stefan had prayed. God was with her when Dever attacked her, when Anne stole her ideas, when Harry the patient went crazy. When Stefan kissed her. Her face burned, even while she allowed a sheepish grin.

All the other Red Cross ladies were in the barracks when she stepped in. Betty finished writing a letter with a flourish and added it to her completed stack. She was such a diligent correspondent. And a nice person. Why didn't Satan feel a need to harass her? Of course, it was a blessing for Betty that he didn't.

Marie stopped her thoughts. Like Stefan said, she shouldn't compare. Betty may have heartaches she knew nothing about.

"Ugh!" Lettie jumped up and threw something onto her cot. "My last pair of silk stockings ruined because I got bits of gravel in my shoes. There's no hope of replacing them."

"Sure there is." Marie pulled a pair out of her locker. "I bought these last week at a shop in town. They're cheap too."

"Where?"

"I need some too."

"Will you be going back there soon?"

Suddenly, all the girls needed new stockings. Since they didn't all have opportunities to go into Reykjavik, Marie offered to shop for them. They lined up, gave her money, and she wrote a list. She shopped for patients, and now she would shop for her friends.

Warmth spiraled through her. She'd had a challenging day, but it was a beautiful evening.

Chapter Twenty-Four

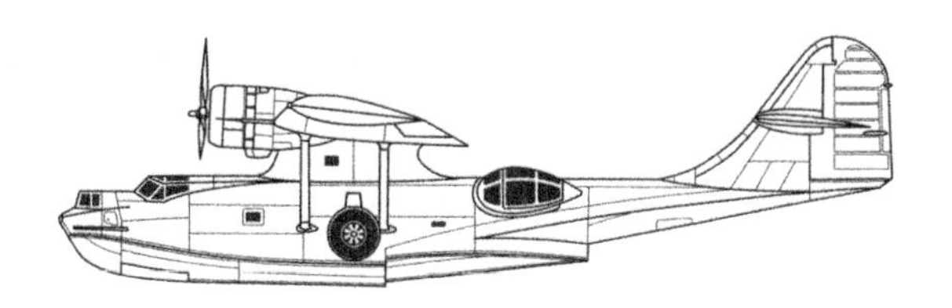

Which was worse? Patrolling the convoys, or patrolling the empty Denmark Strait? Stefan squinted against the glittering sea. To spot a submerged U-boat today would require a miracle.

A miracle. Maybe they were going about this wrong. He pointed to Grant's controls for his copilot to take over while he pulled out his maps.

It made sense for U-boats sailing from Norway to stay north of Iceland and slip down the Denmark Strait. It also made sense for them to traverse the strait during hours of darkness so they could travel on the surface, where they could recharge their batteries and sail twice as fast. He'd also heard they could travel submerged for only two hours.

To avoid detection, they would submerge during daylight. The strait wasn't very narrow. At their closest point, Iceland and Greenland lay about two hundred miles apart, and the strait was over three thousand feet deep. A big area for them to hide in.

Stefan gazed into the distance toward Greenland, trying to think like a submariner. Suppose he had to surface to recharge. Would he hug the coast of Greenland with its sparse population? He angled their course toward the massive island and shared his thoughts with the crew.

"That'll be more interesting than looking at waves." Pennington's words were wrapped in a yawn.

"I've got 'noculars." Lawrenz spoke like he had his mouth full.

Stefan's stomach rumbled. They hadn't eaten since 0400, and it was now—he glanced at his watch—1500. "Flash, are you eating?"

"I'm hungry."

"Did it not occur to you that the rest of us are too?" McQuaid growled. He'd been irritable since reading his mail last night. "Slap together sandwiches for all of us."

"But I'm eyeballing Greenland."

"Quit whining and give the binoculars to Buck Rogers."

Stefan prepared to stop the argument, but Poulos came to his rescue. "I'll make the sandwiches."

"Thanks, Buck." Stefan pulled back on the throttle. "What's on the menu? Sliced Spam?"

"But of course. What else?"

"Yummy, yummy, something good in our tummies."

Stefan shook his head at Pennington's quip.

"I liked the cheese sandwiches we had four weeks ago."

After a moment of silence, everyone laughed at Jenz's quiet comment.

"Four weeks ago?" Grant asked. "Are you sure about that?"

"Oh yes. I've been waiting for them to reappear ever since."

"Poulos, we have tomato soup, don't we?" Stefan said, recalling something Marie had told him.

"Yeah. Should I heat some?"

"Please do."

Marie had dunked Spam sandwiches into tomato soup at the orphanage. Spam was a frequent meal for the children. Cheap, easy to prepare, but not very tasty. The soup made it more palatable.

When Poulos delivered his lunch, Stefan dipped the corner of his sandwich into the cup and took a bite. He nodded. "Much better."

Grant and Poulos watched him eat, and Grant looked back at Poulos. "I'll have soup too, please."

"Yeah, me too. Like ketchup, right?"

Soon they were all eating soup-dipped sandwiches. All except for Lawrenz.

"Hey, where's my lunch?"

"You already ate. If you want more, get it yourself." Poulos didn't let Lawrenz push him around. "I'll take over watching the coastline."

Stefan flew the plane south along the coast for over an hour. They had just passed the Arctic Circle when Lawrenz yelled, "I see something."

Grant rolled his eyes in Stefan's direction before asking, "Could you be more specific?"

"There's an inlet with something man-made," Pennington answered. "A little house or a shed. I don't see any people."

They flew in low. While the place seemed deserted, a firepit near the building must have been used in the last couple weeks since the wind hadn't erased distinctive features.

"Another weather station?" Ramsey asked.

Unlikely. Iceland sat just south of the Arctic Circle, with a small island partially inside the Circle. Stefan didn't think the Germans would be so bold. But they might have another purpose. "Lawrenz, is your camera rolling?"

"You betcha."

Grant studied the water. "It appears calm. Do you want to land?"

Stefan nodded. "Everyone, keep your eyes peeled for signs of life. I have an aversion to being shot at."

After a smooth landing, Stefan taxied deeper into the cove to avoid being spotted from the sea. Then he pivoted the airplane so it'd be ready to take off again. He signaled Ramsey to stop the engines, instructed Pennington and Poulos to set the anchors, then opened his window and listened. Silence.

"Lawrenz, break out a raft. McQuaid, want to lead an expedition?"

"My pleasure." Stefan heard the smile in his voice. "Who should I take?"

"Pennington, Lawrenz, and Poulos. And bring pistols and a radio."

Stefan hoisted himself up through the overhead window and watched them paddle to shore. Grant joined him, and Ramsey emerged through the blister window. Stefan scanned the area with binoculars, spotting many islands and mountains in the distance, but no trees. Much like Iceland.

The radio crackled, and McQuaid's voice came through. "No one's home. It's an empty shed, but they were careless. At the firepit, we found bits of charred paper with German writing."

"Bring it along." He called down to Jenz, "Want to join us in the other raft and set foot on Greenland?"

"You betcha," Jenz said, echoing Lawrenz's favorite response.

When they stepped ashore, Stefan headed east. "Let's see what the view's like from atop this bluff."

The sun hung low in the western sky by the time they crested the hill, and the sea glimmered beneath its light. He estimated they had two hours remaining for a safe takeoff.

When a brisk wind swept over the hills, he wished for one of Matka's hand-knitted caps to protect his ears.

Grant rocked back on his heels. "There's nothing here. Absolute desolation. We could be the only people alive on Earth."

The light diminished in an instant, and Stefan swiveled around in the gathering gloom to see that the sun had dipped behind a distant mountain. "We better head back."

Jenz held up a hand. "Listen."

Initially, only the wind whistled in Stefan's ears, but then, what was that? Some sort of engine? Definitely man-made.

Ramsey stabbed a finger to the northeast. "Look!"

The sea bubbled, and a U-boat emerged.

Excitement filled Stefan. He was right. The Germans did skulk along the Greenland coast and stay submerged during daylight hours.

Dread engulfed him when he realized they were trapped in the cove. If the Germans turned into the cove to visit their shed, they'd find the PBY. Stefan and his crew might be able to hold off a few men in a raft, but U-boats carried fifty men.

Lawrenz's voice floated up the hill, and Stefan sucked in his breath and fumbled for the flashlight on his belt. When he boarded the raft, he didn't know why he'd taken it. Thrusting the flashlight at Jenz, he said, "Morse code them for silence."

"What about the radio?" Grant asked.

Jenz nodded toward the sub. "They might intercept."

Hatches opened on the U-boat and men climbed out.

"Everybody down." Stefan dropped onto the bristly growth. "Even without the sun, we'll be silhouetted."

Using binoculars, he studied the Germans. Why had they stopped? What were they doing here? A few sailors checked their antiaircraft gun. They talked and laughed, unconcerned about possible enemies nearby.

Lawrenz scuttled into their group. "I brought the camera. Wow! Look at that. Is that sauerkraut I smell?"

Stefan exchanged glances with Grant. At least their bubbly crewman was keeping his voice low.

"Make sure the camera doesn't flash."

Ramsey's droll comment caused Stefan to scrutinize the camera. No flash attachment. He breathed slowly. *Stay calm. Think ahead.* They were in a dangerous situation. He brought them here, and he had to get them out.

"What are they waiting for?" McQuaid said, joining them.

"Where are Pennington and Poulos?"

"I sent them back to the plane to be ready to haul the anchors or man the guns after hearing the U-boat's engine. Think the Krauts are waiting for a rendezvous?"

Stefan thought for a moment. "Following this route, they likely came from Norway, so they don't need to meet up with a supply sub. Another U-boat to form a wolfpack doesn't seem probable here in the strait." He glanced at the sky. "The moon's already set and won't rise until after midnight. They've got us bottled up in an unfamiliar cove. If they don't leave soon, we'll have to spend the night."

At a command from the captain in the white cap, all the smoking Germans tossed their cigarettes into the sea. They expected something.

Grant scooted closer. "Is there an Allied ship coming through here that we don't know about?"

Silly question. If Stefan didn't know about a ship, how would he know if it was coming through? The sub lay parallel to the coast. Torpedoes came out the front or back ends, so if the Germans wanted to sink a ship, they needed to reposition.

"Aircraft approaching," Ramsey said. "Sounds like a PBY."

"There it is, following our route," McQuaid said.

A blinking light flashed from the plane. Morse code. What in the world?

"It's giving tomorrow's convoy info." Disbelief filled Jenz's voice.

Swinging the binoculars up to his eyes, Stefan strained to read the plane's number. P-6. Frank Cusson's PBY? Shock reverberated down to his toes.

The airplane passed by, and a rumble indicated the U-boat intended to sail on.

Stefan leaped to his feet. "Back to the plane. Fast. We have to sink that sub."

"Give Pennington two blinks so they'll hoist the anchors."

Stefan didn't question McQuaid's request. He flashed the light twice before training the beam on the ground as they raced for the beach. Jenz stumbled and somersaulted, but the wiry, nimble guy was up and running again without missing a beat. Lawrenz lagged behind, holding the camera in front of him like it was a decorated cake.

They pushed the raft out and tumbled in. Icy water leaked into Stefan's shoes when he stepped into deep water. Everyone grabbed for the paddles. He bit back a grin when Ramsey came up with a leg. Jenz had dived in and remained upended.

"How are you planning on handling this?" Grant asked Stefan as he and Ramsey brought their PBY to life. "They'll hear us and know we're not the other plane. They'll either stay on the surface and fire on us, or they'll dive."

"I'm hoping they'll dive. Then I can send Fido after them."

Stefan understood Grant's stunned expression. They hadn't used Fido before. Fido was a new top secret weapon, an airborne acoustic homing torpedo. It was designed to zero in on the propeller cavitations of a submerging submarine. Air crews were ordered to use Fido only on submerging U-boats to avoid any survivors who might realize the Allies had an advantage.

"I'm hoping they're heading toward the middle of the strait. With maneuvering room, they should dive rather than fight. It's too dark for fighting to benefit them."

Ramsey started the starboard engine, quickly following with the port engine. Stefan adjusted the throttle for the lowest speed possible until Ramsey assured him the oil pressure was good, then opened the throttle to one thousand rpm for the engines to warm up. He was tempted to rush the process, but crashing wouldn't do them or the convoy any good.

"Anchor gear stowed and gun-blister water seals inflated?" Pennington and Lawrenz gave affirmative answers, as he knew they would, but Stefan's nerves were on edge. PBY engines were noisy, and it was a sure bet someone on the sub heard them.

He was grateful the night wasn't pitch black but clear and full of stars. Warfare by starlight. Moonrise remained an hour away, too late to help them. The banks on either side of the cove stood out in different shades of gray from the sky. His takeoff wouldn't be completely blind. He could do this.

Once they cleared the cove, they'd pick up a crosswind. He was ready.

"Okay, on your toes, everyone. Watch for the U-boat. We need to find it fast."

The plane rocked slightly, indicating a beneficial current rolling into the cove from the sea. Stefan started their takeoff run, quickly reaching seventy-five knots. The plane bounded into the air and soared over the strait. "Floats up."

"There it is!" In the bow turret, Pennington had the best view. "Two o'clock position, maybe a thousand yards out."

Stefan banked to the south. Everything he knew about Fido flashed through his mind. They flew low and slow, coming up on the stern. Starlight illuminated a disturbance on the water. The sub was submerging.

He released Fido, and it dropped from the wing.

"Yes!" Grant pumped his fist.

Stefan understood his exultation. Last week, another pilot in their squadron tried to use his Fido, but it hung up in the brackets, only to drop minutes later, too late.

He circled around the U-boat's likely location, and the water erupted.

"Jackpot!" McQuaid said from his window.

Stefan leaned back in his seat. He'd done it! Exhaustion turned his muscles to quivering jelly. He closed his eyes and relaxed. Sleep sought to claim him, but an old flight instructor's admonition rang in his ears. *You can sleep when you're dead.*

He called McQuaid for the route to Reykjavik and adjusted course. Turning control over to Grant, he headed to the back. Buck and Flash sat in the blister windows. He touched Lawrenz's shoulder. "Did you photograph the attack?"

"Sure did, but the photographs are gonna be dark. I hope we can at least see a water fountain. What else could it be out here?"

Stefan nodded before stretching out on a bunk in the living quarters. A traitor on Frank Cusson's crew. Did his friend have any inkling?

He plugged his headset into the interphone system. "Listen up, fellas. Don't say a word to anyone about what we saw. Nothing about a traitor or where we sank that sub. I'll report to Captain Hopley as soon as possible. Any investigation will be up to him. You may be asked to give statements, but beyond that, stay mum."

"Right. Don't want to tip off the traitor that we're onto him." Lawrenz's voice held a chipper tone, as usual.

The crew prattled on, and Stefan didn't stop them. The chatter would keep them awake as they flew in the dark.

Disturbing thoughts swirled in his mind. Had anyone died

because of the traitor? Someone among them, acting like a friend, was stabbing them in the back.

Stefan laced his fingers behind his head. The man needed to be apprehended, but why did he have to be on Frank's crew? Would Captain Hopley believe him? He swallowed hard. Those photos better turn out.

Chapter Twenty-Five

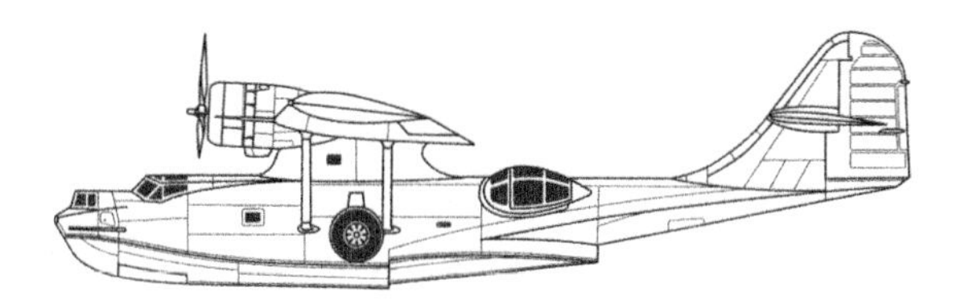

Marie bit her lip as she wrote out the patient's labored words. His letter to his wife sounded like a farewell: where to find his will, who to talk to about settling his estate, how to manage her finances. He'd been at sea for a long time. Surely his wife had learned to carry on in his absence, but maybe he felt better by repeating everything.

"Tell her I've loved her since the day we met, when she was drenched in rain and her wet shoes squeaked."

Marie smiled at the whispered words.

"Live life for both of us. We'll meet again." The poor man sighed.

She stopped writing. That sigh. She reached out, but remembered his burns. Charred skin was extremely painful with even the lightest touch. When she leaned over the man, she realized the breath had left his body. He was gone.

She dropped back onto the chair, thinking of how this sailor had just entered eternity. She'd never been with someone at their moment of death. He'd simply ... slipped away.

His torment had ended, but a new pain would begin for his

wife. Tears welled in Marie's eyes. Brushing them away, she grabbed her pen and scribbled as fast as she could, informing his wife that communicating with her was the last thing he had done and now he was released from the excruciating pain of the third-degree burns over much of his body. She made sure to include that if she needed any assistance, she should not hesitate to call on the Red Cross.

Laying aside her pen, she gazed at the body. What a ghastly way to die. The smell of his wounds was enough to gag her. Were the doctors right to try saving him when they merely prolonged his agony for a few days? She knew about triage—concentrating on the wounded that weren't mortally injured and leaving the hopeless to die. Had they been busier with the savable, would they have filled him with morphine and left him to die?

But if they had, he wouldn't have had the chance to write this last letter to his wife. Marie massaged her forehead.

A doctor glanced into the ward, and Marie waved him over. "He's gone." Her voice wobbled, and an errant tear slid down her cheek. "He asked me to write to his wife, and then he died."

The doctor towered over her as he checked the patient. "His death was inevitable." He stepped back and studied her, softening his expression. "Take the rest of the day off. Go outside, take a walk, concentrate on life."

Ordinarily, Marie would insist on carrying on, but today she heeded his advice. She hurried outside and wandered aimlessly, tears blurring her surroundings. Why did this death upset her? Other patients she'd spoken with had died, but not in her presence. Was that what was differen?

Wisps of memory tickled her conscience. She was three years old and a strange lady told her that her mommy and daddy weren't coming home. They'd gone to Heaven, and she had to be brave. The hollow feeling turned to panic as the woman marched her into the orphanage.

Marie paused by the officers' mess and took a deep breath. She must be empathizing with the seaman's wife.

As she stood beside the mess, a man came out. Stefan's copilot. They were overdue last night, but they'd returned. Her anxiety eased. "You're back. Is Stefan inside?"

He grimaced. "No, he's trying to see the captain. We had a hairy situation yesterday."

She couldn't recall the man's name. Grant and McQuaid were officers, but which was he? When he said no more, she probed. "Is everything okay?"

He rocked back on his heels, shoved his hands in his pockets, and looked skyward at a gull, an incoming plane, a cloud, anything but her. "He ordered us to remain silent, but I can say he really threaded the needle." He finally met her gaze and flashed a grin. "See you around."

Something was definitely amiss, but threading the needle was good. Right? She should pray for Stefan.

Our Father, which art in Heaven, hallowed be thy name. Her thoughts stalled. This was serious. She should make it personal. *Father in Heaven, help Stefan. I don't know what's wrong, but you do. Be with him.*

* * *

Stefan saluted and remained ramrod straight until Captain Hopley acknowledged him.

"All right, Dabrowski, what's so all-fired important that you insisted on seeing me?"

Cold sweat broke out on Stefan's brow. Not an auspicious beginning. He'd planned what to say but now realized his best course was to spit it out fast.

"We landed in a Greenland cove, sir, to investigate a building. While we were there, a German U-boat surfaced off the coast when it grew dark, around 19:30. An hour later, a PBY flew south along the coast, and we saw Morse code flash from the plane. My radioman said time and coordinates were given for today's convoy."

Hopley's fist landed on his desk. "Are you saying the men in one of our airplanes are committing treason?"

Stefan bobbed his head. "At least one man did. I saw the plane's number, P-6. That's Frank Cusson's aircraft, and I know he would never condone treason. But I also know what we saw."

The captain tapped a pen on the desk while staring at him with narrowed eyes. Did he believe him? Would his reputation of being as boring as bathwater help or hurt Hopley's opinion of him?

The captain turned to the door and barked, "Ensign Bishop."

A young man scurried into the room. "Yes, sir."

"Summon Lieutenant Cusson to report here immediately. Ask the admiral to join us and you take notes."

"Yes, sir." The ensign shot Stefan a look of curiosity or empathy—or was it suspicion?—before hastening out of the office.

Time dragged, but the rear admiral and ensign soon took seats flanking the captain behind his desk. Apparently, they didn't intend to invite Stefan to sit. Cusson entered and hesitated at the scene. He stepped alongside Stefan and saluted.

Stefan studied the admiral. Though he hadn't been apprised of the situation, he appeared more curious than irritated at the abrupt summons.

Captain Hopley folded his hands on his desk. "Lieutenant

Dabrowski, kindly tell your story to Admiral Stone. This time in full detail."

Stefan took a deep breath and nodded. "Sir, we flew south down the Denmark Strait yesterday, close to the Greenland coast, where we spotted a small building. We saw no signs of life, but it appeared to have been visited within the past month. We landed in a cove to investigate."

Cusson shot him a wide-eyed glance.

As Stefan related how he'd sent part of the crew ashore to examine the shed, he wondered if the brass would object to him having taken the rest of the crew ashore for the fun of it. Were they guilty of dallying in a foreign country without permission? Was it wrong to have left the plane unattended?

No one interrupted. He continued telling of their hike up the bluff overlooking the strait, and of the submarine surfacing and loitering, trapping them in the cove. The ensign's eyes bulged as he scribbled down Stefan's words. He'd be lucky if he was able to transcribe them later.

Stefan's heart thudded as he reached the point where another PBY appeared and they saw the Morse code flashing the convoy's location. He heard a soft gasp. Cusson had been facing forward, but now he swiveled toward Stefan, his jaw dangling.

The admiral spoke. "Did you see the aircraft?"

Stefan nodded. "Yes, sir. I saw its number ..."

Cusson interrupted. "My plane." His voice cracked, and he cleared his throat. "That would have been my aircraft, sir."

Admiral Stone crossed his arms. "Do you know who would have sent the signals? The bow gunner?"

"Not the bow gunner, sir. The whole crew was subjected to his snoring when we were in that location." Cusson's face lost all color. "It had to be the blister gunner. Carl Graetz."

"Graetz. A German name." For the first time, Stefan noticed Captain Hopley had a crew roster in front of him.

"Yes, sir." Cusson squared his sagging shoulders. "His father fought for the Kaiser in the last war. Carl speaks German."

"Is he an American citizen?" Frost tinged the admiral's voice.

"Yes, sir. He was born in Ohio."

"Have you ever had cause to question his loyalty?"

Cusson sagged again, and Stefan wished they'd offer him a chair.

"I didn't think anything of it at the time, sir, but last week, while we were hunting a U-boat on the fringe of a convoy, Graetz mixed up his directions. He said it was to the right. Another gunner immediately said it was left. Graetz said, 'Left. That's right.' I thought he was acknowledging the correction. Unfortunately, *right* has different meanings. Maybe he wanted to confuse me."

Hopley asked, "Did you get the sub, Cusson?"

"No, sir. It went deep and we lost it."

A moment of silence passed before the admiral said to Hopley, "The sub last night likely summoned a wolfpack to ambush that convoy."

"We sank that sub, sir," Stefan said. "Hopefully before it sent a message."

The captain raised his brows. "In the dark?"

The admiral tilted his head as he scrutinized Stefan. "Perhaps you should continue your story, Lieutenant."

"We ran back to our plane, took off, located the sub, and"—he shrugged—"I fired our acoustic homing torpedo."

"You sank the sub with the acoustic torpedo?" Hopley's quiet voice suggested he didn't believe Stefan.

"If I may, sir." Stefan addressed the ensign. "Will you contact the photo lab and see if our film has been developed?"

The captain's brows rose higher. "You took pictures?"

"One of my men had our N-4 camera, sir."

From the outer office, he heard the ensign say, "We need to contact the photo lab ... Oh, good." He returned to the captain's office with McQuaid on his heels, and McQuaid handed Stefan an envelope with a barely perceptible nod.

The top photo showed a sharp view of the U-boat taken from the bluff. Stefan set it on the desk, and both officers leaned forward.

"This one shows the flashing coming from the aircraft." He could have called it Cusson's plane but opted to leave his friend's name out.

He pulled out another photo and experienced a moment of euphoria. Here was his proof. "This one's awfully dark, but you can make out the water fountain erupting from what most certainly must be the sub exploding."

"Say, this is more like it." A smile spread across Admiral Stone's face. "Those acoustic torpedoes can win the war against the U-boats."

He probably didn't expect a response, but Stefan offered one anyway. "We wouldn't have gotten the sub with depth charges. Not in the dark."

"Yes, that's a job for the homing device. Fido will make a difference in the dark days of winter." The admiral turned to the ensign. "Call the MPs. I want this Graetz arrested and his billet searched. And round up the rest of the crew. Keep them separated."

Cusson's Adam's apple bobbed.

The admiral squinted at Stefan's name plate. "Dabrowski, you may go. Good work."

As he passed behind Cusson, out of sight of their superiors, Stefan touched Cusson's back in reassurance. By exposing an act of treason, he felt like he had betrayed a friend. He hoped discovering a traitor on his crew wouldn't have an adverse affect on Cusson.

McQuaid waited in the outer office. "Everything okay?"

"For us, yes." Stefan sighed. "For Frank? I don't know."

McQuaid put a comforting hand on Stefan's shoulder. Small comfort.

* * *

Marie jumped up from the bench when Stefan exited the office building. His shoulders slumped and his eyes were half-lidded, but a smile tugged at his lips when he spotted her. He wrapped his arms around her, and she hugged him tight. "Is everything all right? Your copilot said you had a hairy situation, but you really threaded the needle."

"Threaded the needle?" He laughed and turned to his crewmate. "What does Grant know about sewing?"

McQuaid snorted.

Stefan placed his palm on the side of Marie's face. She leaned into it and smiled. "Any trouble with the crazed husband?"

"No, I didn't see him. Today a burn patient died after he finished dictating a letter to his wife."

Stefan grimaced before staring at McQuaid. The navigator looked around and up at the sky. "Ya know, I think I'll go hit the sack. It's been a long night."

"Good idea. I will too, in a bit." After McQuaid veered off, Stefan smiled at Marie. "What do you have planned for the rest of your day?"

"I'm hoping to find some mail addressed to me, and then I'll head into town. It seems I've become the designated shopper not only for patients but also for my hut mates, who all want new silk stockings. Do you need anything?"

"Yes, but you won't find it in town." He cupped her face and touched his lips to hers. Soft at first, the kiss gained urgency.

Her toes curled, and her pulse tap danced through her veins. She heard birds sing. No, it was catcalls and wolf whistles rising around them. Her cheeks flamed.

Stefan leaned back and groaned. "Come on, let's check for that mail."

A bonanza awaited Marie. "Four letters! Never have I received so many at one time. Not even around my birthday." She frowned. "Wait a minute. My birthday is coming up. Maybe these are birthday cards. From Sister Marguerite, Francoise, Ozanne, and Lucretia, a nurse at the naval hospital where I worked."

"Does that mean you won't open them until the big day?" Stefan held out his hands while she loaded him down with mail for the rest of the Red Cross team. "Which day is your birthday?"

"The fifth. And no, I'm not going to wait." She pried open a letter. "Francoise says she saw my picture in *Life* magazine. I'm surprised. It's unlikely she subscribes to *Life*. My whereabouts are no longer secret." She thrust the letter at Stefan and opened another. "Sister Marguerite saw it too. And she says it was noted in the newspaper. People at the orphanage are disappointed it wasn't named." Heat surged through her. "The magazine said I was a Quebec orphan, so the newspaper must have too. That's not something I like to advertise."

"Did they send birthday greetings?"

She scanned the letter. "At the bottom, Sister Marguerite closes with 'happy birthday.'"

At least she remembered. That was more important than a

fancy card. Still, disappointment stung. If her parents still lived, would they have sent a card and a present? Had they been together, would her mom have baked a cake? While Marie grew up, would they have given parties for her like her friends at college had talked about?

Stefan knew her birth date now. Would he find a pretty card in Reykjavik? Maybe even a little present?

The top letter on the stack in Stefan's arms started to slide, and she grabbed it. A letter for Anne. She held it up. "Think I can file this one in the trash?" She slapped the letter back on the stack, nearly causing Stefan to drop them all. "When she saw the *Life* article, she made her usual snide remark. Something about how I acted like I'm the only one from the Red Cross and I don't even belong here because I'm a foreigner."

Holding the precarious load against his chest, Stefan nudged her forward. "There's only one itsy-bitsy package here. Don't you gals receive care packages of cookies and brownies?"

Marie cheered up. "Lettie complained about that the other day. Since we're women and women like to bake, no one seems to think we'd like a box of cookies. It's like they think we have kitchen privileges here. I asked Lettie if she requested goodies, and she went silent for a whole ten seconds. Then she said she'd have to do that."

At the Red Cross hut, Marie relieved him of the mail. "You're going to get some rest now?"

"You better believe it. I'll probably have another very early flight tomorrow, assuming I'm not roped into the treason investigation. This evening, though, that'll be our time." She nodded, and he kissed her. "See you."

Inside the hut, Marie walked up and down the aisle, dropping letters on the appropriate cots. Sara entered the hut as Marie debated the fate of Anne's mail. "Oh, good. Sara, I'll let you decide what to do with Anne's letter."

Sara peered at the return address. "Hmph." She shoved the letter into the stove. "It's from her aunt, who is part of the reason why Anne hates you."

Marie stared at her. "What does Anne's aunt have to do with me? That wasn't mailed in Quebec."

"No." Sara plopped onto her bed and scrutinized the ceiling. "Let's see. Anne's father served in France during the First World War. She says the French—and the Brits, for that matter—wanted the Americans to join the fight so they could be cannon fodder and give the French a rest. Never mind about U-boats sinking American ships. Then what?"

She wound a lock of hair around her finger. "Oh, yes. Her dad and his buddies took shelter in a Frenchman's barn during a rainstorm. The farmer must have thought they were Germans and fired at them. Anne's dad was hit in the leg. It didn't heal well, leaving him with a terrible limp."

"So she hates French people," Marie sighed, "even though French Canadians have never been to France."

Sara held up a finger. "Wait. There's more. Her father came home crippled and bitter and became an alcoholic. He was abusive, and Anne's mother killed herself, leaving Anne at his mercy. She's full of bitterness too, and blames the French. You're her scapegoat."

Marie imagined Anne's home life. "Was she ever happy when you were at Hvalfjord?"

Sara twisted her lips. "She'd smile with her mouth but not her eyes. When the guys weren't within earshot, she'd make snide remarks about them. No, I don't think she was ever happy, unless it was with Mr. Perry."

Marie stared at her mail before perusing it. She'd always considered the orphanage to be a necessary evil, but it was a blessing. She was fed and clothed, and Sister Marguerite lavished her with affection. No one ill-treated her.

Poor Anne. However, Marie's new understanding did not extend to wishing her back.

Ozanne wrote that the trees in the apple orchard were heavy with fruit. Marie's mouth watered as she imagined taking a juicy bite. Lucretia sent a pretty birthday card in which she reported all the recent shenanigans at the hospital, naming people Marie knew. Francoise mentioned a cute wounded pilot who had returned home. She sounded more upbeat lately, like she had stars in her eyes. Good for her.

They all sounded well. Life was good for Marie too. She hopped up and grabbed her money. Time to shop.

Chapter Twenty-Six

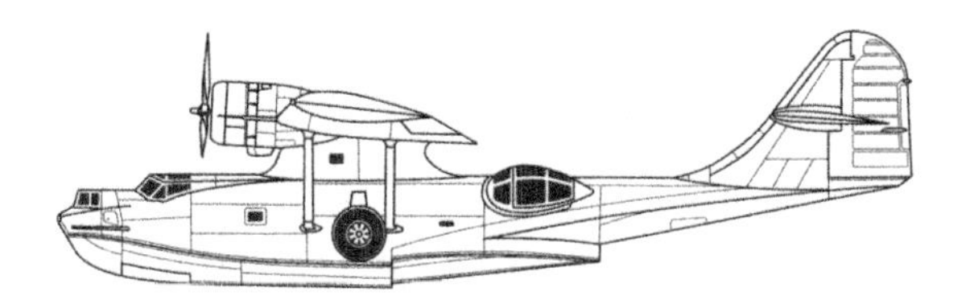

Corporal Wilmer Case was heading out of Camp Kwitcherbelliakin and offered Marie a ride into Reykjavik. He'd been her favorite chauffeur since the day she met Stefan. Whatever happened to the man who dated her and Lettie at the same time? George. His name was all she remembered.

She brushed aside the hair blowing in her face. "You must drive a lot of miles every day."

"Yeah, but it sure beats typing reports or counting cans in the galley. One of my pals is in supply. Boring. I prefer the wind in my face." A sudden shower had him fumbling for the windshield wiper. "Although I do appreciate the canvas top. Where are you off to?"

"My first stop is a store near the photographer you pointed out last time I rode with you. I hope they still have silk stockings. All the girls in my hut need them, and I'll probably buy out their entire stock."

"Can't you get them from the PX?"

"The PX is for the military, not the Red Cross."

"That's not … oh, well …" He finally settled on a swear word. "Ah, pardon my French, ma'am."

Marie grinned. After three meetings, they were familiar enough that she could call him out on his language. *"Désolé, caporal, mais ce n'était pas français."*

He jerked his head toward her, bringing the steering wheel with him. She grabbed the wheel and forced it back. "Please do stay on the road."

His face brick red, Corporal Case straightened out their course and stammered, "I beg your pardon, ma'am. I forgot you're from Quebec. Of course you know French. I'm sorry."

She touched his arm. "Forget it, okay? Let's keep to English for polite society."

In an effort to retrieve their easy camaraderie, she seized the first topic that came to mind. "Have you attended any of the dances?"

He rolled his eyes. "They're mob scenes."

"Are you referring to when the Icelandic girls came?"

"They arrived late, like nine o'clock. Then they peeked in. The men practically trampled themselves to get to them first. Those girls turned tail and ran for their lives. Can't say I blame them. All those guys salivating. I'd run too. The Red Cross ladies lured them back in." He shook his head. "Lured. That's what one of them called it. She felt guilty, like maybe she was leading the Icelandic girls to their doom."

"But did they dance?"

"Yeah, if you can call it that. Guys were constantly cutting in. No one had a chance to get to know them. Some of the girls knew a little English, but not enough for a conversation. I said hi to one girl. She was shy. Or scared half to death. They must have been curious, though, since they came."

Marie sighed. She'd heard thirty girls had come to the dance attended by three hundred servicemen. One girl for ten men. Ideal conditions for chaos.

Corporal Case dropped her off at the same intersection where he'd let her and Stefan off the other day. "I'll be heading back around four. Be at that bench there if you want a ride."

"That's a bus stop."

"So hang back if a bus comes along." He drove off with a grin and a wave.

Marie passed the photography business and hesitated at the window. How long had it been since she and Stefan posed for the camera? He must have picked up the pictures by now, but he hadn't said anything. Did he intend to give her one for her birthday? What a wonderful gift that would be.

The general store offered a dozen pairs of stockings. She took them all. The clerk looked at her askance when she dropped them on the counter. Marie pulled out her list and ran her finger down the names while pushing each pair aside. Offering the clerk a bright smile, she said, "Success. You can't imagine how happy these will make the Red Cross ladies."

The young woman's eyes widened, but she said, "We want to please."

Marie's thoughts scattered in a dozen directions. She wasn't invisible—the clerk talked to her! Did they really want to please the Americans? Maybe she'd been to the dance. Would she welcome a little conversation?

"Do you know where I can buy flower seeds?" What a dumb question.

The clerk tilted her head. "In America?"

Marie laughed. "Yes, but mail is so slow."

"Summer is over. You wish for flowers now?"

"I plant them in cans and put them by the window. It's not

the best climate since the hut can be cold. But I've grown little colorful flowers for a bit of prettiness."

"We have not real flowers if you want pretty color." The clerk pointed to the other side of the store. "Over here."

Marie's first thought was plastic flowers. No thanks. But the girl led Marie to a tiny collection of silk flowers. A rose-colored orchid caught her eye. It was frivolous and expensive. But it was gorgeous. She plucked it from the shelf.

On the way back to the checkout counter, she spotted coloring books. She stopped so suddenly the clerk nearly collided with her. Marie paged through the book as an idea percolated. She reached for a package of eight fat crayons. "I work in the hospital. These might help the men with hand injuries to exercise their fingers while they heal."

Thrusting the items into the startled clerk's hands, she counted her money. Five cents short, but she had enough of her friends' change to purchase the coloring book, crayons, and the extravagant flower. Betty shouldn't mind if she borrowed an aurar worth a nickel.

She left the store with her tote bag brimming, her wallet lighter, and the clerk's smile warming her heart. With time to spare before meeting Corporal Case, she glanced around and spied a church spire. Would the congregation welcome American visitors? Another idea begged for consideration. After a few wrong turns, she located the church.

This wasn't the church that allowed the Americans use of their building for English-language services. She should really start with that one, but here she was. She entered the cool, dark space and let her eyes rise to the vaulted ceiling. A sense of peace prevailed in the edifice, yet unease tapped on her heart as she advanced into the nave. She didn't belong here.

She spun around and gasped, pressing her hand against her

thundering heart. A cleric stood not three feet away. His gaze flickered over her Red Cross insignia. "Help, lady?"

Marie fought her involuntary stiffening at his words. His tone implied he thought she was a lady of the evening. Squaring her shoulders, she raised her chin. "God is everywhere, but I find it easier to feel His presence in His house."

She wanted to add "My mistake." But, no. As Sister Marguerite liked to say, "always assume the best." Instead, she said, "Forgive the intrusion."

Too late, she realized her poor choice of words. Intrusion was similar to invasion. He probably believed the Americans had invaded Iceland just like the British had. She stepped around him.

"Wait."

She pivoted slowly. He didn't appear so confrontational now.

"You wish pray?" He waved toward the sanctuary. "You pray."

Not the most gracious invitation, but maybe he felt as leery toward her as she felt toward him. He gestured forward, and she fell into step beside him as they approached the altar. High above, a statue of Christ held its arms out in blessing.

"'Come unto me, all ye that labor and are heavy laden, and I will give you rest.'" Marie whispered the verse in the still air.

The cleric watched her with unblinking eyes. "You are burdened?"

He knew more English than she thought.

"Our men like to be friends with everyone. Here ..." *Careful. Don't insult him.* "Icelanders are proper, but not cordial to Americans. We know you don't want us here. You want your sovereignty. But in war, we must go where we don't want to go, and the men do not wish to be here. They want to go home. They do not like being treated as if they are invisible."

The man continued to watch her. Did he understand what she said? A minute passed. Two. Then he heaved a sigh that must have totally emptied his lungs.

"Yes, we wish our country to be left out of war. We hear of bad things in Denmark." He inclined his head. "Better to have Americans than Germans occupy our land. We have been rude to your men."

Rude to the women too, but Marie let that slide.

"Christmas is a few months away. That will be a hard day for the men to be far from their families." She hoped she wasn't stepping out of line. "We heard our bases in England are planning Christmas parties for the local children. Santa Claus, treats, singing. Would Iceland's children like a party?"

She held her breath. When the men in the hospital read about party plans in the *Stars and Stripes* military newspaper, their comments rang with sarcasm or false humor. *"What a cushy life those guys in England have. Too bad no one would come if we threw a party. Must be nice."*

No one had authorized Marie to inquire about inviting children to the base. They could hold a party at the church or a community center. Surely the navy wouldn't mind if she instigated a party. The frosty relations with the locals concerned the brass. Whom would she speak to? The general in charge of all US forces in Iceland? He'd greeted the Red Cross ladies but didn't know them individually. No, she'd dump this on Mr. Walton's desk. And offer to help, of course.

The priest stared at the statue of Christ. Seeking divine inspiration? He turned to her, and a hint of a smile cracked his face. "The children would enjoy a party."

Marie let her breath swoosh out. "I'll inform my Red Cross supervisor. Mr. Walton will contact you."

Outside, she couldn't stop grinning. She had meant to ask if a men's choral group could sing at church, but better to ask at the church that welcomed Americans. A children's party! Since they couldn't have hundreds of men crowding into the venue like at the dances, they should first invite the men who were fathers. They'd most appreciate the chance to interact with children.

"You nurse?"

Marie was so engrossed in her ponderings she wasn't paying attention to her surroundings. Two men stood in front of her. They wore drab fishermen-type jackets over dull-colored knitted sweaters and knee-high rubber boots. They smelled fishy.

She shook her head. "No, sorry, I'm not a nurse."

She angled to step around them, but one man reached out and tugged a lock of her hair. His hand was filthy with ... fish guts? Her heartbeat accelerated. "Excuse me."

They wouldn't let her leave. The other man grabbed her arm. "Nice teeth."

Marie spotted a familiar Jeep ahead. Sucking in her breath, she screamed, "Corporal Case."

An engine roared, and Case zoomed up the street. He bounced out and grabbed her hand, pulling her away from the startled Icelanders. "Perfect timing," he said. "We'll be back on base in time for grub."

If she hadn't moved fast enough, he probably would have tossed her into the Jeep. He gunned the motor and they were off. "Who were those clowns?"

"Fishermen, I think. They touched my hair with dirty fingers and said I have nice teeth." Marie worked hard to keep her voice even.

"You do have nice teeth. Have you noticed dental care isn't a priority here? Even young adults have badly decayed or missing teeth. The locals don't realize it, but they encourage me to be quick with my toothbrush."

His prattle calmed her. *Think about what's pure and lovely and honest and good. Count my blessings.* Like Wilmer Case and Stefan and Betty and the rest of the girls in her hut. She glanced at her bulging tote bag. *Think about playing Santa Claus.*

Chapter Twenty-Seven

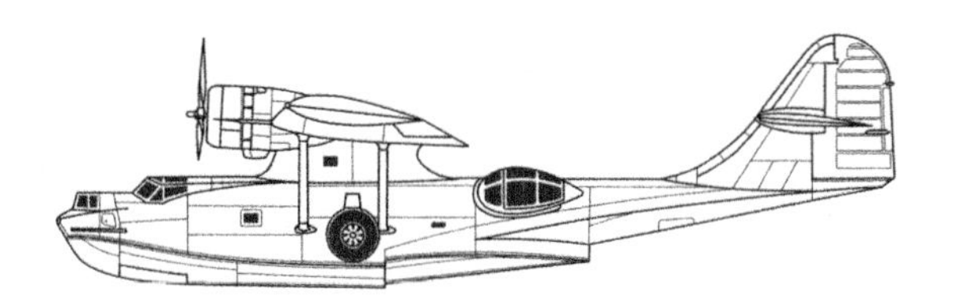

Stefan and Marie boarded his plane while Ramsey and a mechanic checked over its systems. When his engineer gave him a nod, Stefan breathed easier. He led Marie to the living quarters.

"Welcome to our home sweet home."

She stared at the tiny electric stove. "You've mentioned frying fish and Spam, and heating soup. I'm guessing you don't bake cookies."

He laughed. "Not by a long shot. We have had cookies put aboard, though. Plain old sugar cookies, and not exactly fresh. Dunkers for coffee."

"Where's the fridge?"

"No fridge. It's always colder than an ice cube in here, so we don't need refrigeration."

The plane dipped as someone boarded and Dever appeared at the bulkhead. "Aha. Hanky-panky in progress. I knew it. You like to pretend you're a straight arrow, but I know better, Stevie D." He leered at Marie, and Stefan clenched his fist. "Your canary can't handle real men."

Ramsey loomed behind Dever. "Sir, would you toss me that coil of wire?"

Stefan found the wire. "On two." He started his arm forward and pretended to throw it. Dever reached up to grab ... nothing. Before he could react, Stefan launched the coil to Ramsey.

Dever sneered. "What are you doing here, Dumski?"

"Look who's asking stupid questions," he said to Marie. Turning back to Dever, he said, "We're maintaining our plane and minding our own business, a concept that is foreign to you."

A click and a flash. Lawrenz grinned above his camera. "Perfect." He disappeared back to the front of the plane.

"What did he do?" Red suffused Dever's face.

Stefan laughed. The man didn't have the upper hand and was coming unglued. "You've never seen someone operate a camera before?"

"Why did he do that?" Dever yelled, his spit flying.

Stefan grabbed a rag and wiped his sleeve. "Evidence. Of intruders. Maybe saboteurs." He threw the rag back on the shelf. "Get off this aircraft, Dever."

The man narrowed his eyes. "Are you accusing me of sabotage?"

"Out. Now." Stefan nodded to a man now standing behind the other pilot.

Dever spun around, hesitated a moment, then snarled. "Get out of my way."

As he stormed off the plane, the mechanic removed the MP armband from his sleeve. "That guy's a real bowl of cherries."

Stefan stilled. "Has he been on this PBY before?"

"Oh yeah." The mechanic bobbed his head. "He's always snooping around. Not just this plane. Weird, really, because there's no personal or valuable stuff left onboard. I did see him pick up a book from the navigator's desk here and move the bookmark forward several pages." The man rolled his eyes. "So juvenile."

Stefan turned back to the bunks where Marie remained huddled and out of sight. Her face was pale, and she brushed the blanket folded on the bunk with a trembling hand. He shouldn't have brought her here.

It seemed like a good idea at the time. Marie wanted to see the plane. If Dever showed up, Stefan would control the situation by asking Ramsey and Lawrenz to watch their plane. But he upset Marie in the process. He wouldn't make that mistake again.

He held out his hand. "Come on. Let's find someplace private."

They walked past the flight line. The sun had set, so they didn't attempt to go farther. Marie gasped. "Look at that."

Above them, a string of green light topped with purple quivered across the sky. A spurt of color rose and danced above them before swooping low. Wisps of green blazed about, playing crack the whip. The purple fringe turned red. The heavenly display hovered, grew still, and faded.

"Magical." Marie breathed, her hand gripping his. "That was ..."

"Phenomenal? Exquisite? Mind-boggling?"

"Yes. All of that." She continued to stare up into the sky, where stars multiplied like bursting popcorn.

"Aurora borealis don't qualify as geology, but I can tell you about the scientific properties ..."

Her fingers covered his lips. "No. Don't spoil the wonder."

He should be insulted. Instead, he kissed her fingers. The evening wouldn't end on a sour note after all.

* * *

As breakfast concluded the next morning, a messenger told Stefan to report to Lieutenant Commander Arnett's office. That was unusual. More common was Dever's smirk from across the room.

When Stefan arrived at Arnett's office, the commanding officer didn't return his salute. "Dabrowski, you are hereby relieved of the duty of plane captain. A panel will determine whether you will face court martial charges. Meanwhile, you are confined to base."

Stefan nearly stuck his fingers in his ears to wiggle loose whatever was affecting his hearing. "Court martial charges for what reason?"

"Irresponsible conduct, endangering the lives of crew members, and allowing unauthorized civilians onboard a navy aircraft."

He said nothing of Cusson's traitor. Must not have figured out how to pin that on Stefan. The unauthorized civilian must refer to Marie. Dever hadn't wasted any time spewing his venom. From "boring as bathwater" to this, courtesy of someone who took umbrage with his ancestry.

Captain Hopley entered the small office. His let his gaze flicker over Stefan before he frowned at his subordinate. "You wanted to see me, Arnett?"

The man straightened. "Sir, I am convening a panel to investigate bringing court martial charges against Dabrowski."

"Court martial?" Hopley's jaw dropped. "Are you out of your cotton-pickin' mind? Dabrowski's the best pilot we have. Check your action tallies. He has far more U-boat kills than anyone else. He uncovered a traitor in your squadron. I've been waiting for a medal commendation to pass my desk, but you've been dragging your feet. What do you have against this man?"

"I've received numerous reports ..."

"From whom?"

"Lieutenant Dever, sir."

"The pilot loitering outside?" Hopley banged the door open. "Get in here, Dever."

Dever marched in with parade-ground bearing, no doubt expecting praise. Stefan's breakfast curdled in his gut.

"You think you're really something, don't you, Dever? You expect women to fall at your feet, and if they don't, you force yourself on them." Hopley spun to face the CO. "I told you to take care of this. What have you done?"

"I talked to him about it." Arnett shrank.

"Talk, eh? Not even a slap on the hand?"

"His mother asked me ..."

"His mother?" Hopley's voice dropped to a low growl. "What does she have to do with the navy? How do you know her?"

"We're cousins, sir, and ..."

"Cousins?" The captain's roar could shake windows a block away.

He turned his glare back on Dever. "What gives you the right to complain about Dabrowski?"

"Well, sir, he's a Polack—"

The captain turned so red Stefan feared for his health.

"My wife has Polish ancestry." Hopley ground out each word. "*You* are an idiot. Get out of here. I'll deal with you later."

Dever's smirk died. He must be quaking in his boots. His wild salute knocked the cap off his head. He chased it as it rolled across the room, and yes, he looked very much like an idiot.

Silence descended with his exit. Stefan startled at Hopley's now moderate voice. "Arnett, you're not the man to lead this squadron. However, before you go, I believe it's imperative that you understand how a good aircrew performs its duties. You will accompany Lieutenant Dabrowski and his crew on today's mission." He turned to Stefan. "When do you leave, son?"

Stefan gulped. Take Arnett along? "Ninety minutes, sir."

"Be there, Arnett." The captain waved Arnett to the door.

Stefan walked out with Captain Hopley.

"Dabrowski, you don't seem too pleased with the way things turned out."

Stefan pursed his lips and decided on honesty. "I'd rather face a hearing than sit in tight quarters with Arnett all day."

Captain Hopley had the nerve to laugh.

* * *

Marie finished writing the letter with a flourish. "How's that? By ending on a nice, cheery note, your wife should realize you're doing well."

The patient groaned. "As well as can be expected, you mean. I'll limp for the rest of my days." He rolled his head back and forth on his thin pillow. "Can't tell Maeve, though. This is the first pregnancy she's held on to for more than three months."

"I'll get this in the mail right away." Marie patted the man's arm and rose.

And nearly stumbled. Stefan stood in the doorway, looking like he'd lost his best friend. Her mind raced. Had something happened to Daniel or John, his unholy trio pals? Or maybe ... She hurried over.

"Let me guess. Dever retaliate."

"In spades." Stefan glanced at his watch. He offered a quick recap before checking the time again. "I have to go. It won't do to keep the CO waiting. I wanted to see you first, though. Pray for me, Marie." He cupped her cheek, gazing at her like he needed to memorize every feature and flaw. "Maybe

I should bring along a change of clothes and some deodorant. Tangling with the Germans in combat is bad enough. Now I'll have an enemy in my plane breathing down my neck."

He kissed her, hard and swift, and left.

She turned back to the room and found a dozen cheeky grins aimed at her. They faltered, replaced by frowns.

"What's the matter, miss?" The nearest patient sported a leg in traction, wore a body cast, and had both arms wrapped in thick bandages. Other than his hair being singed away, his head was the only part of him left uninjured. "We haven't lost the war, have we?"

Marie forced a smile. "No, seaman. We're going to win this war. It would be a lot easier, though, if there wasn't contention within the ranks."

The man frowned. "Hmm. Not a problem here. Definitely the Krauts who did this to me. Them and their filthy torpedoes."

She glanced around the ward, noting she still had an audience. "Please join me, boys, in praying for the PBYs keeping watch over the convoys today. It's going to be a rough day for my favorite aircrew."

Chapter Twenty-Eight

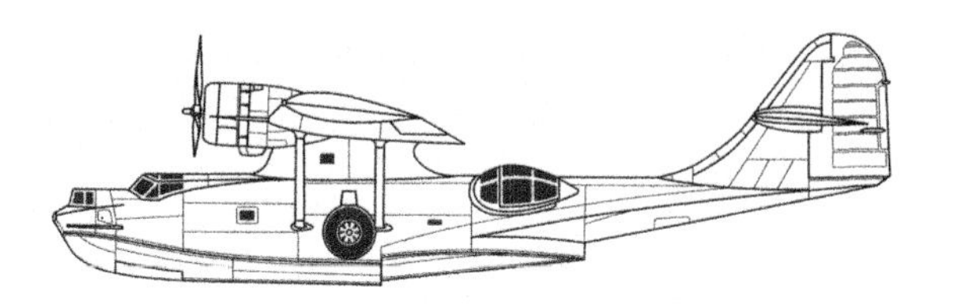

"Do we have to do this?" For all his moments of brightness, Lawrenz still whined like the schoolboy he'd so recently been.

"Orders are orders." Stefan herded his crew onto the airplane. "Here comes our unwanted guest. Everyone, take your places, stay on your toes, and keep the chatter down."

He and Grant ran through the preflight checklist with Ramsey, bringing the plane to life, when Lieutenant Commander Arnett squeezed into the cockpit. Stefan noted the man's sudden stillness at finding Grant in the copilot seat. A sudden chill ran through him. Surely Captain Hopley hadn't intended for Arnett to take over Grant's duties.

Grant tapped a dial, appearing not to notice. "The luminosity is fading here. Jenz—"

"Spare tube coming right up."

McQuaid tried to pass the tube forward, a difficult task with the CO blocking the cockpit. Arnett took the tube from him but didn't hand it to Grant. Instead, he examined it like he'd never seen one before.

Grant still hadn't noticed Arnett. "Where's that tube, Jenz?"

Stefan plucked the tube out of the CO's hand. "Right here. All stations, report in."

His crewmen reported their readiness. Poulos added, "We have an abundant supply of chemical toilet bags and toilet paper."

Stefan smothered a laugh and nearly choked on his saliva. He wouldn't bet against Poulos and Lawrenz anticipating Arnett to wet his pants.

Takeoff proceeded without a hitch, and they winged their way to the rendezvous point with the convoy. Their guest had taken a seat at the unoccupied radarman's station, but now he reappeared in the cockpit and plugged in a headset. "Grant, is it? I'll take that seat now."

Grant shot Stefan a wide-eyed look as he adjusted a control.

"Did you hear me? Why are you still here?"

Stefan gritted his teeth. "Grant and I work together as a team dedicated to efficient flight. Sir."

"I can handle this airplane. Get in the back, Lieutenant."

Stefan offered Grant a minute nod. They couldn't overrule a high-ranking officer. Their flight was bound to be sloppier without Grant's contributions, but maybe that was Arnett's goal—to make them look bad.

"Fear not, for I am with thee. Be not dismayed, for I am thy God. I will strengthen thee, Yea, I will help thee. I will uphold thee with the right hand of my righteousness."

The ancient words from Isaiah scrolled through Stefan's mind, giving him peace. No matter what mischief Arnett had in mind, God would see Stefan through. He could take that to the bank.

An hour passed as they flew southwest. Any moment now,

they'd spot the convoy. He felt the commander's baleful glare. Arnett stared at him, surveyed the view of ocean, scanned the dials, and stared at him some more.

He finally spoke. "It's awfully quiet."

Since the plane created its usual noise, he knew Arnett meant the men. A little conversation was normal. But today, only McQuaid's voice came through the headphones, verifying their route and contact point. Stefan thought better of replying that Arnett had dampened their enthusiasm. He certainly didn't want to reveal the Buck Rogers/Flash Gordon setup in the back. However, he should reply. "It is."

Two minutes later, Pennington's comment changed the atmosphere. "There's the convoy."

"The color of the day is green." Jenz sounded breathless.

Stefan looked up through the overhead window to see a streak of green soar skyward from Ramsey's Very pistol.

"Recognition signals transmitted," Poulos reported. "The Aldis lamp could use a tune-up when we get back."

Grant eased into the cockpit and flipped a switch.

Arnett frowned. "Why did you do that?" He glared at Stefan. "You should have told me to adjust the setting."

The man outranked him, but Stefan was still the plane commander. He wouldn't allow the CO to throw his weight around in his aircraft. "Everyone on my crew knows his duties and does them without being told. That's why we're successful." He grinned as Grant reached between them to adjust the throttles as Stefan descended to fly in a wide circuit around the convoy. "Captain Hopley wanted you to see how we work, not take over. My copilot and I work in tandem without speaking. That's why it would be best if you take a seat elsewhere. Now that we're over the convoy, things can happen fast."

Arnett narrowed his eyes to slits, and his lips formed an

equally thin line, but he thrust himself out of Grant's chair and shoved past him.

Stefan nearly wilted in relief. Grant slid into his seat and shook his hand like he'd handled hot water. Stefan yanked off his headset to be sure Arnett didn't hear his laughter. He leaned over and yelled, "Welcome back."

Grant offered a thumbs-up.

Stefan replaced his headphones. "Okay, Jenz. What's the news?"

"U-boats have been chattering like magpies. The huff duff reports one bearing after another, some close, others far off, and anywhere in between. New contact report coming in now."

"Filthy visibility," Pennington said. "Spotting a sub won't be easy. Even with wave action, the surface is more like a mirror than a window."

The sun hung in the sky like a hazy ball. Squalls were likely. Clouds already rolled in from the east, casting darker patches on the water. Perfect hiding places for U-boats. Fortunately, the German sailors didn't know about the possible camouflage.

Jenz cut into Stefan's musing. "Contact bearing seven degrees starboard. Maybe fifteen hundred yards."

Less than a mile. This U-boat wasn't waiting for either cover of darkness or its pals to converge.

"Periscope! One o'clock."

As he altered course, Stefan wished Pennington hadn't yelled on the radio.

"Conning tower surfacing. Three o'clock." Lawrenz lacked his usual boisterousness. Arnett must have joined him in the blister.

"Two U-boats?" Stefan didn't need the Germans ganging up on him with the CO watching.

"Yes, two separate contacts." Jenz paused. "Huff duff reports a wolf pack seems to be congregating."

Stefan spotted Pennington's periscope just as it dropped out of sight. The sub might dive straight ahead or make a sharp turn. Right or left? The opaque water prevented him from knowing. Wasting his depth charges on a blind guess wasn't an option. Not when another target loomed in sight. He aimed for the surfaced U-boat.

Enemy sailors spilled out of the hatches and raced for their antiaircraft gun. Already, bullets flew at them. Stefan wished for better speed. "On your toes, fellas. The Germans intend to duke it out with us."

Over the noise of his engines, he heard a bullet crash against the fuselage. He skidded the plane to the left. Unlike the heavy bombers that had to maintain a steady course while on their bombing runs to a stationary target, he had no obligation to make life easy for his moving target.

Arnett's voice crackled in his ears. "We are under fire."

Seriously? Stefan wanted to laugh. Technically, they were over the fire.

"It's called combat." That sounded like Pennington, who stood exposed in his turret, firing back.

Stefan circled around the sub, giving Lawrenz a clear shot from the blister.

"Yikes!"

Stefan grimaced at Lawrenz's exclamation. He'd given the Germans a clear shot at his gunner. "Everything okay back there?"

"A bullet came through the bottom of this window and went out the top of the other. I got a real good look at it."

"Where's ..." Grant began the question Stefan wanted to ask but didn't want to voice in case Arnett was listening.

Lawrenz understood. "Hiding in the galley."

"Not quite," McQuaid said. "Heading your way."

Stefan clenched his jaw. The man ought to know better than to roam around the plane during a battle. A quick glimpse revealed a German tumbling to the deck of the sub. He'd match his gunners against the enemy any day. That's what Arnett should have been watching.

In his periphery, he saw a hand plug in a headset. A querulous voice soon filled his ears. "Can't you stay out of the line of fire? You're endangering this aircraft."

"This is combat," Grant answered.

"It's an irresponsible risk."

When was war not risky? Whose side was this guy on?

Past the U-boat now, Stefan climbed into cloud cover before looping back. They popped out of the clouds to find the sub one thousand yards away.

"They're blowing the tanks to crash dive," Pennington yelled.

Good. Stefan preferred them being unable to shoot back. He dropped to thirty feet and released depth charges into the swirling water. Two minutes passed as he circled. His heart sank. He must have missed, or the depth charges were duds. And with the commanding officer breathing down his neck.

"Jackpot! Cha-ching, cha-ching, cha-ching," Poulos yelled on the interphone. "We got us an oil slick. It's spreading out for half a mile. There's even men and other junk in it."

Stefan grinned, relief sweeping through him. One less U-boat to harass the convoy and one less reason for Arnett to complain about him. "Jenz, where's that other sub?"

Jenz offered the coordinates, and Stefan swung around in the tightest circle the plane could manage. Below, ships plodded along in straight lines, like ducks lined up in a shooting gallery at the county fair. All the U-boat had to do was fire a spread of torpedoes, and they'd have an excellent chance of winning a prize.

"What are they doing on that ship? Think they're trying to point to a sub?" Grant grabbed his binoculars. "The seamen are pointing to a spot, and their spotlight is aimed ... There it is!"

Stefan couldn't see it. "You've got it. Take control."

Grant adjusted their course, and Stefan caught sight of a disappearing periscope. "It's coming our way."

He released three depth charges with their fuses set at twenty-five feet.

"We've got a hanger. No, there it goes." Poulos took a deep breath. "One of the garbage cans didn't want to leave us, but it did drop."

"Yahoo! We got a geezer," Lawrenz, of course, yelled through the intercom.

"How about a *geyser*, kiddo?" Despite his droll remark, McQuaid's excitement came through.

"Fine and dandy with me." The correction didn't faze Lawrenz. "I'm taking pictures."

Stefan rotated his shoulders. A quick glance showed Arnett had wandered aft. "Jenz, is the huff duff showing anything in the vicinity?"

"Maybe twelve miles out to the east-southeast. It's submerged."

Stefan flew ahead of the convoy. Deteriorating weather buffeted the plane, and rain slashed the windshield. He yawned. Time to stretch his legs. With a tap on Grant's arm, he rose stiffly.

No sign of Arnett. He paused by McQuaid's desk and pantomimed his question. McQuaid shrugged and pointed to the back.

Stefan looked up at Ramsey in his station in the pylon and gave a thumbs-up with his brows raised. Ramsey grinned and returned the thumbs-up, signifying that everything was working fine.

Jenz remained glued to his window, watching for messages to flash from the lead destroyer.

Lawrenz and Poulos lounged in the blister compartment. When Stefan pointed at the lav, Poulos handed him a Flash Gordon headset.

"Lawrenz thinks the honcho wet his pants, but I think he wet his shirt. He smells real ripe." Poulos flapped his arms and wrinkled his nose. "Either his deodorant expired, or he forgot to use it."

Stefan grabbed a roll of duct tape and recruited the gunners to help tape over the bullet holes to prevent cold wind from whistling through.

Arnett emerged from the lavatory and watched. "How much damage occurred?"

"We won't know until we're back in Reykjavik, of course, but everything's working," Stefan said. "And no one was wounded."

He moved into the living quarters and checked the food supply. Lawrenz followed him. "Time for dinner?"

Stefan nodded. "Looks like pea soup is on the menu. Want to heat it?"

Lawrenz pulled out a pot. "Do we have to feed him?"

"You don't need to serve him. He's quite capable of serving himself."

Stefan was hungry for something other than soup. He pictured Matka's roasted chicken and dumplings and could smell her freshly baked bread. His stomach growled.

After the electrical bomb release mechanism had repeatedly failed on the PBYs, the galley appliances were blamed for using too much current, and crews were restricted to heating coffee or soup. Stefan didn't think the galley caused the drop in battery voltage and allowed the stove's use for heartier meals like fish and Spam once they were finished with convoy patrol. Not today, though. Not with Arnett onboard.

He found a box of rolls and squeezed eight onto the stove around the pot of soup. Lawrenz pointed back to the blister. Oh, right. Nine men aboard. He reached for another and attempted to rearrange the rolls. Larence waved his hand and put the roll back in the box. "He can have a cold one," he yelled. "He won't know ours are warm, and he should know what it's like to have cold food."

Good point. Stefan nodded.

He dropped into his seat with a sigh, resentment gnawing on his soul. His thoughts toward Arnett and Dever were far from charitable. He needed to practice what he preached to Marie about forgiveness.

Father, forgive me, for I do what I know I shouldn't. I remember all the wrongs Dever and Arnett have done to me. Help me lay this burden of misery at the foot of Your cross.

He was called to pray for his enemies, but how? Bullies usually weren't happy, so they made themselves feel better by destroying others' happiness. He could pray that they find peace.

Thankfulness for his own family flooded him. This evening, he would write to his folks and tell them he loved them.

They were approaching Reykjavik when Ramsey announced, "We have a problem. The port wheel isn't lowering."

Stefan recalled the bullets pinging into the aircraft. "Lawrenz?"

"Checking." Five seconds passed. "Whoa! It's been shot. The rubber's shredded and hanging. Some pieces are dropping off."

"All right, then." Situations like this boosted Stefan's love for amphibious planes. "Ramsey, will the wheel retract?"

"I'm not getting a lock. Lawrenz?"

"It did go up, but it's not as tucked in as the starboard."

"Lower floats." Stefan angled for the bay, wondering why the commander hadn't made a snide remark.

Nope. He wouldn't go there. He'd left his burden named Arnett at the cross and refused to grab it back.

The plane kissed the water and skimmed through light waves, settling gently. He keyed his mic. "Anyone spotting little waterspouts from bullet holes, call 'em out."

McQuaid responded, "The port fuselage has a leaky faucet."

Stefan searched the beach and the harbor. A seaplane tender stood off by itself. He headed toward it. The tender crew could hoist them aboard, repair their wheel, and plug their holes. Being in port meant a launch could transfer them to shore instead of remaining on the tender during maintenance. He could spend the evening with Marie instead of Arnett.

A crowd awaited them on the beach. Jenz would have radioed their actions, but sinking U-boats no longer garnered so much attention. Captain Hopley stood in the crowd. Stefan sighed and said to Grant, "Everyone must know about our special guest."

Arnett strode forward and saluted Hopley. "I'm lucky to have made it back, sir."

"Is that so?" Hopley's voice reeked with exaggeration despite his poker face.

"Reckless endangerment. They flew right into fire, and now the plane is damaged."

Lawrenz passed near them on his way to the photo lab, and Hopley hailed him. "How was your flight, young man?"

The young gunner skidded to a stop. "Swell, sir. Sank two

subs and nobody got hurt. Except, sir, that pea soup is kind of disgusting. I'd rather have a pork chop."

The captain released a burst of laughter and leveled a stern look at Arnett before turning his attention to Stefan. "Well done, Lieutenant. You make sinking U-boats look way too easy."

"Thank you, sir. Weather conditions weren't so great for spotting them. Maybe the Germans knew that and grew careless. Surfacing during daylight within sight of the convoy didn't make sense. They did make our job easy."

"And your plane?"

"No major damage, sir, but they'll give it a thorough checkout."

Hopley nodded. "Carry on."

"Yes, sir."

When Stefan spotted Marie making her way through the crowd, he was more than ready to carry on.

Chapter Twenty-Nine

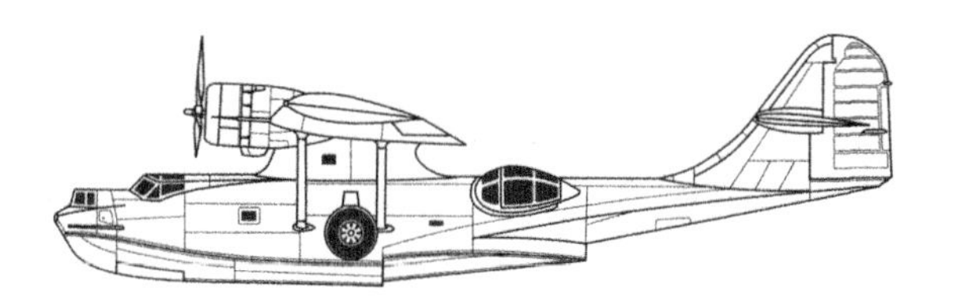

Marie reached for Stefan's hand as she joined him at the edge of the throng. "The conquering hero returns in triumph."

"Shh." He pulled her close. "I don't want anyone thinking they need to knock me off a pedestal."

She searched the gathering but saw no sign of Dever. "Is someone suggesting a need for that?"

He sighed and tucked her hand around his elbow. "Maybe not. Maybe I'm becoming paranoid. We're supposed to be fighting the Germans, but I feel like we're in a competition. The emphasis isn't on how many ships make it to England, but on how many U-boats each pilot sinks. The Germans fear us pouncing on them, so they give us a wide berth. Even Dever may have discouraged an attack."

Stefan was so modest. She could think of nothing to say that might assuage his concerns. "Boys will be boys" would sound belittling. She placed her other hand on his arm and hugged it.

"Are you hungry?" Good grief. Now she must sound like a

grandmother or mother, always trying to feed people. Like food was the cure for everything.

"Yeah, my stomach's wondering what it did to make me ignore it. I do not, however, have a craving for pork chops like Lawrenz. What did you have?"

"Overcooked pasta with cheese."

He groaned.

"And a chocolate sheet cake with white icing."

"Better. Keep me company while I eat? Then we can go dancing or something."

Apparently, the cooks in the officers' mess tried harder to please the fighting men than they did the nurses and Red Cross women. Stefan's macaroni didn't look like spilled brain matter, as Lettie called it. Marie didn't realize she was twisting a napkin until he set down his utensils. "Something or someone bothering you?" he said with a glint in his eyes. "Another unknown husband show up?"

"A supposed unknown cousin."

Stefan lifted his brows. "Really?"

She shrugged. "And then there was the patient who watched me constantly. I guess I looked at him too long, wondering why he didn't wipe his runny nose. He concluded that I was interested in him." She propped her chin on her hands. "Thankfully, his broken leg will keep him from chasing me."

"Tell me about this cousin. What's his name?"

"Gabriel Foubert. He saw the *Life* magazine article. He's in transit to England and was thrilled to stop over in Iceland so he could meet his famous cousin." She slapped her hands on the table. "When I said I have no family, well, that dampened his enthusiasm."

Stefan cocked his head. "You didn't want to visit with him?"

After all this time, didn't Stefan understand?

"I don't have family. No relatives wanted me."

He covered her hand. "How old is he?"

She had to think. "He's just joining the fight now. Eighteen or nineteen?"

"So he's several years younger than us. He wasn't born yet when your family died, so he had no part in rejecting you." He patted her hand. "Here's your opportunity to learn about your family. You may discover you were better off in the orphanage."

She leaned back in her chair, but he kept her hand trapped under his.

"Do you know what unit he's with?"

Gabriel had probably told her, but she hadn't listened. "Army, I think? A Canadian group."

"Must be part of the big buildup for the invasion of Europe. Interesting that he's flying instead of traveling by ship." Stefan shoveled the last bite of cake into his mouth. "Not bad." He wiped his mouth. "Okay. Let's go find your cousin."

Marie had never been to Meeks Field. The air reeked of gasoline and throbbed with the sound of engines. Planes sat everywhere, and men milled about. "We'll never find him."

"Sure we will. These are mostly Americans. Shouldn't be too hard to find a bunch of Canadians."

She trailed after Stefan as he questioned one man after another, each pointing them farther along. A Canadian flag flew over one of the last groups in line. Marie pressed a hand to her abdomen, feeling queasy. She wasn't ready for this. For a lifetime, she'd believed herself unwanted. Gabriel Foubert might either confirm that, or, what? Claim it was all a mistake but no one knew where to find her? Ha!

A group of soldiers eating out of mess kits lounged by a cargo plane with Canadian markings. Marie stopped and gazed around. Of course, the Allies hadn't built a motel for the transits, but weren't Quonset huts provided for them? Did these men have to sleep on their plane? Maybe any guest huts were filled.

Stefan grabbed her hand and tugged her forward. He paused at the edge of the group. "Excuse me, gents. Do you have a Gabriel Foubert here?"

A man hopped to his feet on the far side. Marie's stomach tightened, and she dragged in a deep breath. She could do this. Hear him out, Stefan said. It might be nice to have a cousin.

Gabriel pinned her with his gaze as he approached. She saw anticipation, curiosity, maybe hope in his eyes. Perhaps he wanted to be friends. Or maybe he just wanted a story about poor little Marie for the next family gathering. With a nod to Stefan, he said, "*Bonjour*, Marie."

Stefan studied him. "Yep, I see a family resemblance. You both have the same sprinkling of freckles."

Marie crossed her arms and slid her gaze to Stefan. "Thank you, Stefan, for mentioning that."

Stefan had the audacity to grin before asking Gabriel to walk with them. He waited until they were beyond earshot of Gabriel's pals. The arm Stefan slung around Marie's shoulders calmed her, although maybe he intended to keep her from bolting.

"I'm Stefan Dabrowski. I fly PBY patrols here."

She bit her lip. She should have introduced them.

"What can you tell us about the days after Marie's parents died and no relatives claimed her?"

No small talk. Just *bam*. Trepidation, fear, hurt, and yearning warred within her as she watched Gabriel.

The man leaned back on his heels and pushed his hands into his back pockets. "I first learned about you when I was nine or ten." He directed his words to Marie. "I was looking at the front pages of my mom's Bible where births, marriages, and deaths are recorded. Paul, Catherine, and Louise Foubert were listed as dying on the same day. I asked who they were. Mom said Uncle Paul was Dad's older brother and they'd died in a car accident. My sister said something about how sad that the whole family died, and Mom said another daughter wasn't in the wreck."

Shivers danced along Marie's spine.

"Maggie, my sister Magdalena, asked where you were. Mom said you lived in an orphanage. Maggie wrinkled her nose and said, 'That's creepy.'"

Marie gripped Stefan's hand. Hard. An unknown cousin thought living in an orphanage was creepy. Did she think orphanages equated with insane asylums? Maybe she thought Marie was crazy to be placed in such an institution.

"Did any of the family consider taking Marie in, providing a home for her?" Stefan drilled in with his questioning.

Gabriel dropped his head back as he looked up at stars emerging in the darkening sky. "I wasn't born yet, you realize, so I can't speak for everyone's choices. I can tell you who's in the family." He sighed. "My parents didn't marry until the following year, so they weren't an option. Uncle Augustin was an alcoholic. He lost his job because he was a know-it-all who tried to tell the boss once too often how to run his business. His kids tended to scatter when he came home." He turned to Marie. "You would not have wanted to live there."

Gabriel ticked off his fingers as he continued. "Aunt Agathe died in childbirth with number eight. Uncle Jacques tried to find another wife to take care of the kids, but they were dirt poor and the house should have been condemned long ago. I have a vague memory of Mom dressing the littlest one in a dress of my sister's because hers was indecent, and Mom saying we should take in the poor mite, but we have nine kids in our family. Eleven people with a kitchen table that seats ten. Last one to dinner had to sit at a rickety card table."

"What about your grandparents?" Stefan asked, stopping him. "Where were they in this?"

"Yeah." Gabriel grimaced. "Granny had a stroke around that time. She didn't attend my folks' wedding and died later that year. Granddad lost part of a leg in a farming accident and didn't manage very well. Uncle Charles had to run the farm mostly by himself. That wouldn't have been a suitable place for a little girl."

"I'm getting the picture that no one had financial means." Stefan sounded less like an interrogator and more like a dismayed advocate.

Gabriel snorted. "Uncle Louis's wife wanted to know how much money your parents left. She would have been interested if there was a tidy sum. No, we're simple country folk for the most part. No college graduates. Not even many high school graduates. My brother and I joined the army right out of school because it was a sure job." He shrugged. "Of course, war will be hazardous to our health."

Marie's heart pounded against her chest. Most of her relatives lived hardscrabble lives or were downright ne'er-do-wells. The nuns had scorned a family living near the orphanage, claiming the children were worse off than the orphans and likely to become criminals.

"I remember a woman hugging me," Marie said. "I thought she may have wanted me." Her voice quavered.

"She was on your mother's side of the family." Gabriel studied the stars again. "During a cousin's wedding, someone mentioned you. Said this aunt had four boys, at least, and wanted a girl. But they had no room. Their house had one bedroom. The parents slept on a foldout sofa. Apparently, she died young." He kicked at the ground. "It's not like no one wanted you. In fact, Uncle Felix would have taken you. He had a lot of kids, and they were all expected to be farmhands. I think it was Aunt Judith who discouraged him. She said you'd be better off in the church's orphanage."

By the time Stefan thanked Gabriel for his time, Marie's ears buzzed. As she and Stefan headed back to their base, she felt sick. She smoothed the paper she'd been clenching so tightly and read Gabriel's scrawled address. Should she write to him? Servicemen enjoyed receiving mail. What would it hurt? He was her cousin.

She had family now.

They paused at their spot on the beach. Stefan rubbed her back in soothing circular motions, and she leaned her forehead against his shoulder.

"If I hadn't grown up in the orphanage, I wouldn't have received the scholarship and attended college. I wouldn't have joined the Red Cross and come to Iceland. I'd probably be picking beans somewhere in Quebec with two or three children hanging onto my skirt."

"We wouldn't have met." Stefan cradled her head against him.

She sniffed. "My relatives don't exactly shine like stars."

"Salt of the earth. That's what they are."

Marie almost laughed. "Some sound much too salty." She wrapped her arms around his waist. "I should forgive them, right? Actually, the only thing they might be guilty of is ignoring me. Not even birthday or Christmas cards. They probably didn't want to get my hopes up that someone on the outside might want me after all."

"On the outside?" Stefan stepped away so he could face her. "Sweetheart, you weren't in prison."

They walked along the runway used by the PBYs, which was strangely empty after the hustle at Meeks Field. Hills rose in the distance, barren. She sighed. "I don't know how I feel now. Yes, it sounds like I was better off in the orphanage, but the way they all ignored me as if I was of no consequence, that still hurts."

She pitied herself when she had so much to be grateful for. The bare hills didn't help. "Back in Quebec and New England, the trees will be ablaze with color now. I miss the leaves."

"Why don't you ask one of your artistic patients to paint you a fall scene full of colorful trees?"

Marie laughed and nudged him. Sweet Stefan always looked for the good instead of wallowing in disappointment. She needed to emulate his attitude.

Above them, stars twinkled in abundance. She turned in a complete circle to get her bearings. "There it is. The Big Dipper. And if you follow the outer edge of the kettle ..." She traced a line through the sky with her finger. "There's the North Star."

"The Milky Way is more distinct here than at home." Stefan looped his arm around her shoulders and hugged her close. "I thought about studying astronomy instead of geology but decided earth science had better prospects than space."

His arm tightened as Marie let out a gasp. A ghostly green flared up against the stars. She clasped her hands. "The Northern Lights!"

Two fingers of green waved back and forth for several seconds before wrapping together and fading.

"That's it?" Marie searched the sky. "That's all?"

"Rather wimpy, wasn't it?" Laughter shook Stefan's voice. "I guess that means it's time to turn in. Tomorrow will be a big day."

"It will? Why?"

"My plane's maintenance is forcing us to take the day off.

Let's celebrate. We can go into Reykjavik and have dinner. What do you say?"

Tomorrow was her birthday. Did he remember? Maybe he had a present for her. Maybe a portrait. "I think I'd like that."

As she prepared for bed that night, her thoughts turned to her cousin. He seemed nice. He hadn't painted the cheeriest picture of their extended family, but if enough were like him, family holiday gatherings must have been fun. She should have asked about cousins her age who she might have played with before the accident. She had no memories of any playmates. Would they wish to know her now?

Her father had so many siblings. It still made no sense that none of them ever reached out to her. Since her parents died, she'd never had anyone to count on. Oh, Sister Marguerite had cared about her. And Ozanne and Francoise would always be her friends. But they were busy with their own lives now, and the orphanage sisters had new children to care for.

Maybe she shouldn't hope Stefan remembered her birthday. Better not to hope and be pleasantly surprised than to hope and be disappointed.

Chapter Thirty

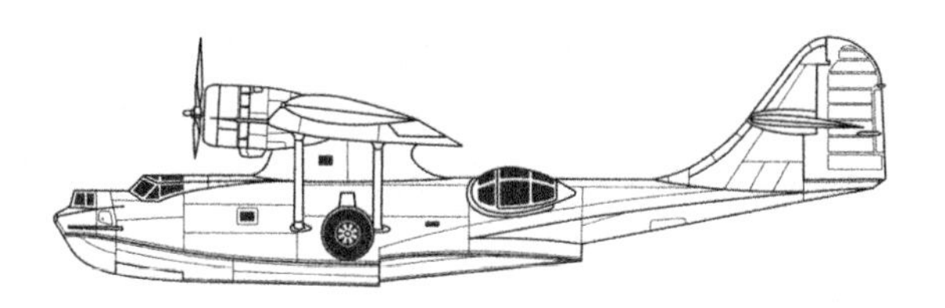

"It's Thursday."

Marie spun around to find Stefan leaning against the Red Cross hut. "Good morning to you too."

He grinned. "Good morning, lovely lady. I forgot to tell you last night. Thursday is when the swimming pool in town is open for Allied troops to use. Bring your swimming suit, okay? We can go after dinner."

His eyes shone with excitement. He'd mentioned before that he enjoyed swimming at the local pool but had never asked her to join him. She'd probably be the only woman. The hot springs had been fun, but other women were there, so she didn't feel so on display.

Quit dithering. He wants to enjoy an outing with you.

"All right, we'll go swimming. On full stomachs."

He laughed. "It'll be great." He paused while the other Red Cross women passed them and entered the nurses' mess. "Now that I have that out of the way, happy birthday, Marie."

She hadn't noticed he'd kept his left hand behind his back. Bringing it forward, he held a present wrapped in newsprint with a string bow. He remembered! Sudden tears demanded release, but she blinked them back.

The box was thin and the size of a large book. Or a portrait. From deep inside, a flock of butterflies emerged, tickling her with their fluttering, ethereal wings. She shivered in delight.

They claimed a table at the edge of the hut, but before she landed in a chair, she carefully pried the paper loose. Stefan had used a copy of *Stars & Stripes* instead of gift wrap, but the habit of saving anything that could be reused had been engrained in her at the orphanage.

Anticipating a photograph, she raised the lid and found ...

"Autumn leaves!" Pressed maple leaves lay on a paper towel. Dark red, lighter red, yellow, orange, even variegated. Eight of them, all perfectly shaped. Grasping a stem between her thumb and index finger, she lifted the largest leaf and twirled it. Did the scent of autumn cling to the leaf, or was she imagining it? "Where? How?"

Stefan sat beside her, grinning. "My sister sent them. She presses leaves every fall for spatter-painting projects in a Sunday school class she assists with. When I learned you missed leaves, I asked her to send a bunch, pronto. They arrived in the last care package I received. When McQuaid and Grant insisted on sharing the goodies, I was afraid they'd discover the leaves, fuss about them, and ruin the surprise."

Eyes misting, she eased the leaf back onto the collection and squeezed his hand. "Thank you, Stefan. I love them."

"You're most welcome." He nodded at the box. "But there's more."

Marie lifted the cardboard tray. Their portrait! She gazed at it in wonder. "It turned out perfectly."

"We look like quite a handsome couple, if I may say so myself." He scooted closer and joined her in examining the photo. "Since we're not wearing fur-lined parkas and Arctic caps, like a lot of the men wear for portraits here, the censor can't object to sending this home, which I've already done. My parents and Dorota will recognize you as soon as you step off the train in Milwaukee."

Marie caught her breath. He talked as though a visit to Milwaukee was a certainty. And perhaps more than a visit. He hadn't asked a specific question yet, but they were definitely headed in that direction. A delicious tingle of anticipation zipped through her from head to toe. He leaned close, and his lips touched hers with a gentle kiss that carried the promise of passion. Someday. Someday soon.

* * *

The day was wonderful. Yes, Marie had to put in her time at the hospital, but breakfast was a hit. She loved the leaves and the photograph. Asking Dorota to send leaves had been an inspiration. They could have been lost or mangled, but his sister had packaged them well, and she must have selected the finest leaves in her collection.

Before leaving for town, Marie gave him a peek into the Red Cross barracks. She tied thread to each leaf stem and taped them to the ceiling over her bed. Her hut mates were envious. Lettie pouted when Marie declined to hang a leaf over each bed, ignoring the fact that there weren't enough for all of them.

After an early dinner at the Vik Hotel, they arrived at the public pool when it opened for their use at six o'clock. Stefan pulled out his wallet and paid their fees of one kronar, fifty aurar each. He pointed Marie to the ladies' room before heading for the men's room. "You'll exchange your ticket with the dressing room attendant for a towel and locker."

"An attendant? I've never heard of any nurses using the pool. What does she do with the time?"

Stefan shrugged. "Maybe the girl who sells the tickets at the entrance booth has to hustle down here to assist you."

Marie wrinkled her nose, and he laughed.

He quickly changed into his swim trunks, locked up his clothes, and used a big safety pin to pin the key to his trunks. He wanted to arrive at the pool before Marie in case a lot of men were already there. They were likely the first ones here, and no one should give her a hard time, but he refused to take chances.

She peeked out of the changing room and scurried to his side, her towel wrapped around her. "No one else is here?"

"For the moment." Tossing his towel onto a bench, Stefan reached for hers. She surrendered it slowly. "Come on. The water is great."

She dipped in a toe. "It's warm."

A big pool, beautiful water, a luxury waiting just for them. No sooner did he think it than the door behind him clicked open.

"Hot diggity dog. We got us a mermaid to swim with."

Marie stiffened, and Stefan clenched a fist. He turned to find a half-dozen young men entering the pool area. Enlisted men, no doubt. He hadn't noticed them in the locker room. One of them was Jenz.

Jenz sized up the situation. "Forget it, Toad. She's the lieutenant's lady." He dropped his towel on a bench and dove into the deep end.

Toad screwed up his face but continued to watch Marie.

Stefan sighed. "We better submerge and stake a claim to the far lanes."

Wearing the same modest turquoise-print swimsuit she'd worn at the hot springs, she did resemble a mermaid. No reason for those boys to ogle her, though. Were they Jenz's friends? Barracks mates, maybe. He'd never noticed Jenz here, but then, swimming with one's face planted in the water wasn't conducive for visiting with other swimmers.

He and Marie swam several laps before they began a lazy breaststroke, allowing them to keep their heads above water and chat. She kept her voice low. "That Toad keeps looking over at me. I'm sure it's a nickname, but it's a good one. To think that only a few decades ago our swimwear would have been illegal for showing too much skin."

"Would you like to wear an old-fashioned swim dress?"

"Too much material. Think how heavy it would be." She sighed. "But the way that Toad guy watches me makes me wonder what the Red Cross ladies in the United States or England have to contend with. Plenty of civilian women are pleased to date servicemen. The men shouldn't be so obsessive about the women in the Red Cross."

Stefan stilled. "Anxious to leave Iceland?"

She smiled and reached across the lane marker to touch his arm. "No, but we were told we wouldn't be here longer than a year. We arrived in March."

They reached the wall in the deep end, and Marie pivoted like she was performing an aquatic ballet. "You don't expect to stay here for over a year, do you?"

"No. The navy transfers the squadrons around. I like to think the brass wants to even out the times spent in hardship locations and highly sought assignments. I'm sure we'll be gone in less than three months."

Marie's lips thinned as she stared ahead. "Where do you hope to go?"

"We were in Newfoundland before coming here, so I'm sure we'll go to a warmer climate. My friend Daniel is in northern Brazil, and there's a PBY squadron nearby. I wouldn't mind being near him." They turned around at the shallow end.

"Far more squadrons are in the Pacific, though. I won't be surprised if we're sent out there."

He'd known all along that Iceland wasn't a permanent assignment, and now his departure quickly approached. Departure from Iceland and from Marie. The war could drag on for another year or more. Come summer, the Allies would surely invade Europe. Then the army would have a hard row to hoe, fighting the Germans all the way to Berlin. He and Marie would be separated for all that time. The thought cast a gloomy cloud over him.

They stopped at the deep end to tread water. He inclined his head. "What about you? Where do you hope to go from here?"

Marie grabbed the edge of the pool and let her legs float to the surface. "We don't necessarily stay together. The Red Cross offers positions in clubs, which would be most like here, except in one location instead of little outposts scattered about. Then there are clubmobiles traveling around to air bases in England, and rest homes where aircrews can go for a week of R and R. And of course, hospital work."

She studied her toes poking out of the water. "I'll probably go back to the States. As Anne was fond of pointing out, I'm not an American citizen. Our predecessors here were the first group to travel overseas as recreation workers. They were pioneers, really. When it was time to relieve them, I was asked to come because they appreciated my work at the hospital in Washington. The navy has hospitals in southern California." She grinned. "It would be nice to be near a beach. Maybe Pearl Harbor. Is there a chance you'll be based there?"

Slim to remote.

"Pearl is a backwater now. Many PBYs are painted black and called Black Cats. They're in the thick of things, fighting the Japanese at night. While Iceland is cold and dark much of the time in winter, it's not terribly dangerous, so I doubt we'll draw another leisurely assignment."

Marie rubbed a hand across her face. Did her eyelashes glisten with pool water, or tears? He reached for her hand and pulled her closer.

"Hey, Lieutenant!" Jenz grinned at him from the next lane. "I hear we're flying early in the morning."

Beyond him, the other boys watched them. Good grief, he'd been about to kiss Marie with an audience. He tried to smile at Jenz. "So it's an early night for us. I guess it's a good thing we're about to be kicked out of here."

As he spoke, an attendant came into the pool and announced their time was up. Ten servicemen climbed out of the pool. Stefan and Marie took their time swimming to the stairs, enjoying a final moment without the leering Toad.

* * *

Dried off and dressed, they went outside and passed a long line of Icelanders waiting to enter. Marie blinked. So many waited. She had no idea swimming was so popular. The men and women chatted among themselves, but none made eye contact with them. The now-familiar feeling of being invisible wrapped around her, and she laced her fingers with Stefan's. He squeezed her hand, and she smiled. At least someone cared.

Back on base, they stopped at headquarters so Stefan could review his orders. "Early departure, all day in the air." He yawned. "Just thinking of it makes me tired."

"So I'll say good night and let you get some rest." She beamed up at him. "Thank you for a wonderful birthday."

His lips brushed over hers. Soft. Respectful. Mesmerizing. Then he angled his head and deepened the kiss. Her insides turned mushy. She was a goner with Stefan Dabrowski. And he was leaving in three months. How would she survive? She watched him stride away after escorting her to the Red Cross barracks.

She'd survived the loss of her parents. Marie raised her chin. This, she hoped, would be a temporary separation. She could survive this too.

Chapter Thirty-One

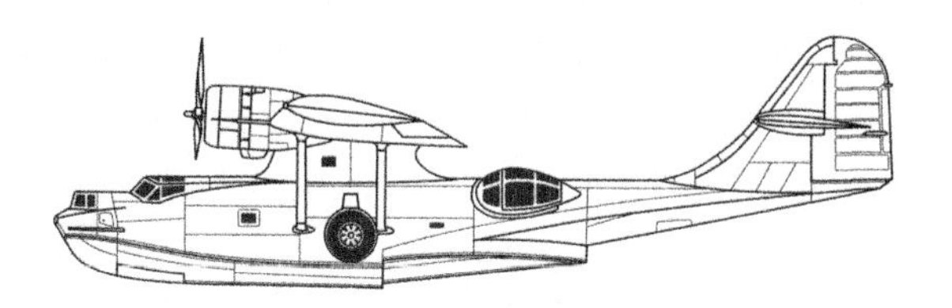

The airplane roared into the sky and Stefan settled onto their course. "Interesting strategy today. We've never done a five-plane sweep in front of a convoy before. Makes me wonder if a wolfpack is waiting to pounce."

Grant set the throttles. "How would the navy know about it? The convoy escorts have their huff duff and sonar, but how would they know in advance?"

"Maybe intelligence has broken the Krauts' code," McQuaid said. "The ships are told to grab a U-boat if possible instead of sinking it. Get your hands on their codebooks, and we're in business."

That would be sweet. Of course, the Germans would become suspicious if the Allies always showed up and clobbered them. They'd change their codes, and how long would it take to crack the new one? Stefan studied the ocean. Mild wave action. If they discovered a U-boat today, they could take full credit and not share the triumph with some broken code.

The gunners chatted as they flew. Poulos mentioned someone in their barracks got in a fight, was punched in the jaw, and lost a front tooth. Stefan scoffed. Fights usually resulted from too much beer, but Iceland was dry. The US military allowed each enlisted man to buy 3.2 percent beer at the PX once a week, on Fridays. Two bottles per man, and the bottles were opened at the counter to keep them from being accumulated. The gunners couldn't have been drunk.

He tuned back into the conversation. Pennington claimed to have been hit in the face twice with no damage. Lawrenz admitted his brother suffered a chipped tooth when he was showing off on a pier, slipped, and fell into the lake.

"How about you, Lieutenant Dabrowski? Did you ever lose a tooth?" Saving him and Marie from embarrassment last night must have emboldened Jenz to ask personal questions.

Fine. He didn't mind. "Why, yes, I did. A girl swung a mean right hook and knocked out my tooth."

"What?" A chorus of disbelief rose in his ears. "What happened?"

"My best friend Daniel's little cousin Gloria and his sister Theresa always followed us around. Gloria got mad one day and walloped me instead of Daniel. Of course, I was seven, and it was a loose baby tooth, so no harm done. Still, I got a lot of mileage out of it, holding my jaw and groaning for weeks afterward. She was properly chastised. Now Gloria's a navy nurse, but before healing people, she beat 'em up."

He needed to tell Marie that story. She'd love it. She'd love his friends.

McQuaid broke into the laughter to point out they'd arrived at the start of their sweep. They flew at the southern edge of the broom, ahead of a convoy consisting of fifty-eight merchantmen bulging with food, fuel, and munitions.

"Okay, everyone on your toes." Stefan shifted in his seat. "I don't want any U-boats sneaking through our sector."

Hours ticked by as they swept the ocean. At one point,

Lawrenz insisted he spotted a whale. He was probably using up their film to prove it.

"I'm hearing about men in a life raft." Jenz returned to his business-only voice. "A pilot reports seeing a lot of men approximately sixty miles south of us."

"That's a fair distance." McQuaid's words were muffled, as if he were busy with his maps. "The wind will be pushing them farther south."

"Jenz, are any ships able to assist them?" Stefan didn't mind attempting a rescue with the favorable ocean surfaces, but he needed permission to break off from the convoy sweep.

Five minutes passed before Jenz answer. "We're cleared to go after them. The four other PBYs will spread out their sections to cover ours."

Stefan veered south. "Okay, Pennington, keep your eagle eyes peeled. Hopefully the raft is equipped with a flare so they can signal us."

Half an hour later, Ramsey spotted them. "Flare going up at two o'clock."

A lot of men, Jenz had reported. That put it mildly. The raft was packed. Arms waved at them, lacking energy and reminding Stefan of seaweed undulating in light swells. They must have been floating for a while.

"Can anyone make out the nationality of their uniforms?" Stefan wouldn't put it past the Germans to stage a crew in distress and have a U-boat ready to surface and attack.

"They're not all wearing uniforms," Poulos said. "Maybe they're merchant seamen."

Maybe, but Stefan doubted it. Unless a ship had foolishly sailed on its own, making it easy pickings, the convoy escort should have reported the missing vessel. Even a ship that broke down or became lost from a convoy would have raised an alarm with the escort.

"Ramsey, watch the sky. Poulos, watch for subs. I'll try to circle lower for a better look." Stefan didn't want to descend too low. Banking a plane with a 104-foot wingspan required precision and nerve. He wouldn't attempt the maneuver with a low cloud cover or heavy swells.

"I think they're Brits. That one guy's wearing an RAF uniform, isn't he? Oops," Lawrenz muttered.

"What's going on back there, Flash Gordon?" McQuaid was on edge, leaving Stefan to wonder why.

"I lost my balance and hit the fuselage. Now I can't turn off my headset."

"All right. Just don't serenade us with a belching demonstration." Stefan grinned at Grant's smirk. "Anyone else verify RAF?"

"There might be a second uniform," Pennington answered. "But most of them are huddled under a blanket."

This could still be a German trap.

"All right. We'll land, but have your guns ready in case they're Germans with weapons under that blanket. Ramsey, lower floats." Stefan circled farther out, checked the swell movement for the direction of the wind, and lowered the plane.

A smile crossed his face as the PBY settled gently. Poetry in motion. Boy, did he love flying amphibious planes. Marie had flown in a PBY when she was evacuated from the Red Cross field trip, but that was a runway landing. He needed to take her flying before leaving Iceland, because they wouldn't likely have another chance. Maybe when a plane needed a test flight after maintenance, he could sneak her aboard.

"Any popped rivets?"

"Are you kidding me? That was smoother than a runway landing." Lawrenz sounded indignant, as though he had executed the landing. The thought tickled Stefan.

A mechanical sound filtered through Lawrenz's headset. "Port blister window opening."

Several yards away from the raft, Lawrenz shouted, "Who are you?" A moment later, he snorted. "They're Canadians from a bomber that ran out of fuel two days ago."

"Seriously?" Grant shot Stefan a skeptical look. "Have they removed the blanket?"

"Yep. Lots more RAF uniforms in evidence, and no guns."

"Permission to come aboard. Any wounded get the bunks." Stefan slid open his side window, wishing for a better view of proceedings. "McQuaid, oversee the boarding."

The plane lurched as ten chilled, hungry men were pulled aboard. Through Lawrenz's open headset, Stefan heard him encourage the men to use the ladder he'd let down. The men seemed too numb to manage. One man suffered from a leg injury, and McQuaid directed Lawrenz and Poulos to help him into a bunk.

McQuaid also sent some of the men forward to balance the plane. One of them crawled up to the cockpit. "Thank you for picking us up," the man said. "I didn't think anyone would find us."

He wore pilot's wings. A hefty scab on his temple hinted at the headache he must have endured from a rough water landing. Stefan swallowed hard and nodded. *There but for the grace of God ...*

McQuaid sounded in his ears. "All aboard, nothing of value in the raft, blister closed, no room to breathe. Lawrenz, serve coffee to our guests. We're ready to go."

Ten men. Say 170 pounds each. Seventeen hundred extra pounds onboard. Not a problem.

While Stefan taxied into the wind, Grant turned and called to their guest, "Which way were you going?"

"East to England."

"What do we do with them?" Grant directed his question to Stefan. "Land beside a convoy escort so they can continue on to England, or take them to Iceland?"

"We'll take them to Iceland. The wind's picking up. I'd rather not attempt another water landing."

The aircraft finally lumbered into the air.

They'd been back in their sweep for an hour when Jenz burst through the headphones. "P-1 on the north end is going after a U-boat. It's on the surface and firing at Dever. They've taken a lot of hits. P-4 is trying to flank the sub, and the sub's submerging."

Grant broke in, "I feel like I'm listening to a baseball game."

"P-4 is sitting on the sub, and Dever is running for home. They might not make it."

Silence reigned for fifteen minutes.

"You're not going to believe this," Jenz exclaimed. "P-1 is down, and we've been asked to pick 'em up—bring all the rescues back in one plane."

Overhead, clouds billowed on top of one another. Below, the ocean churned with five-foot swells. The beautiful day had turned grim. And they wanted him to land with a plane already stuffed to overcapacity, pick up eight more men, and safely take off in washing-machine waves?

Being an amphibious pilot was not for the faint of heart.

Stefan circled Dever's life raft as the weather continued to worsen. This was doable. If he repeated those words often enough, he might believe it. "What happened with his landing?"

Jenz sighed. "Rough landing cracked open the hull. One of the crew is badly injured."

Lawrenz snorted.

Stefan took a deep breath. No point in putting off the inevitable. "Here goes nothing."

He flew in a long, shallow glide at minimum speed. Close to the surface, the swells neared eight feet. The plane splashed onto the crest of a swell, which swished them into a trough. He grinned. Best rough water landing he'd ever executed.

Or maybe not. Lawrenz's urgent call dashed his self-congratulations. "Pencils! Shove 'em in all the popped rivet holes."

"Report!"

"No worries, Lieutenant. Great landing, but you know, some rivets have to be spoilsports."

A rocking-horse motion caused someone to retch. Stefan wrenched open his window. In a packed ship, they didn't need chain-reaction seasickness creating a malodorous environment.

"Lawrenz, open the blister and be ready with a monkey fist."

"Aye aye, captain." Lawrenz was in his element. "Hey, you guys want a ride?" He grunted, indicating he'd thrown the weighted line. "Grab the rope and we'll pull you in."

Stefan heard McQuaid instructing their first rescues to move farther forward. "Pack in tight. Look on the bright side. You won't be cold. If you feel sick, please don't puke. Ramsey, can you host another homeless waif up there?"

Beside him, Grant chuckled. "I'm glad I don't have to deal with the chaos."

Sounds of the P-1 crew boarding came over Lawrenz's open headphone. "*Oofs*," "*ows*," and "move overs." Dever's querulous tone came through loud and clear. "It's crowded in here."

"You think?" Lawrenz skirted on disrespect. "You're not our first pickup. The best seats have been taken."

"Move aside. I'll go up to the cockpit."

"Not possible." Lawrenz must be gritting his teeth. "All of our guests are forward."

Grant made a face at Stefan. "Figures he'd want to come up here. He'd probably demand to take over. And after wrecking his plane. Did he learn nothing from his cousin getting sacked?"

"Who's flying this plane?" Dever's question surprised Stefan. He hadn't noticed the crazy-eight number?

"The best. Lieutenant Dabrowski."

Silence.

"Okay, Lieutenant. The blister's closed. The wounded guy is laid out in Poulos's tunnel compartment. We're as ready as we'll ever be."

"Good job, Flash."

Now to take off. Stefan stared at the churning sea. *Don't think about it. Remember your training. You can do this.*

To lighten their weight, he released the depth charges from their wings. Then he eased the throttles forward, and the plane accelerated like a drunken sailor. They hammered through waves with colossal thuds that could tear them apart. The succession of crashing waves threw a curtain of water over the forward window, obscuring his visibility. After one shuddering thud, McQuaid yelled, "Lawrenz, pass the pencils forward."

Stefan wondered if they'd ever get up on the step. The suction underneath held them in its grip. He porpoised back and forth, trying to break the suction. They'd climb onto the front of a step only to crash back into a trough. When a gigantic wave tossed them into the air, he yelled, "Full power." Grant nearly tore the throttles off. They must have covered six miles before their airspeed was sufficient to keep them airborne.

Stefan sagged back in his seat, noticing his drenched clothes. His arms and legs quivered. With shaky fingers, he keyed his interphone. "Damage report."

"A few more waterspouts," McQuaid said. "And the drift-meter housing tore loose. We're fine."

From the blister, he heard Dever whine, "I'd like some coffee."

"Sorry, it was first come, first served. Our larder is empty." A grin flavored Lawrenz's voice. "But not to worry. We're heading back to base to restock."

The flight back to Reykjavik stretched out like a marathon. The guest sharing Pennington's compartment fidgeted constantly, trying to get comfortable on the cramped, hard floor. Behind Stefan, the bomber pilot sat with his arms around his bent legs. Every time he tried to straighten out a bit, he bumped Stefan's seat. Iceland never looked so welcoming.

When they landed, the rescued men filed off the plane in silence. The bomber crew was dazed and silent after their ordeal, and Dever's crew failed to make eye contact with anyone. They'd lost their plane. Nothing to be proud of. Dever dallied on the tarmac, glancing toward the cockpit. What did he want?

Stefan taxied to the hangar for his faithful workhorse to receive the tender, loving care it needed. Then he headed straight to his barracks and collapsed onto his cot for a nap.

Chapter Thirty-Two

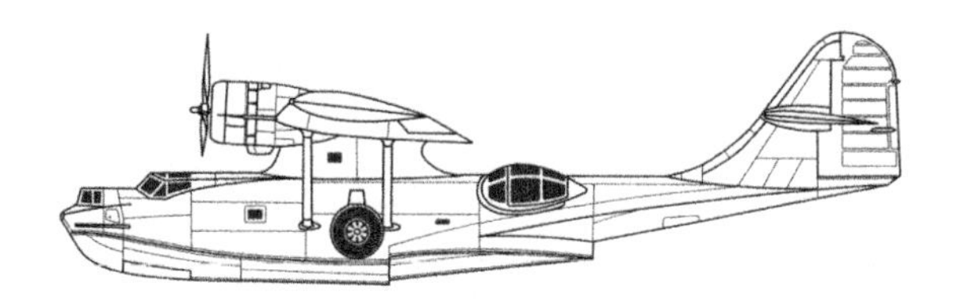

Marie shifted on the plank-on-barrels bench outside Stefan's barracks. David McQuaid had told her he was exhausted from a strenuous flight. She peeked at her watch. Almost time for supper. Should she wake him? Let him sleep around the clock?

A telegram lay on her lap, its message in Polish. She recognized two words: "Ojciec" and "Matka." Stefan's mother wrote about his father. That couldn't be good.

That's what she'd told the intelligence officer who brought her the telegram with suspicion lurking in his eyes. Just because no one in his office knew Polish, he suspected the worst of Stefan. She wondered if he had someone watching her, waiting for Stefan's reaction to the missive.

The telegram arrived through the Red Cross, and Intelligence became involved because of the language. She visualized the intelligence officer snatching it away from Mr. Walton. Why hadn't the Red Cross representative in Milwaukee advised Mrs. Dabrowski to use English?

A bird flew overhead, and Marie jumped to her feet. A puffin! She'd never seen one in the vicinity of the airbase. Maybe, like the dove after the flood, this bird brought tidings of good news. Perhaps Stefan's father still lived. She exhaled a laugh at the fanciful hope.

"What's funny?"

She whirled at Stefan's voice, gravelly from sleep, and clutched the telegram to her chest. "Um, I just saw a puffin."

He searched the empty sky before turning his gaze to her and quirking a brow.

Marie bit her lip and held out the telegram. "This came for you."

Trepidation pinched Stefan's handsome face. He scanned the message and staggered backward, dropping onto the bench and bending over the scrap of paper. "Six days ago."

She touched his shoulder. "What happened?"

"Pops had a heart attack," he sighed.

So he was still alive. At least he was six days ago. By now, he might be doing well. Or be in the grave. Marie squeezed onto the plank beside Stefan and offered a hug.

He leaned against her. "We're in a war. Lots of people are dying. Men I knew, that I trained with, have died. We expected it. But I also expected to return home and be welcomed by my dad."

He might still be alive. Marie opened her mouth to say so but clamped her jaw. The best response was quiet companionship.

The crunch of footsteps on the gravel pathway caught her attention. A bespectacled young chaplain paused beside them. "Is something wrong?"

Since Stefan continued to stare at the telegram, Marie answered. "Bad news from home."

Stefan roused. "My father's in his fifties. Always healthy. Six days ago, he had a heart attack."

After a quiet moment, the chaplain murmured, "I see." He glanced around. "Why don't we head to the mess hall? We'll gather a team of prayer warriors and lift your father to the throne of Heaven. The prayers of righteous men are powerful and effective."

A smile hinted at Stefan's lips. "Where two or three are gathered in God's name, He is with them."

"Indeed, He is. Come along. No time to waste."

Marie gripped Stefan's hand as they hurried after the chaplain.

The number of men who rose from their meal and joined them for prayer at one end of the mess hall astonished Stefan. More were acquaintances than friends. Some attended chapel services. Now they gathered around, their heads bowed. Frank Cusson stood behind him, his hand on Stefan's shoulder. Everyone prayed for his father.

Stefan recalled a day he must have been four years old. Ojciec came home from work, and Stefan ran outside to greet him. Pops picked him up and swung him around, saying, "How's my boy?" Tears threatened at the sweet memory, and Stefan squeezed his eyes shut.

After praying, the men murmured words of comfort and offered him and Marie solitude. Stefan's appetite had fled, especially with grilled Spam on the menu, but he sat at an empty table and sampled a spoonful of bean soup. It actually was tasty. Mindful of Marie's anxious gaze, he continued spooning it up.

For dessert, they ate squares of sheet cake with chocolate icing. One of the cooks must have had time on his hands. In the center of each slice sat a piece of fruit from a can of fruit cocktail. His slice boasted a scarce maraschino cherry.

The cherry triggered another memory. Pops loved maraschino cherries. When they made ice cream sundaes, he insisted they weren't complete without a cherry on top. Stefan's brother Jed didn't want one, but Pops pushed one in. Jed ate the bite with the cherry and screwed up his face, his eyes crossed. Pops roared with laughter.

Oh, Ojciec, I know Heaven's better, but don't go just yet.

As he and Marie left the mess, Dever stopped him. "That was some good flying you did."

He spoke like a flight instructor analyzing Stefan's performance.

"Thank you. Glad you approve."

Dever frowned. Not the response he expected? Too bad. Stefan angled Marie to bypass him.

Dever took a step forward. "Thank you for picking us up."

The hurried words stopped Stefan.

"I'm sorry about your dad," Dever added.

All the aggravation the man had caused Stefan bubbled over. "What? No 'the world will be better off with one less Polack' wisecrack?"

His adversary actually squirmed. "Sorry, man. It wouldn't matter to me if something happened to my old man. I was just a punching bag for him until he finally went away to the big house for robbing a liquor store."

As they watched Dever slink away, Marie whispered, "Wow."

Dever's story helped explain his behavior but not excuse it. Stefan shrugged. "Let's go to the beach."

On the way, he told her about the day's flight. "I don't know how the convoy faired or whether our sweeping tactic did any good. I do know a sub shot down Dever, which I guess is better than losing a ship."

He stopped short of the water lapping over their shoes. The moon's gravitational pull continued to generate the Earth's tides without fail. The thought was comforting in the midst of a ferocious war all over the globe. A world where a too-young father suffered a heart attack. A world where small children lost their families.

He turned to Marie and laid his hand on her cheek. Her eyes widened, but she shifted her face to kiss his palm.

"I love you." He should have cleared his throat, for his voice was little above a whisper.

Her smile bloomed. "I love *you*."

He pressed his lips to hers. He couldn't get enough of her.

They were both breathless when he leaned back. "Will you marry me?"

* * *

Marie blinked. As did Stefan, as though he'd surprised himself with the sudden proposal. Not wanting to give him a chance to change his mind, she laced her fingers behind his neck. "Yes, I'll marry you."

"I never imagined when I received my orders to come to Iceland that I'd marry here."

"Marry *here*?" Her voice squeaked.

"Of course." He locked his arms around her. "It'll mean a long separation when we pull out, but that's no different than all the wives on the home front. Besides, we'll never have your friends and my crew together again. Don't you think a Christmas wedding sounds nice?"

Maybe his proposal wasn't spur of the moment. He had thought this through. "What about your family?"

His happiness dimmed for only a moment. "My parents will throw us a party when we arrive in Milwaukee. Maybe in the fall, when the autumn leaves are full of color."

"I think a Christmas wedding sounds beautiful."

Epilogue

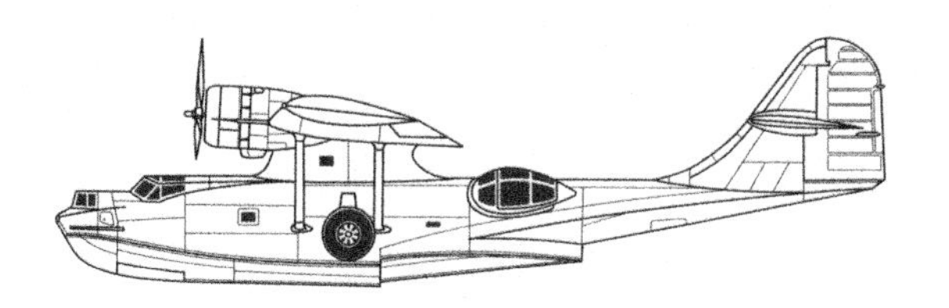

Pearl Harbor, Territory of Hawaii
June 1945

Marie hurried to the pier. Stefan was coming! His ship would dock very soon. She looked at the lei clutched in her hands. Goodness, she was crushing the delicate plumeria. She draped it around her neck before she damaged it further.

The fact that she was here in Honolulu still amazed her. When she requested Pearl Harbor for her next posting, she expected to be turned down. Apparently, few other women were interested in island life. After a brief stop in Washington to visit Red Cross headquarters and arrange for her stored belongings to be sent to Milwaukee, she'd been in Hawaii since leaving Iceland.

She loved the tropical island. It didn't have autumn leaves like Quebec and New England, but at least the trees and palm fronds proved to be a lovely substitute. And now Stefan would join her.

He was assigned to a Black Cat squadron in the Pacific, as he'd expected. His letters were full of hair-raising experiences. A mine-laying mission during which they'd nearly flown into a mountain still gave Stefan nightmares. Or the time a downdraft dropped them so low they'd almost collided with an enemy destroyer. Comic moments too, like Buck Rogers and Flash Gordon dropping empty soda bottles to whistle down on the Japanese, depriving them of sleep on nuisance raids. It was dangerous work, and they were shot down.

Shot down!

The thought still chilled her. Besides being full of enemy sailors, the Pacific Ocean was populated with sharks. She'd worked with men at the hospital here who'd been bitten.

The telegram informing her of her husband's arrival described him as ambulatory, so his injuries weren't too serious. Maybe he wouldn't even need to stay at the hospital.

"There it is." A dockhand nodded to a ship nudged along by a tug. Around her, ambulance attendants stubbed out their cigarettes and returned to their vehicles.

A woman in civilian attire sagged beside her. "Finally." She smiled at Marie. "My husband is part of the ship's crew. It takes forever to make the crossing from Australia or one of those little islands out there. Sometimes it takes as long as two weeks to travel one way." She glanced at Marie's Red Cross uniform. "Are you helping with the patients?"

"I'm waiting for my husband." She waved at the ship. "He's a navy pilot and was shot down. I haven't seen him in a year."

"Oh." The woman formed the word with her mouth, but Marie didn't hear it.

Sailors on the ship tossed lines to those on the mooring quay. In quick order, the ship was secured. A door in the side of the ship opened, and a steady stream of wounded were carried off. Stefan wouldn't need a stretcher. Being ambulatory, his feet should be fine.

"Marie!"

There he was. She bounced on her toes and tried to wave with decorum.

Standing on the deck with his left arm in a sling, he waved. "Be right there." He disappeared back into the ship as the gangway was positioned. Orderlies pushed some patients in wheelchairs while the walking wounded followed. When Stefan appeared in the hatchway, she rushed to the end of the gangway.

Stefan strode down the ramp. He dropped his seabag to the side and pulled her against him with his right arm, claiming her lips with his.

He was here. Alive and well, if his amorous greeting was any indication. "Your arm?"

"Forget it. My shoulder, actually, but it's hardly sore. I don't know why they insisted on sending me back, but I wasn't about to complain. I've seen enough of my crew. I only want to see you." He gave her another kiss that curled her toes.

She remembered the lei and transferred it to him. "Do you have to go to the hospital?"

"Yes, at least to check in."

They boarded a bus provided for the walking wounded. Marie sat on his right and hugged his arm. "The military took over the Royal Hawaiian Hotel during the war. It's reserved for those who have performed hazardous duty at sea. That's mostly sailors, marines, and sub crews, but you're included. I was able to reserve a room for us if you don't need to stay at the hospital."

His smile broadened and his eyes glittered. "We'll take that room even if I have to go AWOL."

As they waited for a doctor to check him out at the hospital, he told her about his experience. "The Japs got us with a lucky shot. One of our parachute flares in the aft was hit, and the resulting fire ignited all the other flares. Everyone came forward, and we closed the bulkhead hatches, but we went down. We weren't able to grab any life rafts or even life jackets. Somehow, I banged my shoulder."

He paused, his eyes distant. "Poulos was with us. But in the water, when we formed a circle to hold hands and tread water, he wasn't there. Maybe he was injured by the fire. Must have drowned. It was just after dark, so no one saw him slip away." Stefan caressed her hand with his thumb. "Anyway, another crew saw our fire and circled back to look for survivors. They landed and picked us up. All except our Buck Rogers. Lawrenz is really torn up over his death."

Marie lowered her head against his shoulder. She didn't know Poulos well but remembered his dark hair and quick smile.

"By that time, my shoulder was on fire," Stefan continued. "Couldn't move my arm at all. We were far from base and a hospital ship was closer, so they dropped me off there." He grinned. "And who should I see but Gloria, my friend Daniel's cousin." He raised his left hand high enough to cover his mouth. "I told the doctor, 'Don't let her hit me and knock out another tooth.' You should have seen the look on the doc's face. And hers! She raised her fist and threatened to really knock out a tooth."

Marie laughed with him. She looked forward to meeting the feisty nurse. "Oh! Your parents sent some photos."

She pulled out the older couple's portrait, and Stefan stared at it for a long moment. "I'm glad I had leave when I transferred from Iceland and was able to visit them. Pops looked good three months after his heart attack, but here, he's good as new."

He spent some time studying the picture of Dorota and her beau. "My little sister's grown up."

"She's a faithful correspondent. I hope we'll become good friends in person."

"No doubt about that. She's always complained about not having a sister." He flipped to the photos of his two brothers, and a telegram slipped out. "What's this?"

"The best news of all. Bron is alive. After V-E day, he was found in a Dutch hospital. He's been ill, but the medical staff told the Germans he was worse than he really was. They knew if he was transferred to a POW camp, he likely would die. All three of you survived the war, and your parents are ecstatic."

Stefan leaned his head back against the wall. "Thank you, God." He dragged in a deep breath. "It was a year ago we heard his ship was strafed and he disappeared. I was sure he was a goner."

They sat quietly, wrapped in each other's arms. Marie had trouble grasping her good fortune. Her husband had returned from the war, and soon they would journey to Wisconsin where a big, happy family awaited them. She was pen pals with Gabriel and two other cousins. No longer was she an unwanted orphan.

A nurse called Stefan to an exam room, where the doctor poked and prodded Stefan's shoulder. Marie noticed the effort Stefan made to remain stoic. The doctor looked at her then back at Stefan. "If you have other lodging arrangements, that's fine. Come back on Monday."

They caught a taxi for the ride to the Royal Hawaiian. The pink hotel glowed in the sunlight. They were shown to a room overlooking the ocean. Martial law was repealed the previous October, but barbed wire remained on the beach. It didn't matter, because the beach was open to the public.

Stefan turned to her, his smile growing as he pulled her

close. "A year and a half after our wedding, and we can finally enjoy a honeymoon."

Marie didn't require a mirror to know her face warmed to a glowing pink that must match the hotel. "Welcome home, Lieutenant Dabrowski."

Author's Note

Most World War II novels take place in Europe. The war, however, was worldwide, in places like Brazil, Iceland, and the South Pacific. Little is known about the war in Iceland, so the research was challenging. I was especially fortunate to find two out-of-print sources full of fascinating insights.

Without the American Christian Fiction Writers and its critique groups and conferences, I would never have succeeded in my writing. Special thanks to Jenny Erlingsson, Connie Cortright, Teresa Haugh, Erin Stevenson, Lana Christian, and Cindy Peter for reading and critiquing this book. Thank you to the Scrivenings team, including Linda Fulkerson, Amy Anguish, and Denica McCall.

If you're on Pinterest, see my board for Novel: No Leaves in Autumn for views of Camp Kwitcherbelliakin, Red Cross workers, Reykjavik, and PBYs: www.pinterest.com/terri-wangard/

I hope you enjoyed *No Leaves in Autumn*! Would you help others enjoy this book too? Help other readers find this book by recommending it to friends in person and on social media.

Review it. Reviews can be tough to come by these days. You, the reader, have the power to make or break a book.

Connect with me on Facebook: www. facebook. com/AuthorTerriWangard. Visit www.terriwangard.com and sign up for my newsletter.

Thank you so much for reading *No Leaves in Autumn* and for spending time with Stefan and Marie.

In gratitude,
Terri Wangard

About the Author

Terri Wangard grew up in Green Bay, Wisconsin, during the Lombardi Glory Years, but she didn't appreciate the Packers until she moved away.

Libraries have always held a special place in her heart. She has fond memories of visiting Green Bay's North Branch library, and looking for Maj Lindman's *Flicka, Ricka, and Dicka* books. She scribbled stories in a notebook (fortunately, not saved) and her first Girl Scout badge was the Writer. No surprise, she has a master's degree in library science.

She has lived in Michigan, Utah, Southern California, and is now back in Wisconsin, where her research for her first

WWII series included going for a ride in a B-17 Flying Fortress bomber. The series, published in 2016, features B-17 navigators and the women they fell in love with. Terri has also written a novel about the *Lusitania*, far more interesting than the *Titanic*, and a companion novel set in World War I.

She won the 2013 Writers on the Storm contest and 2013 First Impressions, as well as being a 2012 Genesis finalist. *Classic Boating* Magazine, a family business since 1984, keeps her busy as an associate editor. In her spare time, she enjoys bicycling, reading, photography, travel, and genealogy. She is a member of the American Christian Fiction Writers, and serves as secretary for her local chapter and is a category coordinator the First Impression and Genesis contests.

Also by Terri Wangard

Seashells in My Pocket

Unsung Stories of World War II—Book One

German-Brazilian Isabel Neumann delights in creating seashell art, but it's her mathematical ability that lands her a job at the American air base in Natal, northern Brazil, during World War II. She doesn't need a calculator to determine the correct weights and balances for the Air Transport Command's cargo planes.

Daniel Lambert, an American transport pilot based at Natal, endures the taunts of combat pilots that he is "allergic to combat." His flying skills win him respect, however, and his friendship with Isabel deepens, even as a new source of trouble looms.

Isabel is caught in the crosshairs of a German saboteur who is obsessed with her. He insists that she belongs with him, and demands that she help him sabotage the Allied base. Her growing relationship with Daniel angers the Nazi, who will do anything to get rid of him. What will happen to Isabel if the madman captures her?

You May Also Like ...

A Song of Deliverance—by Donna Wichelman

The Singing Silver Mine Series—Book One

Born into the Irish system of landholding that favors the moneyed class, Anna Sullivan has no dowry and no chance of marrying the man she loves. Poor and heartbroken, she flees Ireland to tend to Uncle Liam's house in Colorado and take on her deceased aunt's sewing business.

But when Anna arrives in Georgetown, she discovers a mine disaster at the Singing Silver Mine has killed her uncle. Orphaned and destitute again, she gathers her faith, courage, and ingenuity to establish a life in the community. Only one person stands in her way —the mine's owner.

A wealthy, grief-stricken widower of European nobility, Stefan Maier threw his energies into making his mark as a silver mining baron in Colorado when his wife and child died at sea, emigrating to America.

Now, everyone blames him for the mine disaster that killed nine men. But how does he convince the lovely and opinionated Irish woman of his innocence?

Will Anna's heart soften towards Stefan? Will Stefan prove himself worthy of Anna's affections? Each will have to risk everything to attain what they want and need most—love.

Get your copy here:

https://scrivenings.link/asongofdeliverance

* * *

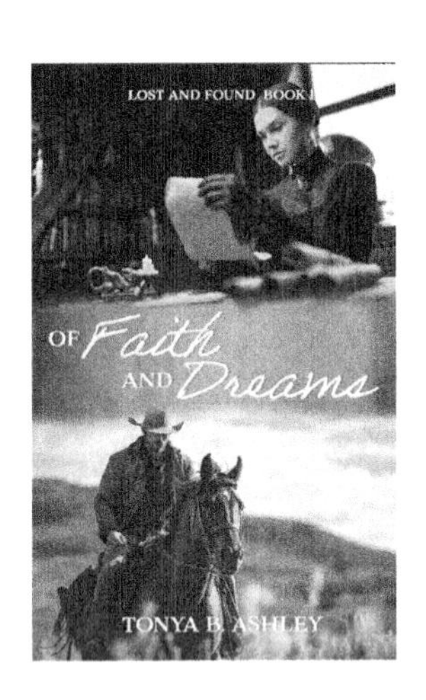

Of Faith and Dreams—by Tonya B. Ashley

Lost and Found series—Book One

When Van Buren, Arkansas, is inundated with Forty-Niners seeking to outfit themselves with horses before heading west, Justin Hogue sees it as the perfect opportunity to step out of his father's shadow to establish a horse ranch. The same influx of prospectors ushers in a competitive horse trader who wants him out of the way. Further complicating things, Justin is challenged with a new tenant at the Hogue family boardinghouse.

Eliza Dawn is an independent, headstrong seamstress who claims to follow the prospectors west to sell her garments. Justin believes she's hiding something. After all, a few dollars for shirts isn't worth the risk. So, he keeps his distance until a mysterious letter and an intriguing ring unite them in searching for an unknown prospector.

Can they find one man in a thousand before the gold expeditions leave town? What will put Justin's dreams at greater risk–conflict with the horse trader or Eliza Dawn's secrets?

Get your copy here:

https://scrivenings.link/offaithanddreams

Scrivenings
PRESS
Quench your thirst for story.
www.ScriveningsPress.com

Printed in Great Britain
by Amazon